The Summer Nanny

Holly Chamberlin

KENSINGTON BOOKS
www.kensingtonbooks.com

KENSINGTON BOOKS are published by

Kensington Publishing Corp.
119 West 40th Street
New York, NY 10018

eISBN-13: 978-1-4967-0157-2
eISBN-10: 1-4967-0157-7
First Kensington Electronic Edition: July 2018

ISBN-13: 978-1-4967-0156-5
ISBN-10: 1-4967-0156-9
First Kensington Trade Paperback Printing: July 2018

10 9 8 7 6 5 4 3 2 1

Printed in the United States of America

Outstanding praise for the novels of Holly Chamberlin!

THE SEASON OF US

"A warm and witty tale. This heartfelt and emotional story will appeal to members of the Sandwich Generation or anyone who has had to set aside long-buried childhood resentments for the well-being of an aging parent. Fans of Elin Hilderbrand and Wendy Wax will adore this genuine exploration of family bonds, personal growth, and acceptance."
—*Booklist*

"Chamberlin successfully portrays a family at their best and worst as they struggle through their first holiday without a beloved husband and father and have to redefine their relationships."
—*Library Journal*

THE BEACH QUILT

"Particularly compelling."—*The Pilot*

SUMMER FRIENDS

"A thoughtful novel."—*ShelfAwareness*

"A great summer read."—*Fresh Fiction*

"A novel rich in drama and insights into what factors bring people together and, just as fatefully, tear them apart."
—*The Portland Press Herald*

THE FAMILY BEACH HOUSE

"Explores questions about the meaning of home, family dynamics and tolerance."
—*The Bangor Daily News*

"An enjoyable summer read, but it's more. It is a novel for all seasons that adds to the enduring excitement of Ogunquit."
—*The Maine Sunday Telegram*

"It does the trick as a beach book and provides a touristy taste of Maine's seasonal attractions."
—*Publishers Weekly*

Books by Holly Chamberlin

LIVING SINGLE

THE SUMMER OF US

BABYLAND

BACK IN THE GAME

THE FRIENDS WE KEEP

TUSCAN HOLIDAY

ONE WEEK IN DECEMBER

THE FAMILY BEACH HOUSE

SUMMER FRIENDS

LAST SUMMER

THE SUMMER EVERYTHING CHANGED

THE BEACH QUILT

SUMMER WITH MY SISTERS

SEASHELL SEASON

THE SEASON OF US

HOME FOR THE SUMMER

HOME FOR CHRISTMAS

THE SUMMER NANNY

Published by Kensington Publishing Corporation

As always, for Stephen
And this time also for Kimberly and Colleen

Acknowledgments

My sincere thanks yet again to John Scognamiglio for his wise and unflagging support. And to all of the nurses at Brigham and Women's, as well as at Maine Medical Center, my thanks for their kind and good care of Stephen and me.

Character cannot be developed in ease and quiet.
Only through experiences of trial and suffering
can the soul be strengthened, vision cleared,
ambition inspired and success achieved.
—Helen Keller

Chapter 1

Beautiful spring weather came late to southern Maine and now, when it had finally made its appearance in mid-April, Leda Latimer was taking full advantage by opening all the windows in her studio to let in fresh air for the first time since the windows had been shut tight the previous October. Just the week before, the vibrant yellow forsythia bushes had mellowed into lush green. The first and then the second robin had been sighted, and the ubiquitous muck of mud season had begun to dry out, leaving ruts in the driveway and along the path around the side of the house. Ruts Leda could handle. Wallowing in wet ground she could not.

Leda was a lifelong resident of Yorktide. She wore her dark hair in a ponytail or in a casual updo. At forty she didn't yet need reading glasses, though she suspected she would need them before long. Doing the sort of work she did put a strain on the eyes, for Leda was a craftswoman, as her mother had been before her. In fact, Leda had learned all of the basic skills she knew from her mother, and while making a living by crafting was a bit laborious, Leda could imagine no other way of spending her time. She would have liked her daughter to express an interest in craftwork, too, but Amy had less than no interest. Many years before, Leda had tried to teach Amy how to sew a button on a blouse. Blood had been spilled. Leda's blood.

Leda was proficient at a variety of skills, from rug hooking to embroidery, from beading to sewing. She made particular clothing items for Amy and made alterations to her own clothes, both of which cut down considerably the cost of maintaining their wardrobes. As for work that paid the bills, there were two main categories—what Leda called the custom and the commercial.

The custom work itself could be divided into two categories: work produced from Leda's original designs and that skillfully copied from famous works of art. When a customer wanted a particular item and couldn't find it in a brick-and-mortar or an online store, she came to Leda's studio and browsed through her ready-made designs or worked along with Leda to get the vision in her head onto paper. This process could be anything from exhilarating to frustrating, but in the end the results were almost always gratifying for both Leda and her client.

The second part of Leda's custom work was the reproduction of popular works of fiber art, from designs produced by William Morris in the nineteenth century, to works dating much further back in history. For example, people were mad for the famous Unicorn Tapestries. The originals, created between 1495 and 1505, were masterpieces of needle and thread, color and design, and Leda never tired of the challenge of re-creating the beautiful and poignant scenes depicted in the seven works. She and her clients were particularly interested in images pulled from *The Unicorn Is Found*, *The Unicorn in Captivity*, and the Lady and the Unicorn tapestries. Because of the time, effort, and artistry that went into each of these meticulous re-creations, Leda was able to charge a healthy price for each of them.

On occasion, interesting commission work led to more commercial enterprises. For a local woman who was proud to trace her ancestors to Scotland, Leda had copied several of the surviving bits of embroidery stitched by Mary, Queen of Scots, during her long incarceration in England. Once word had gotten around that Leda could produce such small masterpieces without the aid of a kit, orders came flooding in. The most popular of the images were without a doubt the ones that featured animals. The Catte, Jupiter (one of Mary's pet dogs), Delphin (a dolphin), Frogge, and Eape were clear favorites.

Leda's bread-and-butter work, however, was making originally designed rugs, pillows, chair pads, table linens, and accessories like eyeglass cases and change purses. These she sold locally at home-decorating shops such as Wainscoting and Windowseats, owned by her friend Phil Morse. Leda also sold her work at The Busy Bee quilt shop and a few of the tourist stores in the area. She did have a website—LatimerCreations.com—though it didn't get significant traffic. Leda wasn't exactly good at self-promotion. In fact, she had set up the website only at her daughter's urging. "Everyone has an online presence these days, Mom," Amy had argued. "You'll be totally left behind if you don't have a website."

"Left behind what?" Leda had been tempted to ask, but she knew what her daughter meant. Only weeks earlier she had learned the meaning of FOMO; Vera, her closest friend, had explained it in context of an article she was reading about current trends in the food industry. "It means fear of missing out. It pertains to those people who need to be tuned in to media of all sorts 24/7." Leda had laughed. "I *live* to miss out," she exclaimed, to which reply Vera had given her a look Leda found disconcerting. Maybe keeping one's head in the sand wasn't always the smartest thing.

Still, Leda did all right. It didn't hurt that her mortgage was small, as her parents, Anne and Paul Gleeson, had paid off most of it before they died; when Amy was seven, the little house on Hawthorne Lane came to Leda in their will. The house suited Leda's and Amy's needs perfectly. There were three bedrooms and a full bathroom on the second floor. Amy had the largest of the bedrooms, Leda the second largest, and the smallest was kept as a guest room. The first floor comprised a cozy kitchen, big enough for a table at which to eat meals; a living room; and Leda's studio. Three of the studio's walls were mostly windows, allowing for plenty of light.

An ear-piercing scream of the feline sort caused Leda to jump. The noise had come from Winston Churchill, though it might equally have come from Harry, aka Henry 8th. Both were large and grumpy and demanded constant attention. They were suspicious of visitors, even ones they knew, which was probably why Winston had let out a warning.

Indeed, a moment later Leda heard the back door, the one that led from the small hall off the studio into the yard, open and shut with a bang. Vera Cecil had a way with doors. A moment later Leda's assumption was confirmed when Vera appeared in the doorway of the studio. Her short, dark hair was sticking up like a rooster's coxcomb, and she was wearing an old plaid shirt Leda knew for a fact she often wore to bed.

"Well," Vera announced, throwing her hands in the air. "It's over. Another relationship bites the dust."

"What happened?" Leda asked, putting down her embroidery hoop. "I thought things were going really well for you two."

"So did I," Vera admitted. She strode into the room and flopped into the armchair on which one of Leda's hand-stitched quilts was draped. She was no sooner seated than Harry was on her lap. "You'll read about it in the paper tomorrow, but I might as well tell you now. The charming Kitty Doyle is a bank robber. Well, she was a bank robber, back when she was known as Katie Dunn."

"Wait," Leda said. "What?"

"You heard me. The police turned up at the door first thing this morning with an arrest warrant. You can imagine my surprise. I hadn't even had my first cup of coffee. It wasn't until after ten o'clock, three hours after the cops dragged my girlfriend off to the slammer, that it sunk in. I'd been harboring a criminal without knowing it."

"A bank robber? Really?" Leda shook her head. "Where do you find these people? Wait. Don't tell me. I don't want to know. I hope the police believe that you had no knowledge of Kitty's past."

Vera rubbed her eyes with the palms of her hands. "They seemed to," she said, "but my lawyer will press the point."

"It's kind of too bad really," Leda said thoughtfully. "I liked Kitty. True, she had that slightly freaky way of watching people out of the corner of her eye, but now that habit is explained."

Vera sighed and gave Harry a stroke. "She made a mean beef stroganoff. I'm going to miss that beef stroganoff."

"You'll meet someone else," Leda said soothingly. "You always do."

"Nope," Vera said. "After this latest debacle, I'm resigning myself to being an old maid. I have spectacularly bad taste in women, and I can't see that changing no matter how many self-help books I read."

"You've been reading self-help books?" Leda asked.

"For years," Vera admitted. "It's been my dirty little secret, but I'm dumping them all now. Fat lot of good they did me."

"Maybe you should let a friend set you up," Leda suggested. "That way at least you'll know the person is halfway sane. Well, assuming you trust the friend."

"Nope. I'm done." Vera suddenly got up from the armchair, sending Harry flying. He landed on his feet. "I don't know why I'm so bad at meeting normal people. I had a perfectly fine childhood. My parents loved me. They even spoiled me, and maybe that somehow made my judgment go bad, assuming my judgment was ever good. It's a mystery for the ages."

"A mystery I wish I could solve for you."

"If wishes were horses . . . Well, I'm off. Just wanted to give you the big news." Vera came to a sudden stop and turned around. "It just dawned on me. What am I going to do with Kitty's stuff? Even if she gets out on bail, she ain't living with me."

"Send it to her family?" Leda suggested.

"That would be a great idea if I knew anything about her family, and I don't. What a mess!"

And with those words Vera was gone, letting the back door slam behind her.

Some people have really rotten luck in love, Leda thought, turning back to her work. If only a little bit of the luck Vera enjoyed in the financial sector could be inserted in the sector of romance, Vera might be a whole lot happier.

For many years Vera had worked in various administrative office positions until about eighteen years ago, when she had inherited a fairly large amount of money from an aunt that allowed her to quit her job and move to Yorktide, where she set up her dream restaurant. Over Easy, a high-end breakfast place, closed in mid-October, after the last of the leaf peepers had gone home, and reopened in late May to catch what business the very earliest vacationers might bring. During the dreaded Maine winters Vera traveled, visiting her parents in Arizona and indulging in spa retreats in Santa Fe. She often asked Leda to join her, all expenses paid, but Leda, while not stupidly proud, wasn't comfortable taking expensive gifts from anyone, not even her dearest friend. If ever she could afford to join her friend on a spa retreat, she would. Until then she would be content with stories of hot stone massages and naked yoga classes. Well, the naked yoga stories she could do without. Too much flapping around.

Vera had come to Yorktide not long after Leda's husband, Charlie, Amy's father, had passed. She had met Leda at the real estate office where Leda was working as a receptionist. The two women grew friendly, and over time Vera had become a sort of aunt and even a friend to Amy. Like Amy, Vera was interested in au courant fashion, something Leda wasn't particularly, so she made a better shopping buddy for Amy than her mother.

Leda went to her worktable and opened one of her sketchbooks. A vague idea had come to her the night before as she was on the verge of sleep. Now, pencil poised over the blank page, Leda tried to empty her mind of all extraneous noise, but it was not so simple. Vera's news of her latest romantic fiasco had brought to the fore of Leda's mind her own romantic situation—or lack thereof. She had been on her own since Charlie's death not long after the birth of their child Amy, now twenty-one and soon to graduate from college. In odd moments, but only in odd moments, Leda felt a pang of loneliness. Growing old might not be a lot of fun and games, but if you were in a couple then at least you weren't alone when arthritis made it difficult to get into and out of the car or gastrointestinal issues took much of the fun out of eating dinner out.

Still, Leda knew that being on her own was a far better way to live her life than to spend it side by side with someone she didn't love or who didn't love her. She knew that without a shadow of a doubt.

Shadows. Moody, crepuscular light. That idea that had come to her the night before just as she was about to fall asleep. . . . Leda began to draw.

Chapter 2

It was a beautiful spring day with temperatures reaching the low sixties for the first time since who could remember when. Purple and yellow crocuses had bravely begun to poke their little heads above ground and the rare daffodil had been spotted, a sure harbinger of better weather to come.

Hayley Franklin, otherwise sensitive to beauty in all of its shapes and forms, was untouched by the scent of green wafting through the open window of her car. She was on her way to meet her boss, Judy Speer. Hayley had a bad feeling in the pit of her stomach. She knew that she had done nothing wrong. Still, when your employer summoned you to the office for a chat, things could not be good.

Hayley stopped at a red light and immediately became aware that the guy behind the wheel in the car to her right was staring at her. She ignored him. She was used to the effect she had on men. The bolder sorts did more than stare. For the pigs, Hayley always had a few choice words that managed to shut them down. The unwanted attention drove her crazy.

But what could she expect when she looked the way she did? Hayley was five feet, ten inches tall and slim, with long legs, a small waist, and what she had once been told was an "enviable bust." The ridiculousness of that assessment had almost caused her to smack the woman who had said it to her—a body part enviable? An intellect, sure. An excellent moral character, yes. But a body part?

The light changed and Hayley drove on, glad to be leaving the creep in the other car behind.

For the past four years Hayley had been working for Squeaky Clean, a small local company that specialized in cleaning private homes. Judy Speers had started the business when her husband had run off with another woman, leaving her to support two little children on her own. Hayley's pay was good, but the work could be exhausting and sometimes a bit stomach turning. A surprising number of otherwise civilized people didn't seem to mind hair accumulating in drains or spatter marks on toilets and floors. And on occasion the people whose houses Hayley cleaned could be a bit high-and-mighty with her and the other women on her crew. Hayley resented this borderline callous treatment, but she always remained polite and took pride in doing her job thoroughly. After all, she had no choice but to keep quiet and carry on. She couldn't afford to be fired.

Hayley still occasionally babysat in the evenings, though when her father was in one of his bad states she stayed home. It wasn't safe for her mother to be alone with Eddie Franklin when the demons were upon him. Her longtime clients understood that she couldn't always be available and had never abandoned her for the simple fact that Hayley was great with children. And maybe also because they felt bad for Hayley and Nora Franklin. Hayley didn't like being pitied, but when it came to an extra forty or fifty dollars now and again she could ignore the pity. You did what you had to do.

And that was a lesson her mother had learned all too well. Nora Franklin was forty-seven years old. Photographs proved that she had once been attractive, but the joy in her smile was long gone, her once shiny hair was now dull, and the lines around her mouth were deeper than they should be.

For the past nine years Nora had worked as a bagger at Hannaford, the local grocery chain. The job was steady and Nora was treated well. The only trouble arose when the family found themselves temporarily without a second car due to Eddie's failure to make a loan payment or some other Eddie-instigated disaster. Then, if Hayley couldn't drive her mother to and from work, Nora had to rely on a fellow Hannaford employee.

Hayley's mouth set in a grim line as she drove past Forest Road. The Franklin family had lost their home on that quiet little street to foreclosure when Hayley was ten. She didn't know the details of how it had been taken. All she knew was that you couldn't dwell on what had once been, good or bad. You had to keep facing ahead. You had to be ready for whatever was to come.

Like more substandard living quarters. Since losing the house Hayley's family had been living in a series of apartments in buildings that were once grand single-family homes but that had become generally run-down and broken up into strangely configured living spaces. One apartment had only a stall shower and no tub. One apartment was so small there was no room in the kitchen for a full-size fridge. Another apartment had an illegal second bedroom about the size of a large closet in which Hayley was forced to sleep. At least she had had some privacy. Her brother had slept on the old couch in the living room, his long legs draped over the couch's arm.

Hayley's relationship with Brandon, six years her senior, was pretty much nonexistent. He had never been the least bit interested in being a big brother, and when he wasn't ignoring Hayley he was torturing her in ways he thought were funny—tripping her when she came into a room, taking her stuff without asking permission, once even cutting her hair when she was asleep. Their mother had tried in vain to control him. Their father had paid no attention whatsoever to his son, other than to take him along to the pubs when Brandon came of age, where too often they ended up getting into fights with other patrons, which most often resulted in their being tossed out into the street, markedly worse for wear.

No, there was none of that Hallmark domestic coziness in the Franklin residence, none of that sense of loyalty you were supposed to find in a family, the knowledge that no matter what happened, someone had your back. A long time ago Hayley had decided that happy, devoted families were the rarity after all, in spite of those holiday commercials that depicted laughing grandparents bonding with doting grandchildren while moms and dads looked on fondly.

Dads. The sad truth was that Hayley had only one memory of "special" time alone with her father and she would never share it with anyone, not even her closest friend, Amy Latimer. It was too pathetic.

Back when she was about eleven there was a popular show on network television called *Prison Break*. It probably wasn't an appropriate show for a kid her age, but no one had protested when she had joined her father in front of the old TV. Her father would sit on the couch, right in the middle, his legs spread wide. Hayley would sit on the floor. He never spoke to her during the commercial breaks other than to tell her to get him another beer from the fridge. He never thanked her when she did. But he never told her to go away.

A child would take what attention she could get and interpret it as affection. At least that was what Hayley had done, until one night Brandon came home about halfway through the show, boasting that he had scored thirty bucks. Eddie Franklin had turned to his son, eyes suddenly bright. Then he reached for the remote, turned off the TV, and taking his son's arm had led him to the door. "Let's go to Mike's Tavern," he had said.

When her father and brother had left the apartment, Hayley continued to stare at the blank television screen. Deep down she supposed she had known all along that the weekly hour in front of the TV hadn't meant anything to her father. Still, to have her intuition proved in so final a manner had hurt.

Hayley pulled up outside the Squeaky Clean headquarters, located in a tiny strip mall, and went inside. Judy Speer was sitting behind the old card table that served as her desk. "Hayley," she said. "Thanks for coming in. I hope it wasn't inconvenient."

Hayley assured her that it wasn't. She was anxious for Judy to say what she had to say. The sooner you knew bad news, the sooner you could start to figure out how to handle it.

"I've decided to retire at the end of June," Judy announced, "and I'm closing down the business. My daughter is due in July, and without the father around she's going to need all the help she can get." Judy shook her head. "It's far from an ideal situation, but I know it's my duty to do what I can for Charlotte and the baby."

Judy's reason for retiring was one you simply couldn't argue against, Hayley thought. Besides, the company was hers to do with what she wanted. Judy didn't owe her anything. "I understand," she said.

"I've prepared a reference for you." Judy handed Hayley a typed sheet of paper. "You'll see I've given you a glowing recommendation. You're the best employee I've ever had by far."

After thanking Judy for her consideration, Hayley took her leave. Grimly she got into her car. This was bad news. Similar jobs paid far less than what Hayley had been paid working for Judy. But she wasn't really surprised at this turn of events. Nothing good ever happened no matter how hard she tried to make it happen. Hayley started the car and headed for home. If it could be called a home.

Chapter 3

"Where is it?" Amy asked her room. Her room did not reply, though if it could it might have said, "If you ever bothered to put things back where they belong you might have found your headband by now."

Clothes were strewn across the unmade bed, heaped on the rocking chair, and spilling out of the closet. The trash can overflowed with used tissues and makeup removal pads. An empty bottle of juice had been sitting on the windowsill for more than a week. A crumpled candy wrapper had been lying on the rug since Amy had dropped it there the night before. A slipper had gone missing over a month ago and had still not made an appearance.

"There it is!" Amy cried, spotting the missing headband in a corner.

Amy Latimer was five foot, three inches tall, neither overweight nor underweight. Her dark curly hair was unruly but not problematically, which was good because hair products were seriously expensive. Her eyes were dark like her father's eyes had been. As for her personality, well, she was open and friendly and honest, and her mother was those things, too, though Leda Latimer was a better judge of character than Amy had ever been. In that way, too, Amy was like her father, happy to think everyone she met was as nice as she was. Not that Amy remembered her father, having been a baby when he died. But her mother and grandparents had told her all about Charlie Latimer, and Amy had loved hearing the stories.

Amy went to her small desk, the one her mother had used as a child, and opened her laptop. Checking her bank statement was a task she dreaded. There always seemed to be a nasty surprise. This time was no different. Amy frowned. How could she have so little in her savings account? Okay, she had sort of lost track of her goal of putting away one hundred dollars every week—or had it been every two weeks?—but still. Her expenses weren't huge. Her mother paid the mortgage and electric bill and whatever else needed to be paid to keep the house running. Sometimes Amy bought the groceries, but only sometimes. And her mother paid her tuition, too. Whatever money Amy made from a variety of part-time jobs was earmarked for day-to-day expenses, like coffee drinks and lunch at the college cafeteria and gas for her car, which her mother owned outright because it had once belonged to Amy's grandfather, who had paid off the loan before he died.

And then Amy remembered. She had bought that new leather wallet earlier in the month, hadn't she? Not that she had really needed a new wallet but it was the prettiest shade of purple. And she had also bought those cool sandals in two colors, black and light brown, because you needed some things in multiple colors. You just did.

"Darn," Amy muttered. She was supposed to be saving for her move to Boston come September. She would be sharing an apartment in Allston with three girls she knew from school and working at a cool new clothing shop called The Aces. Her mother had promised to help cover the cost of the move, but the last thing Amy wanted was to take advantage of her. Maybe she could find two jobs for the summer. The question was, What sort of jobs would pay the most? Maybe she would ask around at school. Someone might have a brilliant idea of how to earn a lot of money in just a few months.

School. Amy had almost forgotten that there was an assignment due the next day. She reached for the spiral notebook on the floor by the desk and began the search for a pen. It was ironic. Here she was, an average student at best, about to graduate with a degree from a four-year college while Hayley, always an excellent student, hadn't even been allowed to complete a two-year course at the community college. Life, Amy thought, could be so unfair. Though it hadn't really been unfair for her. In fact, life had been pretty darn good so far.

Chapter 4

"A bank robber?" Amy said, handing her mother a can of peeled tomatoes. "As in someone walks into a bank holding a gun and wearing a ski mask?"

"I can't be sure about the ski mask," Leda admitted as she put the can into the cupboard and then reached into the second grocery bag. "But I'm pretty sure a gun is required."

Amy sighed. "Poor Vera. Why does this sort of thing always happen to her?"

"I don't know," Leda admitted. "She's so savvy in every other way, but when it comes to romantic partners, her discrimination fails. That or she falls in love with someone expert in fooling people into thinking she's normal."

"Rats!" Amy exclaimed, holding up a box of cereal. "I got the wrong kind. I like the kind with raisins, not almonds."

Leda smiled. "Did you take a moment to actually read the box before tossing it into the cart?"

"Probably not," Amy said. Then her phone rang. "I have to get this, Mom." Amy dashed from the kitchen, leaving her mother to continue the unpacking.

And if Amy couldn't be relied upon to read the label on a package of cereal, Leda thought, how was she going to handle living on her own (roommates didn't count), reading bills carefully before paying them and remembering to turn the oven off before going to bed? Leda sighed. Amy was a rather naïve young woman, still a virgin, impressionable, and prone to see only the positive and the obvious. And she was terrible with managing money. Rather, she was terrible about spending it before it could be managed. Leda continued to try explaining the basics of home economics and personal financial responsibility but to no avail.

As for a direction in life, Amy had never expressed an interest in a particular career path. In fact, it almost seemed as if she didn't much care what she was doing as long as she was making money and having a good time doing it. There was nothing wrong with that attitude, even if some people might consider such a life as directionless.

Leda experienced a pang of guilt. There was no doubt in her mind that she was partly responsible for her daughter's immaturity. She and her parents had coddled the poor fatherless child Amy had once been, and it had been a difficult habit to break. But now it was high time for Amy to grow up. So, while Leda was nervous about Amy's moving to Boston in the fall, she was also supportive of her daughter's decision. Amy needed to learn how to live an independent life.

Amy returned to the kitchen as suddenly as she had gone. "Sorry, Mom," she said. "That was Stacy. She wanted to remind me that Victoria's Secret is having a major blow-out sale this weekend. We're going to drive to South Portland on Saturday."

"What do you need at Victoria's Secret?" Leda asked, hoping her tone didn't betray the trepidation she felt. None of the items in that store were necessary, and all were overpriced. At least they were overpriced for the Latimers.

Amy shrugged. "Nothing, really. But I'll find something to buy."

Leda gathered the empty bags and began to fold them neatly, one into the other. So much, she thought, for her lessons in home economics.

Chapter 5

Hayley stopped at a crossroad as a driver was supposed to do, not that many drivers on these back roads obeyed such commands—like the man who cycled on past her on his makeshift three-wheeler. Raymond Windermere was the eccentric owner of a tumbling-down old farmhouse in the back of beyond. Sticking out of the wicker basket strapped behind his seat was a haphazard pile of books. It was said that Raymond Windermere was insanely rich, but the only thing he seemed to spend money on in Yorktide was books.

Hayley could understand such passion. She yearned for money with which to buy every book she had ever wanted to read and a copy of all the favorites she had already read. Thank God for the library. It had been her haven since she had first been able to read. In fact, Hayley remembered keenly the very moment her interest in history was born. Her mother had dropped her off at the public library in Yorktide while she kept an appointment with the doctor. As childminders, librarians were perfect for the parent with little or no money to spare. The eight-year-old Hayley had wandered from the tiny children's section into the not-much-larger section of adult books. On one of the blond wood tables there sat a thick book with an interesting title—*Peter the Great: His Life and Legacy*. Hayley took a seat at the table and opened the tome. Within minutes she was captivated by the written contents as well as by the glossy images. If some of the vocabulary was new to her, and most of the names of people from foreign lands impossible to pronounce, the story was compelling enough to keep her turning pages.

Suddenly her intense concentration had been disturbed by the appearance of an adult at her side. The woman smiled and pointed to the open page. "What's a little girl like you doing reading a big book like that?" she asked. "You should be reading one of those nice books written especially for children."

For a moment, Hayley hadn't known how to respond. Was she doing something wrong? And then it came to her very clearly that she *wasn't* doing anything wrong. "Did you know," Hayley asked the woman, "there was a person called Peter the Great who ruled Russia for forty-two years? He was almost seven foot tall." The woman seemed disconcerted by Hayley's reply and rapidly walked away.

The incident was burned into Hayley's brain. It was when she had first learned that there were activities that certain people were not supposed to engage in. People like children, girls, old people, poor people, African American people, immigrant people. The list of who should not be doing X or Y just because they were who they were went on. It was when Hayley had first learned that the world was full of arbitrary rules and regulations, and while you might not be able to change all or even some of them, if you were smart you could learn how to circumvent and even to ignore them.

Since that afternoon at the library Hayley had read every bit of European and American history she could get her hands on while keeping up with schoolwork, holding down sometimes two jobs at once, and being a good daughter to her mother if not, in her father's opinion, to him. For Eddie Franklin's fatherly approval Hayley would have to abandon everyone (even her mother) and everything (even her reading) that didn't directly pertain to his creature comforts, and Hayley was not in the least bit interested in being her father's devoted personal servant any more than she was compelled to be by circumstances.

Hayley steered her car around a significant hole in the road, all too common after a long Maine winter. This intense intellectual interest was the thing that most differentiated Hayley from her parents and brother, none of whom seem to have any passions at all, certainly not intellectual passions. She often wondered where she came from. Who in her family had intelligence like hers? Was it someone on her father's or her mother's side? A great-great grandmother or a great-great-great grandfather? There had to have been *someone* in her lineage with a passion for learning. Or had she been switched at birth? Had the child really born to Nora and Eddie Franklin been handed over to civilized and cultured parents, while the child born to that civilized and cultured couple had been handed over to the Franklins? But no. One look at the shape of her hands, exactly like her mother's, and one look at the color of her hair, exactly like Brandon's, and one look at the color of her eyes, exactly like her father's, was enough to convince Hayley that for better or worse—and it was for worse—she was indeed of Mackenzie–Franklin blood.

Hayley turned onto Hawthorne Lane. The Latimers lived at number 22. No sooner had Hayley parked her car in the drive than Amy was beckoning to her from the porch.

"Come up to my room," she said. "I want to show you what I got at the Victoria's Secret sale."

Hayley followed Amy to her room on the second floor. One thing Hayley knew for sure. If the room were hers she would keep it far neater than Amy was in the habit of keeping it. With a mew of distaste, Hayley picked up a bit of orange peel with her fingertips and dropped it into the already full trash can.

Amy showed her two form-fitting T-shirts, one pale pink and the other white. "Aren't they pretty?" she asked.

"They're nice," Hayley said mechanically. Could there be two more impractical colors?

"What's wrong?" Amy asked, eyeing her suspiciously and tossing the T-shirts across the room.

"I lost my job," Hayley said bluntly. "Judy is closing the business at the end of June."

"Ouch. Sorry."

Gingerly Hayley sat on the edge of Amy's bed, half afraid of what might be lurking under the covers. "It's the story of my life," she said. "One step forward, two steps back. It gets boring after a while, you know?"

"Don't be depressed," Amy said heartily. "I have a way we both can make a ton of money this summer."

"What? And don't say we'll buy lottery tickets. You know I'm against gambling."

"Nothing like that," Amy assured her, plopping down next to Hayley. "This girl I know from my psych class told me she's been working as a summer nanny on Nantucket for the past two years. She says it's a great way to earn money without having to be cooped up in an office staring at a computer or standing on your feet waiting tables all day."

Hayley frowned. It was bad enough cleaning the houses of the well-to-do but to be compelled to cater to the whims of their spoiled brats? "No thanks," she said.

"What do you mean?" Amy asked. "You're great with kids. Look, my friend told me how to go about finding a job as a nanny. It's super easy."

"The idea is absurd," Hayley said. "Rich people seeking a caretaker for their children would never hire someone like me, with my casually criminal family and lack of education."

"Don't be silly. I don't even have babysitting references like you do," Amy pointed out, "but that's not stopping me. Look, my friend got to go with one of her families to Aruba for two weeks. She said it was fantastic. We could get a free vacation!"

"Nothing is ever really free, Amy," Hayley pointed out. "Your friend paid for that holiday in hard labor, you can be sure. She wasn't the one lazing on a beach chair sipping piña coladas or whatever it is people drink in Aruba."

Amy sighed. "Why do you always have to be so negative?"

"Practical," Hayley corrected. "And if it comes across to some people as negative, I can't help that."

Amy looked genuinely crestfallen, and Hayley felt a surge of guilt for having quashed her friend's enthusiasm. "All right," she said. "I promise to think about it. But don't hold your breath."

"Why would I do that?" Amy asked.

Hayley rolled her eyes heavenward. "Never mind."

Chapter 6

Leda was taking a brief respite from her work, but only a brief one, because one of her longtime clients was anxious for the delivery of the embroidered place mats and matching napkins she had ordered. Carolyn's college nemesis was coming for luncheon at the end of the week and she was eager to impress. Leda thought the idea of impressing someone you hadn't seen for over forty years was slightly ridiculous, but she had held her tongue.

Now, resting on the love seat in her studio, Leda found herself gazing at her formal wedding portrait. She kept it on a shelf over her worktable. Leda and Charlie had married only months after meeting in the lobby of a small movie theatre in South Berwick. They had taken to each other right away. The eighteen-year-old Leda had been desperately seeking a refuge after the awful thing that had happened to her the previous summer, and marriage to Charlie had provided that refuge, if only for a short while.

Leda's cell rang. It was Phil Morse from Wainscoting and Windowseats.

"I just sold the last of your eyeglass cases and tissue holders," Phil told her. "You wouldn't by chance have any more at hand?"

"No," Leda told him, "but I can easily make up at least five of each in the next few days. Just as soon as I finish a custom order for Carolyn Cheswick."

"Great. And I'll probably sell those quickly, too."

Leda smiled. "Impulse purchases."

"And they're perfect as little gifts to the self for the customer who's in need of retail therapy," Phil pointed out. "Do you want me to pick them up when you're done?"

"I'll drop them off," Leda told him.

"Thanks, Leda," Phil said.

After the call ended, Leda finished her cup of tea and went to her desk to record Phil's order and to schedule the work into her weekly planner. When you ran your own one-person business, organization was key. Leda was pleased that her accessory items continued to sell briskly. It cost her very little to make eyeglass cases, tissue holders, and even coin purses. She used scraps of material left over from larger projects, and she always kept a good stock of buttons and zippers and snaps on hand. Accessory items brought a tidy profit for very little work and expenditure.

Leda rose from her desk and went over to her worktable to resume work on Carolyn's order. Amy had told her that Hayley had lost her job with the cleaning company. Hayley would land on her feet, of that Leda felt sure, but she so wished that something magical would happen for her, if not in the shape of a knight in shining armor—because that scenario hardly ever worked out—then in the shape of a solid opportunity for advancement. It saddened Leda to see a bright young woman so burdened with her family's woes.

Thankfully, family woes were something with which Amy had never had to contend. True, the death of her beloved grandparents had hit her hard, but both had been in ill health for some time so their passing wasn't entirely unexpected. Even at the age of seven Amy had been sensitive enough to realize that Grandma and Grandpa hadn't been enjoying much quality of life and that in some ways their deaths were a blessing to them.

"It's me."

The unexpected whisper almost made Leda jump out of her skin.

"I didn't hear you come in," Leda said to Vera, her hand to her heart. "The door didn't slam."

"Shhh!" Vera hissed. "I think I'm being followed." Vera tiptoed toward one of the windows that looked over the side yard. "I think I saw someone watching my house this morning," she said. "And when I went to the post office there was a strange man staring at me from across the street."

Leda shook her head and wondered if her eminently sane friend was finally losing her mind. "Who could possibly be watching you?" she asked.

Gingerly, Vera pushed aside the sheer curtain less than half an inch and peered out. "The police," she said. "Or one of Kitty's old criminal cronies."

Leda got up from the worktable and took her friend's arm. "Come away from there," she said. "What you need is a nice cup of tea to calm your nerves."

Vera looked at her with wide eyes. "Haven't you got any whiskey?" she asked.

Chapter 7

Hayley was only a few blocks from home. Rather, from the apartment in which the Franklins were currently residing. No place had felt like home for years. Homes were places in which you could let down your guard and feel secure. No one could feel secure with Eddie Franklin on site.

And the truth was that the current situation in which she and her mother found themselves was the fault of one long-ago, very bad romantic mistake on the part of Nora Mackenzie, a naïve and innocent young woman who had been taken in by a handsome face and a quicksilver tongue.

As for Hayley, she was not looking for or expecting love. And caring led to grave mistakes. The last thing she wanted was to get trapped in a ridiculously bad marriage like her mother had. When you let your emotions get involved, even the smartest person got stupid and fast. Hayley had no intention of getting stupid, which is the main reason she had never had a boyfriend. She wasn't a virgin, but what sex she had engaged in had been on her own terms and had most definitely not involved the heart.

When Hayley reached 16 Rockford Way she parked in the small lot behind the building, next to her neighbors' beat-up vehicles. Wearily she walked around to the front of the building, pushed open the door, and stepped into the small, dark foyer. She could hear the old woman in the tiny first-floor apartment warbling along to a radio set to a country music station. Heavy footsteps overhead told her that one of the two young guys who rented an apartment on the second floor was home. Hayley went over to the narrow wooden table against the wall on which the mail carrier deposited the tenants' letters, bills, and coupon flyers. She sorted through the mess and extricated anything addressed to the Franklins. Two bills, a catalogue addressed to Edward Franklin or Current Resident, and a letter-sized envelope addressed to Nora Franklin.

Hayley frowned. She recognized the handwriting on the envelope, large and awkward. It belonged to her brother. It was odd that he would write a letter rather than call, and for a moment Hayley wondered if Brandon was seriously ill or in terrible trouble with the law. She might not feel affection for her brother, but she didn't wish him harm. If he was sick or in trouble then it might be better for her to read his letter before passing it on to her mother. Hayley could foresee a scene of panic if her mother received bad news about her son without first being prepared.

With a glance at the steep stairs covered with a dirty carpet, Hayley opened the envelope. Inside she found a single sheet of lined paper torn from a small notebook. *Mom*, it said. *It's me Brandon. How are you? I am fine. But I need money bad. Send me what you got. Like five hundred dollars would be good. Brandon.*

Hayley frowned and shoved the letter back into the envelope. She should have known. Her bum of a brother, currently living in Augusta, needed money. More likely he *wanted* money, probably for booze or some stupid purchase he would only wind up breaking or losing.

No doubt about it, she had done the right thing by opening the letter. If her mother had seen it she would immediately have sent off whatever money she had in her purse whether the family could spare it or not. Her hands trembling with anger, Hayley tore the envelope and letter in half and in half again. Then she left the building, went around back to where the garbage cans shared by the building's tenants were located, and buried the pieces of paper in an open plastic bag poking out of one of the cans. Her hands felt filthy, and not only because of the brown banana peel, damp paper towels, and other refuse she had accidentally touched while making her brother's selfish request go away.

Hayley went back into the building and began the climb to the third floor. Her mind was made up. Things had to change. She would take Amy's advice and apply for a position as a summer nanny. With any luck, she would get a position that paid really well and she would hold on to the money. And one day, one wonderful day, Hayley and her mother would walk away from Yorktide and all the sad memories it held for them. And they would never look back.

Chapter 8

"Guess what?" Amy said, taking a carton of milk from the fridge. "I'm applying for a job as a nanny this summer."

Her mother frowned. "Are you sure that's a good idea?" she asked.

"Why wouldn't it be? I could make a lot of money if I'm lucky."

"I saw Noah Woolrich in town earlier," her mother said brightly.

"That's nice," Amy said, joining her mother at the table and adding some milk to her cup of tea. She knew why her mother had changed the subject. Leda Latimer harbored a desire for her daughter to fall in love with Noah Woolrich. He was super nice and smart and good-looking, but for some reason Amy herself didn't understand she wasn't able to return his feelings.

"He looks good," her mother went on. "He looks so robust and healthy."

Amy sighed. "Mom. Please. So, is Vera in the clear with the police? I mean, they don't think she was Kitty's accomplice, do they?"

"No, she's not a suspect. But she did think she was being watched by either the police or one of Kitty's criminal buddies."

Amy shook her head. "It would be funny if it weren't so sad."

"I've got to run this box over to Phil's shop," her mother said, reaching for her bag. "I'll be back soon and we can talk more about that nanny position."

Amy laughed. "There's nothing to talk about."

When her mother had gone, Amy wandered into the living room with her cup of tea. On the credenza there was a portrait of her grandparents taken on their wedding day way back in 1974. Her grandfather had been like a father to Amy. He had definitely been the man of the house, the one who fixed the food disposal when a chicken bone got caught in it; the one who mowed the lawn; the one who kept an eye on the boiler in the basement. Amy couldn't remember one time they had had to call in a professional fix-it guy. And her grandmother had been like a second mother. When Amy's mom was at work at the real estate agency, Grandma had been the one to remind Amy to put her dirty clothes into the laundry hamper; the one to make Amy's lunches to take to school; even the one to review Amy's homework. It had been an idyllic upbringing in a lot of ways, and Amy was grateful for what she had enjoyed, never more so than when she listened to Hayley talk about her own troubled home life.

Poor Hayley. Amy hoped she would seriously consider the idea of working as a nanny. They could have so much fun hanging out together with all the kids. In fact, it might just be like summer camp. Amy had never gone to summer camp, but she knew that the counselors and the kids had a great time together, doing crafts and going swimming and making s'mores over a roaring fire. And on the Fourth of July they might have a bonfire and set off fireworks, or if that was too dangerous at least they could all wave around sparklers. How different was a nanny from a camp counselor? Probably not all that different. It was probably oodles and oodles of fun.

Amy finished her tea and went to the kitchen to put her cup in the sink. She had a very strong feeling that this summer was going to be the absolute best summer of her life.

Chapter 9

Leda sat at one of the two looms in her bright and airy studio. The cats were sprawled at her feet, relaxing after a brutally challenging morning of eating and chasing each other up and down the stairs. The house was quiet; Amy had gone off to class just after breakfast. It was the perfect atmosphere in which to work on the latest project for one of her longtime clients, but Leda's mind simply would not focus on her craft. Instead, it insisted on returning to a pivotal moment in the long-distant past.

Leda knew her fears were irrational. There was no logical reason why Amy's working as a nanny this summer should carry with it any greater risk of danger than her working as a waitress or a checkout person. When you thought about it, walking dogs was probably far riskier than looking after someone else's children in the security of their own home. Dogs could turn on you and bite. Leda frowned. Just like people.

The thing was, Leda was scared that the past was poised to repeat itself. She had never told this to Amy, but at the age of seventeen she had taken a job as a summer nanny for a family from upstate New York. Lance Stirling was a fairly well-known painter, and his wife, Regan, looked after the home and their one-year-old daughter, Rebecca. That summer, Regan had explained, the family needed to hire a nanny so that Regan could spend her time pursuing an online degree in Egyptology. The Stirlings treated Leda politely, and Rebecca was an easygoing child. The money was adequate, and Regan even provided a homemade meal each day. Everything seemed just fine, if, in fact, a little boring. But it didn't remain boring for long.

Looking at the loom before her, Leda saw not strands of cotton of varying color, width, and texture but her teenaged self, intensely drawn to the man who was her employer. In her infatuation, she had thought that Lance's artfully wild hair made him look like one of the Romantic poets or, better yet, a rock star. His hand-rolled cigarettes had made him seem exotically European. His black moods had made him seem deep and soulful. His eyes, a penetrating green, had seemed to divine her most secret thoughts. Leda had done her best to hide her attraction, but when she noticed that Lance was spending a fair amount of time following her with those penetrating eyes, she allowed her own gaze to linger.

Abruptly, Leda got up from the loom and crossed to the window that faced the small backyard with its stone birdbath, its ancient lilac bush, its recently mowed grass. Sadly, the lovely scene had no power to quiet her troubled emotions. Even after all these years the memories of what happened that summer still had the power to anger and embarrass her. But once the memories had come to the forefront of her mind, Leda had no choice but to let them play out.

Staring unseeingly at a small yellow bird perched on the edge of the birdbath, she remembered how it wasn't long before Lance Stirling began to request her company in his studio while his daughter napped and his wife studied at her computer. He told Leda that her presence soothed him. He told her that because she was an artist with an artist's soul she understood him in ways his wife could not. When Leda protested that her fiber work was simply a hobby, he scolded her for her lack of self-worth and told her that she was wonderful. Special. Beautiful. He made sketches for her and signed them with a flourish. He picked wild flowers and wove them through her hair. He wrote her poems. He told her that he loved her, that she was his muse, that they were fated to be together. He began to speak in husky whispers when they met, to touch her arm surreptitiously when they passed in the hall, to kiss her urgently behind the half-closed door of his studio. He told her that he loved her.

One of the cats rumbled in his sleep, and Leda jumped. Once again, she had slid so deeply into her foolish youth. . . . Leda put her hands to her temples as she remembered what had come next. She had felt guilty about what was now undoubtedly an affair. But at the same time, she had also felt elated, powerful, and sure. How could being in love ever be wrong? The world would forgive any transgression made in the name of love. It *had* to forgive. And so, one day when Lance's wife was away visiting a friend, Leda had gone to bed with him.

Leda turned away from the window and its view of her serene backyard and wandered over to the comfy love seat. She sank onto it and pulled an embroidered pillow onto her lap. What had happened then was the very worst part of the whole mess. The day after she had been with Lance, she had gone to the Stirling home literally tingling with excitement, anticipating more protestations of love and passionate embraces behind half-closed doors. But instead of greeting Leda with his provocative smile, Lance had told her that he was too busy to waste time chatting with the nanny and had retreated to his studio, closing the door behind him. Leda was devastated by this sudden coldness, which only grew icier by the day. One afternoon, less than a week after Leda had lost her virginity to Lance Stirling, she confronted him, begging to know what she had done to cause him to reject her.

"It's run its course," Lance had told her harshly, stabbing at a canvas with his brush, hand-rolled cigarette dangling from the corner of his mouth. "Let it go."

"I can't let it go," Leda remembered crying out. "I won't!"

Lance had turned from his canvas. Even from the depths of her misery Leda had been able to recognize the look of disgust on his face. "That's enough," he snapped. "Get ahold of yourself."

But Leda could not get ahold of herself. She threatened to tell his wife what had happened between them.

"Go ahead," Lance said with a laugh, turning back to his work. "It won't make any difference."

Leda had run from the studio then, fighting nausea. She knew she didn't really have the nerve to approach Regan Stirling with the truth. She had no idea how she would finish out the summer working in such close quarters with Lance and his wife. Before she could give the immediate future any further thought, Regan and little Rebecca returned from their daily walk.

"I need to talk to you," Regan said to Leda.

Leda had gone numb with fear. She had no idea what to expect from Lance's wronged wife.

"Look," Regan had gone on. If not exactly sympathetic, her tone betrayed no anger. "You're not the first kid Lance has seduced and you won't be the last. He's an artist. He has no time for the restricting social conventions of the middle class. The fact is you mean nothing to him, just as all the others in the past meant nothing and just as all the ones to come will mean nothing. It's me he loves and me he'll never leave. Me and Rebecca. His family."

It was then that Leda heard a noise in the hall behind her and turning caught sight of Lance, paintbrush stuck behind his ear, the ubiquitous cigarette in hand. He glanced at her as he passed, shrugged, and continued on. It was at that moment that Leda Latimer finally understood that she had been merely a notch on Lance Stirling's bedpost.

Leda ran from the house and never went back. She didn't call to tender her resignation. She didn't write a note demanding what salary she was owed. She put her head down and waited for repercussions, but none came. Lance and Regan Stirling left Yorktide at the end of the summer and she never saw or heard from them again.

The weeks immediately after the debacle had been the worst in Leda's life. She told her parents that she had been let go because the Stirlings had changed their mind about needing a nanny. If her mother or father suspected the truth or something like it, they chose not to question her, and for that Leda was thankful. She could never have admitted to her parents that she had been so foolish as to fall for a married man, or so cruel as to interfere in someone else's marriage, but even if she had been able to confess, what good would telling them have accomplished? The deed could not be undone.

Full of self-loathing, Leda abandoned her plans to attend Yorktide Community College that fall and took a menial job in a small, local factory. Before the end of the year she had begun to date a nice local boy named Charlie Latimer. They married the following spring. And she still thought of Lance Stirling with longing. She knew that something was deeply wrong with her for not being able to let go of feelings for a man who had treated her so badly, but she just couldn't seem to help herself. The longing was stronger than the anger.

By summer Leda was pregnant; Amy was born when Leda was nineteen years old. And before Amy had celebrated her first birthday, Charlie was gone. He broke his neck in a fall from scaffolding while working a construction site. Leda mourned his death, but not for very long. She hadn't really known the man she had married. The one and only good thing that resulted from Charlie's sudden death was that it served to completely kill all feelings for Lance Stirling that still lingered disturbingly in Leda's heart. Charlie's untimely end had catapulted Leda into adulthood.

Leda rose from the love seat and went to her loom, determined to return to the responsibilities of the present. Of course the past wasn't necessarily doomed to repeat itself. That was superstitious thinking. Still, it was hard to shake off the feeling of deep anxiety that had burrowed its way into her chest since Amy had announced her intention of taking a position as a nanny this summer. At twenty-one Amy was even more naïve than Leda had been at seventeen. It was entirely likely that Amy might fall prey to an unscrupulous employer as had her mother. But there was nothing Leda could do to stop her daughter from pursuing the path she had chosen. She was, after all, an adult. Leda could only hope that whoever hired Amy was not a predator like Lance Stirling had been. That wasn't too much to hope for, was it?

Chapter 10

Hayley was on her way to the Goodwill shop in Wells. She had considered asking Amy to come along but had then thought better of it. Amy's enthusiasm for shopping could wear on Hayley's nerves. She had never seen anyone get so excited by such trivial things as sequins on socks and blouses with cut-out shoulders.

She was on her way to Goodwill because, through the employment agency Amy's friend had suggested, Hayley had almost immediately been offered interviews with three families. Interviews meant clothing that wasn't worn through in spots and faded in others.

The first interview was with a Jon and Marisa Whitby. They were already renting a house in Ogunquit, though they didn't require the services of a nanny until mid-June. They had two-year-old twin girls, Lily and Leyla. Jon Whitby was the founder and CEO of Whitby Wealth Management, a firm based in Greenwich, Connecticut. Marisa Whitby, currently a full-time mother, had worked as a translator for a Paris-based publishing house before the birth of her children. On paper, they were a formidable couple. Who knew how disconcerting they would be in person?

Hayley hadn't told her mother that her job at Squeaky Clean would be ending shortly. Nora had enough to deal with without worrying about her daughter's lost income. When Hayley landed another job, she would break the news. And if she was lucky, that might be soon.

Once inside the store, Hayley resisted the temptation of the book section. She was here to buy clothes suitable for work. For a moment, facing what seemed like acres of options, she regretted not having asked Amy to come along. She had always been in awe of how Amy knew how to accessorize. It was a creative flair she had probably inherited from her mother. She could take any old T-shirt and jeans and transform the two basic pieces into an "outfit" by tossing on a long scarf and wearing high-heeled sandals instead of sneakers.

But Hayley *hadn't* invited Amy, and so here she was, on her own. She began to flip through the racks of clothing. She figured that a nanny needed clothes that were practical and befitted her position in the household of a wealthy family. It was almost forty minutes before she had selected what she thought might be appropriate items and brought them to the dressing room.

She tried on the taupe A-line dress first; the neutral color seemed a smart choice. And as Hayley looked at herself in the full-length mirror she felt a very alien spark of specialness. She looked good. Very good. And then she frowned. These new clothes were not to make her look pretty. They were in service of a specific goal. And if she didn't achieve that goal the clothes would go to a resale shop and she would hope to make back a portion of the money she had spent.

Still, Hayley wondered what her father would say when he saw her in the new clothes, assuming of course he would even bother to notice. If he did notice, no doubt he would rant about her spending his hard-earned money, which was of course ridiculous. She was spending *her own* hard-earned money. But her father's feelings were beside the point. What had to matter most was that she was taking what might turn out to be a big step toward improving her life and her mother's life as well.

In the end, Hayley bought the taupe dress, a pair of chinos, three T-shirts, and a lightweight cotton jacket for a grand total of sixty dollars. If that wasn't smart shopping, Hayley didn't know what was.

Chapter 11

Amy yawned, this time so widely she heard her jaw crack. Something in her head, anyway. The semester was nearing its end. Exams and final papers were killing her, but she thought she was doing okay. If only she could stop yawning and pay attention to her work and not focus so much on the summer ahead. But that was seriously difficult.

The thing was, Amy and Hayley had signed on with a reputable employment agency that specialized in placing nannies with appropriate families. So far, Amy hadn't gotten even one interview and always for the same reason. A lack of experience. Amy knew she was a good person. If only someone would give her a chance to prove herself!

Amy returned to the employment agency's home page and read for what seemed like the millionth time the official description of the job. *A nanny is responsible for following a parent's instructions regarding the care of his/her child. A nanny is responsible for meeting the child/children's needs be they emotional, physical, intellectual, or social. A nanny . . .*

Maybe applying for a job as a nanny had been a silly idea in the first place, Amy thought dejectedly. Hayley was faring way better. She already had three families interested in her. Well, that was to be expected. She was so smart and had so much more work experience.

Amy exited the site and checked her e-mail account. She didn't use it much and sometimes forgot to look at it for weeks on end. But now she was very glad that she had, because there in her inbox was an offer of an interview from a family seeking a nanny for the summer.

The e-mail had come from someone named Cressida Prior. The name sounded vaguely familiar, but Amy didn't waste time trying to figure out where she might have heard it. She read the brief e-mail several times with interest. Cressida Prior had found Amy's name and contact information via the employment agency and in the interest of "preserving her valuable time" had decided to contact Amy directly. Ms. Prior was seeking a nanny to look after her two children, a boy age eight and a girl age ten. Amy felt her spirits rise. She wouldn't have to change diapers or give the children baths, and she would definitely have fun taking them to the beach and building sand castles and going for ice cream after. Children that age were cool. There was no mention of a father or of any household staff. There was no mention of the children's names.

Cressida Prior told her to be at The Atlantic promptly at 12:15 on Thursday. It struck Amy as a bit odd that Ms. Prior assumed she would want to apply for the job, but the fact was that she *did* want to apply. She would have to reschedule an appointment she had made for a pedicure, but that was no problem.

The Atlantic! It was a seriously high-end restaurant. There was no way Amy and her mother could afford to eat there. Well, maybe they could share an appetizer without breaking the bank, but that was about all. Now the question was, What should she wear to an interview in such a fancy setting? Amy ran to her closet and began the search. Homework could wait.

Chapter 12

"Coffee's ready," Leda announced. She brought the French press to the table, where Amy was devouring a cinnamon Danish. Leda was only sorry that Amy hadn't thought to buy a Danish for her mother as well.

"Thanks, Mom," Amy said when Leda placed the pot on the table and took a seat across from her daughter.

Leda took a sip of the hot coffee. After having been turned down by three prospective employers, Amy had finally been granted an interview with a family in search of a summer nanny. Leda did not feel great about this.

"Are you absolutely sure you want to work as a nanny this summer?" Leda said with a poor attempt at sounding casual. "There are plenty of other jobs around town. Maybe Vera could hire you. You know waitstaff are always coming and going."

"Mom," Amy wailed, wiping her hands on her napkin, "we've been over this like a million times! I want to be a nanny. And I told you I have an interview."

"You could get a job at the Starfish," Leda said somewhat desperately. "I hear they pay well."

Amy smiled. "Doing what? Being a chambermaid? I have enough trouble making my own bed. Who came up with the idea of fitted sheets? Do you know how many nails I've broken trying to make my bed?"

"I could see if Phil needs help at Wainscoting and Windowseats," Leda offered.

Amy rolled her eyes. "I don't understand why you're so down on the idea of my being a nanny," she said. "It's a great way to make money, and there can be all sorts of perks. I read that sometimes employers give their nannies use of their own cars to run errands. I might even get to drive a car made after 2010."

Leda sighed. "Are you sure you won't just consider asking Vera for a job at Over Easy?"

"Totally sure," Amy said firmly. "I'd much rather spend my days watching over a child in someone's fancy house than waiting tables. You're on your feet for hours at a time and you have to deal with some really fussy customers, people who send their pancakes back because they don't look like the pancakes their mother made."

"Caring for someone else's children is also hard work," Leda pointed out. "And you might get saddled with really fussy parents who make doing your job nigh impossible."

Amy shrugged. "I'll deal with all that. You know I'm pretty easy-going."

"It can be a difficult thing," Leda said carefully, "being thrust into a family with its own dynamic so different from your own."

"Yeah, but I'm not applying to be a live-in nanny. I'll be home every night." Amy reached across the table and squeezed Leda's hand. "Don't worry, Mom. I'll still have my own life."

"Be as careful choosing the family as they'll be choosing you. It needs to be a good fit for both parties."

"I know, I know. I'm not stupid."

"I didn't say that you were," Leda protested. "What's the name of this family with whom you're interviewing?"

"Cressida Prior is the mother. I don't know yet if there's a father around."

"Something about that name sounds familiar," Leda noted.

"I know," Amy said. "I thought so, too."

"I wonder why she's asked to interview you at a restaurant? Why not interview you at her hotel?"

"Mom! What does it matter where we meet?"

Leda smiled. "You're right. It doesn't matter." What mattered, she thought, was that her daughter was hired by decent, respectable people. And for that she could only pray.

Chapter 13

Hayley reached into the top drawer for a can opener. Her mother loved baked beans, so once a week she made a meal around them. Tonight she would serve the beans with a salad and a pan of corn bread she had made from a convenient mix. And even though Hayley didn't care whether her father ate dinner or not, she always made sure to prepare enough for three. It was for her mother's sake that she did this. Her mother cared whether Eddie Franklin had a hearty meal at the end of the day.

As she prepared the meal, Hayley considered her experience earlier at the Whitby home. She had approached the interview with an uneasy mix of hope and resentment, ready to find Marisa Whitby a smug, self-satisfied woman who would view Hayley through the lens of privilege and find her sadly lacking. All through the time they had spent together, both alone and with the children, Hayley had been waiting for the revelation of high-handed snobbery, but it had never come.

Hayley remembered getting out of her car—she had worn the taupe dress she had bought at Goodwill—and looking up in awe at the house the Whitby family was renting. It was very large. Its shingles were mellowed with age to a soft, silvery gray. There was an old-fashioned wraparound porch on which were grouped white wicker chairs and wooden rocking chairs. Four large pots of flowers were placed at intervals along the portion of the porch facing the road. Hayley counted three chimneys.

She had lifted the brass knocker in the shape of an anchor and knocked twice. Marisa Whitby had opened the door a moment later, wearing a pair of cargo pants rolled at the ankle and a loose button-down shirt. In one hand she held a dishtowel, and in the other a spatula. "Come in," she said with a smile. "I had a hankering for pancakes," she explained as she ushered Hayley into the house. "Would you like some?"

Hayley had declined the offer but had accepted a cup of coffee. The interview had been held at the kitchen table, where Marisa had scarfed down four pancakes in an impressive few minutes. Hayley had appreciated her straightforward way of asking questions and her attentive way of listening to the answers. Marisa had explained that she had agreed to teach a course that summer at Yorktide Community College, which was the reason she needed to hire a nanny. "It's a favor," she explained. "The director of the Romance Languages Department and I went to graduate school together and we've stayed friends. Her husband is going through chemotherapy, and being Tom's caretaker is a full-time job right now. When the guy Deb had lined up to teach the course bailed at the last minute, she turned to me."

After they had spoken for half an hour, Marisa led Hayley to the twins' bedroom on the second floor. They had just woken from a nap and were sitting up in their cribs, quietly playing with plush toys. They were truly adorable little girls with their mother's strawberry blond hair. They were not identical; one had blue eyes and the other's eyes were distinctly green, and one was noticeably smaller than the other—Lily, Hayley was to learn. "It's hard not to spoil your children," Marisa had admitted in a whisper. "I want them to grow up to be women people like and respect, not women known for spoiled and selfish behavior. But sometimes I look at those chubby little cheeks and I almost can't help but squeal."

Hayley had spent almost two hours with Marisa and the girls. After giving the girls a snack they had toured the house, passing through the first floor, on which there was a living room, a dining room, a kitchen, a bathroom, and a guest bedroom, then moving on to the second floor, which featured a very large master suite complete with a deck facing the ocean, two smaller but still substantial bedrooms, and another full bathroom. After that they visited the patio off the kitchen and the beautiful garden beyond it, filled with gorgeous plants and flowers, many of which Hayley couldn't name.

"I'm sorry there's no pool," Marisa had said at the end of the tour. "I did buy a small plastic wading pool for the girls to splash around in." Hayley had assured her that was not a problem.

Marisa had promised to let Hayley know her decision within twenty-four hours, for which consideration Hayley was grateful. If she didn't get the position with the Whitby family, she would simply go ahead with the other two interviews she had lined up. It took more than one rejection to ruin Hayley Franklin's motivation.

The sudden sound of a key in the lock on the door to the apartment caused Hayley to flinch. A half a moment later she heard the door quietly opening and then closing. Hayley sighed in relief. It was her mother. It would be so nice to live without a knot in her stomach, without the constant anticipation of chaos. It would be so nice to be able to relax in her own home.

"I'm in the kitchen, Mom," Hayley called out. "Dinner is almost ready."

A moment later Nora Franklin was standing in the doorway to the kitchen. "Is that corn bread I smell?" she asked with a smile.

Hayley returned the smile. "You bet," she said.

Chapter 14

Amy arrived at The Atlantic at ten minutes after noon, five minutes before she was scheduled to meet Cressida Prior. She had no idea what the woman looked like; she had forgotten to Google her. Anyway, Amy figured she would be able to recognize her; it was preseason, and there were very few nonlocals in Yorktide at the moment. And if she had any difficulty identifying Ms. Prior she could always ask one of the restaurant's staff to help her.

Amy had decided to wear one of the narrow bodice, full-skirted sundresses she so loved. A headband helped control her wildly curly hair, which she had gotten trimmed for the occasion. Closed-toe espadrilles with a sensible one-and-a-half-inch wedge completed the look, which Amy hoped was both professional and approachable. No one wanted to hire a starched monster to care for her children. Right?

When a scan of the restaurant's imposing foyer revealed no one likely to be the woman she had come to meet, Amy approached a passing waiter, who pointed her to the bar area, where Amy found a very tall woman looking down at an iPhone in her hand. The woman was very thin, almost runway model thin. Her dark hair was cut super short; when Amy looked more closely, she saw that the hair was actually quite sparse. She was wearing a dress Amy was pretty sure she had recently seen in *Harper's Bazaar*, and she immediately recognized the woman's bag as Chanel.

Amy took a deep breath, walked purposefully toward the woman, and stuck out her hand. "Ms. Prior?" she said. "I'm Amy Latimer. It's a pleasure to meet you."

Cressida Prior's lips slid into a momentary fine line of a smile. "I don't care for shaking hands," she said. "It's a convenient way to spread germs."

Amy's hand dropped to her side. She could feel her cheeks flame. Of course it was a dirty habit. Why hadn't she ever thought of that before?

"Come. I've reserved a table by the window."

Mutely Amy followed Ms. Prior's rapid strides across the dining room. A waiter followed. After announcing they would each have a coffee, Cressida dismissed the waiter. Amy had thought they were meeting for lunch. It was almost twelve-thirty after all. But that was okay. She would have lunch when she got home.

And then the proverbial lightbulb went on in Amy's head. "I thought I recognized your name!" she said excitedly. "Cressida Prior of Prior Ascendancy! We learned about you in a course I took two semesters ago. It was about how entrepreneurs use social media to help start and build their businesses."

Cressida smiled. "I'm glad to know colleges these days teach the important things, not only airy-fairy academic nonsense. Do you know that Prior Ascendancy is the ultimate in one-stop shopping for meeting and convention directors of a majority of the big medical associations in the country? Of course, we also have a long list of clients in the corporate sector."

In spite of Cressida's statement, Amy still wasn't entirely sure what it was that Prior Ascendancy did, but she was not about to admit that. "I know," she said, though she hadn't known. "It's very impressive."

Cressida bestowed a more robust smile on Amy, and the interview flowed more easily from that point on. Cressida asked a few basic questions—how old was she; had she lived all of her life in

Yorktide; what was her favorite television show—and encouraged Amy to talk about one of her favorite topics, fashion.

"I have a good feeling about you," Cressida announced after a mere fifteen minutes. "And I'm never wrong. You've got the job."

For a moment, Amy didn't quite believe what she had heard. "I do?" she said. When Cressida nodded, Amy said, "Thank you! I mean . . . thank you!"

"No need to thank me. I'm sure you'll prove me right by being a great help to me."

Amy hesitated. She felt embarrassed to be asking, but . . . "The agency said there would be a contract for me to sign?"

"I prefer to leave the agency out of this, as you might have gathered from my contacting you directly. Our agreement will be just between us, an arrangement that will save us both time and money. The agency people need never know that we met. And there's no need for a contract. Any deal that can't be closed with a handshake isn't worth closing." Cressida smiled. "A figurative handshake, of course. And you can call me Cressida."

Amy nodded. "Thank you," she said again.

"As for pay, I think you'll find I can be generous, especially when there's no middleman to pay." Cressida took a small leather-bound notebook from her Chanel bag and with a beautiful pen, also pulled from her bag, she wrote something on a page. When she was done, she tore the page from the notebook and slid it across the table to Amy.

Amy gasped. "Thank you!" she breathed. "Thank you so much." She thought she might cry. She would be paid on an hourly basis and would receive her wages in cash at the end of each week. The sum was more than she had ever hoped to make, ever.

Cressida paid the bill and then handed Amy a small printed booklet. "Read this carefully," she said. "You'll start the Monday of the second week of June. If you have any questions in the meantime, my contact information is on the back page, as are the names of the children and my husband. I'll notify you when I've chosen a house so you'll know where to show up. Let's say eight a.m."

Amy began to extend her hand before remembering that Cressida didn't care for handshakes. She followed Cressida out of the restaurant. With a brisk nod, Cressida walked off toward a bright red Tesla. Amy waited until she had pulled out of the lot before getting into her fifteen-year-old Honda Civic. She could barely contain her excitement. *The* Cressida Prior had chosen her to be nanny to her children, whatever their names were. Amy flipped to the last page of the booklet Cressida had given her. Jordan and Rhiannon.

Amy started the car's engine. She couldn't wait to tell her mother the good news.

Chapter 15

Leda was in the kitchen making a cup of tea when she heard the front door open and shut. A moment later Amy burst into the room, cheeks flushed like a schoolgirl's.

"I got the job!" Amy cried. "Can you believe it?"

Leda took the tea bag from her cup and dropped it into the garbage. "What do you mean?"

"I went to the interview and Ms. Prior, I mean Cressida, offered me the job right then and there!"

"She didn't say she was going to check your references?" Leda asked with a frown.

"Nope," Amy said. "She said she had a good feeling about me."

"Doesn't she have to go through the employment agency before making the offer official?"

"She told me there's no need for the agency," Amy explained. "Didn't I tell you she contacted me directly?"

This was strange and possibly worrisome news. "No," Leda said. "You didn't."

"Huh. I thought I did. Anyway, Cressida said an agreement between just the two of us would save us both time and money. Something about there being no middleman."

Leda managed a smile. "Well," she said, "I suppose congratulations are in order. So, what's she like? Did you meet Mr. Prior, if he exists? The children?"

Amy sat at the table and reached for one of the apples piled in a ceramic bowl made by Leda's friend Missy. "Nope. It was just Cressida at the restaurant. And Mom, she's fantastic!"

"In what way?" Leda asked, joining her daughter at the table.

"Well, she's super elegant and chic, for one. And remember how we thought her name sounded familiar? That's because she's the founder and president of Prior Ascendancy. Or maybe she's the founder and CEO." Amy shook her head. "Something like that. Isn't that awesome? I can't wait for you to meet her. I'm sure I'll be able to introduce you guys at some point."

Leda wasn't at all sure Cressida Prior would be eager to meet the mother of her summer nanny. She glanced down at her baggy linen trousers and wondered at what point her daughter had started finding CEOs awesome. "By the way," she asked, "what sort of company is Prior Ascendancy? I've never really been clear on that."

Amy frowned in concentration. "She explained it to me. It's sort of like one-stop shopping for people setting up conventions. I think. I can't really describe it, but that doesn't matter. You'll never believe how much money she's paying me. Go ahead, guess."

"Why don't you just tell me," Leda suggested.

"Okay. Ready?" Amy named a sum that would have sent Leda reeling if she hadn't already been seated.

"That's very generous," she said. "*Very* generous. The job description must be very detailed." *Exhaustive even*, Leda thought. "I could take a look at your contract if you'd like. Two heads are often better than one in these matters."

"There is no contract," Amy told her. "Cressida said we didn't need one. She said that if a handshake, a figurative one, isn't enough to seal a deal, then the deal isn't worth sealing. Or something like that. I forget exactly."

Leda frowned. If Ms. Prior had hired Amy through the employment agency there would be an official contract. A legal one. "But it's usual for there to be an agreement in writing," she pointed out. "A contract is for the protection of both parties, you know. It seems odd to me that a professional like Cressida Prior would dispense with something so basic to doing business."

Amy laughed. "I'm not worried. Mom. This is Cressida Prior we're talking about, *the* Cressida Prior! If she says we don't need a contract, I believe her."

Though Leda wasn't at all happy about Cressida Prior's refusal to hire Amy through the employment agency, or to give Amy a written contract, or about the fact that Amy hadn't been introduced to the children and the children to Amy, Leda decided to let the subject drop for the moment. But only for the moment. "Well," she said, "congratulations again. I hope everything works out."

"Why wouldn't it? Oh, Mom, I can't believe my luck! Working for such an awesome, amazing person is like, I don't know, a dream come true!"

"It will be the children you'll be spending your time with," Leda pointed out. "Not their mother."

"I know, but still. Oh, I almost forgot! Cressida gave me this to read." Amy pulled a small booklet from her bag and tossed it onto the table. "I'll look at it later. I can't wait for school to be out so I can start my new job!"

"Don't let visions of an idyllic summer get in the way of studying for final exams," Leda warned.

"Really, Mom?" Amy got up from the table and went to the fridge. "I'm going to get something to eat. An apple is so not enough for lunch."

"I thought Cressida was taking you to lunch," Leda said.

"I thought so, too," Amy admitted, pulling a jar of peanut butter and one of jelly from the fridge, "but we only had coffee."

Leda watched as her daughter quickly and messily made a sandwich. The money Cressida Prior was offering would be a big temptation to anyone but especially to someone as financially clueless as Amy. She wished Amy would be earning a more reasonable amount of money so she wouldn't be tempted to spend too much on unnecessary items when there were so many important things to be paid for.

But wishes were dangerous things.

Chapter 16

Amy had hurriedly ushered Hayley into the house. "Wait for me in the living room," she instructed. "I have to take the cookies out of the oven in like two seconds."

Hayley had gone into the living room as directed. No sooner had she sat on the couch than Winston made himself at home on her lap. Hayley liked cats and dogs. One day, she would like to adopt an animal. That is, if she were ever able to live on her own without worrying about her family, and most days that seemed like an impossible dream.

"Ready for my big news?" Amy asked, suddenly standing in the doorway. Hayley had never seen her look so excited. "I got the job working for Cressida Prior!"

"You got the job?" Hayley was surprised. She was very fond of her friend, but she wasn't at all confident that Amy would make a successful nanny.

Amy plopped into an armchair. "Yup. And don't you recognize the name?"

"Nope," Hayley admitted.

"Cressida Prior of Prior Ascendancy. It's this huge successful company she founded all on her own."

Hayley scratched Winston's chin more vigorously. "She thinks pretty highly of herself, doesn't she? Ascendancy? Gods ascend. People don't."

"I think it's a good name for a company," Amy said robustly. "It sounds important. Anyway, how did your interview go?"

"Fine. I should know by later today if I got the job."

"What was Mrs. Whitby like?" Amy asked.

"She was pretty down-to-earth," Hayley told her. "Not what I expected."

"I'm sure you'll get the job," Amy said firmly. "Wait, did I tell you how much I'm getting paid?"

"No, and I don't need to know. A person's salary is a private matter."

"Come on," Amy cried. "You're my best friend. I'm going to tell you, so get ready."

Amy did tell her, and for a terrible moment Hayley felt her entire body buzz with jealousy. The salary Marisa Whitby was offering didn't come near what Amy had been offered, but it still was significant. "That's a lot of money," she said neutrally. "What did your contact at the employment agency say about it? I mean, is it usual for a client to be so . . ." Hayley had been about to say "generous," but somehow the word didn't seem right.

Amy laughed. "OMG, I forgot to tell you, too! Cressida hired me privately. I mean, she found my name through the agency, but our agreement is totally between us."

"Is that right?" Hayley commented. Every alarm bell in her cautionary system was going off, but she had known Amy long enough to be sure that nothing she could say right now would make her friend take a closer and more critical look at the situation in which she found herself. "You should be able to save at least five thousand dollars by the end of the summer."

"Yeah, but I'm also going to buy some things I've been totally wanting. Hey, I almost forgot. I saw your father the other day. He was driving an old Mustang. Since when does he have a cool car?"

"Since never," Hayley told her. "It belongs to one of his cronies. I don't know what's wrong with the guy to have loaned it to my father. He's got to know the car's going to come back damaged or worse."

Amy sighed. "I know I shouldn't speak ill of your father, but he really is a scoundrel."

"Scoundrels have charm," Hayley corrected. "My father has about as much charm as a slug."

"I wonder why your mother married him. There had to be something that made her blind to his faults. Love, I suppose."

"Lust," Hayley corrected. "My father was good-looking back then, before he got all bloated and bleary eyed with booze. I've seen pictures. My mother's head must have been turned by his flashing eyes, because he certainly didn't have anything else going for him."

"Did your mother's parents ever try to intervene once she married your father?" Amy asked with a frown.

"I don't know," Hayley said. "Anyway, what could they have done? I do know they were totally against the marriage. My grandmother told me once when my mother took Brandon and me to visit. And when my grandparents died, all my father wanted to know was if my mother was left any money."

"Was she?" Amy asked.

"About enough to bury her parents and to pay off a few outstanding debts," Hayley said. "My father wasn't happy. He has this huge sense of entitlement, like the world owes him something simply because he's alive. The world doesn't owe anyone anything."

"That's a grim way of looking at things," Amy said.

"Not grim," Hayley argued. "Just realistic." She ran her hand down Winston's silky back. Life was fundamentally unfair, she thought. There was no such thing as a magic wand, and miracles only happened in movies. The sooner you accepted that, the better.

Suddenly, Amy jumped to her feet. "I think we should celebrate! The cookies should be cool by now. Come on!"

Dutifully, Hayley followed Amy to the kitchen, only after extricating herself from under eighteen pounds of annoyed cat.

Chapter 17

Amy parked in the lot behind the old-fashioned pharmacy and set out in the direction of The Yellow Buttercup. She was on a pre-shopping mission in preparation for the days in the not-too-distant future when she would have real disposable income, not the occasional few dollars she had now. With all the money Cressida would be paying her, there would be more than enough to spend on fun extras. And, of course, some left over to put in the bank.

The night before, Amy had spent over an hour reading up on Prior Ascendancy, but she still wasn't 100 percent clear on how the company worked. And she hadn't bothered to check out Cressida's reputation on any of the nanny websites like her mother had suggested. Cressida Prior was famous. She had won her first award from an organization that recognized excellence in business before she was thirty. Of course she would be a fantastic boss.

Amy was just outside The Yellow Buttercup when she spotted Noah Woolrich across the street, standing outside the new artisanal candy shop and talking on his cell phone. Everyone in Yorktide knew that Noah's romantic interest in Amy dated back to their grammar school days. In first grade he had given her an envelope in which he had put three pennies and a note written in blue crayon. The note had read: *yur friend noah.* It was the first of many small gestures that had continued until, in seventh grade, Noah had gathered his courage to ask Amy to be his date to the spring social. Amy had said no. She thought that Noah was nice, but she was in no way ready to like boys "in that way." And from that point on Noah had seemed content to admire from afar. It wasn't until he had moved back to Yorktide in early May that he had really spoken to her again. They had run into each other in Hannaford. Amy had felt genuinely glad to see him, and they had parted with vague promises to get together at some point.

Amy was about to wave when a very pretty young woman she didn't recognize came out of the candy shop and joined Noah. Amy felt a strange twinge in her stomach. But that was silly. She wasn't interested in Noah, so she couldn't be jealous. Amy watched as Noah enveloped the young woman in a hug. And then she turned abruptly and climbed the two low steps to the store.

A bell above the door tinkled prettily as Amy stepped inside. She immediately saw that she was the only customer. The store was crowded with merchandise, mostly beautiful clothing and accessories but there were also displays of scented candles, home decorating books, and handmade soaps. Amy wandered slowly through the offerings. She had never been able to afford anything at The Yellow Buttercup, but before too long she would be able to buy, say . . . Amy's eyes widened. Four hundred dollars for a cotton scarf? Even if she had as much money as Cressida Prior, she wasn't sure she would feel comfortable spending four hundred dollars on a scarf. But maybe she would. Everything was relative. Hayley was always saying that.

Amy roamed on, occasionally picking up an item to examine it more closely. She avoided making eye contact with the well-dressed saleswoman behind the counter at the back of the store. She was a little embarrassed that she wasn't there to actually buy anything. Not that she was wasting anyone's time or anything. . . .

The saleswoman suddenly cleared her throat, and Amy startled. Maybe the saleswoman thought she was a shoplifter. Maybe she knew that Amy couldn't afford a single thing in the store, not even a fifteen-dollar scented candle. Slowly but purposely Amy walked to the door and left the store, half-expecting the saleswoman to follow her out and demand to see the contents of her pockets. But the saleswoman did not follow, and Amy felt annoyed with herself. Why had she felt as if she didn't belong in The Yellow Buttercup? Her money was as good as anyone's. Rather, the money she would have before long.

Noah and the mystery woman were nowhere in sight. Amy was glad. She was also curious. But just a little bit.

Chapter 18

It was a cool, rainy afternoon, more like late September than June. Leda was in her studio working on a set of cushion covers one of her neighbors had ordered. Her thoughts, however, had again drifted to Amy and the situation she had accepted from Cressida Prior.

Leda's daughter had few faults, but the biggest one was that she was not the best judge of character. To be fair, there were times when even the most astute judge of character was fooled into believing an unethical person ethical or a criminal person innocent, but Amy had made too many bad calls for her mother's comfort. There was, for example, the time when, in spite of education about the dangers of going off with strangers, a ten-year-old Amy had been just about to get into the car of a couple who claimed they could best find their lost puppy only with her help, when miraculously Vera had come along and saved the day. "But they were so sad," Amy had told Vera, who was leading Amy home by the hand. "How could I say no?"

Then, when Amy was fifteen, her head had been completely turned by an eighteen-year-old senior who had beguiled her with tales of his selfless work in an unnamed nursing home and his volunteer services at an unnamed no-kill animal shelter, until one afternoon Amy had come tearing into the house only to tell Leda that this paragon of virtue had been arrested for illegal possession of a firearm. "And I almost said yes to a date with him!" Amy had cried. "How could I not have seen the truth?"

Most recently, in her freshman year of college, Amy had found herself the victim of a Mean Girl plot; the new friend from English class who had seemed so interested in getting to know Amy had one day cruelly cut her off. "She wouldn't even look at me," Amy had complained to her mother that evening, in genuine distress. "I said hello like I always do, but she just turned away. What did I do wrong?"

But there was little Leda could do now that Amy had taken the position other than offer mild warnings and hope that Amy didn't react by doing just the opposite of what her mother was warning against.

The back door banged open and shut, and a moment later Vera appeared in the studio. She was wearing a bulky knit sweater and a beret. "I love days like this," she said. "If it weren't for the money I earn in summer, I'd want it to be fall all year round."

Leda smiled. "Wouldn't you miss lazy afternoons sunning yourself at the beach?"

Vera dropped into the old armchair that had once belonged to Leda's grandmother. "Like I ever have an afternoon off? So, how did Amy's big interview go?"

"Funny you should ask," Leda said, and she told Vera about Amy's getting the position immediately and how Ms. Prior, founder and president "or something" of Prior Ascendancy, had told Amy there was no need for a written contract or for the employment agency to be involved.

"What crap," Vera said, reaching down to scratch Harry's head as he leaned against her leg. "You'd better believe she's got an army of lawyers hashing out even the tiniest business transaction she makes. And without the agency there's no referee, as it were, to negotiate if problems arise. What's she playing at, I wonder."

"Taking advantage of a young woman who's clearly not the savviest person you'll meet?" Leda suggested.

"Well, not that I want anything bad to happen to Amy, but if she *is* taken advantage of by this woman it's a lesson learned. What does Prior Ascendancy do, anyway?" Vera asked.

"Don't ask Amy. She doesn't know. As far as I can make out, Prior Ascendancy organizes conventions and annual meetings for groups like dentists and food wholesalers."

Vera grimaced. "That doesn't sound very glamorous."

"And get this. Amy wasn't introduced to the children. I don't know about you, but if I were hiring someone to care for my children I'd want to be sure they took to the person before I went ahead and took her on."

"That is odd," Vera said. "For Amy's sake let's hope the kids aren't undisciplined monsters."

"And she didn't ask to see Amy's list of references. For all Cressida Prior knows, she could have been hiring a criminal. I don't know, Vera, nothing about this situation seems right."

"I agree there are some strange things about it. But keep in mind that given your history you were prejudiced about Amy's working as a nanny from the start."

"I know. Still, take a look at this." Leda handed her friend the booklet Ms. Prior had given Amy.

Vera flipped through the booklet, occasionally stopping to read a page closely. After a moment, she looked up. "There's nothing in here about the care of the children," she said. "This is ridiculous. *Don't bring chips or other snacks into the house. Be sure to use hand sanitizer before leaving the bathroom. No shorts. No halter tops.* Who wears halter tops these days?"

Leda frowned. "I have a feeling this summer is going to prove very interesting. Now, how about a cup of hot chocolate to go with this autumnal weather we're having?"

Chapter 19

Hayley was engaged in scrubbing the kitchen sink when her cell phone rang. Hurriedly, she wiped her hands on a towel that had seen better days and then answered.

"Hayley?" a pleasant voice said. "This is Marisa Whitby."

"Oh," Hayley said. She was aware of a slight fluttering of butterfly wings in her stomach. "Hello."

"I'm calling to offer you the position as nanny to Lily and Layla," Marisa said. "Your references were impeccable, and I really enjoyed our conversation yesterday. More, the girls seem to take to you. So, what do you think? I hope you're still interested. I wanted to call as soon as possible in case you were offered another position."

Hayley leaned back against the sink. She felt downright faint with relief. "I think, I mean, yes, thank you," she said. "Thank you very much. I'd love to work for you this summer."

"I'm so glad!" Marisa went on to outline the terms of the agreement they had discussed the day before and promised to drop off two copies of a contract later that day.

"No," Hayley said quickly. Marisa could not come to her home. Ever. "I mean, thank you, but I'll come by and pick it up if that's all right."

Marisa agreed, and they ended the call.

Hayley stood against the sink and allowed this monumental news to sink it. The idea of finally being able to get out of Yorktide—her mother in tow—seemed almost like a real possibility now. Almost. If she could work as a summer nanny for a few years, she might just be able to save enough money to make a clean break. And who knew whom she might meet while working for wealthy people like the Whitbys? Someone who might recognize her intelligence and her thirst for knowledge and decide to sponsor her education, someone who might . . .

With a sharp tug, Hayley reined in her excitement. She was too practical and had experienced too much hard luck to believe in wonderful things happening for her. And she was still wary of the Whitbys, in spite of what she had seen of Marisa. People with the kind of money they had couldn't be as decent as Marisa seemed to be.

Hayley walked rapidly to her room in order to change into something presentable. She couldn't show up at the Whitbys' home wearing her old cutoff jean shorts and a tank top. And in spite of the wariness that was natural to her, she realized that she felt the need to celebrate this moment. On her way back from the Whitbys' house, she would stop at Dunkin' Donuts and buy one of those seriously overpriced frothy coffee drinks. Maybe. Probably not.

Chapter 20

Leda did a quick mental check to see if there was anything she had forgotten to set out. Amy's graduation party had to be perfect. Vera had provided the food, so that wasn't a worry. Leda had picked up the cake from Bread and Roses that morning. Phil had provided gorgeous arrangements of pink and white roses as his gift to Amy. The drinks table was well stocked. The only thing that might be considered missing was music. Leda didn't have a sound system that could handle parties.

Amy's diploma was temporarily stuck to a piece of board displayed on an easel set up in the kitchen. After the party, Leda would have the diploma properly laminated. She was proud of her daughter. Academics didn't come easily to Amy, but she had graduated with a respectable grade point average. No more could be asked for.

Leda took a sip of the very nice wine that Vera had been able to provide with a major discount and looked over to where Amy was chatting with the girls she would be living with in Boston come September. Amy had known all three of them since freshman year. Tracy would be attending law school. Stella had plans to work as a hostess in an upscale restaurant. Her father was the one who had set aside an apartment for the girls in one of the buildings he owned in Allston; he was giving them a significant cut on the rent.

The third girl, Megan, would be continuing on the path to becoming a licensed physical therapist. They were all smart and decent young women, and Leda had no worries about one of them evolving into a bad influence on the others.

Hayley, too, had come to the party, but without her mother. That was no surprise. Increasingly Nora Franklin had become a bit of a recluse. Word around town was that she no longer even attended church on Sundays. Leda knew for sure that many years ago Father Mark and members of Saint Matthew's Women's Council had tried to stage an intervention of sorts but that it had come to nothing.

Poor Hayley, Leda thought, as she walked across the freshly mown yard to say hello. It had to sting, not receiving a diploma of her own.

"I'm glad you could make it," Leda said when she had joined her.

Hayley nodded. "This is a big day for Amy. I wouldn't miss it for anything."

"Amy tells me you got a good position working for a family called the Whitbys. Congratulations."

"Thanks," Hayley said. "The girls are adorable. Mrs. Whitby seems very nice. I haven't met Mr. Whitby yet, but he won't be at the house a lot."

"Amy is over the moon about working for the illustrious Cressida Prior this summer," Leda told her.

Hayley looked to where Amy stood chatting with her future roommates. "I'm guessing Ms. Prior will be a formidable employer," she said. "No one achieves that level of success without being an exacting boss. And no one pays that kind of salary without demanding a pound of flesh."

"I agree. I have to admit I'm a bit worried about how Amy will handle the job, and the money." Leda shook her head and smiled. "But this is a party. We should be focused on the good things."

"Yes," Hayley said with a bit of a smile. "We should be."

"Do you want to take a piece of cake home for your mom?" Leda asked. "I'm sorry she couldn't join the celebration."

"Thanks," Hayley said. "That would be nice."

"Not that the cake is anything like the cakes Nora Franklin

used to make. I remember all those years she won first prize in the annual Yorktide bake-off."

"That was a very long time ago," Hayley said, and then she moved off.

Leda sighed. She regretted having called up the memory of Nora Franklin in earlier times, before the full awfulness of her life had descended on her.

"Mom!" Amy was waving wildly from across the yard, a pink rose from one of the arrangements stuck behind her ear.

Leda smiled and went to join her daughter.

Chapter 21

Hayley was nervous. Of course, all first days on a job were notoriously anxiety ridden, but there was an awful lot riding on this particular job. She tried to put all other thoughts from her mind as she drove to number 1 Overlook Road, but one refused to budge. The memory of Amy's graduation party. Hayley hated herself for it, but she had felt a distinct note of resentment watching Amy and the girls who were going to be her roommates in Boston this autumn. They were getting out. They weren't burdened with parents who could barely function on their own. It was wrong to resent another person's happiness or success, but sometimes it was very difficult not to.

Difficult, Hayley reminded herself, pulling into the drive before the big old house overlooking the ocean, *but not impossible.*

Marisa let her in, wearing what might have been the same cargo pants and shirt she had been wearing the first time they had met.

"I don't think I told you why Jon and I chose Maine this summer," Marisa said conversationally as they headed toward the kitchen. "We were watching an old black-and-white movie set on a wild and rocky coast somewhere and we thought, Why not Maine? And here we are."

Hayley smiled. "There are far worse places to be in summer."

"I agree! I think I told you that Jon won't be here all that often."

Marisa smiled. "Some might say he's a workaholic, but it's not that. It's more that he feels a personal duty to tend to the company he founded. Anyway, that's neither here nor there."

Marisa went on to explain that Hayley would largely be left alone to manage the girls, and that arrangement suited Hayley just fine. Marisa then detailed the girls' current meal and nap schedule, provided important contact information in case of emergency, indicated each child's favorite toys, and gave Hayley permission to take the girls to the beach as long as they were slathered in sunblock and wore their sunhats. "Layla hates to wear a hat," she warned Hayley. "It will be a struggle to keep it on her head." Marisa smiled. "I know I said this before, but your references from the families for whom you've babysat were really glowing."

"Thanks," Hayley said. "I like children." But it was more than just liking children, Hayley thought. In truth, she had a fierce need to protect the young and vulnerable, a need that stemmed from having been a frightened and benignly neglected child.

"I'd better get changed," Marisa said suddenly. "I can't show up at work wearing my knock-around clothes, though I wish I could."

After Marisa had gone off to the college for a day of meetings before classes began the following week, Hayley found herself feeling a bit stunned. For a brief moment, she allowed herself to imagine that she was the owner of the lovely old house. Haley wasn't prone to fantasizing; she thought it was time that would be better spent doing something productive. But every once in a rare while she allowed herself to indulge in imaginary scenarios in which life was far less difficult than it really was. Returning from those scenarios to the actuality of her life was always accompanied by a severe deflation of spirits, a very good reason to keep imagination in check.

Sweet childhood chatter burst from the kitchen's baby monitor, alerting Hayley to the twins' waking. She hurried to their bedroom on the second floor, ashamed that she had allowed herself the indulgence of fantasy. Not again, she warned herself. Never again.

Chapter 22

Amy got out of her car after checking for the millionth time that she had the right address: 10 Hilltop Close. She was nervous. She had dressed with care, following as best she could the suggestions Cressida had made regarding her working wardrobe. She wasn't sure how active the children would be—in fact, she had absolutely no information about the children whatsoever aside from their names and ages—so she had brought along a change of clothes in case she would be playing tag in the backyard or tossing a Frisbee at the beach. She would leave the bag in the car for now.

The house that stood at the top of the rise before her looked to be made of concrete and was painted a gleaming white. There were lots of windows. The roof was flat, and only three long, low steps lead to the front door. The front lawn was perfectly mowed; there were no flower beds, shrubs, or trees. A wide path of white gravel led from the edge of the lawn around the side of the house.

Cressida answered the door before Amy could ring the bell. "You're right on time," she noted, looking at her watch. It was a Rolex. She was wearing a thin silk blouse, unbuttoned far enough for Amy to see the bones of her chest, and a pair of slim-fitting black slacks.

"Thanks," Amy said.

Cressida nodded. "Let me show you around the house."

Cressida led Amy from the kitchen with gleaming stainless-steel appliances and white stone countertops to the smallest of three bedrooms on the second floor, a room painted white from floor to ceiling. It didn't take Amy long to realize that the house was entirely bare of carpets, rugs, wall hangings, even curtains. Everything seemed spare and hard-edged; even the window shades were made of what appeared to be an inflexible material, maybe some sort of plastic.

"What do you think?" Cressida asked when they had completed the tour.

Amy wasn't quite sure how to reply. In truth, she didn't much like what she had seen—the house was too stark for her tastes—though she did like the fact that there was a huge swimming pool in the middle of the patio and that the view of the ocean was amazing. "It's very modern," she said finally.

"It's very clean is what it is," Cressida said. "I can't tolerate dirt or mess. You'll need to keep that in mind."

"Yes," Amy said. "I will." It was in the booklet Cressida had given her after the interview.

"This house is absolutely a dream," Cressida said when they were once again in the living room. "Still, before I agreed to rent I stipulated that all unnecessary fabrics and knickknacks be removed before I would take up residence."

Amy smiled. "My mother loves being surrounded by knickknacks. She's a professional fiber artist. She makes rugs and tapestries and pillows and things like that. Sometimes she'll make a quilt for a birthday or wedding anniversary."

Cressida looked off into the middle distance before turning again to Amy. "How nice for her," she said, "but I'm sorry to say that all such things are unhygienic, collectors of dirt and bugs and dead skin cells. I require that sheets and towels be changed and washed daily. Will takes care of that. And the children are not allowed plush toys that aren't machine washable, and of course I won't tolerate pets."

Amy decided this would not be the time to mention Harry and

Winston. Surreptitiously she glanced down at her navy skirt, wondering if it was decorated with a stray cat hair or two. She would have to be extra careful to remove all traces of the boys before leaving for the Priors' each morning.

"Some people might think I'm being finicky," Cressida was saying, "but in fact I'm just a highly discriminating person, and often people like me are misunderstood."

"I'm sorry," Amy said, not sure if that was the right thing to say.

"I don't mind. Having taste is worth being misunderstood."

"Um, where are the children?" Amy asked. She was eager to meet them, eager and more than a bit nervous. What if they didn't like her? She really had very little experience with children, and she had a sneaking suspicion that some of them were probably smarter than she would ever be.

"I believe my husband took them to the beach." Cressida gestured over her shoulder. "There's a hose on the patio he uses to wash them down before they track sand and who knows what else into the house."

"Are they particularly messy children?" Amy asked. "My mother says that I was always coming home with muddy shoes and grass-stained knees."

"Not in the least," Cressida said sharply. "I've taught them to be extremely hygienic." And then she rolled her eyes. "But their father can be a bad influence, which is why I demand he use the hose."

Cressida offered nothing more about the children and their habits. Most of Amy's day was spent following Cressida from room to room and learning what changes she had required before agreeing to the rental. At one point, Cressida had gone into her office and locked the door behind her, leaving Amy to sit in one of the straight-backed chairs in the upstairs hall, figuratively twiddling her thumbs. Cressida had emerged from her office half an hour later looking much refreshed.

Only at four o'clock did Will Prior return to the house with Jordan and Rhiannon. By this point, Amy had very little idea of what to expect from Cressida's children. She half imagined they would be dressed in clothes from another century, Jordan in knee breeches and a stiff collar, Rhiannon in a starched white dress and highly polished Mary Janes.

But the children who greeted her were very much residents of the twenty-first century. Jordan seemed a bit shy, if his biting his lip was any indication. His hair was a startling shade of yellow blond, and his eyes were pale brown. He was, Amy thought, a beautiful child. He was dressed in a T-shirt with an image of a cartoon character Amy didn't recognize and a pair of cargo shorts. As for Rhiannon, she was her mother's mini-me if you focused on her facial features and the way she stood with her back ramrod straight. She was wearing a black T-shirt and black jeans; she definitely would stand out from the other children in town this summer. Her light brown hair was severely scraped back into a low ponytail. Overall she gave the impression of a joyless child, but Amy tried not to make a snap judgment. She was so often wrong when she did.

"This will be your nanny for the summer," Cressida announced. "Her name is Amy Latimer. Amy, this is Jordan and Rhiannon."

"Hi," Amy said. "I'm Amy."

"I know," Rhiannon said in a strangely flat voice. "My mother just told us your name."

Amy flushed. "Sorry. I mean, it's nice to meet you both."

Jordan suddenly stuck out his hand as if an electric shock had reminded him that it was the polite thing to do. Amy took it and Jordan pumped once before releasing his grip. He did not meet her eye.

Amy then turned to Rhiannon, expecting the girl to perform the ritual of greeting as well. But Rhiannon kept her arms at her side. "I don't shake hands," she said. "I don't like germs."

"Oh," Amy said. "Okay." So Rhiannon was like her mother in more ways than appearance.

Cressida suddenly sighed the sigh of a long-put-upon woman. "There you are," she said to the man who had just joined them in the living room. "You've kept us waiting. Amy, this is my husband."

Amy was again surprised. She hadn't really known what to expect Cressida's husband to look like, but it wasn't this youthful, good-looking man with a shock of hair the same color as that of his son's. His eyes were pale brown as well. He was narrow hipped and wiry, like he probably spent a lot of time on a bicycle or hiking trails rather than in a business suit in some corporate office. Like his son, he wore cargo shorts and a T-shirt. He gave her his hand to shake and welcomed her warmly.

No sooner had Will released Amy's hand than Cressida spoke sharply. "Shouldn't the children be getting to their homework?"

"Right." Will ushered his son and daughter from the room.

"They have summer homework assignments?" Amy asked. She wondered if she would be required to help them with math problems. The guidelines Cressida had given her didn't mention anything about solving math problems.

"I've set them a course of study. You can't let your mind get flabby." Cressida glanced at her Rolex. "Well, you can go home now. And Amy? You did a marvelous job today."

"Thank you," Amy said. "You're sure you don't need me to help with dinner or . . ."

"No. That's Will's job. And I should mention that there's no need for you to be spending time with my husband. I'm your employer. If you need something or have any questions, you come to me. Is that understood?"

"Yes," Amy said. "It's understood."

For a moment, Amy wondered if Cressida was worried that she would flirt with Mr. Prior, or maybe Cressida knew that her husband had a roving eye and she was giving Amy a veiled warning. But this was *the* Cressida Prior. What woman in her right mind would try to steal her husband? And what man married to Cressida Prior would be crazy enough to leave her for another woman?

"I'll see you at eight tomorrow morning," Cressida said, leading Amy to the door.

Amy got into her car. It had been a strange day all around; she hadn't really done anything and yet Cressida had praised her work. The meeting with the children had disconcerted her. Rhiannon seemed oddly self-possessed for her age, and Jordan was the kind of shy that could make other people uncomfortable. As for Will

Prior, he seemed okay, though she was having trouble accepting Will and Cressida as a couple. True, she had only just met them, but they seemed so vastly different.

With a shake of her head Amy decided right then and there that her first day had been a great success. As she drove back to Hawthorne Lane she found that she was very much looking forward to going back to 10 Hilltop Close the following day.

Chapter 23

Since morning Leda's mood had been a bit off. Part of that she attributed to worry about Amy and her first day on the job. Another part she rather ashamedly contributed to long-held self-doubts having to do with her work as a craftswoman. The fact was that even after all these years of earning a living by her talents, Leda still had trouble thinking of herself as a professional.

The event that had triggered this swelling of self-doubt was an article Leda had come across that morning in one of the many online magazines she read regularly. Andrea Black, all-around craftswoman, was featured in a five-page spotlight, complete with photos. Leda had always admired Andrea's work, and yet as Leda read she had felt a twinge of envy. Leda knew it was both foolish and wrong to be envious of someone who had genuinely earned her recognition and reward. It had occurred to Leda that maybe if she was more comfortable with her own decisions regarding her career she would be of a more generous spirit toward her fellow craftspeople. Phil was always urging her to spread her wings and explore her own definition of success, but change was difficult and sometimes it felt downright impossible.

Now, almost five in the afternoon, Leda was again at her desk, checking e-mail and urging herself into a better frame of mind. Suddenly, an e-mail popped up from an old acquaintance. There was a friendly greeting, followed by information about an event the following weekend at the Cornhusk Theatre. Josiah Marks had pursued Leda romantically some years back, but when she had expressed no interest in return he had gracefully backed away. There had been other potential suitors over the years, but none had managed to capture Leda's attention, despite that the majority had been the kind of man any intelligent and good-hearted woman might find acceptable.

Andrea Black. Josiah Marks. Leda had often wondered if her fear of professional success as well as her reluctance to get romantically involved could both be traced back to what Lance Stirling had done to her that long-ago summer. The possibility was disconcerting.

Firmly, Leda closed her laptop and headed for the kitchen. She was making one of Amy's favorite meals for dinner, chicken pot pie with peas and carrots. It would be easier to buy a frozen pot pie from the grocery store, but Leda believed in celebrating important events like the first day of a job and the last day of school. Her own mother had felt the same. It was a family tradition Leda hoped Amy would keep when she was married with her own family one day.

Leda sighed as she turned on the oven to heat. Noah Woolrich. The poor young man had been carrying a torch for so long, but there was a limit to even the deepest devotion. If Amy didn't come around soon, she might find her suitor-in-the-wings had set his sights on another, more welcoming woman.

Chapter 24

There was a refreshing breeze that evening. Amy was sitting in the narrow, high-backed rocking chair Mrs. Latimer had painted a peaceful blue, and Hayley was perched on the top step of the Latimers' small front porch.

"And there's this amazing pool," Amy was saying. "I'm hoping I'm allowed to use it. Cressida didn't say anything about it, and I didn't want to ask."

Amy had been going on about her first day working for the Priors for close to twenty minutes and yet there had been no mention of the children for whom she had been hired to care. Hayley found this odd.

"So, you didn't actually spend any time with Cressida's children?" Hayley asked when Amy stopped for a breath.

"Well, no," Amy admitted. "But I did meet them at the end of the day. They seemed nice. Well, Rhiannon was kind of cold actually and Jordan seemed pretty shy, but that's probably just because I'm new. I'm sure we'll all get along just fine. Hey, how was your first day?"

"Good," Hayley told her. "Marisa was around for a while, and then it was just me and the girls. They're very well behaved. Smart, too. Their language skills are pretty advanced. I've known some two-and-a-half-year-olds whose vocabulary was limited to two or three words."

"Guess what I bought with the money I've made so far?" Amy said suddenly.

"You got paid already?" Hayley asked, wondering if Amy had heard one word she had said.

"Well, no, but at the end of the week Cressida will give me cash for the hours I've worked."

"So you spent money you don't actually have?" Hayley remembered her brief conversation with Mrs. Latimer at Amy's graduation party. It seemed that her concerns were justified.

Amy sighed. "I do have it. I mean, I'll have it on Friday."

"All right, what did you buy?" Hayley asked.

"A fur hat. I drove to this consignment shop in Biddeford that sells designer stuff donated by rich women. When I saw the hat I just fell in love and had to have it. It was ninety dollars, but like the saleswoman said, it is an investment."

"Smart saleswoman," Hayley said dryly.

"Actually, the hat isn't meant to be worn for warmth even though it's fur. It's like one of those hats Kate Middleton wears, the ones tilted to the side of her head. It's for fancy occasions. It comes with a pin to help keep it on."

Hayley was absolutely certain she had never seen anyone in the state of Maine sporting such a thing. "So, where do you plan on wearing this hat?" she asked.

Amy shrugged. "It would be perfect for a winter wedding." Then she frowned. "Why are you looking at me like that? All judgmental."

"I'm not judging," Hayley lied. "How you spend your money is no business of mine."

Amy beamed. "Thanks, Hayley. It's so chic and elegant. I just know you'll love it."

"Yes," Hayley said. "I'm sure I will."

Chapter 25

The second day on the job is bound to be more about the children, Amy thought as she climbed the stairs to the front door. Before she could use the key Cressida had given her, the door opened. Amy wondered if Cressida had been watching for her. This morning she was wearing another thin silk blouse and slim tan pants. Diamond studs sparkled from her ears.

Cressida smiled. "I admire punctuality in a person," she said by way of greeting. Then she turned, and wordlessly Amy followed her upstairs to the room Cressida was using as her office.

"You're a very nice-looking girl, Amy," Cressida said as they went along, "so I know you won't take offense if I suggest that you would look even better if you lost five or ten pounds."

Amy was not offended. "You're right," she said. "I probably would."

"And the silhouette of that dress makes you look a bit too chubby. You should avoid a full skirt, at least until you drop some weight."

Amy glanced down at her 1950s-inspired sundress. Her mother had made it to Amy's specifications. "Yes," she said. "I see what you mean."

Cressida's office was painted an even brighter white than the other rooms in the house. At the moment the sun was shining in full force through the floor-to-ceiling windows that composed the room's fourth wall, windows that offered a spectacular view of the ocean. There was only one desk, at which was placed an ergonomic swivel chair covered in clear plastic. Amy wondered where Will did his work, assuming he had any to do, like bills to be paid or even stuff to look up online. Maybe in the master bedroom. The master bedroom was off-limits to Amy.

Suddenly Cressida pointed a perfectly manicured finger, interrupting Amy's musings. "What is that you're wearing around your wrist?" she asked.

Amy couldn't quite read Cressida's tone. It sounded like a mix of curiosity and horror, but that was silly. "It's a bracelet my mother made," Amy told her. "She used a traditional Japanese technique called Kumihimo. I'm probably not pronouncing that right. It's not easy to make something like this."

"I don't care for what's euphemistically called fashion jewelry," Cressida said. "I wear jewelry made of only important materials. Here, let me show you a few pieces from my collection. Shut the door, will you?"

Amy did as she was told. Cressida went to a narrow wooden chest about three feet high. "I bet you didn't know that this is a safe," Cressida said with a sly little smile. "It's bolted to the floor, of course. I have one like it at home in Atlanta. You should know that I don't show my pieces to just anyone."

"Oh," Amy said. "Thank you."

With her back to Amy, Cressida opened a small door in the front of the safe and punched the security code into a little keypad. There was a loud click, and Cressida pulled open what was essentially the front panel of the chest. From the safe she removed a beautiful tan leather box. Cressida chose a key from the set she wore around her wrist and unlocked it.

"When I travel I bring only a few essentials," Cressida explained before she lifted the box's lid. "My wedding rings, of course." Cressida thrust her left hand close to Amy's face.

Amy had noted the diamond-encrusted band and the large cushion-cut solitaire that sat atop a second band the moment she had met Cressida. A person would have to be blind to have missed the rings. "They're beautiful," she said.

"They are. I had them made to my exact specifications." Cressida laughed. "The rings Will gave me years ago were just pathetic. I sold them for scrap."

Amy didn't quite know what to say to that, so she held her tongue.

"And I never travel with copies like so many people do," Cressida said, opening the leather box. "This, for example, is a necklace from Tiffany's T collection."

Amy's eyes widened as she looked at the long gold chain draped across Cressida's hands. "It's so pretty," she said.

"I adore the collection. And this," Cressida said, returning the necklace to the box and choosing another piece, "this is a bracelet from their Hardware collection. I'm not entirely in love with it, but it was only a few thousand dollars so no cause for regret."

Amy didn't quite know what to say to that, either. Instead, she pointed to a gold bracelet settled against the cream-colored velvet that lined the box. "This is nice," she said.

Cressida laughed. "It's more than just nice. It's a Cartier Love bracelet. I have several. I stack bangles from Cartier with those from Hermès. And this," she said, lifting a necklace with what looked to Amy like flowers set at intervals, "is from the Van Cleef and Arpels Vintage Alhambra collection. It was introduced in 1968, you know."

Amy nodded, though she did not know and had never heard that word before. All-hamber?

"This, of course, is Bulgari," Cressida went on, displaying a large gold ring set with various colored stones. "The style is unmistakable."

"Unmistakable," Amy said.

"The image you present to the world is paramount," Cressida said, returning the ring to the box and folding her arms across her chest, her tone suddenly serious. "You have to decide what message you want to be sending to others. A person who chooses high quality over mere sentimentality is a person whom others can safely look up to and emulate. She is a person who announces to the world that she *matters*."

Amy felt slightly embarrassed; self-consciously she pulled the left sleeve of her blouse over her mother's bracelet. More, she felt grateful to Cressida for having taken the time to clue her in on a matter as important as one's public image. "I'd like to be that sort of person," she said. "A person people want to emulate."

Cressida bestowed on Amy a magnificent smile that put all of Amy's doubts to rest. "Excellent," she said. "Just what I'd hoped to hear." Cressida returned the box to the safe.

"Should I check on the children?" Amy asked. She hadn't seen Jordan or Rhiannon, or Will for that matter, since she had arrived that morning.

"Oh, they're not here," Cressida said with a wave of her hand. "I sent them all to some program at the historical society in Wells."

Amy was curious. She wondered why she hadn't been asked to accompany Will and the children on their excursion. Before she could frame the question in a way that wouldn't sound like a complaint, Cressida clapped her hands.

"Let's go to the kitchen and make kale shakes," she said. "We'll have so much fun!"

"Sure," Amy said, forcing a smile. Amy thought that kale was gross, but at least the shake would be slimming. With a hand on her rounded stomach, Amy followed Cressida from the room.

Chapter 26

Leda was in the kitchen, preparing dinner. Suddenly out of the corner of her eye, she caught a glimpse of Amy, arms loaded with what looked like heaps of fabric, passing in the hall.

"Amy?" she called.

Amy came to a halt, and Leda saw now what she was carrying. "What are you doing with those sundresses?" she asked.

"Bringing them to the thrift store," Amy said.

"Why? The yellow one is almost brand-new."

Amy sighed. "I'm tired of them. I don't like the style."

"What do you mean?" Leda asked. "You've always loved sundresses. And you look so pretty in them."

"They make me look too curvy," Amy said dismissively. "I want to look more streamlined. I want to be seen as someone with, I don't know, more purpose."

Leda strongly suspected that Amy was parroting someone else's opinions. Cressida Prior's opinions? "What sort of purpose?" she asked.

"Purpose in general," Amy replied.

"I see." Leda took a deep breath. "Look, do me a favor and hang on to the dresses for a bit. You might change your mind."

"I doubt it." Amy sighed. "And they're taking up so much room in my closet. But okay, if you insist."

Leda watched as Amy turned around and headed for the stairs, dresses in tow. She felt a bit hurt. Had Amy forgotten that her mother had made two of those dresses and that she had altered a few of the others so that they fit perfectly? Who else but Cressida Prior could have been the one to put the ridiculous notion about looking too curvy in Amy's head? She thought about the insanely large amount of money Cressida was paying Amy and hoped that Amy wouldn't waste it on clothing to please her employer when there were so many essentials she needed to purchase for her move to Boston come September.

Amy came into the kitchen, dresses gone, and began to roam, opening cupboards and staring at their contents, peeking into the breadbox, examining what was stored in the freezer.

"Dinner will be ready in a few minutes," Leda said.

Amy shrugged. "I'm fine."

"What did you have for lunch?" Leda asked.

"Cressida and I made kale shakes."

Leda, who was not constitutionally opposed to kale, nevertheless had some difficulty with the notion of drinking it rather than chewing it. "What else was in it besides kale?" she asked.

"There was some chopped garlic. And Cressida put in some protein powder or something."

"How did it taste?" Leda asked.

"Fine," Amy said.

Leda knew when her daughter was lying. "Still, you must be hungry if that's all you had for lunch."

"It was very filling, actually. Cressida said that sometimes she has only a kale shake a day for weeks and never feels tired or hungry."

Leda frowned. "That doesn't sound very healthy."

"Cressida says it is."

"And if Cressida said that the moon was made of green cheese, would you believe that, too?" Leda wanted to say this, but instead she brought the meal she had prepared to the table. "No kale was involved in the making of this dinner," she said lightly. "Still, I think you'll find it healthy."

"What's on the asparagus?" Amy asked suspiciously. "That's not butter, is it?"

"No," Leda lied. "Just lemon juice."

Amy took her usual seat at the table and with a gesture that appeared to Leda as almost surreptitious, she reached for a piece of bread, tore it in two, and stuffed one of the pieces into her mouth.

"So how did it go with the children today?" Leda asked, taking her own seat.

Amy swallowed before replying. "Actually," she said, "they weren't there. Will took them to a museum or something."

Leda placed a piece of cod onto her plate. "What did you do all day?" she asked carefully.

"I helped Cressida."

"Helped her with what?"

Amy poked a spear of asparagus with her fork and stuffed it into her mouth. "Things," she muttered around her food.

Leda took a bite of her cod. She didn't know exactly what sort of situation her daughter had gotten herself into, but it didn't seem—as her father used to say—on the up-and-up. Still, it was too soon to make any real judgment.

"There's apple pie for dessert," Leda said. "Vera made it this morning."

Amy put her fork on her plate, next to the cod from which she had only taken a few bites. "No thanks," she said. "I'm done."

Chapter 27

Taking a cue from Marisa Whitby's laid-back around-the-house style, Hayley was wearing an old pair of jeans, a white T-shirt, and sneakers without laces. Her hair was tied up in a loose bun, and her face was covered with a mud mask that had come in the mail the day before, a promotion for some new company or other. Hayley had decided to give it a try; you only had to leave it on for twenty minutes and you were guaranteed a glowing complexion. Not that Hayley believed a word of the hype, but it seemed silly to let the product go to waste, and as long as she was alone in the house doing nothing more exciting until the twins woke than tidying up the kitchen and unclogging the toilet in the powder room . . .

Hayley eyed the plunger with disgust. It had seen its day. She would put it in the trash and mention to Marisa that it needed to be replaced. Holding the plunger as far away from her body as possible, Hayley came out of the powder room and made her way toward the kitchen, where the garbage bin was kept by the back door.

No sooner had she passed through the open doorway than she came to a crashing halt. There was a man standing in the middle of the kitchen. He was tall and good looking. He was wearing cargo shorts and an untucked button-down shirt with the sleeves rolled up, and there was a travel bag at his feet. He had very large, very blue eyes and wavy auburn hair. Most important, he was a total stranger.

"Who the hell are you?" Hayley demanded, raising the plunger as if it were a weapon. "And what are you doing here?"

The man grinned. "I'm guessing you're the nanny," he said. "Either that or a plumber who for some bizarre reason likes to give herself a facial while on the job."

Hayley frowned. "You haven't answered my question."

"Right. I'm Ethan Whitby. Jon Whitby is my father. Didn't anyone tell you I'd be visiting this weekend?"

Hayley lowered the plunger and resisted the urge to touch her mud-packed cheek. "No," she said. "I didn't even know you existed."

"Ouch."

"Sorry. How did you get in?"

"I rang the doorbell but no one answered, so I tried the door. It was unlocked. So, you *are* the nanny?"

"Yes. The girls are upstairs taking a nap. I should go check on them." Hayley moved toward the doorway, careful not to turn her back on the stranger. She had only his word that he was indeed Jon Whitby's son. For all she knew he could be a psychopath intent on murder and mayhem. Fine, then, he could kill her but he was not getting anywhere near the children.

"Wait," the man calling himself Ethan said. "You haven't told me your name."

Hayley hesitated. She looked at him closely. His expression was open and candid, but that didn't necessarily mean anything. "Hayley," she said finally. "Hayley Franklin."

Ethan came forward and extended his hand. "Nice to meet you, Hayley Franklin. I'm sorry I startled you."

Hayley hesitated a moment before extending her own free hand. "It's okay," she said. "I really should get upstairs . . ."

"And I should put my bag in the guest room. By the way, where is the guest room?"

"There are two," Hayley told him. "One down the hall there, and one on the second floor."

"I'll take the one down here. Guess I'll see you later."

Ethan Whitby picked up his bag and headed down the hall. Hayley headed for the twins' bedroom on the second floor. She had had no idea that Mr. Whitby had an adult son. A very attractive adult son at that. And what a first impression she had made on him, with her face plastered in mud and a grimy old plunger in her hand. With a start, Hayley realized that she was still wielding said plunger and grimaced.

Chapter 28

"But Mom, I only want to hang out at their house for an hour. Dad said they seemed nice. He said it was okay if it was okay with you, so . . ."

Amy was with Cressida in the office when Rhiannon had come in, asking permission to spend part of the afternoon at the house of a family she, her father, and her brother had met at the beach. The family had a girl Rhiannon's age. The girl was learning how to play guitar and had promised to show Rhiannon some chords.

But Cressida was having none of it. "I said no. And that's final. I don't trust your father's judgment. Until I meet these people myself you aren't to speak to them again, do you hear?"

Rhiannon stamped her foot. "But Mom!"

Amy took an involuntary step backward as Cressida flew from her chair and came around the desk. "Go to your room," she yelled, grabbing her daughter's arm in a tight grip and shoving her toward the door. "And don't come out until I tell you to!"

Rhiannon lowered her eyes as she stumbled past Amy on her way out of the office. Amy's heart was beating rapidly. Cressida's reaction had seemed overly harsh. After all, Rhiannon had done nothing but—

"Children cannot be allowed to defy their parents," Cressida said calmly, resuming her seat. She seemed perfectly composed, as if nothing upsetting had happened.

"Yes," Amy said nervously, continuing to stand with her hands folded before her. Cressida hadn't invited her to sit and was now staring intently at her computer screen as if she were alone. Amy glanced around the bright, white room and suddenly realized that every framed photo was of Cressida. No portrait of her husband. No cute shot of the children at Disneyland. No group shot of the family seated around a Christmas tree.

Maybe Cressida felt that family photos might distract her from the important work at hand, Amy thought. Maybe the photos of her accepting an award wearing a designer suit; clothed in a stunning glittery gown; wearing a bikini while lounging on a sailboat were reminders of how much she had achieved by hard work, focus, and determination. Yes, Amy thought. That was probably it.

Suddenly, Cressida looked up from her computer and gave Amy a big smile. "Come and sit down," she said, gesturing to the chair on the other side of the desk. Amy did. "I want you to know that I will be a mentor to you this summer, Amy. And you will be my protégé. How does that sound?"

"Thank you," Amy said earnestly. Acquiring a mentor had been the last thing she had expected from this job, but it sounded pretty good. She thought that protégé was spelled with accent marks, and that always made a word seem more important.

"Lesson number one," Cressida went on. "The secret to my success is that I do what I want. I refuse to sacrifice anything for anyone." Cressida laughed. "Especially my husband. Remember, Amy, negotiation is for the weak."

Amy nodded. What Cressida had just said went against everything she had learned from her mother and her grandparents. But she would definitely give Cressida's lesson some thought. After all, Cressida was the one who had founded Prior Ascendancy, not the Gleesons.

"I have no tolerance," Cressida went on, "for women who bitch and moan about feeling guilty for spending so much time at the office. I feel absolutely no guilt about being away from my family.

That's what Will is for, to see to the children." Cressida gave Amy a conspiratorial smile. "Frankly he's not good for much else."

Amy smiled back, but in truth she was shocked by the casual way in which Cressida had made the remark. She folded her hands more tightly in her lap, wondering what words of wisdom Cressida would impart next.

"Even in this so-called enlightened day and age," Cressida said, leaning back in her chair and swiveling slightly, "women are primarily defined by their physical functions. What are we in the eyes of the world but our reproductive organs?"

"I guess I've never given it much thought," Amy admitted.

Suddenly, Cressida leaned forward over the desk. "You have to be aware of these things, Amy," she said fiercely. "You have to be tough."

Tough, Amy thought. Maybe Cressida was smart to impose a harsh punishment on her daughter for a minor transgression. Maybe she was grooming Rhiannon for a successful future by practicing "tough love." Amy had certainly never experienced tough love from her mother or grandparents, but maybe people who wanted to train their children to achieve great things in life used tough love regularly.

"I bet you want Jordan and Rhiannon to work for you one day," Amy said, not quite sure why she did.

Cressida laughed and sat back again. "God, no! I want them to excel in a career, but the last thing I want is for either of them to work for me. No, if I do my job properly, those two will have established professional lives entirely independent of me."

Amy thought of all the local families she knew where children had followed their parents into the family business. There were the Gascoynes, for one; three generations of the family were currently running the fishing enterprise and the restaurant. And there was Noah, helping out at his uncle's clam shack, and there were lots of other examples, too.

"Come with me," Cressida said suddenly, getting up from her chair. "I have something for you."

Amy followed Cressida into a small room next to the master suite. She had not been in the room before. Along three of the walls stood the kind of racks you might see in a department store; each rack was laden with clothing. Cressida went to one of the racks and pulled out a cream-colored blouse on a wooden hanger. Of course there would be no padding on Cressida's hangers.

"Here," Cressida said, thrusting the blouse at Amy. "You can have this. I have no use for it anymore."

Amy took the blouse. It was unmistakably silk, the really high-quality kind. It was also a size 6, way too small for Amy. "Thank you," she said earnestly. Now she had even more incentive for losing those five or ten pounds Cressida had suggested she lose.

"Remember everything I told you today, Amy," Cressida said, fixing Amy with her penetrating eyes, "and you'll go far in life."

Silently, Amy followed Cressida out of the room. No one had ever told her that she would go far in life. In fact, Amy doubted that anyone had ever believed that she *could* go far in life. She felt grateful and proud at that moment. She had a mentor. Who else in Yorktide had one of those?

Chapter 29

Leda was putting out coffee and a plate of bite-sized cranberry scones when Vera popped by the studio in her usual way.

"Expecting a guest?" she asked.

"A potential client," Leda told her. "Her name is Margot Lakes."

"I could leave," Vera suggested.

"No, stay. Any word on the bank robber?"

Vera shuddered. "My lawyer tells me I'm totally in the clear, and that's all I need to know."

"This is one of the reasons I stay single," Leda said, arranging the sugar bowl and the creamer next to the press pot of hot coffee. "It's far less risky. No more men for me."

Vera frowned. "Surely you haven't written off all men because of that one louse?"

"Of course not," Leda said, but not without the consciousness of lying. "Anyway, they were both louses, the husband and the wife, and maybe she was worse, allowing the seduction of a young, innocent girl under her own roof. I shudder when I think of how she's raised her own daughter."

"I know plenty of artists, and the vast majority of them are totally decent people. What a crock, I'm an artist so I can treat people like dirt."

"I know. It's hard to imagine anyone really buying into that nonsense."

"Other men have been good to you since then," Vera pointed out. "Charlie, for one. You told me so. And your father and Phil. Why do you continue to allow that creep who could be dead now for all we know determine your life?"

"He doesn't determine my life," Leda argued. "It's just that there are some experiences you can't entirely get over."

"Maybe so. Ooops, there's the bell. I'll get it."

Vera dashed off and returned to the studio a moment later with Leda's potential client. Margot Lakes was new to the area and had purchased a condo in downtown Portsmouth for which she wanted a few wall hangings and comfy throws. She had heard about Leda's custom work through a woman who regularly shopped at Wainscoting and Windowseats.

Leda stepped forward and offered her hand. Margot looked to be in her midforties. She was tall and slim with an air of easy sophistication that was impressive without being intimidating. She was dressed in a perfectly fitted dove gray pantsuit and wore a silk scarf around her neck. Her jewelry was structural and silver.

Leda and Margot spent a productive hour going through samples of various materials and poring over images collected from home decorating magazines. Vera looked on from a comfortable chair, munching scones and drinking coffee. It wasn't lost on Leda that Margot snuck more than one interested look Vera's way and that when she did, Vera turned her head.

Before Margot left she placed an order and made a second appointment to consider a custom bedspread with matching pillow shams.

"Well, looks like you've got a new client for life," Vera commented when Leda returned to the studio after seeing Margot off.

"Let's hope so." Leda looked closely at her friend. "Margot seemed to take to you, but you seemed oblivious."

"I was not oblivious," Vera admitted. "But that way lies madness. I told you I'm going to be celibate for the rest of my life. I'm done getting involved with loonies."

"How do you know if she's a loony? She seemed eminently sane to me."

"If she's interested in me," Vera said firmly, "she's crackers. Well, I gotta go. Thanks for the snack."

When Vera had gone, Leda cleared away the coffee things and considered. What if she could somehow prove to Vera that Margot Lakes was sane and normal and perfectly safe for her to date? It wouldn't be difficult to ask around discreetly. Margot said she was new to the area, but that didn't mean people hadn't heard stories or formed opinions. Leda had never acted as a matchmaker before, but how hard could it be to nudge two nice people toward each other? Probably not hard at all.

Chapter 30

"Why is this crap always littering up the house!" Eddie Franklin wiped his mouth with the back of his hand. "This place is disgusting!" He reached for the book sitting on the little end table, grabbed a thick chunk of pages, and tore them from the binding. Roughly he threw the pages into the air. Slowly, they fluttered to the worn rug, to the seat of the old armchair, to the top of the scarred coffee table.

"That book belongs to the library!" Hayley cried.

Eddie snorted. "Spending your time with your nose in a book when you should be out working for the good of your father. You're a waste."

Nora, standing stock-still in the corner, shot Hayley a wide-eyed look, as if, Hayley thought, begging her not to further antagonize the man.

"Clean that mess up," Eddie Franklin commanded. "What's this world coming to when a man can't even come home to a clean house after a hard day's work?"

"You've never done a hard day's work in your life," Hayley muttered. Her father, already clomping toward the kitchen, hadn't heard her comment. If he had, he would not have let it go unremarked.

Hayley's mother hurried over and knelt to gather the scattered pages.

"Mom. Let me." Hayley reached down, took her mother's elbow, and helped her to her feet.

"I'll go and . . ." Nora's words trailed off as she followed her husband into the kitchen.

With shaking hands Hayley gathered the pages, badly torn along one edge. She wondered how she would explain the destruction to the staff at the Yorktide Library. And then she realized that she wouldn't need to say a word. Everybody knew her as Eddie Franklin's daughter. Everybody would assume that he was in some way the author of the crime. It might at least be more face-saving if she blamed herself.

Hayley stacked the last torn page with the others and retrieved what was left of the book itself from where it lay under the coffee table. No, she thought. No one who knew how highly she regarded books would ever believe she had been so careless. If asked she would tell the bald truth, that her father had destroyed the book in one of his rages. She would accept the financial consequences. And she would promise that in the future she would keep materials borrowed from the library hidden from Eddie Franklin.

Hayley went to her bedroom and closed the door. She sat on the edge of the narrow bed and put her head in her hands. Maybe her father was right, she thought. Maybe she was a waste. How crude, wearing a mud mask while on the job. She wondered if Ethan Whitby would rat her out to his father or his stepmother, and while she hadn't actually done anything wrong, still, she wouldn't want Marisa Whitby to think she didn't take her work seriously. She didn't want to lose a job that paid well, a job that allowed her to function in a clean and pleasant environment, a job that . . . a job that reminded her all too clearly of what she would never, ever have.

Chapter 31

Though Vera was well-off by many people's standards, she lived modestly in a bungalow that had been built in the 1940s. The first floor comprised a small living room, a kitchen, and a bathroom. A narrow hall led to a deck at the back of the house. On the second floor was Vera's bedroom, across the hall from which was her home office. Amy thought the most impressive part of Vera's home was her garden. It was such a peaceful, shaded place, like something out of a fairy tale. Except without goblins.

Vera, Amy, and her mother were on the deck. Vera was manning the charcoal grill, on which she was preparing corn on the cob and burgers. For dessert there were brownies, but Amy had resolved not to have any. And she would skip a toasted bun with her burger. Corn was starchy enough. Cressida would probably skip the corn as well, but Amy knew her own powers of self-denial weren't half as strong as those of her mentor.

"The roses are stunning this year," Leda said. "What's that one over there?"

"That's Constance Spry," Vera explained. "Perfect for a cottage-style garden, which as you know is what I go for."

"Cressida thinks Floribunda roses are the best," Amy announced. She didn't know what a Floribunda rose was, exactly, but she hadn't felt comfortable admitting her ignorance to Cressida.

"What does she mean by the best?" her mother asked.

"Just, you know, better than everything else."

"Better than other types of roses," Vera asked, "or better than any other flower?"

Amy felt flustered. "I don't know exactly."

Vera brought the platter of burgers and buns to the table. "I always thought that in the matter of flowers it came down to personal taste. But that's just me."

Amy took the smallest burger and removed it from its bun.

"What's wrong?" Vera asked.

"Nothing's wrong. I'm just limiting my carbs."

Vera shuddered. "The thought terrifies me."

"Me too." Leda Latimer reached for her burger and the jar of mustard.

"I bought a new vacuum today," Vera announced. "How exciting is that? It's a Bissell."

"According to Cressida," Amy said, "Bissell vacuums are totally unreliable. You should have bought a Dyson."

"And her reasons for this judgment are what?" Vera inquired.

Amy pretended she didn't hear the question and using her fork put a piece of burger in her mouth. Cressida's pronouncements, all of which were stated in such a sure and definitive way, made asking for an explanation somehow impossible. At least impossible for Amy. She wondered if Will ever argued with his wife's opinions or contradicted her when she got a fact wrong, and she must sometimes get a fact wrong. Everybody did now and then. But maybe Cressida was an exception. In any case, she was an awesome mentor. And she believed that her protégé had the potential to go far.

"Rats. I got mustard on my pants. Be right back." Amy's mother hurried into the house.

"It's funny," Vera said when she was gone, "but just last night I was thinking about my first job out of college. I was an admin at a law firm in my hometown, and my boss was from hell. She had these horrible mood swings and treated most of the other admins with contempt, but for some reason she liked me."

Amy made no comment. She had finished her burger, the smallest ear of corn, and a teaspoon of coleslaw but was still hungry.

"After a while I began to feel as if she was preying on me," Vera went on. "She hated that I had a life of my own. She threw a major fit one day when I told her I couldn't join her for lunch because I had a doctor's appointment. And that was it. I quit that very day."

Amy looked away from the plate of brownies she had been studying and frowned. "Why are you telling me this?"

"No reason," Vera said, eyes wide. "The memory just popped into my head is all."

"That's not why," Amy said. "You and Mom both think there's something wrong about my relationship with Cressida. I can feel it."

"Not wrong necessarily," Vera corrected. "Though we do question how Cressida is treating you."

"She's treating me fine," Amy shot back. "I make good money and she gives me extras like, well, the other day she gave me a silk blouse. It's a little too small for me, but I should be able to fit into it by the end of the summer."

"But you're not doing the job you were hired to do," Vera pointed out. "You were hired to be a nanny to her children, not to be, well, whatever it is you are to Cressida."

"A protégé," Amy said. "Cressida said she's my mentor this summer. Anyway, it's not as if the kids are being ignored. Their father is with them all the time."

"Mentor?" Vera frowned. "She hired you under false pretenses. That's deception."

Amy stared at the brownies again. It didn't feel as if Cressida was deceiving her. How could a successful woman mentoring a younger woman be wrong? Every young person needed an older and more experienced person to believe in her.

"How is Hayley faring with the Whitbys?" her mother asked when she had returned to the table.

"Okay," Amy said. "She met Mr. Whitby's son from his first marriage."

"What's he like?" Vera asked.

Amy shrugged. "All I know is that he works for his father's company and showed up for a weekend visit."

"Well, I hope he's not one of those spoiled, rich-kid predator types who think he can have his way with the help. Not that Hayley can't take care of herself." Vera frowned. "I just realized I have no idea if Hayley's ever had a serious boyfriend."

"She hasn't," Amy said. "I can't remember her even having a crush on anyone."

"Sadly," Leda added, "I suspect Hayley regards being in love as an unnecessary indulgence."

"She's afraid to fall in love," Amy explained. "She thinks that love leads to disaster. Look at what happened to her mother."

Vera sighed. "How depressing." And then she turned to Leda. "Did you know that La Prior has announced she'll be acting as Amy's mentor this summer?"

Leda frowned. "You're supposed to be a nanny, not a protégé."

"You guys!" Amy cried. "Come on!"

Her mother reached across the table and took her hand. "I'm sorry," she said. "I'm just being overprotective."

Amy smiled. She could never stay mad at her mother for long. "You never were any good at tough love. Cressida is all about tough love."

Vera reached for a brownie. "No doubt she is."

Chapter 32

Leda was having breakfast with Phil Morse at Over Easy. The restaurant wasn't inexpensive, and there was no way Leda would be able to afford to eat there on a frequent basis if she weren't the owner's closest friend.

The restaurant was cozy in the extreme. Vera had gone for a French provincial atmosphere. The furniture featured scrolls and molding. Surfaces were done in earthy colors like mustard yellow, cranberry, and sage. Table runners were made from a white and blue toile fabric. Farm animal paintings by local artists hung on the walls. The tiny ceramic salt and pepper shakers on each table were shaped like elegant little birds. The napkins were linen and patterned with images of tulips. One of Leda's tapestries, the largest she had ever done, had pride of place on an exposed brick wall. It was a still life depicting a table filled with platters of fruits and vegetables; a pitcher held a bundle of wild flowers. It was purposely reminiscent of Flemish still lifes of the seventeenth century but without the addition of dead animals and birds.

Phil gently pushed the creamer across the table. "I asked you here today for a reason," he said.

Leda smiled and poured a bit of cream into her coffee. "Not just to enjoy my sparkling company?"

"As pleasant as that company is, I have an ulterior motive." Phil leaned in, and his handsome face took on his serious, down-to-business expression. "The Fiber Arts Fellowship just announced the categories in this year's competition. There's a new category called Best Emerging Talent, and I think you should submit one of your tapestries."

"I couldn't," Leda said automatically. It wasn't the first time she had made that reply to one of Phil's suggestions that she seek more recognition for her work.

"You can," Phil said, sitting back in his chair. "You choose not to."

"I'm a little old to be considered emerging," Leda pointed out.

"No, you're not," Phil argued. "Toni Morrison published her first novel at the age of forty, as did George Eliot, aka Mary Ann Evans. Grandma Moses didn't start to paint in earnest until she was almost eighty when arthritis got in the way of her embroidery and quilting."

"I didn't know any of that," Leda admitted.

"So, what do you say?"

Leda was about to protest yet again when she remembered that Cressida Prior had announced her intention of being a mentor to Amy this summer. Leda had always assumed that *she* was Amy's role model. "Okay," she said. "I promise to think about it."

"Good. Get on the website and you'll find the details for submitting your work. If you have any questions I'm sure we can figure out the answers together."

Vera came by bearing their breakfast. Leda had ordered the poached eggs; poached eggs were a dish she had never been able to master at home. "So? Did you convince her yet?" Vera asked, taking the seat across from Phil and next to Leda.

"She's a stubborn one," Phil said, reaching for his fork and knife. "But I've made a start."

"Eat your eggs while they're hot," Vera instructed.

Leda picked up her fork. "So, you two are in this together?"

"We have your best interests at heart, yes," Vera confirmed.

"Phil," Leda said suddenly, "do you know anything about Cressida Prior, the founder of Prior Ascendancy?"

Phil looked up from his French toast. "No. Other than the fact that Amy's working as nanny to her children this summer. Why do you ask?"

Leda looked to Vera and then back to her breakfast. "No reason," she said. "I was just wondering."

"Well, if I do hear anything of interest," Phil said, "I'll be sure to let you know. My customers do tend to talk."

"That's what I like in a man," Vera declared. "A good ear for gossip."

Chapter 33

Before Marisa had left for the college earlier that morning she had told Hayley that Ethan had arrived late the night before. "He's still in his room," she had said while filling her water bottle at the sink. "Don't let him get in your way," she had added with a smile. "He can be quite chatty."

Hayley had smiled in return, hoping her unease wasn't obvious. She wondered if Ethan would tease her about the plunger and mud mask. She had left out those details when she mentioned to Amy that she had met Mr. Whitby's son.

About midmorning Hayley settled on the back porch while the twins napped. The baby monitor was on the small table next to the white wicker chair in which she sat. This sort of peaceful moment, however brief, was something Hayley rarely experienced and certainly never while at home. But her reverie was broken by the sound of the sliding door that led into the house being opened. She didn't turn around. She knew who it was.

"Mind if I join you?" Ethan asked as he came into view.

"It's your house." Hayley silently cursed herself. So much for charm. "I mean, no, of course not."

Ethan sat in the matching white wicker chair on the other side of the table. He was rather beautiful in the way that some men could be. There was a sort of masculine grace about the way he moved; his hands were expressive, and there was a poignancy to his face Hayley hadn't noticed the first time she had seen him. The depth of her physical attraction rattled her.

"What's that you're reading?" he asked.

"It's the third volume of Peter Ackroyd's *History of England*," she told him.

Ethan's expression brightened. "Looks like we have something in common. I'm a total history buff."

"You are?" Hayley said quickly. She was surprised, but she knew that she shouldn't be. Why wouldn't a person who worked in finance also harbor an interest in subjects that had little to do with—well, with whatever it was exactly that Ethan did?

Ethan laughed. "I am. I've had to put up with teasing from some of my friends for being such a nerd. What about you?"

Hayley hesitated. The only one who had ever teased her for her interests had been her father. Rather, he had mocked her intelligence and her intellectual curiosity. But that was not something Ethan Whitby ever need know. "No," she said. "I've never been teased, though I'm pretty much the only one I know who prefers reading nonfiction to fiction."

"I enjoy both equally," Ethan told her. "During spring break in my junior year at Harvard I took a road trip on my own to the Folger Shakespeare Library in D.C. It was great. I caught a production of *As You Like It*, which has always been one of my favorite of the comedies, and I got to hear the Folger Consort perform a program of baroque music. The Folger is a fantastic institution," Ethan went on excitedly, "but try telling that to the majority of spring breakers who have their hearts set on hookups and drinking games."

"I've never been to D.C.," Hayley said. She felt embarrassed admitting this and wasn't sure why she had; most schoolkids counted Washington, D.C., as a guaranteed destination. But when her grammar school had planned a bus trip for the seventh grade, Hayley's parents hadn't been able to spare the few hundred dollars the trip cost. Hayley remembered overhearing a phone call from someone, she never knew who, who seemed to be offering to pay for Hayley to go along with her classmates. But Nora Franklin had hurriedly turned down the offer. Hayley had never asked her mother why. Pride? Her father certainly wouldn't have said no. Eddie Franklin would knock over his own grandmother to be the first to grab a dirty coin from the sidewalk.

"You should put D.C. on your list of places to visit," Ethan said enthusiastically. "You could easily spend weeks at the Smithsonian alone. Have you been to Paris?"

"No," Hayley said with a forced smile. "Not yet at least."

"I was there just last year. When you go be sure to visit Napoleon the First's tomb at the Hôtel des Invalides. I'm not a huge fan of Napoleon, but you don't have to be to appreciate the baroque style of the building and the contents of the Musée de l'Armée itself. The costumes and paintings and old regiment standards, the maps and old cryptograph machines. It's all so interesting and pretty moving."

Hayley suddenly remembered something she had read back when she was in college and studying European history. "Doesn't the museum have armor supposedly worn by the future king Henry II?" she asked.

Ethan's eyes widened. "Yeah, it does!"

Hayley smiled and felt a rush of pride. She might not have a college degree, but she was not ignorant.

"I can't help myself when I visit museums," Ethan went on. "I spend a small fortune on books in the gift shop."

Hayley felt a flash of annoyance. She wondered what Ethan considered a "small fortune." She had never had *any* fortune to spend on books. With a bit of effort Hayley got control of her knee-jerk annoyance. "Money spent on books is never a waste," she said.

"I agree," Ethan said. "The only problem is I can't seem to ever let go of a book. I've still got all of my college texts and even a bunch from high school. One day I'm going to have to have an entire room in my home for books."

Hayley recognized all too well the tone of keen passion in Ethan's voice. "All this interest in history and you didn't go into academia?" she asked.

"Gosh, no," Ethan said. "I'm not a rigorous intellectual, just an enthusiastic amateur. I work in finance because, frankly, math and economics come easily to me. And I like working for my father. I know he wants me to take over the business once he retires. The idea is kind of daunting, but I'd hate to let him down after all the hard work he put into founding the company."

"You respect your father," Hayley said.

"More, I like him."

"So, he would be disappointed if you didn't want to take over when he retires?"

"I think he would," Ethan admitted, "but he would never force me to do what I didn't want to do."

Hayley looked down at the book in her lap. Ethan's relationship with his father could not be more different from her relationship with hers. The notion of leaving a positive legacy for his children clearly had never occurred to Eddie Franklin. As for a sense of loyalty, Eddie Franklin certainly had never installed *that* in either of his children.

Ethan suddenly stood. "I'll let you get back to your book. Before long the girls will be awake and you won't have a moment to yourself."

"It's what I'm getting paid for, to work," Hayley said sharply. There it was again, that ingrained tendency to take offense, to protect herself. "I mean," she went on, "thanks."

Ethan smiled, but the smile didn't seem quite as genuine as it might have been. But maybe Hayley imagined that. And then he went back into the house.

Hayley felt unnerved. She didn't know what exactly she expected from Ethan Whitby, but it certainly wasn't genuine companionship. And not once had his eyes roamed to her breasts or her legs. Ethan seemed oblivious to her physical charms. Well, that was a good thing. The last thing she needed was to be dodging the wandering hands of the son of her employer.

Chapter 34

"I think that from now on I'm going to call you Aimee."

Amy looked up from the presentation she was collating. "I'm sorry?" she asked.

From across the desk Cressida replied with a tight smile. "I said that I've decided to call you Aimee. The French pronunciation is so much more sophisticated. Remember what I've said about appearance and presentation. Aimee can open doors Amy cannot."

Amy didn't know how to respond. She had always liked her name. Anyway, what did an unsophisticated person need with a sophisticated name? But like Cressida said, appearances and presentation were super important. Amy was sure she looked more important since she had put away her sundresses. Aimee. It did sound nice. And it might also be spelled with an accent, like protégé.

"You don't have a problem with it, do you?" Cressida pressed.

"Of course not," Amy said hurriedly.

Amy went back to the collating. She felt flattered. People who were close had affectionate nicknames for one another. If that's what Aimee was, a term of affection. Maybe Cressida just liked the way it sounded, more sophisticated like she had said.

"Aimee?"

It was a moment before Amy looked up again. "Oh," she said. "Sorry. It's just that I'm not used to it yet."

Cressida got up from her ergonomic chair. "You'll get used to it," she said. "Now, I'm going for a run. Finish collating those presentations and then take them to Federal Express. They need to be at the Atlanta office tomorrow morning."

When Cressida had gone, Amy realized something. If her mother had been more of an achiever they might have been able to travel and afford important jewelry and designer clothes and maybe even a house with a pool. But Amy was soon to be on her own, and Cressida was offering a glimpse of what she might achieve if she turned away from Leda Latimer's unambitious way of getting through life and embraced Cressida Prior's go-getter attitude. If Amy truly turned away from Amy and became Aimee, she just might go far.

Amy smiled. Very far.

"Your mother makes the best lasagna. Be sure to thank her for me when she gets back from Vera's." Hayley frowned. "Why aren't you eating?"

"I'm eating," Amy protested.

"You had two bites. Oh well, more for me." Hayley put another serving of lasagna on her plate and dug in.

Amy took another small bite of lasagna and put her fork on her plate. "Cressida has decided to call me Aimee," she blurted. "That's the French way to say Amy."

"I know what it is," Hayley said shortly. "Why didn't you say no? She has no right to change your name."

"It's not really changed. It's just different. Besides, I like it. I was thinking that maybe I'd go by Aimee with everyone and not just Cressida."

Hayley laughed. "You have got to be kidding me! Suddenly, after twenty-one years of being Amy Latimer you're going to go around Yorktide to all the people who have known you since you were born and tell them to call you by a new name? I've never heard of anything so pretentious. You are who you are, Amy, and that's just fine. Wait, you're not going to ask your mother to call you Aimee, are you?"

"No," Amy said hurriedly. She wasn't dumb enough not to realize that her mother might be insulted that she had decided to change her birth name. "No, of course not. Don't say anything to her, okay?"

"No worries. By the way, when was the last time you had a day off?"

"What do you mean?" Amy asked.

"It's a simple question, Amy. When was your last day off? We've been working for over two weeks now."

Amy picked up her fork and put it down again. "I haven't had one, actually."

"Why not?" Hayley pressed.

"I don't know," Amy admitted.

"You don't have a formal agreement about that, either, do you?" Hayley asked. "Was it another figurative handshake with Cressida saying, yeah, you'll have time off but not setting a schedule in advance?"

"It doesn't bother me," Amy said defensively. "I'm sure if I want to take a day off, Cressida would be fine with it."

"She had better be! Look, why don't you ask her to discuss a schedule with you."

Amy was beginning to feel annoyed. "I said it doesn't bother me. I'm sure Cressida will give me time off soon."

"But how do you get anything done in your real life if you can't plan ahead?"

"Being with Cressida *is* my real life, a part of it anyway," Amy argued. "And you're forgetting that she pays me hourly. The more I work, the more money I make. That counts for a lot."

"Granted, but there is such a thing as fair treatment."

"I *am* being treated fairly," Amy said. "Seriously, Hayley, why are you so down on Cressida? You, my mother, and Vera."

"Because something doesn't seem right about the setup. But hey, if you're happy, I'll butt out."

"I *am* happy, so thank you for butting out."

The two young women sat in uneasy silence for a moment until Hayley got up from the table. "I should get going," she said, taking her empty plate to the sink. "Thanks again for dinner."

Amy managed a smile. "Sure," she said. When Hayley was gone, Amy remained at the table, her hands in her lap, her shoulders slumped. The excitement and determination she had felt only that afternoon at Cressida's, her mentor's, now seemed like a very distant memory. Why did the people who said they loved her the most feel the need to burst her bubbles? It wasn't fair, Amy thought. It just wasn't.

Chapter 35

Leda had begun her informal background check of Margot Lakes. Just that morning she had run into Clare Thomas in the grocery store. Clare, a former neighbor on Hawthorne Lane, worked in downtown Portsmouth. It was a small city, and there was every chance that Clare might have met Margot in passing. "It's funny you should ask," Clare had said. "We got to chatting last week at my nail salon. She seems really nice. We exchanged cards and said we'll have lunch some time."

While Clare's estimation of Margot wasn't proof positive of Margot's sterling character, it did go some way in affirming Leda's own assessment of her as a worthy potential romantic partner for Vera.

But Vera's romantic life would have to take a backseat at the moment. Ever since Phil had suggested that Leda enter the competition held by the Fiber Arts Fellowship, or the FAF as it was commonly known, she had been agonizing about what to do. Part of the problem with simply saying yes, I'll enter my work, was that she felt no real separation between herself and her creations. Phil was always trying to help her adopt a healthy distance from her work, at least as far as other people's judgment of it, and no doubt he was right. If a customer didn't like the wares on display in his store and said so, Phil didn't take the opinion of one person as criticism of himself or of his artistry in creating a beautiful shopping environment. That was professionalism, and professionalism was something Leda had failed thus far to attain. Maybe it was too late for her to become a true professional, though if she voiced that concern Phil and Vera would forcefully remind her that it was never too late to change.

Leda frowned. Even her daughter seemed interested in making a change, even if the change wasn't her own idea. Amy was a keen reader of fiction; as far as Leda knew she had never read one bit of nonfiction outside of what was assigned in school. But the day before Leda had come upon her reading *The 7 Habits of Highly Effective People*. "Cressida said it's an essential if I'm going to succeed in life," Amy had told her mother. "And I want to succeed."

Amy's comment—even if it had been put in her head by her employer—had prompted Leda to ponder the notion of success. She had never accepted the common and overly simplified definition of success as the earning of vast sums of money. So then, what did success really mean? Success could imply failure; one person's win was another person's loss. Success could imply mastery of a subject or even mastery over a person. In the sense that Leda had achieved mastery over certain aspects of her art, she supposed she could be considered a success, at least by fellow artists.

It seemed to Leda that the only intelligent way to define success was according to your own desires. The challenge was to identify those desires and then to pursue them. But Leda had never been what people termed a go-getter.

Not, she thought, like Cressida Prior.

Chapter 36

Hayley let herself into the house with the key Marisa had given her on her first day. Marisa had somewhat embarrassedly told Hayley that they often neglected to lock the door, even at night. "It's so peaceful and idyllic here," she had said. "There's just no crime in this part of the world."

Well, Hayley thought as she walked through to the kitchen, that might be true of this neighborhood, with its large houses, well-kept lawns, and gorgeously planned gardens, but it certainly wasn't true of the neighborhood in which the Franklins currently made their home. If you lived on Rockford Way you would be seriously foolish to leave your doors unlocked at any time of the day or night.

Marisa was seated at the counter with a cup of coffee when Hayley came into the kitchen. "Good morning," she said brightly.

"Good morning. Did Mr. Whitby get in all right last night?"

"Yes," Marisa told Hayley. "But not until almost eleven. Some issue at the office. Anyway, he should be down soon. We thought we'd have breakfast at Over Easy and then check out a movie. It's been ages since we've been to a movie theatre. Most times we just stay home and watch something on Netflix or Acorn."

Hayley removed the cotton sweater she had worn against the morning chill and slipped a long apron over her head. "What are you going to see?" she asked as she set about preparing the girls' daily snacks.

Marisa laughed. "I almost don't care what we see. I'm just craving popcorn with bad-for-you butter flavoring."

Hayley heard footsteps on the stairs and someone whistling loudly and off-tune. She didn't know what exactly to expect from a man who owned a thriving investment firm. In any case, as she had been with Marisa, she was prepared not to like Mr. Whitby all that much. A moment later he strode into the room.

"Hello!" he said, coming toward Hayley with a hand extended. "You must be Hayley. Very nice to meet you."

Hayley, expecting a brutally firm businessman handshake, was pleasantly surprised that her hand was released intact. "It's nice to meet you, Mr. Whitby," she said. She saw the resemblance between father and son right away; both men shared a strong aquiline nose and piercing blue eyes. While Ethan's hair was deep auburn, his father's hair was steely gray, and he still had an awful lot of it. There were deep lines at the corners of Jon Whitby's eyes. Either he never wore sunglasses, Hayley thought, or he was in the habit of smiling a lot. Did seriously successful wealthy men smile about things that had nothing to do with one-upping other successful wealthy men?

"Jon, please," he corrected. Then he went to his wife and kissed her on the cheek. "I'm in the doghouse," he told Hayley with a smile and a twinkle in his eye. "I woke the twins when I came in last night."

"He tripped over the umbrella stand in the front hall," Marisa explained, looking up to her husband. "Luckily he wasn't hurt."

Jon looked at his watch, a modest round dial on a worn, brown leather band. "We'd better get a move on," he said. "If we don't linger over French toast we can catch an eleven o'clock showing of that new comedy with what's his name, that comedian I like."

Marisa laughed. "We have our cell phones should you need us," she said, reaching for her bag on the counter.

"Enjoy the movie," Hayley said as hand in hand the Whitbys hurried from the kitchen.

"Thanks!" Jon Whitby called.

When they had gone, Hayley continued to prepare the twins' snacks and to plan their lunch. What she had just witnessed of the relationship between Jon and Marisa Whitby presented such an enormous contrast to the relationship between her parents. Eddie Franklin was no friend to Nora. Hayley doubted he cared much for his wife at all. And how could her mother possibly be a true friend to someone who treated her with such habitual disrespect?

Hayley went to the fridge for a bunch of green grapes. She simply couldn't imagine Jon Whitby ever raising a hand against his wife. True, appearances were often deceiving, and abusers came in all shapes. Still, the image refused to form in her mind, though she could all too well visualize her father lifting a hand against her mother. All she needed to do was to call up a memory.

The fact that Nora Franklin had refused to press charges each time her husband had assaulted her haunted Hayley. She couldn't help but wonder if her mother felt she deserved bad treatment. It was not a question Hayley could ask her. The answer might be too difficult to bear. More upsetting was the well-known fact that the habit of abuse tended to run in a family, whether because of learned behavior, psychological predilection, or a combination of both. Hayley saw how her brother's conduct mimicked her father's, and sometimes she worried that one day she might allow herself to be mistreated like her mother. Though Hayley knew she was strong—she had proved it time and again—a tiny part of her deep down inside worried that in a circumstance of extreme stress her strength wouldn't hold. Hayley was smart enough to know there was no possibility of completely throwing off one's past, but there had to be ways to move into the future relatively unencumbered by traumas experienced when one was young. There had to be.

A sudden sound from the baby monitor on the counter alerted Hayley to the fact that the girls were waking from their morning naps. Hurriedly she headed for the stairs to the second floor. She was eager to see their little smiling faces. Children were such very precious gifts. They were to be cherished and protected. Both in spite of and because of her own haphazard upbringing, Hayley truly believed that.

Chapter 37

"Aimee, I need you to do me a big favor this morning."

Amy, sitting across the desk from Cressida, smiled brightly. She loved being needed. Hayley had often called her a people pleaser, as if that were something to be ashamed of. "Sure," she said.

Cressida handed her a slip of paper on which was written a phone number with an area code foreign to Amy. "This is the number of my great-aunt Emily's nursing home. Call and let them know I won't be at Emily's ninety-fifth birthday celebration as promised."

Pretty much the last thing Amy wanted to do was deliver a disappointing message to an elderly woman, but she realized she was sort of afraid to refuse. "Okay," she said. "What should I say if they ask why?"

Cressida laughed incredulously. "They have no right to ask why, and if they do you can tell them it's none of their damn business."

Amy flinched. "Okay," she said.

Cressida suddenly smiled. "You're a lifesaver, Aimee. I hate how those people try to make you feel guilty for having your own priorities that don't include them."

"What people?" Amy asked. "Nursing home staff?"

"No, old people. They're the most self-centered things you can imagine." Cressida rose from her chair and announced that she was going out for a while.

Amy remained seated at the big desk in the bright office. She thought of her grandparents, who had been the most unselfish people she had ever known, next to her mother. She thought, too, of Mr. Sampson, an elderly neighbor who was always doing nice things for Amy and Leda, like giving them fresh catnip from his garden. Maybe some old people were self-centered but not the ones Amy knew. Cressida must have had a really bad experience with an older person; that's why she considered them all self-centered. It wasn't right to judge an entire group of people based on an experience with one member of that group but . . .

Amy got up and began to pace the length of the office. She hoped she could give the message to a member of the staff without having to speak to Cressida's great-aunt personally. She hoped the woman wouldn't be too disappointed when she learned that her great-niece wouldn't be attending her party. But maybe Emily didn't like her family. Maybe she wouldn't care that Cressida was absent.

It was with a sick feeling in the pit of her stomach that Amy punched the number of the nursing home into the phone. As luck would have it a perky receptionist put her in touch with an aide rather than with Great-Aunt Emily directly. Amy stumblingly delivered her employer's message, and though Cressida had not authorized her to apologize Amy did, several times. The aide didn't seem surprised to learn about the cancellation and politely thanked Amy for calling.

That unpleasant chore accomplished, Amy busied herself with the trivial tasks she had been set until, almost an hour later, Cressida returned from wherever it was she had gone.

"Did you make the call?" she asked abruptly. Her eyes were bright, and there was a sheen of sweat on her face.

Amy told her that she had.

"Family can be such a huge liability," Cressida stated, stalking over to the enormous window that looked out on the Atlantic.

"I only have my mother now," Amy said. "My father and grandparents are gone."

Cressida turned sharply. "You should feel grateful for the fact that it's only the two of you. So much less grasping and whining to deal with. People are such a burden."

Amy had never considered people as a burden, let alone her family members. In fact, she had often wished that she had siblings or cousins, and she missed her grandparents if not the father she never really knew. But Cressida was her mentor and Amy was here to learn, so . . .

Suddenly, Cressida strode over to Amy. "You deserve a treat," she said with a big smile. "Let's browse the Tiffany website."

Amy returned Cressida's smile. "All right," she said. "Sure."

Chapter 38

Leda frowned at her laptop. She had spent the last twenty minutes scanning mentions of Cressida Prior and Prior Ascendancy, and so far she had come up with not one bit of damning information about either. What had she been hoping to find? That Cressida was living under an assumed name, in hiding from a syndicate of drug lords she had cheated out of millions of dollars? Something so outrageous that even her besotted daughter would take notice and quit Cressida Prior's employment immediately?

But here was something potentially interesting. Leda clicked on the link that had appeared at the bottom of the screen and scanned the article, the gist of which was that three years earlier several employees at Prior Ascendancy had brought a lawsuit against Cressida Prior in which they claimed to be victims of age discrimination. In the end the case was settled out of court. The writer, while feigning impartiality, had not been able to refrain from suggesting that something about the whole affair seemed fishy. Had Cressida Prior paid off her accusers because they were in possession of documented evidence that could damage her? Or had she simply not wanted the bother and greater expense of a court case?

The back door opened and banged shut, and a moment later Vera appeared in the studio.

"You look grim," she noted, leaning against Leda's desk. "What's up?"

Leda told her about what she had just read. "Do you think I should tell Amy?" she asked.

"No," Vera said flatly. "She'll believe the charges were made up and that Cressida was perfectly innocent. Which, for all we know, she was, as disappointing as that might be."

"Still," Leda said, "I might just mention it to her."

Vera shrugged. "Go ahead. But it won't get you anywhere. Just saying."

"Why did you come by?" Leda asked. "Not that it isn't nice to see you."

Vera stood away from the desk. "Almost forgot. Can I borrow your stapler? Mine broke."

"Sure." Leda opened a drawer and handed her old metal stapler to Vera.

And then Vera was gone, letting the back door slam behind her.

All afternoon Leda had wrestled with the notion of telling Amy about the article she had come across earlier. Vera was right. There was probably no point in speaking, but in the end, Leda found that she simply couldn't keep the information to herself.

"I read an article earlier that mentioned your employer," Leda said, passing the salad to Amy that evening at dinner.

Amy smiled. "Did she win another award?"

"Not quite." Leda told her daughter what she had learned, careful to keep her tone neutral. "I just thought you should know," she finished.

Amy put down her fork. "I can't believe you would take those malicious rumors seriously," she said with a laugh.

"They were more than rumors," Leda pointed out. "A lawsuit was filed."

"So? That doesn't mean anything. Those employees were probably just jealous of Cressida and wanted to punish her for being more successful than they could ever be."

"I doubt that was the case," Leda argued. "People don't just sue other people for the fun of it. At least the majority of people don't."

Amy rolled her eyes. "Look, I'll ask Cressida what happened. I'll prove to you there was no truth to the accusations."

Leda restrained a sigh. "I don't think that's a very good idea," she said. "If she tells you anything, it will only be a version of the truth her lawyers concocted for public consumption."

"You're so cynical!" Amy cried.

"I'm not cynical," Leda protested. "I'm just—cautious."

"Don't you remember what Grandpa used to say, that you shouldn't believe everything you read?"

Leda sighed. "I remember." Clearly, there was no point in arguing further. Leda went about eating the seafood casserole she had prepared, aware that Amy was picking at her own dinner, scraping the bread crumbs from the top, picking out the bits of cheese and dropping them onto her napkin. Leda had thought she might mention the FAF competition to Amy that evening but now thought better of it. She doubted that Amy would care. Until—if—she decided to enter, she would keep quiet about the competition. If she decided not to enter, she didn't want Amy to be further disappointed in her mother's lack of drive and ambition. Drive and ambition were traits Cressida Prior had in abundance. Amy had told her so.

"Don't you like the casserole?" Leda asked, though she knew full well why Amy was picking apart her meal.

Amy sighed. "I wish you hadn't put bread crumbs on top. I told you I'm cutting carbs." Suddenly Amy threw down her napkin and got up from the table. "You know what the real problem is?" she said. "You've never believed in me. Cressida believes in me. She says I have potential."

"That's so not true," Leda cried. "I've always believed in you!"

"Have you?"

And with that, Amy marched from the kitchen, leaving Leda alone at the table, stunned. Vera had been right, she thought. She should never have mentioned the lawsuit to her daughter.

Chapter 39

Hayley mumbled and pushed her cheek farther into the pillow. She was almost asleep but that distant noise, whatever it was. . . . She lifted her head and peered into the dark. The noise was becoming louder.

"Damn," Hayley muttered, as she tossed the sheet from her and sat up on the edge of the bed. Uneven footsteps, a stumble, a curse far more colorful than the one Hayley had just uttered, and spoken in an all-too-familiar growl. Hayley yanked the cord on the secondhand lamp on the secondhand night table and a dim yellowish light filled the small room. She heard a door open softly and envisioned her mother scurrying through the apartment, eager to let her husband inside as soon as he reached the third floor.

"For God's sake, not again," Hayley said, more loudly than she had spoken before. She got up from the bed and hurried into the living room. Her mother was standing a few feet from the apartment door, clutching the neck of her threadbare cotton robe around her thin, stooped shoulders, her feet in the ratty old slippers she had been wearing for more years than Hayley could count.

"Mom," Hayley said.

Nora Franklin turned with a start, her eyes wide. "He's . . ."

"I know what he is," Hayley said sharply. Eddie Franklin had reached the third-floor landing. Hayley could hear him grumbling and guessed that once again he could not find his keys. A sudden pounding against the wooden door confirmed her suspicions.

"Let me in!" he shouted.

Nora Franklin darted forward, but Hayley grabbed her mother's arm and held her back.

The pounding continued. "What the hell is wrong with you two? Let me in!"

"Hayley," her mother begged. "Please open the door."

"Why?" Hayley hissed. "So he can come in here and slap you around and call me foul names?"

"He'll fall asleep soon enough," her mother argued. "Please!"

The pounding had now become kicking. Hayley wondered how long it would be before her father lost his footing and fell over backward, hitting his head on the floor of the hall or maybe even tumbling down the stairs. . . .

"Let him sleep in the hallway," she said. "He's got to learn that he can't treat us like this."

Nora began to cry. "Please, Hayley! Please open the door and let him in!"

"Franklin!" The voice came from the floor below. It was one of the two young men who shared an apartment. "If you don't stop that racket right now, I'm calling the police."

"Not the police," Nora whispered harshly. "Not again."

Hayley sighed. She released her mother's arm and unlocked the door. Eddie Franklin lurched forward and stumbled into the apartment.

"You go to bed, Mom," Hayley directed. "Now. I'll get him onto the couch."

With a nervous backward glance, Nora Franklin hurried off in the direction of her bedroom. Luck was with Hayley that night. Her father seemed to have worn himself out trying to knock down the door. It was relatively easy for her to guide him to the battered old couch they had found discarded on someone's front yard two years earlier. He went unprotestingly to his makeshift bed. Within moments he was snoring harshly. He had not thanked his daughter for letting him in or for covering him with the quilt Mrs. Latimer had made for Hayley's sixteenth birthday.

Hayley went back to her room and, leaving the yellowish light on, lay down on her bed and drew the thin sheet over her. Though she was exhausted, her mind was too fraught for sleep. "I've got to get out of here," she whispered to the four walls. "I'll lose my mind if I don't."

Self-pity was not an emotion Hayley liked to indulge, but no one who knew the Franklin family even a little bit could deny that all of Hayley's life she had been behind the eight ball, working long hours at menial jobs to pay her parents' bills, suffering through the foreclosure on the family's house and then the subsequent evictions from various cramped apartments, forced at one point to sleep in a homeless shelter, several times having to endure the embarrassment of her father's and brother's incarcerations. Yet all the while Hayley had made it a point to be scrupulously honest, never taking unfair advantage of a person or a situation even when it might have benefited her. For Hayley Franklin, honesty was a point of honor.

But where has that good behavior gotten me? she thought, looking across the room to the narrow closet that had no door, to the desk that was only a piece of plywood laid across two stacks of old wooden crates. Nowhere.

Hayley shifted on the pillow. In the faint amber light she could make out the titles of a few of the books on her small makeshift bookcase. At the far end of the top shelf there was a battered paperback she had bought at a yard sale. *The Call of Duty* was a stirring, well-written novel about a near-destitute mid-eighteenth-century widow who married a wealthy man she didn't love or even like very much in order to lift her children and her aged father out of poverty. Though Abigail Trenton had forsaken love and even affection, she had achieved the salvation of those she held dear. She had died knowing that she had suffered for the best of causes.

Like the heroine of the novel, Hayley Franklin knew an awful lot about duty and responsibility and self-sacrifice. Some in Yorktide would say she knew too much for a person so young, though. . . .

Hayley sprang up and pushed aside the thin sheet. It was an outrageous idea, but . . . why not? Like Abigail Trenton had done, why not marry a rich man as a way out of the dismal life she and her mother had been leading for so very long?

And thanks to Amy, who had been the one to suggest they take jobs as summer nannies, Hayley knew a wealthy man, didn't she? Ethan Whitby. Ethan was intelligent and good looking and nice, even funny, and they both loved history, which gave them something to talk about. And Hayley had met Ethan's father, a successful man who genuinely loved his wife and children. To have such a man as a father-in-law might go far toward helping Hayley forget she had ever lived under the same roof as Eddie Franklin, that poor specimen of a husband and father.

A sudden and slightly hysterical laugh escaped Hayley's lips. What an outlandish idea! Since she had been old enough to realize what sort of man her father was, she had been determined to prove herself the total opposite of the scheming, self-serving Eddie Franklin. To undertake such a reprehensible, immoral measure as to manipulate a good man into marriage would require some serious self-convincing, not to mention a radical change in character. And did she really want to change for the worse, even if it was for the sake of her mother's happiness?

No, Hayley thought. Definitely not. But . . . Hayley lay down again and pulled the sheet over her bare legs. It couldn't hurt to play devil's advocate for a moment, could it? After all, there was plenty of precedence in the real world for a poor or disadvantaged girl marrying a rich man for practical reasons; such a situation didn't exactly make the news. And she reminded herself that even in the twenty-first century women often had to be crafty and deceptive in order to get what they wanted, and if that meant making a marriage of convenience, so be it. There was a valid argument that real feminism was about a woman being able to make her own choices, conventional or unconventional. And, Hayley thought, it wasn't as if she would prove an abusive wife to a wealthy man, especially one as decent as Ethan Whitby seemed to be. No, she would be good to him; she would treat him with care and respect in return for the tangible benefits marriage to him would afford her and her mother.

And even if a marriage to Ethan Whitby didn't last long—and

Hayley suspected that it might not; lies always outed, and the union would have been based on a lie—a divorce settlement would likely be hefty, and by that point Hayley would already have been introduced to a world of power and influence. Maybe she would even find another wealthy man and sell herself to him. There was no point in denying the fact that selling herself was what she would be doing, but at least she wouldn't be spending the rest of her life protecting her mother from the blows of her drunken father and trying to clean up after the stupid antics of her delinquent brother. No, she and her mother would be safe and secure somewhere far from Yorktide, and they would never, ever come back.

Hayley laughed again, but this time without the note of hysteria. What strange thoughts came to a person in the middle of the night! Was it three a.m. already, the witching hour? Had she just experienced a version of the infamous dark night of the soul, a time when all hope and consolation seemed gone and despair could take hold of even the most sensible person, causing her to think desperate thoughts?

Whatever the case, Hayley was having none of it. She knew from long experience that everything appeared different in the light of day. A grim situation didn't look quite so grim once the sun was high in the sky and a drastic decision appeared for what it really was, a *wrong* decision. A bizarre and crazy idea.

Hayley looked toward the door of her room and listened hard for any sound from her parents' bedroom or from the living room. She could hear nothing. All was well, at least for the moment. She yawned and turned off the light. Before long, she slept.

Chapter 40

The White Hart had opened less than a year earlier but had quickly become one of Yorktide's most popular nightspots. It was done up to resemble a classic British pub, from the painted wooden sign hanging out front depicting a crudely drawn white hart against a dark blue background, to the big stone fireplace from which hung copper pots in a variety of sizes, to the portraits of the queen at every stage of her long reign. The menu, however, paid little attention to popular British pub food; chips were called French fries, and there wasn't a bottle of malt vinegar to be found. The beer selection was composed largely of local brews, from pale ales to hearty stouts.

This evening a group of young women working locally as summer nannies were gathered at The White Hart; Amy had heard about the get-together from her former neighbor Michelle, also a nanny, who was tuned in to the friendly and informal network. It had taken some doing, but Amy had convinced Hayley to join her.

The group had been at the pub for only fifteen minutes but already the large, round oak table was crowded with a half-empty pitcher of beer, glasses of wine, a plate of nachos, and a basket of onion rings. Amy hungrily eyed the nachos and the onion rings. Cressida Prior would definitely not approve of bar food. Just that morning Amy had caught Cressida observing her closely as if trying to determine if Amy had lost any of the weight she had suggested

Amy lose. So far, Amy had not lost any weight, but it wasn't for lack of trying.

The others at the table were making short work of the food. Hayley, on Amy's right, was devouring the nachos. Cathi—about thirty years old, Amy guessed—was busily munching onion rings, as was Michelle. Madeleine Huppert, French-born nanny to the children of Colin McNabb and Frank Luther, had ordered a Cobb salad, which came with a crusty roll upon which she had spread a good deal of butter. Amy frowned. Cressida refused to allow butter in the house. Sarah, who had told Amy she was spending her second summer in Ogunquit with the Frey family from rural New Jersey, had just been served a bacon cheeseburger. Elizabeth, the only career nanny of the group and thirty-six years of age, claiming she had eaten dinner, was enjoying a piece of The White Hart's famous blueberry pie.

Amy glanced again at the food on the table. She hadn't been able to find one thing on the menu that Cressida would find acceptable other than an undressed garden salad. The problem was that Amy was seriously hungry, and the thought of ordering what was essentially a small bowl of lettuce just did not appeal. Amy took a gulp of her water. Water, Cressida said, was the best thing for you. She drank a full gallon of water every day.

"So, what's it like working for the Priors?" Cathi asked Amy, wiping her hands on her napkin.

"Fantastic," Amy said promptly. "Cressida Prior is an amazing woman."

"And the husband?" Sarah asked, taking a bite of her burger.

"He's okay," Amy told her. "I don't have much contact with him."

"What about the children?" Madeleine asked. "There are two, yes?"

Amy nodded. "Jordan is eight and Rhiannon is ten. They seem sweet."

"What do you mean they 'seem' sweet?" Michelle asked. "Don't you know for sure yet?"

Before Amy could answer, Michelle went on. "I heard there was some trouble last summer. Seems the Priors' nanny, this super highly regarded woman from one of the best agencies around, walked out after only a few days. I read about it on ILoveBeingaNanny.com. This woman who quit said Cressida Prior was a complete whack job."

Cathi nodded. "I saw that post, too. The Priors hired another nanny through a different employment agency, but they fired her almost immediately. I was never able to discover why. There was nothing on any of the websites. Maybe Cressida Prior intimidated her into silence! Anyway, I'm not sure what happened after that."

"I am," Sarah announced. "The Priors went back to Atlanta. They must have lost a ton of money abandoning the lease on the house, but from what I know they have plenty to waste."

Madeleine frowned. "No amount of money is worth working for a bitch like Cressida Prior. My bosses know someone who got badly burned in a business deal with her. Colin and Frank told me if they ever found themselves under the same roof as Cressida Prior they would walk right out."

"Cressida is not a bitch," Amy said fiercely. What did these people know about a woman who had become the CEO or whatever of her own global company by the age of thirty? "She's fabulous. And I should know, because I spend hours with her every day."

"Doing what?" Cathi asked.

"Whatever she needs done. Like when she's on a business call I sit on the other side of her desk in case she needs me to take notes or to look something up online."

"Doesn't she have a personal assistant?" Michelle asked.

"I'm sure she has one at her office," Amy said, "but when she's working from the house she has me."

"What else do you two do together?" Cathi asked, with what Amy thought was a bit of a sly look. She wasn't sure she liked Cathi.

"All sorts of things," Amy said. "She shows me her wardrobe—she has all this amazing designer stuff—and we shop online. Well, Cressida shops and I help. I mean, she asks my opinion sometimes. And we talk. She tells me how she started her business and how she built it to be such a success. And the other day we went to the spa on Main Street."

"She treated you to a massage?" Sarah asked, eyes wide.

"No," Amy admitted. "She had a massage. I waited for her in the lounge. And we have lunch together almost every day."

Hayley, who had been silent until now, grinned. "I thought you said Cressida doesn't eat."

"I didn't say she doesn't eat," Amy snapped, her eyes darting to the almost empty plate of nachos. "I said she's very serious about her health. She says fat people don't live long. The other day we made kale shakes for lunch."

"I'd rather die happy eating a bacon sandwich than live to be one hundred by drinking kale shakes!" Michelle announced.

Elizabeth finally spoke. Her tone was mild and almost incurious. "You say you spend a lot of time with Cressida. What about the children? Weren't you hired to take care of them?"

"Yes," Amy admitted, "but their father is with them pretty much all the time, so . . ."

Elizabeth made no reply. She put her fork across her empty plate and neatly folded her napkin next to it.

"So," Hayley asked, glancing around the group, "the question seems to be, why does the illustrious Cressida Prior need a nanny in the first place?"

Amy spoke angrily. "It's Cressida's right to hire a nanny if she wants one. She's a very important person. She deserves to have whatever sort of help she wants."

Madeleine raised an eyebrow. "It's usually the husband the nanny falls in love with, not the wife. *L'amour fou.*"

"What does that mean?" Sarah asked.

"Crazy love."

The group broke out into laughter, and Amy felt her cheeks flame with embarrassment. No one understood the relationship she had with Cressida Prior. Not one other person, not even her mother. Especially not her mother, going on about that stupid old lawsuit. What had Cressida said about family being a liability? "Don't be ridiculous," she said fiercely. "I'm not in love with Cressida. It's just that I'm grateful. She's offering me opportunities I've never been offered before."

"Like what?" Sarah asked. She had finished her burger as well as the fries that had come with it.

Amy wasn't sure how to answer. In truth, she hadn't really been asked to do anything particularly new or difficult or exciting. Not yet, anyway. "Like lots of things," she said defiantly.

Hayley suddenly put her hand on Amy's arm. "Come on, Amy, we're just teasing."

Amy pulled her arm from Hayley's touch. There was one tortilla chip left on the plate in the middle of the table. There was a bit of cheese on the chip. *To hell with it,* Amy thought, but before she could reach for the chip it had made its way into Michelle's mouth.

Chapter 41

Folding laundry was one of Leda's favorite domestic chores. There was something very soothing about it, and it was one of those finite tasks. When it was done, it was done. Until the next time laundry needed to be folded. So much for finite.

Leda shook out one of Amy's T-shirts and placed it in the laundry basket. Since she had mentioned the lawsuit against Cressida Prior, Amy had been even more vocal about her employer's superpowers, mentioning several times in one evening the fact that Cressida ran five to seven miles a day and that when she had given birth to her children she had done so without any painkillers. "How nice for her," Leda had commented over and over, but Amy hadn't noticed the sarcasm in her mother's tone. Leda felt bad that she had displayed her jealousy as she had but not bad enough to apologize. After all, Amy hadn't apologized for accusing her mother of not believing in her.

It dawned on Leda then, as she smoothed and folded a pillowcase, that envy could be a catalyst for action. The desire to one-up another person, to show that you could possess what they possessed and more. . . . To date such motives had been entirely foreign to Leda. She had never been a competitive sort, and after that disastrous summer of being in thrall to Lance Stirling what tiny competitive spirit she might have possessed had been quashed.

But a competitive spirit wasn't a bad thing to have in this world. It was just that cooperation had always come more naturally to Leda, and cooperation was fine except when it morphed into self-abnegation. Again, she thought about the notion of success and how it could be defined in so many ways. She remembered how Charlie used to say that as long as he had his wife and his daughter he felt he was the richest man in the world. His career ambitions had been limited, but his understanding of success had been, Leda thought, simple and wise. In Charlie Latimer's view, to love and to be loved in return was what made a life a successful one. It was too bad Amy seemed to be forgetting that.

Leda picked up the basket of folded laundry and climbed to the second floor. After stowing the clean towels in the linen closet, she opened the door to her daughter's room and carried the fresh sheets to the bed Amy had stripped that morning. As she turned to leave the room something on the top of the dresser caught her eye. It was a sort of hat, like a fascinator but made of fur. What, Leda wondered, was Amy doing with such a thing? She picked it up and looked at the label sewn onto the silk lining of the hat. It had been made by a milliner in Paris. Leda frowned. How much had Amy paid for this? And where would she ever wear it?

Leda returned the hat to the dresser and left the room. How Amy spent her money was no business of hers as long as Amy was putting aside enough to cover the cost of a move to Boston. But was she? Leda didn't think she would get very far by asking.

Chapter 42

For the past fifteen minutes or so Lily and Layla had been sitting on the carpeted floor of the den, happily occupied building and then knocking down towers of old-fashioned wooden blocks. Hayley had been observing the girls closely since the first day she had met them. There were more differences between them than just size and eye color. Lily, for example, was a whiz with puzzles and seemed never to tire of asking questions like "What's that?" and "Why?" Layla was by far the more physically active of the two and seemed to have no fear. She was like a little monkey, climbing on anything in her way, while Lily preferred to stay grounded, though she could walk up the stairs to the second floor unaided and her dexterity was on a par with her sister's. Both girls were heard to say "I do it!" several times a day, and when for some reason or another Lily or Layla could not do what she believed she could, there might be a small tantrum. But only a small one.

Hayley, sitting in one of the many high-backed rocking chairs scattered around the den, found herself wondering what the twins' brother was doing at that very moment. She knew so very little about Ethan Whitby and how he spent his time other than the fact that he was passionate about history. Only that morning she had found herself looking forward to asking Ethan if he had ever read Peter Ackroyd's biography of Thomas More, but that was assuming he would want to engage in conversation. Their past conversations could be chalked up to simple good manners on Ethan's part.

Hayley felt her face flushing at the memory of the crazy idea that had come to her the other night. Getting Ethan to marry her? Just as she had expected it would, in the illuminating light of day the fantasy of the night seemed absurd.

It wasn't that Hayley was holding out for true love. She had never dreamed of finding a soul mate and walking hand in hand into the proverbial sunset. People like her weren't made for such things. They were made for more prosaic ends. They were made for drudgery and mediocrity. True romance played no part in the lives of the Franklins. Brandon regarded women as bedroom playthings and not much more. As far as Hayley knew, her brother had never gotten a girl pregnant, which seemed a bit of a miracle. The fact that her father didn't cheat on her mother was also a surprise. Hayley supposed she should feel grateful that her mother was spared the particular indignity of a cheating husband, but feeling grateful for anything as far as her father was concerned was a serious struggle.

Layla swiped the latest block tower to the floor, and Lily clapped. Suddenly, Layla climbed to her feet and toddled over to Hayley. With a big grin she pulled up her shirt and said, "My tummy!"

"Yes," Hayley said quite seriously, "that is your tummy."

Lily then climbed to her feet and lifted her shirt. "My tummy, too!" she announced.

Hayley laughed. Most times she would so much rather be with small children than with adults. At least, she thought, an image of Ethan crossing her mind, most adults.

Chapter 43

There was more than the usual traffic on the road this morning, and Amy was worried she would be late arriving at Cressida's house. She wasn't sure Cressida would accept any excuses for a lack of punctuality other than something major, like death. That was silly. Illness would probably be an acceptable excuse. Maybe.

Amy's mood wasn't the best. The women's teasing the night before had upset her and not only because she had been hungry. The problem was that she wasn't quite able to put her finger on what about the teasing had gotten to her. Whatever it was, Amy had decided not to tell the others that Cressida was acting as her mentor that summer, or that Cressida had chosen to call her by the French version of her name. The other nannies didn't deserve that information.

When Amy had gotten home after leaving the pub she had gone straight to the freezer, where she found an unopened pint of chocolate chocolate-chip ice cream. She had eaten the entire thing. After, she had felt guilty and had realized that before she had met Cressida Prior, pigging out on a carton of ice cream wouldn't have made her feel anything but happy and full. But that's because before she met Cressida Prior she lacked self-control. Cressida was teaching her about self-control as well as about self-respect.

Amy pulled into the driveway and parked. It was exactly eight o'clock. Cressida was waiting for her just inside the door as she often was, wearing leggings, a tank top, and running shoes.

"I need you to undertake a very important mission for me, Aimee," Cressida said by way of greeting.

Amy smiled. No one had ever asked her to undertake an important mission before. Certainly not her mother. "Sure," she said eagerly.

Cressida turned and walked in the direction of the kitchen. "I need you to hand-deliver a very sensitive document to one of my company's lawyers in Hartford."

"Connecticut?" Amy asked, following her employer.

"Yes. I'm asking you to do this because I trust you, Aimee. And there are not many people I trust."

Amy felt a glow of satisfaction. What would those other nannies say if they could hear Cressida right now? "When do I go?" she asked.

"On Wednesday. But we'll talk more about that later." Cressida came to a sudden stop and turned around. "Right now, I want to talk to you about curating your life. Do you know what I mean by that?"

"Not really," Amy admitted. She had only ever heard of curators in museums and wasn't quite sure what they actually did. "But I'd love to learn."

"Good. Let me just juice a few cucumbers for us and we'll begin."

Amy smiled, though she didn't relish the idea of drinking cucumber juice. But it was probably very slimming, and she still hadn't lost the weight Cressida had told her to lose, so she would drink the juice as her mentor suggested she do. And she would learn about curating her life.

And on the way home that afternoon she would stop at The Yellow Buttercup and buy the sequined evening bag she had fallen in love with weeks ago. It was only $150 and would definitely come in handy once she was living in Boston and meeting other people who believed in her potential to succeed.

Chapter 44

Amy frowned and poked at one of the embroidered pillows piled on the couch. "Cressida is a highly discriminating person," she announced.

"Oh?" Leda said, prepared to be annoyed. She had been enjoying a good mystery novel until Amy had come into the living room and begun to wander, sighing as she went. "How is she discriminating?"

"She thinks about everything very carefully before she does it. Like how she dresses and what she eats and how she spends her free time. She curates her life."

"How interesting." Leda cast a longing eye at the novel in her hand.

"I've been thinking, Mom," Amy went on. "Maybe we should clean up the place a bit, get rid of some of this junk."

Leda laughed. She didn't know why. She was not amused. "Excuse me?" she said. "Nothing in our home is junk. And the house is cleaned from top to bottom every week."

"I don't mean that it's dirty," Amy explained. "Just that it's kind of stuffed. Like, what about all the throws on the couch and chairs? Do we really need them? And maybe we could toss a few of the pillows in here."

"I like this place just the way it is," Leda said stoutly.

Amy sighed. "Okay. It was just an idea. Cressida was telling me today about this amazing woman named Marie Kondo who came up with this amazing way to tidy up your life. Something about only keeping things that give you happiness. Or maybe it was joy. Anyway, did you know there's something called the National Association of Professional Organizers? You can hire someone to come into your home and totally clean it up. You can even hire someone to organize your thoughts!"

Leda wondered if the thought organizer, too, was amazing.

"When I'm in Boston," Amy went on, "I'm going to keep my room seriously clean and spare. I just hope the other girls aren't too messy. Mess means a lack of self-respect."

Leda refrained from asking if Amy had gotten around to cleaning out her room right here in Yorktide. She had recent evidence that it was still pretty much the opposite of clean and spare. For a moment she was tempted to ask Amy about the fur hat she had found but decided not to. Not yet, anyway.

"Harry!" Amy cried. "Get off that chair!"

Leda frowned. "Amy, you know full well that's Harry's chair."

"But he'll shed all over it," Amy complained. "I'll sit in it and get cat hair all over my clothes, and Cressida can't stand animals."

"Then don't sit in the chair," Leda advised. "Harry, stay where you are." Harry did, and Leda put her novel aside. She would get back to it later. She got up and headed to the kitchen.

"What's for dinner?" Amy asked, following her.

"Spaghetti with carbonara sauce."

Amy grimaced. "I can't eat that."

"What do you mean?" Leda asked as she set about finishing the dish in the big, black cast-iron pan she had inherited from her mother. "You love spaghetti carbonara."

"I did like it once, but I was talking to Cressida today and she said that there's a new study that proves once and for all that eggs are bad for you."

"What new study?" Leda asked.

"I don't know. She didn't say."

Leda's patience felt very close to snapping. "Amy, an egg here and there is not going to kill you."

"I'd rather not, Mom," Amy said. "I'll make myself a salad. Cressida eats a lot of salad but without dressing. The dressing has empty calories."

Leda watched as Amy inexpertly sliced half a cucumber and half a tomato and tore several leaves from a head of lettuce. She scooped the simple ingredients into a soup bowl and set it on the table.

"There are red peppers in the fridge," she said lightly. "And an avocado."

"Cressida said that avocados have too much fat."

Leda thought of the empty ice-cream container she had spotted in the recycling bin and decided not to comment on it. "I believe avocados have what's known as the good sort of fat," she said instead as she brought the cast-iron pan to the table, took her seat, and put a liberal portion of the spaghetti on her plate. "Bon appétit," she said brightly.

Amy speared an uneven slice of cucumber with her fork. Leda was torn between laughter and pity. Amy was twenty-one. Her ability to judge and separate out the preposterous from the reasonable should be far more developed than it was. In spite of four years of courses that were supposed to teach critical thinking, Amy had graduated as pretty much the same person she had been when she had entered college.

"What did you have for lunch?" Leda asked.

"A glass of cucumber juice," Amy said, cutting away a bit of brown, wilted lettuce.

Leda lifted her glass of wine to her lips to hide her frown.

Chapter 45

Hayley took one of the three knives the Franklin family owned from the drawer by the old toaster. The blade was dull even though Hayley had recently sharpened it using the heavy steel sharpener Nora had inherited from her mother. The knife really should be tossed, but the cost of a good replacement was prohibitive. As long as it was even partially functional it would suffice.

With only half a mind on the task Hayley began to slice the bunch of carrots she had already peeled. She was still wrestling with her conscience. The notion of marrying for money was absurd, but for some reason it wouldn't go entirely away. Maybe it was because almost every moment of every day was a harsh reminder of the miserableness of her life. Take, for example, her stop at the public library that afternoon to return the book her father had destroyed. She had offered no explanation for the destruction, though she had apologized profusely and paid for a replacement copy. The librarian, one of those who had worked there for well over twenty years, had asked no questions, only smiled sympathetically as she accepted Hayley's money. Nevertheless, the experience had been mortifying.

Hayley looked to where her mother was scrubbing a stubbornly dirty pot. This latest apartment didn't feature a dishwasher, nor was the hot water always hot. But there was some bit of good news for the Franklin household. Miraculously, her father had gotten a job on a construction site where a friend of a friend was foreman. Eddie Franklin was not skilled, but he could handle basic tasks if closely supervised. Personally, Hayley wouldn't trust him within ten miles of a power tool, but that wasn't her concern.

"I hope Dad doesn't blow this job like he blew the last one," she said. "Who gets fired from a dishwasher position?"

"He didn't blow the job," her mother corrected mildly. "The man in charge of the kitchen staff was very rude to him, and your father has too much pride to stand for someone treating him rudely."

Hayley restrained a sigh. "When's he supposed to be home?" she asked.

"Well," Nora said hesitatingly, "I'm not sure. He said something about the site closing at three, but he also said not to expect him home for dinner."

Hayley knew what that meant. It meant that when the day's work was over her father would be heading directly to the pub—one of the few that hadn't banned him—where he would get happily drunk until he was unhappily drunk. Which meant that either he would pass out somewhere between the pub and home or one of his cronies would drive him to the apartment, and that meant that Hayley would have to stay awake in order to keep him from disturbing her mother and everyone else who lived in the building until he was passed out on the couch.

"We're going to make rent next month," Hayley said. "Dad's paycheck can help with the electric bill. He will be giving his paycheck directly to you, won't he, Mom?"

Nora Franklin suddenly found a spot on the pot she was washing deeply interesting.

Hayley didn't bother to restrain her sigh this time around. Her parents' checking account—they had no savings account—was of necessity in Nora's name; if her husband had access to the account it would always be empty. This bit of progress hadn't come about without a fight. When Hayley had announced the new plan, her father had raged that as head of the house he had the right to make the big decisions. Her mother, too, had privately argued that by removing her father's access to the money Hayley would be insulting his manhood. "Manhood?" Hayley had scoffed. In the end, through sheer force of will and a bit of luck thrown in—her father came down with a bad case of the flu and was more than usually incoherent for a few days—Hayley had gotten her way.

Of course, with no bank account in his name, whatever paycheck Eddie Franklin might earn could not be directly deposited anywhere but his grubby fist. Still, Nora's earnings were now safe from Eddie's grasp, except for the occasions when he managed to wheedle or bully sums out of her. It was a constant struggle to maintain control of the household finances, one Hayley often despaired of ever truly winning.

"Do those people you work for treat you nicely?" her mother asked suddenly, turning from the sink. "I was talking to Sally, one of the girls who work in the bakery department, and she said she heard that all sorts of terrible things go on in those big homes with those people having so much money."

"The Whitbys are very nice people," Hayley assured her mother. "Look, I'll finish making dinner, okay? And put down that pot. You look as if you could fall asleep on your feet."

Nora smiled gratefully. "Thank you, Hayley. Will you be going out after dinner?"

"No," she said. "I've got a book I want to start. It's about the scientific advancements in the last forty years of the seventeenth century."

Her mother smiled blankly. "That's nice." Then she went off, and a moment later Hayley heard her bedroom door close.

Hayley finished slicing the carrots and filled a pot with water for boiling. Her mother had graduated from high school and had even completed two years of college before Eddie Franklin barreled into her life. But sometimes Nora acted as if she had had no education at all. It wouldn't surprise Hayley to learn that years of domestic fear and misery could alter a person's intelligence for the worse.

And that was something else to think about. Marrying an educated, wealthy man might help elevate her both intellectually and morally. Environment mattered enormously; no one could deny that. There was a limit to the refinement of thought, feeling, and behavior she could achieve living the way she did, in a series of substandard apartments with two parents who needed continual managing.

The bare lightbulb that illuminated the kitchen suddenly blew out. Yes, Hayley thought. There was a limit.

"My father didn't come home last night."

It was a little after one, and Hayley had come into downtown Yorktide on an errand for Marisa, who was grading papers at the house. She had run into Amy, in town on an errand for Cressida. Marisa had asked Hayley to pick up two lobsters for their lunch. Cressida had asked Amy to pick up a prescription for a diuretic.

"Again?" Amy said with a frown.

Hayley nodded. "Again. My mother was upset, but I think it's wonderful when he disappears. For minutes at a time I can forget he even exists. But then I see the broken toaster he swore he'd fix and the crack in the bathroom door where he kicked it and I remember that he's not gone for good."

"It really stinks that he's the way he is," Amy said feelingly. "I wish I could wave a magic wand and transform him into a—"

"A decent, hardworking human being?" Hayley sighed. "It's always puzzled me why my father doesn't seem to want the respect of his children, but he's never even tried to earn our respect. And why doesn't he want to be proud of us in return? He never supported Brandon or me in anything. He actually seems to enjoy dragging Brandon down to his level, and whenever he catches a glimpse of something about me that hints at my intelligence he belittles it. It's like he wants us to be as useless and as hopeless as he is."

Amy shrugged. "Misery loves company?"

"Whatever the reason," Hayley replied, "the whole thing is driving me mad. I've told my mother a million times to ditch my father, but she never listens. She keeps claiming he's a good person at heart and that he'll change, and then when he does something stupid again she's disappointed like she really expected anything different."

"Maybe she won't divorce him because she takes her marriage vows seriously," Amy said. "Didn't you tell me she's a Catholic?"

"Yeah," Hayley admitted. "But she hasn't been to church in years. I don't even know if she believes in God anymore."

Amy shrugged. "Maybe she really does love your dad. Maybe it's as simple as that. Love triumphs over all the bad stuff."

Hayley didn't answer. She didn't want to admit the possibility that love triumphed over "all the bad stuff," as Amy put it. Because if that were true, then everybody was likely doomed to spend the rest of their days with someone totally unworthy of the love bestowed upon them. That scenario sounded way too close to martyrdom for Hayley, and she had never been able to see the point in martyrdom, not that she criticized those for whom it was a divinely ordered necessity, like Edmund Campion, the sixteenth-century Jesuit priest. That was what reading so much about times past did for you. It brought you into intimate contact with people who, while so like you in some ways, were so different in others. It made you more broadminded. It—

"Hayley?" Amy said. "You in there?"

"Sorry."

"I'd better get going," Amy said, already beginning to back away in the direction of her car. "Bye."

Hayley walked to her own car, bag of lobsters in tow. And she wondered if a marriage contracted between two people, one of whom did not love the other but who was marrying for material gain alone, would be any better than the marriage that existed between her parents? Would such a marriage be inherently worse because it was based on a lie? She recalled what she had been thinking about the night before, how a person's environment could depress or elevate certain elements of character and intellect . . .

It was all so complicated. Hayley's stomach growled. One thing was not complicated. She was hungry. And it was very generous of Marisa to include Hayley in her craving for lobster.

Chapter 46

"Let me get this straight," Vera said. She was sitting across from Amy in the Latimers' kitchen. Amy's mother was in the living room talking on the phone with a client. "She wants you to drive all the way to Connecticut and back to hand-deliver a document to one of her lawyers?"

"That's right," Amy said. "It's an important document."

"No doubt. Still, she could safely send it via Federal Express or some other reputable shipping concern. She could probably just e-mail it for that matter."

"I guess," Amy said, "but she wants me to deliver it by hand."

"Does she expect you to take your own car?" Vera asked.

"I don't know," Amy admitted. "She didn't say."

"You mean she didn't suggest you take her car?" Vera frowned. "Then I advise you to ask for compensation on top of your salary for gas and tolls and whatever other incidental expenses you might incur."

"You're as bad as my mother and Hayley," Amy said with a laugh. "Cressida is my friend. I'm doing her a favor. You don't get paid for doing favors."

"No," Vera said, "but there's usually a degree of reciprocity involved in the doing of favors. Will this Prior person be willing to do a favor for you in return?"

"Of course she would!" Amy replied, but she knew that she would never ask Cressida for anything. She didn't have the right to ask a person like Cressida Prior, her mentor, for anything more than what Cressida already gave her. And really, she was a very generous person. Only the other day Cressida had taught her so much about the importance of organizing your life down to the tiniest detail.

"Well," Vera said, "enough about Ms. Prior. How are those nice young women you'll be sharing an apartment with this fall? Have you gotten together to talk about housework and meals and all the other potentially problematic issues that arise when people live together for the first time?"

Amy hesitated. The truth was she hadn't thought of Tracy and Stella and Megan in weeks. And she hadn't spoken to them since her graduation party. Stella had sent her a text a week or so ago but . . . Amy realized she had never responded. She couldn't even remember what the text had said.

"They're fine," she said. "We have plenty of time to talk about stuff."

"How is Hayley doing?" Leda asked when she returned to the kitchen. "I haven't heard you mention her in a few days."

"She's fine," Amy said. "But her father is still being a jerk. He didn't come home the other night."

Vera sighed. "That poor girl. She takes so much upon herself. I'd like to give that Nora Franklin a stern talking to. She's never been a proper mother to Hayley or to Brandon."

"Nora does what she's capable of doing," Leda said.

"Cressida says that people use that argument as an excuse for failure," Amy pronounced. "She says people who allow themselves to be taken advantage of like Mrs. Franklin does deserve what they get. Not that she knows Mrs. Franklin personally. She was just talking about people who allow themselves to be victims."

Suddenly Amy was aware of both Vera and her mother looking at her strangely. "What?" she asked defensively.

"That's a cruel attitude to take," her mother said forcefully. "Until you walk a mile in someone's shoes you simply cannot judge her behavior."

"Your mother is right," Vera seconded. "Above all, be kind. It's not rocket science."

"I need something in my room," Amy announced suddenly. She got up from the table and left the kitchen. She was annoyed with her mother for expressing what Amy used to think was a valid point of view but that she now saw as naïve. The thing was, she was changing and change was always difficult both for the person doing the changing and for those who liked her just fine the way she had been. People wanted to hold you down so you would remain the same person they had known and loved—or the same person they had been taking advantage of. Not that her mother or Vera had ever been anything but nice to her, but like Cressida had said one afternoon, the people closest to you could easily become your worst enemies. Family was a liability, whether they believed in you or not.

When Amy reached her bedroom, she paused at the threshold and looked at the hastily made bed, the dirty clothes in a pile on the floor, the empty juice bottle on her dresser. And then she strode inside, determined to start the curating of her life. Determined to change.

Chapter 47

When Amy had left the kitchen, Vera turned to Leda. “When you were on the phone I tried to talk to Amy about this crazy errand Cressida wants her to run. And I got nowhere.”

“I didn’t even try to question it,” Leda admitted. “I don’t think I’ve heard an original word come out of her mouth since she started working for Cressida Prior. It’s all, Cressida said this and Cressida thinks that.”

“Amy’s never exactly been a critical thinker,” Vera pointed out. “She’s always been too easily swayed by other people’s opinions. Sadly, Ms. Prior’s opinions seem to be of the seriously odious sort.”

Leda sighed. “I know Amy is legally an adult, but the fact is she’s living under my roof. I just don’t know to what extent I can advise or interfere in her life without crossing a line and alienating her. Do you know what she said to me the other night? That I never believed in her. The almighty Cressida Prior believes in her, though.”

“Kids can be cruel to their parents,” Vera pointed out.

“And there’s another thing that worries me,” Leda said. “I suspect Amy hasn’t been saving as much money as she should be. I came across the most impractical of fur hats in her room, and then she showed me a black sequined evening bag she bought at that totally overpriced store with the creepy mannequin in the window. Why does she need a black sequined evening bag?"

"You know, Abraham Lincoln supposedly said something like, 'I'd rather be a little nobody than an evil somebody.'"

Leda laughed. "Are you saying I'm a little nobody?"

"Not at all. I am saying that Cressida Prior is an evil somebody. At least, she's a very unpleasant somebody. You know Annie Lehrmitt, the woman who owns the toy shop on Clove Street? She was in the restaurant the other day and she told me that Cressida Prior literally ran into her on the sidewalk, smashed into her shoulder as she passed and didn't say a word of apology, just kept barreling on. The episode really shook Annie up."

"Poor woman." Leda sighed. "Even if I told Amy about what happened with Annie she wouldn't believe me, just like she wouldn't believe those former employers of Prior Ascendancy had a legitimate cause for suing. It's not like I can force Amy to quit. I could hope for Cressida to fire her, though that would cause some distress, too. And Amy would probably find a way to blame me."

"Well, let's see how Amy feels when she gets home from a round trip to Connecticut," Vera advised. "The experience of Hartford traffic might open her eyes to the reality of her situation as a so-called protégé."

Vera said her good-byes and Leda went to her studio, by far her favorite room in the house. Because she had lived at 22 Hawthorne Lane all of her life, she had no first memory of the studio. It seemed as much a part of her as her hands or her feet. You could say the same for the rest of the house, too, but the studio reigned supreme in Leda's heart. It was where she had discovered her artistic passion and absorbed her first lessons at her mother's knee.

Suddenly, standing in the middle of the room, Leda knew what she had to do. Though she was pretty sure—no, she was certain—she wouldn't win in her category, she would enter the competition sponsored by the FAF. She was not unaware that one of the reasons for her decision was rooted in her jealousy of the relationship between her daughter and Cressida Prior. Jealousy wasn't the best of motives for taking action, but it was a motive all the same. If she should by some crazy chance win the prize for Best Emerging Talent, maybe Amy would remember that her mother was as worthy as her amazing new employer, a person who believed that victims got what they deserved.

And then Leda realized that there was another, far more surprising reason for her decision to submit her work in the competition. She *wanted* to win the prize for Best Emerging Talent. She wanted to win for *herself*. That was a difficult thing to admit, that she believed she was worthy of recognition and acclaim. But she *was* worthy of recognition and acclaim. And she wanted both. She did.

Chapter 48

Hayley pulled open the door of the building and stepped onto the cracked pavement that led to the sidewalk. At the best of times it was hard to ignore the signs of neglect on the property, but now they seemed to leap at her and cause her almost physical distress. The paint on the building was peeling in long strips. What grass there was in the minuscule front yard hadn't been cut in weeks. Lying in the tall grass was a dented soda can, an empty pack of cigarettes, and a crumpled bag that had once contained potato chips. Cigarette butts littered the broken front steps.

The whole thing was just so grim. Hayley frowned. How could people have such little respect for their home? There was an answer for that. The people living in this building had no investment in it. They didn't own their apartments. They didn't plan on staying for long. Some of them had probably lost hope of ever living in a nicer place. Not all people who rented their homes had such lack of respect, only the sort of people with whom the Franklins seemed to wind up living in close proximity.

Hayley got into her car and began the fifteen-minute drive to the Whitbys' rental home. She parked in the space reserved for her, and before getting out of the car she gazed at the scene before her. Everything looked so calm and pretty. The grass was perfectly trimmed, and the flowers were laid out neatly in their beds. A

Japanese maple was fully leafed out. The azalea bushes were full and healthy. Filmy white curtains hung neatly in each window. On the porch, a bright red milk can held a spray of dried Bells of Ireland.

Hayley sighed. Why couldn't her life be filled with beauty? Of course, in any life there were times of difficulty and strain as well as times of ease and joy. But at least if she were a part of *this* world, the world of people like the Whitbys, in the hard times she could take consolation in a clean and orderly home; in a personal library of books that no one would dare to tear to shreds; in clothes that hadn't been worn by other people before finding their way to her closet; in bills that were paid in full and on time; in a backyard with a rose arbor, a stone birdbath, and a big oak tree where under the leafy branches she could find cool respite on hot summer days.

Hayley's hands tightened on the steering wheel. She thought of the black circles under her mother's eyes that morning, of the cardigan Nora Franklin had been patching for the last ten years, of the nervous cough her mother had developed.

It was at that moment that Hayley really and truly decided. Yes, the situation was morally complicated, but she would do it, or at the very least she would try to entice Ethan Whitby into marrying her. And if she succeeded in becoming Mrs. Ethan Whitby she would be kind and grateful and maybe even one day she would come to truly care for her husband. It would be the least she owed Ethan for having rescued her from the sorry life she was currently living.

Hayley felt a huge sense of excitement come over her as she looked out at the Whitbys' perfect summer home. She felt a sense of power she had never felt before when she was just being a dutiful daughter who scrubbed floors for a living.

Hayley checked her watch and saw that she would be late if she sat there any longer. She got out of the car and walked toward the house. Now that the decision had been made, all she had to do was convince Ethan that marrying her was what he wanted more than anything. Not that Hayley had any specific idea of how to go about this. She had never been a flirt, and she knew all too well that her nature was blunt rather than coy or seductive. Maybe if she simply toned down her manner a little bit she might come across to Ethan Whitby as charmingly without pretense rather than as obnoxiously uncouth.

As Hayley climbed the stairs to the front porch she noted with pleasure the wicker rocking chairs in a neat row and the pretty hanging baskets overflowing with red and purple flowers. She was doing the right thing. You had to take risks in life if you wanted to succeed. Hayley knew that from her reading. She thought about what Matilda, daughter of Henry I of England, had risked in order to take back the crown from her usurping cousin Stephen. She had even managed to escape prison not once but twice, the first time disguised as a corpse. Matilda never actually got the crown, but it wasn't for lack of trying, and after Stephen's death her son became King Henry II, so in a way Matilda had won in the end.

And Hayley could win, too. She opened the front door and went directly to the kitchen. Marisa had left a note saying she had taken the girls for a stroll and would be back shortly. There was a bouquet of flowers on the counter with a card propped up against the vase. The message read: *I'm happier every day with you. J.* Not once in the twenty-one years Hayley had known her father had he given his wife flowers. Not once.

Standing alone in the well-appointed kitchen Hayley's momentary high spirits fell. She would stand a chance with Ethan only if she kept most of the truth about her life a secret. Still, she would have to be careful not to tell outrageous lies that might trip her up in the end. She had been born and raised in Yorktide. People knew her. She would have to hope that Ethan would stay away from the locals who might inadvertently let slip a fact she would not want Ethan to know, like that for a few weeks many years ago the Franklins had been forced to stay at a shelter. The memory of those dreadful weeks still haunted Hayley, and she was sure they would continue to haunt her until she drew her final breath. Not that anything traumatic had happened—well, anything more traumatic than being homeless in the first place. The staff was kind and hardworking, and there were a few fellow residents who had comforted Nora Franklin when she couldn't stop her tears from flowing. Still, Hayley had been scared. She had never been so scared.

"We're home!"

Marisa's voice brought Hayley back to the moment with a start. Those memories had been an all-too-forceful reminder of the enormous gap between her and the Whitby family. She took a deep breath and hurried to meet Marisa and the girls.

Marisa smiled brightly when Hayley joined her in the hall. "It's a beautiful morning, isn't it?" she said.

"Yes," Hayley said, returning Marisa's smile in spite of her conscience nagging at her. With an effort, she shook aside the feelings of guilt and lifted Lily from the double stroller. After all, she deserved a decent life as much as Marisa did. Didn't she?

Chapter 49

Just before six a.m. Amy was ready to leave for her journey to Connecticut. First, she was to stop at Cressida's house to pick up the document she was to deliver to the lawyer's office in downtown Hartford. She had looked at a map online for the best route to take during morning rush hour and had written out the directions in large print on a sheet of white paper. Her car didn't have a GPS unit; her mother's car did, but Amy didn't want to ask to borrow the Subaru. She was a little nervous about driving in big-city traffic for what would be the first time, and if she was going to do something stupid like hit the car in front of her she wanted it to be with her own vehicle and not someone else's.

Amy yawned. Mornings were not her strong point. She had gone to bed early the night before in the hopes that a few additional hours of sleep would make getting up at five easier, but the plan had backfired. She had lain awake until almost midnight, too keyed up to drift off. Even after two cups of coffee this morning Amy felt almost dizzy with tiredness. She would have to stop on the road at least once for another cup of coffee, and maybe she would treat herself to a doughnut as well. The sugar might help revive her. She just wouldn't tell Cressida she had eaten something so full of empty calories.

Amy flinched when her phone alerted her to a text. It was from Cressida. The delivery was off. Amy felt a sudden rush of disappointment. Part of her had been looking forward to this little adventure. She was also, she realized, a tiny bit annoyed. If she had known last night that the trip was off she could have slept later this morning. And then she realized that she might be facing an unexpected day off. Though she loved spending time with Cressida, it would be nice to have some time to herself. Hayley did have a point about it being the norm for an employee to have certain days off so she could live her life.

And then came another text from Cressida. Amy was to be at the house at seven. So much for going back to bed. With a sigh, Amy poured a third cup of coffee and then went to the bread box, where there was a loaf of cinnamon raisin bread. A few slices of that with real butter, not that diet stuff she had started using on Cressida's recommendation, would be almost as good as a doughnut.

Cathi nodded toward the small stage. "The bass player is so cute. I love burly guys. He looks like a Viking with that thick blond hair and that gorgeous beard."

Amy was at The White Hart with Cathi, Michelle, and Sarah. At the last minute, Hayley had begged off without a reason, which probably meant that she felt it was necessary to stay at home with her mother. Eddie Franklin must be on a tear.

Thinking about Hayley's lack of explanation for not being at The White Hart that evening, it had dawned on Amy that Cressida hadn't apologized or offered an explanation for the last-minute change in plans. But that was okay. Cressida had let her go at three instead of four, and before that she had let Amy look through her closet on her own. Cressida Prior, founder of Prior Ascendancy, trusted her.

"Who is he, anyway?" Sarah was saying.

"His name is Noah Woolrich," Michelle told her. "He went away to college in New Jersey. I wonder what brought him back here. I mean, most people who leave don't come back. I know I probably wouldn't."

"Maybe he wants to be near his family," Amy suggested. "His parents aren't in great health, and his uncle isn't getting any younger and he is a widower."

Michelle nodded. "Noah is a gentle giant. I mean, he could probably flatten anyone in this pub with ease, but you know he would never lift a hand in violence."

"Is he seeing anyone?" Cathi asked.

Michelle looked meaningfully at Amy. "No. He's saving himself for our Amy!"

"He is not," Amy protested.

"So, are you interested in him?" Cathi asked.

Amy shrugged. "Not really. I mean no. Maybe someday. I don't know."

The others laughed, though not unkindly. Amy looked toward the band again to find Noah smiling at her. She wiggled her fingers in a wave. She was glad she hadn't had to drive to Connecticut and back today. If she had, she would probably have been too tired to meet her fellow nannies at The White Hart and then she would have missed seeing Noah. He really was awfully cute.

"I wonder what the illustrious Cressida Prior would say about this place," Michelle said. "As far as I can tell, no one is brokering big business deals and the only money being spent is on beer and French fries, which would make it pretty insignificant on her radar."

Amy felt a flush come to her cheeks. She couldn't argue with Michelle. Cressida *would* turn up her nose at The White Hart, and maybe she would be right to. Amy moved her left foot and felt the sole of her espadrille stick to the floor.

Cathi raised an eyebrow meaningfully. "Forget about The White Hart. I wonder what La Prior would make of Amy's Noah Woolrich."

Sarah laughed. "From what I've heard she pretty much loathes and despises all men, though she's not above using them when she needs something."

Amy suddenly remembered what Cressida had said about men seeing women as no more than their reproductive organs. Was that what Noah saw in her, a potential mother for his children and no more? She glanced again at the stage, a frown on her face.

"I wonder why she bothered to get married in the first place," Cathi said. "Any insights, Amy?"

Amy shook her head. The question had fleetingly crossed her mind once or twice but she had ignored it. No doubt Cressida had had very good reasons for marrying Will, even if now they seemed an odd and mismatched couple.

"Hey, wait a minute," Michelle said. "Weren't you supposed to go to Connecticut today on some crazy mission for La Prior?"

Amy felt herself blush. She had kind of bragged to her fellow nannies about Cressida's entrusting her with the delivery of an important document. She had been hoping that no one would mention the aborted mission.

"Yes," Amy said matter-of-factly. "But it wasn't necessary for me to go after all."

Cathi frowned. "What do you mean, it wasn't necessary?"

Sarah raised an eyebrow. "She means Cressida decided Amy wasn't trustworthy enough to carry a top-secret document out of the state."

"That's not it at all," Amy snapped. "It's just—"

"Shhh!" Michelle hissed. "I love this song!"

The others focused on the band's cover of a song by Nirvana. Amy felt grumpy and full of self-doubt. Maybe Cressida *had* changed her mind about her protégé. Maybe Cressida no longer believed in Amy and found her untrustworthy. Maybe, Amy thought, she should just get up and go home. She glanced again at the stage and decided she would stay a little bit longer. It was nice to see Noah.

Chapter 50

Leda had asked Vera to join her and Amy at dinner that evening. She felt the need to make a bit of a big deal about her announcement to enter her work in the FAF's annual competition. Tooting one's own horn wasn't always a bad thing, Leda thought as she brought a pitcher of lemonade and a bottle of wine to the table. Not that she would take a page from Cressida Prior's notebook and make a habit of it.

Vera used the tongs to put a heap of fresh green beans on her plate. "So," she said, "no road trip yesterday, I hear."

Amy shrugged. "It had to be cancelled at the last minute."

Leda came to the table with a platter of roasted chicken and vegetables. "I have some big news to share with you both," she said as she took her seat.

"What is it?" Amy asked, eyeing the platter of food with a frown.

"Well, after a lot of thought and some urging from Phil, and from you, Vera, I've decided to enter one of my original tapestries in the FAF's annual competition. The prize for Best Emerging Talent is a thousand dollars and a mention in the monthly newsletter. I'm pretty nervous about the whole thing and I know I won't win, but I thought I'd give it a go."

Vera reached across the table for Leda's hand. "I'm so glad to hear this, Leda," she said. "And don't say you know you won't win. You don't know any such thing."

Amy gave her mother a distracted smile. "That's nice, Mom," she said. "You know what Cressida did today? She closed a multi-million-dollar deal with—well, I can't remember who with, but what matters is that she closed the deal."

Leda concentrated on keeping the annoyance out of her voice. "Is that all you have to say about my entering the competition?" she asked. "That it's nice?"

"Well, it is nice. A thousand dollars is a lot of money for people like us."

"It's not about the money," Leda replied testily. *People like us?* "You know I've never put my work out there to be judged against the work of other fiber artists from around the country. It's kind of a big deal."

Amy picked a string bean from her plate and inspected it closely before taking a bite. "Sure, Mom," she said. "Did you know that last year Cressida won an award for the biggest growth in the industry? Or something like that. I mean, that's pretty amazing."

Leda took a deep breath. Was it any wonder that jealousy was her strongest motivation for entering her work in the competition? She was seriously disappointed in her daughter for her thoroughly uncritical worship of Cressida Prior. And feeling disappointed with your child was a terrible way to feel.

"You've told us all about Cressida. What's the father like?" Vera asked. "I'm having trouble imagining the partner to this woman."

"It's funny," Amy said. "The other nannies were asking about him at The White Hart. Actually, I haven't seen much of him. He's nice, but he's not good for much but watching the kids when Cressida is working."

Leda choked on her wine. When she had recovered enough to speak she said, "I hope you don't voice that opinion anywhere but here. And frankly, I'm surprised you'd make such a harsh judgment only knowing the man for a short time."

"I'm only repeating what Cressida said about him," Amy argued.

"And since when is taking care of young children something to be dismissed as unimportant?" Leda asked.

Vera frowned. "This Cressida person really talks about her own husband in such unflattering terms? And to a stranger?"

"I'm not a stranger."

"Well, you're not a friend, either," Vera pointed out.

Before Amy could protest this statement—and she looked as if she was going to do just that—Leda spoke. "Will Prior is your employer. It's not good policy to bad-mouth your employer, especially when what you're saying is based on hearsay."

"Will *isn't* my employer," Amy said. "Cressida employs me. She explained from the start that I worked for her and not Will."

"You're splitting hairs, my girl," Vera said.

"To get back to the competition," Leda said hurriedly, "I think I've decided which of my original tapestries to submit. I'm going to go with Stars Streaming. It's a good mix of abstract design and identifiable symbols. Hopefully it will speak to judges with a range of tastes."

"I love that design!" Vera enthused.

Leda looked to her daughter. "What do you think about my choice?"

Amy shook her head. "Sorry, Mom, I wasn't listening. I was just thinking about something Cressida was saying this afternoon. She told me that to get anywhere in this world you need to take risks, especially if you're a woman."

"And that's exactly what your mother is doing," Vera pointed out. "Aren't you proud of her for taking this step forward in her career?"

"Sure I am," Amy said. "But it won't really be a step forward unless she wins. I mean, success is only proved by winning. Cressida said something like that."

Leda sent a warning look across the table to Vera, whose face was a thundercloud of disapproval. "Aren't you having any chicken?" she asked as neutrally as she could manage, though she could hear the note of anger in her voice.

Amy made a face. "It's got the skin on it. Do you know how bad fat is for you? Cressida never eats fat, and when she does it's the good kind."

Leda ignored the contradiction.

"Peel the skin off," Vera snapped.

"Another glass of wine?" Leda asked her friend, whose face was now alarmingly red. And she thought that if Amy said one word about Cressida not drinking alcohol she would probably throw the bottle at the wall.

Chapter 51

"How about a cup of tea?"

Hayley smiled gratefully at Mrs. Latimer. "Yes," she said. "Please."

As Amy's mother took two ceramic mugs from a shelf and fetched tea bags from a tin canister, Hayley noted again how warm and homey the kitchen felt with its cheery yellow curtains and a big blue pitcher full of wild flowers on the table. The entire house exuded a sense of warmth and safety.

It was what she wanted. Warmth, safety, stability, beauty. And she might very well get those qualities of life being married to Ethan Whitby. Assuming she ever saw him again. He hadn't made an appearance since his last brief visit when they had talked about a shared love of history.

"How's your mom?" Mrs. Latimer asked, as she brought a small pitcher of milk to the counter.

"Okay," Hayley said. "You know."

"You're still not thinking of getting your own place?"

"No," Hayley said shortly. "I can't."

The teakettle whistled, and Mrs. Latimer poured the boiling water into the mugs. "By moving out you wouldn't be abandoning your mother," she said, replacing the kettle on the stove. "You might actually be forcing her to stand on her own two feet. Certainly, staying on in that house isn't doing you any good. I'm sorry.

Maybe I shouldn't have said that, but I've known you a long time and I've seen what I've seen."

"Amy told me about your entering that competition," Hayley said. Mrs. Latimer would forgive the abrupt change of topic. "I think it's great."

"Amy told you about that? Huh. She didn't seem very interested when I gave her the news."

Of course she hadn't, Hayley thought. All Amy could think about these days was Cressida Prior. "Marisa Whitby bought one of your pieces at Wainscoting and Windowseats," she said.

Leda smiled. "Really? So, do you like working for her?"

"I do. She's decent, which is more than you can say about a lot of people."

Mrs. Latimer sighed. "Hayley, try not to be so negative."

"Sorry," Hayley said with a bit of a smile.

"No apology necessary. I've got to get back to work. Give my love to your mom." Mug in hand, Mrs. Latimer left the kitchen.

"I don't know how you can drink hot tea in this weather." Amy appeared in the kitchen, fanning her face with a drugstore flyer, her curly hair pulled back from her face. "Let's go out back," she suggested. "It'll definitely be cooler than it is in here."

Amy was right. It was cooler in the yard than it was in the house. Hayley took a seat at the little round table covered with a red-and-white-checked cloth. Amy, still fanning her face, sat across from her. "Cressida never seems to feel the heat," she said.

"Hmmm," Hayley replied. She had not come to talk about Cressida Prior. She had come to see Amy with a purpose. She knew from her own experience that if you told someone your intention to act, you felt more bound to go through with that act. It was something to do with the power of a witness. And because Hayley couldn't shake her discomfort with her plan to seduce Ethan Whitby into a proposal of marriage, telling Amy, who no doubt would disapprove mightily, might just force her to defend her decision and thereby boost her courage and determination.

It was worth a shot, anyway. "I've come to an important decision," she announced.

"About what?" Suddenly Amy smiled. "Are you going to splurge and get those ankle boots you liked the last time we were in DSW?"

Hayley refrained from rolling her eyes. "Something a bit more important than shoes. I'm going to get Ethan Whitby to marry me." The moment she had spoken the words out loud Hayley realized how totally absurd they sounded.

Amy laughed. "You're joking, right?"

"No," Hayley said. "I'm dead serious."

"You can't really mean it. It's . . . It's insane!"

"I think it's very sane," Hayley countered. *If unethical,* she added silently.

"Why do you want him to marry you? You hardly even know him! You met him what, once? Twice?"

"I want to marry him so that I can get away from the life I've been leading for the past twenty-one years," Hayley said. "So that I can finally be free of the—of the degradation."

Amy frowned. "Degradation? Isn't that a bit strong?"

"No," Hayley said forcefully. "It's not."

"How are you even going to do it?" Suddenly a look of horror bloomed on Amy's face. "Wait a minute. You're not going to get pregnant, are you?"

"God, no! I'm just going to . . . I'm going to make him like me."

Amy gave Hayley a look that shamed her. For the first time in their relationship, Hayley felt herself to be the less sharp minded of the two.

"You're going to have to do a lot more than just make him like you," Amy said. "You're going to have to make him fall in love with you, or at least think that he has."

"How hard could it be?" Hayley replied with a confidence she didn't at all feel. Maybe telling Amy her intentions hadn't been such a good idea after all.

Amy sighed. "Okay, let's say he does find you attractive, and he probably will. Everyone does. Even so he'll never marry you. He'll think you're not good enough for him, in spite of the fact that you're way more intelligent and kind than most people. Except when you're trying to trap some poor, unsuspecting guy into marriage! Look, I'm just trying to save you from an embarrassing disaster."

An embarrassing disaster. Is that what her so-called plan would come to in the end? Hayley sighed. "I don't care if he doesn't love me. I want him to marry me. That's all."

Amy shook her head. "Who are you? I've never heard you talk like this. You sound so . . . so cold."

"It's the new me," Hayley declared. "I'm tired of waiting around for something significant to happen. I'm going to *make* something significant happen."

Amy eyed her shrewdly. "Did something bad happen at home?"

"Something bad is always happening at home."

"You know what I mean," Amy pressed. "Something really bad. Something other than your father being a jerk and your mother letting him get away with it."

"No," Hayley said. "More of the same. But something changed the other night. I thought, Why not *take* from the world instead of always giving?"

Amy leaned forward. "Hayley, I know you must feel that everything is always against you, but what you're planning is so unbelievably self-serving. You can't use people for your own ends."

"Why not?" Hayley countered. "Plenty of people do just that and they live perfectly happy lives." *Did they?* Hayley wondered. Or were they haunted by the fact of their immoral and unethical behavior?

"You'd have to sign a prenup, you know," Amy pointed out, "and that would be humiliating. I'm sure the Whitbys' lawyers know all about protecting their clients from gold diggers."

Stupidly, Hayley hadn't thought about the possibility that the Whitby family would want to protect its assets from a lowly person like her. But Amy didn't need to know that. "Look," Hayley said, "don't say anything to your mom about this, okay? I mean it. Nothing."

"All right," Amy said after a moment. "But you know she'd tell you the same thing I'm telling you. That it's insane. You're better than this, Hayley."

Am I? Hayley asked herself. "How's it going with Cressida?"

"Fantastic," Amy said, her expression brightening.

And as Amy launched into a paean in praise of the illustrious head of Prior Ascendancy, Hayley found herself wishing that she had never applied for a position as nanny this summer. She would never have been tempted to pursue such a crazy scheme as conning someone into marriage if she had simply found another job scrubbing food stains off other people's backsplashes.

"What is this crap always cluttering up the place?"

"This crap as you call it is a book," Hayley shot back, snatching the volume from her father before he could ruin it. "Or aren't you familiar with books other than to destroy them?"

Eddie Franklin laughed nastily "All that stuff you read, history and politics. What does any of it have to do with you? You're just Hayley Franklin. You're not important. I know what you think. You think you're better than your own father, but you're not."

Yes, Hayley thought. *I am better than you.* But she chose not to argue. Her father wouldn't pay attention to the content of her argument; he would only hear sounds that would infuriate him because he wanted an excuse to be angry with the daughter who shamed him by her intelligence. And the consequence of that anger would very likely be retaliation against Nora, his blameless wife, someone Eddie knew would never resist his blows. True, Eddie Franklin didn't always resort to physical violence, but when he did things got ugly and fast.

No, let her father think—if he ever really used his brain—that his daughter was an ungrateful bitch who gave herself airs. It was of no consequence to Hayley, not now. Amy's protestations had had the desired effect after all. Hayley felt more determined than ever to pursue her plan.

"I'll be at the Axe and Grind," her father muttered, stalking toward the door of the apartment and letting it slam behind him.

Only then did Hayley's mother emerge from the bathroom, where, Hayley suspected, she had been hiding from her husband. "Was that your father leaving?" she asked.

"Yeah," Hayley said.

"I suppose he's going to the Axe and Grind."

Hayley was about to make a snide remark about Eddie Franklin and the local pubs, but the look of exhaustion on her mother's face made her hold her tongue. “Forget about him, Mom,” she said. “You look worn-out. Tough day at work?”

“Well, yes,” Nora said, “now that you mention it. Three customers complained about the way I packed their groceries. One made me take everything out of her bag and start over again. She was very rude.”

“I’m sorry, Mom,” Hayley said, reaching out and placing a hand gently on her mother’s shoulder.

“Hayley? You won’t leave me, will you, now that you’re working for those rich people?” her mother asked. “You won’t let them turn your head and decide to go away from me?”

No, Hayley thought. She would not allow her head to be turned. She was not naïve like Amy. She was manipulative and self-seeking. She was setting out to snare a decent man into a marriage with a woman who wanted him only for his money and his status. A twinge of severe embarrassment ran through her. What would Nora Franklin think if she knew what her daughter was planning for the sake of them both?

“No, Mom,” Hayley said firmly. “I won’t abandon you.”

Nora Franklin smiled feebly. “You’re all I’ve got,” she said.

“I know, Mom,” Hayley said. “I know.”

Chapter 52

For the past thirty minutes Cressida had been working on her computer at her desk, a frown of concentration adding additional lines to her already lined forehead. Amy, sitting idly across from her employer, had nothing else to do but to observe Cressida's flying fingers and to wonder why Cressida was wearing a sleeveless top. Sleeveless was not a great way to go for someone whose arms were so thin. But no doubt Cressida had a very good reason for wearing a sleeveless top, and it was no business of Amy's to criticize. Especially since she still hadn't been able to lose the pounds Cressida had suggested she lose. Amy didn't know why. She had cut way back on lots of foods, but the weight refused to go away.

"I want you to listen in on a very important phone call I'll be making," Cressida announced suddenly, closing her laptop with a click.

"Okay," Amy said. She felt relieved. At least there was something on today's agenda. So far Cressida hadn't assigned her any tasks, and with Will and the children out of the house yet again, Amy had been feeling pretty useless.

"I'll be terminating someone," Cressida went on, "and it will do you good to hear how such things are done. On no account are you to say anything. You're just to listen to him and me, understood?"

Amy nodded, though what she really wanted to do was to emphatically say no. To be a witness to someone losing his job seemed very wrong, especially given the fact that she didn't work for Cressida's company. It was more than wrong. It was—what was the word? Callous? Cruel?

But this was the world of big business. This was the world of *successful* people, not people like Amy's mother, who were content to spend their lives toiling away in near anonymity. Then again, Amy remembered, her mother had decided to enter that competition. Amy supposed that was something, but it didn't have anything to do with *real* power, not the kind that Cressida wielded.

"I'll make the call at one o'clock sharp," Cressida announced. "Until then go through that box of back issues and throw out anything older than three months."

"Yes," Amy said, though she doubted performing such a simple task as tossing old issues of *Forbes* and the *Atlantic* would help take her mind off the impending phone call.

Cressida smiled. "You're a dream, Aimee. I'm going for a run."

As the morning became early afternoon, Amy's discomfort grew until she felt as if she might be sick to her stomach. Even if Cressida's employee deserved to lose his job he was a person with feelings. He had the right to be treated fairly and with dignity. There was no doubt in Amy's mind that if he knew someone was listening in on his dismissal he would be miserable. But what could she do? Saying no to Cressida just wasn't possible.

At precisely three minutes to one o'clock Cressida appeared in the doorway of the office. Amy's heart began to pound in her chest.

"I changed my mind about making that call," Cressida announced. "I'm going to fire him in person when I next see him."

Without further explanation Cressida turned and walked off. Amy literally sagged with relief. And then she scolded herself for being so naïve. Maybe Cressida's asking her to witness the firing wasn't in fact cruel. Maybe it was meant to be a lesson from mentor to protégé. Maybe feelings had to be ignored in order to get important things done. That must be it.

From the office window Amy could see three other massive houses along the coast, each more beautiful than the other. She thought of Hayley wanting to enter a world of money and influence. What if she succeeded in joining that world, whether by marrying Ethan Whitby or through some other way Amy couldn't even imagine? Would it radically and fundamentally change her? It was almost impossible to imagine Hayley doing or saying some of the things Cressida did or said. Hayley was strong but she wasn't . . . Amy frowned. Hayley wasn't like Cressida. Take, for instance, the light in which Hayley viewed her mother's victimhood. Though it might annoy her, she never ignored her mother's plight. Cressida, Amy thought, wouldn't be so . . . Cressida couldn't afford to be so kind because . . .

Amy glanced at her watch. She wished it were four o'clock, the time Cressida usually dismissed her. Suddenly, there was no place more she wanted to be than in her bedroom—messy though it still was—with one or both of the cats—furry as they were—on her lap. Things always seemed more certain when she was home. Things always seemed . . .

Chapter 53

Amy had gone off to the Priors' house after breakfast, during which she had regaled her mother with tales of the great Cressida Prior's past and present accomplishments. Leda had exercised a good deal of patience over her coffee and toast but had almost lost hold of that patience when Amy revealed that Cressida had fired the pool maintenance service because she thought one of the crew had sneered at her. "You can't have that sort of insubordination in an employee," Amy had pronounced sententiously.

Now, Leda was settled in her studio, Harry and Winston asleep on the old love seat in the corner. She had just cleared her mind of all else but the work she had planned to do that morning when her cell phone rang. Leda didn't recognize the number but answered the call nonetheless.

"Leda Latimer?" a woman asked. "My name is Diane Freeman and I'm calling from the *Journal of Craftwork*. Perhaps you've heard of us?"

"Of course," Leda said. "I have a subscription."

"Good," the woman went on. "I'm one of the new staff writers and I'm putting together next month's Artists to Watch column. I'd like to feature you in the piece as someone who's yet to gain real media coverage. Would this be a convenient time for you to answer a few questions?"

For a moment, Leda didn't know how to answer. A magazine wanted to feature her in a profile? "Yes," she said finally. "I guess so. But how did you get my name?"

Diane Freeman laughed lightly. "A good reporter never reveals her sources, but in this case I think I can make an exception. A great fan of your work suggested you to our editorial department. Cora Flowers. You do know her?"

"Yes," Leda said. "I do." Cora Flowers had been one of her earliest supporters; indeed, she had been a fan of Leda's mother's work as well. Leda wondered why Cora hadn't told her that she planned on approaching the *Journal of Craftwork*; maybe Cora thought Leda would protest, given her well-known aversion to publicity.

The reporter went on to ask Leda a few basic questions: How old had she been when she first got involved with fiber arts? Was crafting a family tradition? Did she prefer working on her own, or was she a member of a crafting circle? Leda answered as clearly as she could, all the while half doubting the interview was actually taking place.

When the interview was over and Diane Freeman had thanked Leda for her time, Leda sat for a moment in stunned silence. It seemed her reputation had been growing without her being aware of it. She felt thankful and more than a little proud, and she wondered how Amy would react when she learned that a major crafting publication had reached out to her mother.

But then Leda frowned. She doubted that Amy would care in the least.

Chapter 54

Hayley had welcomed any chance at research while in college. Even in high school she had gone out of her way to scour sources when writing papers for history, English, and sociology classes. And she hadn't limited her research to online sources, helpful as they might be. No, she had hunted down magazines, journals, and real books, the kind with worn covers and crinkly old pages, when seeking information and opinion.

So, when it came to setting out to more fully understand the world that Ethan Whitby inhabited, Hayley had planned carefully. First step, investigate Whitby Wealth Management. Using her ancient laptop she had logged onto the company's website, where she learned that WWM provided financial and investment advice, accounting and tax services, and retirement and estate planning. Clients worked with a single wealth manager to ensure their assets were well looked after. A further search told Hayley that Jon Whitby's personal philanthropic efforts were significant. He regularly contributed to no fewer than four charitable organizations and sat on the board of two of them. On paper at least, he was a man of integrity and energy and focus.

Second step, find out how the upper half lived, and that involved reading through copies of magazines such as *Town & Country*, *W*, and *Vanity Fair*. Magazines like these weren't sources of hard fact, but they could give a glimpse, if a slightly distorted one, of how a segment of society saw and presented itself. For obvious reasons, Hayley hadn't wanted anyone to recognize her poring over the glossies, so she had chosen to visit the library in South Berwick.

She had already paged through two issues of *Town & Country* when she heard her name being spoken. Hayley looked up almost guiltily. So much for researching incognito. "Yes," she said. The woman was wearing a gold chain around her neck with matching gold disc earrings. She didn't look like someone Hayley knew from her usual rounds in Yorktide, certainly not someone she would run into at the Laundromat down the street from her family's apartment.

"Barbara Ross," the woman went on. "We met at Hannah Fox's house. Remember?"

"Yes," Hayley said with as bright a smile as she could muster. "I remember." She did, sort of. Usually when she was at work scrubbing someone's floors or rinsing out their shower stalls she didn't pay much attention to anyone who might come and go. You could hardly shake hands with someone while wearing rubber gloves covered in ammonia-based cleaning fluid. But now that she thought about it, she did remember Ms. Fox introducing her to her friend. It had seemed odd at the time, not to say awkward. "How are you?"

"I'm fine, thanks." Barbara peered down at the magazine open on the table before Hayley and laughed. "*Town and Country*. That's a bit of an unusual choice for you."

Hayley bristled. "It's for a project," she said. "It's about the ethical issues behind expendable income in the upper classes," she said.

Barbara looked momentarily puzzled. Then she smiled vaguely and moved on. Hayley felt annoyed. Why shouldn't she be reading *Town & Country*? Just because she was the daughter of unspectacular parents didn't mean she wasn't allowed to learn about those who were . . . No. Not better than Hayley Franklin. Just . . . different.

After forty minutes of perusing the stack of magazines she had gathered, the fruit of Hayley's efforts was a handful of fairly useless observations. First, the publications seemed pretty obsessed by the British and European royal families. And heiresses, debutantes, and socialites.

Jewelry was important to the readers of these magazines, too. Hayley had come across a photograph of a pink, oval-shaped diamond that stretched all the way from the base of the model's finger to beyond her knuckle. Then there was a necklace coming to auction at one of the big houses; it was expected to sell for $12 million. The sum had made Hayley feel slightly ill. She had looked at the woven bracelet that Mrs. Latimer had made for her and wondered if she would be able to wear such a piece if she were to succeed in inserting herself into a world like the one described on the pages of these magazines. Or would she be required to wear only what one article referred to as "important jewelry"? Important, of course, meaning outrageously expensive.

Another observation Hayley made was that seriously wealthy people seemed to attend events almost every day of the week, whether it be a charity ball or a party on a yacht the size of a football field. And you couldn't just show up to certain events wearing any old thing. If a man expected to be allowed in the Royal Enclosure at Royal Ascot he had better be sporting a black or gray top hat. And if a woman wanted to be at his side she had better not be wearing a dress with spaghetti straps.

Of course, travel was a vital part in the lives of the seriously wealthy. In Marrakech, you could book a villa for a sum that amounted to a little more than Hayley's yearly salary, and that was a salary in a good year. In Ireland, you could hire a luxury train. Destination spas were popular.

And, Hayley had learned, seriously wealthy people were subject to the changing whims of home decorating ideas. It seemed that in 2017 separate master bedrooms were a "thing." Hayley wondered how that worked. Did a husband and wife have to agree on separate bedrooms? She could foresee a fair amount of divorces resulting from hurt feelings and misunderstandings unless separate bedrooms stopped being a "thing" by next season.

Food and wine, too, meant a lot to the seriously wealthy. Rather, food and wine that was in vogue. There was something called a

Yubari King melon that sold for between thirty and fifty dollars in Japanese department stores. White truffles cost between $3,000 and $5,000 per pound. Osetra sturgeon caviar would set you back about five hundred dollars per serving.

And if you were wealthy enough to buy white truffles and Osetra caviar, you were wealthy enough to afford clothes by designer houses like Versace and Gucci and Saint Laurent. Hayley looked down at her thrift store chinos and frowned.

After a mind-numbing two hours, Hayley gathered the stack of magazines and returned them to their slots in the wooden bookcase alongside ragged copies of *Sports Illustrated*; *O, The Oprah Magazine*; and *People*.

How rich, she wondered, did you have to be to be considered a part of the infamous 1 percent? A billionaire? A multibillionaire?

Trying to ascertain the habits of the rich was pretty daunting, Hayley thought as she slid behind the wheel of her humble Kia Spectra. Suddenly she recalled a line from a short story called "The Rich Boy," written by F. Scott Fitzgerald. She had read it in high school sophomore English class, along with *The Great Gatsby*. The line went: "Let me tell you about the very rich. They are different from you and me." Indeed, if the content of the magazines Hayley had just perused was anything to go on, the divide between those born to privilege and those not seemed an impossible divide to breach.

Hayley started her car and pulled slowly out of the library parking lot with the unhappy conviction that it would take a person far savvier than herself to even attempt such a feat.

Chapter 55

The temperature was already well into the eighties and it was only ten o'clock in the morning. Amy hoped that she wasn't sweating through her linen blouse. Cressida, walking at her usual breakneck pace through downtown Ogunquit toward the parking lot where she had left the car before her eight o'clock massage appointment, didn't seem to be aware of the rising temperature. Maybe she could handle the hot weather because she was so skinny. Maybe, Amy thought, if she lost the weight Cressida had advised her to lose, she wouldn't sweat so much.

"Sometimes I just want to shake that man," Cressida was saying.

Amy hadn't been able to hear all of what Cressida was saying, not with lagging behind her long and purposeful strides. She assumed that Cressida was taking about Will again. On the ride into town Cressida had been listing her husband's latest mistakes and misdeeds. Amy, while nodding and making what she hoped were appropriate murmurs of agreement, had actually been doing her best not to listen too closely. Her mother and Vera were probably right about it not being cool of Cressida to bad-mouth her husband to her employee.

"He's the most ineffectual person I've ever met, and I'm afraid the apple didn't fall far from the tree," Cressida went on. Suddenly, she looked over her shoulder. “Well?” she demanded. “Aren’t you going to ask what I mean?”

Amy’s step faltered. “Sorry. Are you talking about Jordan?” she asked.

“Of course I’m talking about Jordan. That boy is too much like his father for his own good. Sometimes I think he’s a lost cause. I’ll have to pin any hope I have of raising a successful child to Rhiannon, though there are times I despair of her, too.”

Amy gulped. Jordan and Rhiannon were only children. It wasn’t right to judge children so harshly. But there was that word again—successful. Cressida knew about what it took to be successful in everything she did, including parenting.

Thankfully, they were forced to come to a stop by a red light. Amy tried to catch her breath without letting Cressida know that she was winded. Cressida shifted impatiently from foot to foot. Suddenly Amy saw a familiar black pickup truck just across the street. She smiled when she saw Noah Woolrich striding toward it. As he began to climb into the driver’s seat he spotted Amy and waved. Amy returned his wave and watched as Noah started the truck and then pulled slowly into the traffic of Main Street. The license plate read WOOLY. It had been Noah’s nickname in grade school.

“Who in God’s name was that?” Cressida asked as she stepped into the street with the green light. “That creature with the black truck.”

That creature? “His name is Noah Woolrich,” Amy said. “We went to school together.”

Cressida frowned. “He looks like one of those awful professional wrestlers, the ones who prance around the ring in those ridiculous costumes pretending to fight one another. I mean, how many tattoos does he have? And that beard! Revolting.”

“Actually,” Amy ventured, “Noah is a gentle person. He’d never get into a fight.”

“A coward, then. What can he possibly do for a living?”

He’s not a coward, Amy said, but she spoke the words silently. “He works at a craft mead brewery. He’s a product developer.”

Cressida laughed. “He makes *mead*? Really? That’s disgusting.

What does he eat for breakfast, gruel? I certainly hope you would never get involved with someone like that. You're worth more than to throw yourself away on a . . . on whatever it is he thinks he is. Here's the car. I can't wait to get back to the house and away from these pathetic tourists."

Silently, Amy slid into the passenger seat.

Amy sat slumped at the kitchen table, a half-empty glass of iced tea in front of her. She usually put a teaspoon of sugar in her iced tea, but since starting work for Cressida she had eliminated that bad habit. Iced tea just wasn't the same without sugar, but that was the least of what was bothering Amy.

She was really bothered by what had taken place earlier that day. She knew that in the past she had proved not the best judge of character, but in this case she knew for a fact—everyone in Yorktide knew!—that Noah Woolrich was a genuinely good person.

Cressida had had no right to call Noah a coward. She didn't know anything about him. She didn't know that back in high school Noah had saved the life of a little boy by dashing into the street to snatch the child out of the path of an out-of-control truck. The little boy was unharmed, but Noah had suffered a broken arm for his pains. Now, if that wasn't courage, what was? Cressida also didn't know that in his time off from the brewery Noah worked at his uncle's place, The Clamshell, for no pay. That was Noah Woolrich, always willing to lend a helping hand. And Amy liked his beard. It was well groomed. And his tattoos weren't images of devils and naked women. They were really beautiful, Celtic symbols and ivy vines and the name of his long-gone but still beloved grandmother.

Amy rubbed her temples. She felt ashamed for not having stood up for someone she knew to be a good person. Why had she accepted Cressida's harsh and unfair judgments without protest? She had remained silent when Cressida had mocked Noah's appearance, and there was no excuse for that. She had learned when she was quite small that to mock a person for the way he looked was wrong and never, ever justified. So why had she so casually ignored that lesson? What was it about being with Cressida that made her act . . . well, that made her act in a way she would be ashamed for her mother or Hayley or Vera to know about.

"Hi. I didn't hear you come in earlier."

It was Amy's mother. She was wearing a pair of denim overalls and her feet were bare. Cressida Prior wouldn't be caught dead in overalls and bare feet.

"Hi," Amy muttered. She wondered if she had ever really congratulated her mother on being interviewed for that magazine, whatever the name of it was. She couldn't remember.

"I thought I'd start dinner." Her mother looked at her closely. "You okay?"

Amy felt the blood rush to her head. "I'm fine!" she cried. "Why are you always asking me if I'm okay?"

Leda Latimer stuck her hands into the pockets of her overalls. "I wasn't aware that I was doing any such thing."

Amy took a deep breath. It was wrong to transfer the frustration she felt about her own conduct to her mother's innocent behavior. "Sorry, Mom," she said. "I guess I'm just in a bad mood."

Her mother removed her hands from her pockets and went to the fridge. "Did anything upsetting happen at work?" she asked.

"No," Amy lied. "Work was fine."

"A frittata for dinner okay?"

"Sure," Amy said. "Just don't put any cheese in it, okay? I don't need the calories."

Chapter 56

The morning had dawned much as any other morning, with two enormous felines pawing at Leda's face and demanding breakfast with a series of earsplitting howls. But as Leda stumbled out of bed and went to the kitchen to feed the beasts and start the coffee, an idea had come to her, less of an idea really than a sort of internal mandate and one that took her very much by surprise.

Now, cats fed and watered and her own breakfast consumed, Leda sat at her computer in her studio, ready after twenty-odd years to confront Lance and Regan Stirling, the two people who had caused such a radical redirection in her life. Why now? The answer was clear. The fact that the *Journal of Craftwork* had approached Leda had given her an undeniable degree of courage. She was considered an artist to watch. People she admired for their skill and devotion to craft thought her work worthy of notice. This moment was a landmark in Leda's life, and she was smart enough to recognize it as such.

Sitting taller in her chair, Leda chose a search engine. To date, it hadn't been difficult to avoid any mention of Lance Stirling in the media; he was popular but not hugely popular and certainly not a name that would turn up with any frequency on the websites or blogs devoted to crafts that Leda routinely followed. But with a few keystrokes, the Wikipedia page devoted to Lance and Regan

Stirling was on the screen. Much of the article focused on solo gallery shows Lance had mounted to critical acclaim. The last show the article mentioned had been at a small gallery in New Hampshire five years earlier. The article had been updated since then, so perhaps Lance Stirling's time in the spotlight had ended.

It was a bit like exorcising ghosts, Leda thought as she scrolled through the article. Lance and Regan Stirling were only people, not gods, and they were certainly no longer a threat. Leda said their names aloud, and as the syllables disappeared into the air of her studio she felt a lightening of the burden she had been carrying for almost her entire adult life. She scrolled back to the top of the page, where there was a recent photo of Lance, and she felt absolutely nothing, not anger or fear, not the sad remnants of love or the vaguely smoldering fires of passion. Lance hadn't aged very well, Leda noted; his skin looked sallow, and there was a dark blotch on his left cheek. The eyes she had once found so penetrating and commanding she now found rather unremarkable. And they were oddly far apart. She had never noticed that before. No doubt she hadn't noticed many things about Lance Stirling, and what she had focused on had been transformed into glorious things under the influence of teenaged infatuation. A tendency to be short-tempered had been in Leda's eyes proof of Lance's great artistic abilities. A habit of sneering at visitors to the house had been a sign of an understandable impatience with lesser mortals. And his penchant for tossing his dirty clothes over the stair rail rather than bringing them downstairs to the washing machine had been evidence of his innate rock-star soul. Love was blind. And as for lust, Leda thought, that was blind, deaf, and dumb.

Next to the photo of Lance Stirling was one of his wife. Regan Stirling, the woman who had supported if not encouraged her husband's habit of infidelity, didn't look too great, either. Leda thought she saw in the woman's eyes a sense of defeat that had nothing to do with the ravages of age. But maybe she was imagining this. Maybe Regan Stirling felt no remorse for the behavior she had allowed under her own roof. Anything was possible.

Leda scrolled to the end of the article and was pleased to find a mention of the little girl she had been hired to care for that long-ago summer. Rebecca Stirling, now in her early twenties, was currently earning a Ph.D. in environmental science. *Good for her*, Leda thought. She had often wondered what Rebecca would feel if she were ever to learn of her parents' behavior toward innocent young women. To discover that your own parents were predators. . . . In such a case, ignorance might indeed be bliss.

Leda closed the Wikipedia page and went offline. She felt proud of herself for having looked her demons in the eye. And she felt proud of herself in another way, too. Some people, in a desperate and maybe unconscious attempt to erase or to make right what bad deed had been done to them, found it necessary to hurt someone else in return, someone as innocent as they had been when they had been abused. But Leda had always lived her life by the Golden Rule. She had always treated other people with the courtesy and respect with which she wanted to be treated by them. It hadn't always been easy, but it had always been worth the effort. Leda got up from her desk and stretched her arms over her head. It was always worth the effort.

Chapter 57

Hayley peeled a second banana and began to slice it in rounds of about a quarter of an inch thick. The girls loved peanut butter on banana rounds. They would be up from a nap before long and ready to replenish with this snack, and not long after that Hayley would be busy supervising puzzles and games and splashing in the wading pool.

Preparing a snack didn't exactly engage Hayley's mind in any taxing way, so she was free to cast her thoughts in another direction—that of Ethan Whitby. She had begun to wonder if she would ever see him again. She couldn't very well flirt with someone who was absent. But then just that morning Marisa had mentioned that Ethan was paying a flying visit, so there was at least a chance she might encounter him. There was at least a chance she might—

"Hi."

A slice of banana fell from Hayley's fingers. She turned. It was Ethan. His auburn hair was tousled. He was wearing jeans and a chambray shirt open at the neck; the sleeves were rolled up. She realized that she liked his face. It had character. A smile came to her own face. It was automatic, not artful.

"Hi," she said.

Ethan sat on one of the stools at the counter. "How have things been going here?" he asked with a smile. "Are the girls running you ragged?"

"Not at all. The girls are a dream and your parents are great. I mean, your father and stepmother. Sorry."

"You can just say parents. It's easier. So, I have to apologize to you," he said.

"For what?" Hayley asked. They had hardly spent any time in each other's presence. For what could he possibly need to apologize?

"For not asking the basic questions a person is supposed to ask when they meet someone new. Like, have you lived in Yorktide long?"

Hayley's stomach was suddenly home to butterflies. At least she could answer this question honestly.

"Yes," Hayley replied promptly. "I was born here."

"It's a beautiful place to live."

Hayley smiled. "Not necessarily in the winter."

"None of us who live in the Northeast get off easily in winter," Ethan agreed. "But I'll grant you that Greenwich isn't as hard hit as Maine must be. So, any siblings?"

Hayley hesitated, and then the words just came popping out. "I have one brother. He's a lawyer in Augusta. He's six years older than me, so we've never really been close."

"What kind of law does he practice?" Ethan asked, stealing one of the banana and peanut butter rounds.

I can't do this, Hayley thought desperately. *I can't continue this lie.* But she forced herself to conjure an image of her mother with a bruised jaw and blackened eye, an image she had seen all too often in reality. She had to do this. She had no choice. If Ethan knew the truth about her, he would never bother to speak to her again and she would be stuck battling near poverty and the constant threat of physical abuse for the rest of her life.

"He specializes in wills and estates," she said.

"Do you live with your parents?" Ethan asked. "Or do you have a place of your own?"

"I live alone," Hayley said quickly. Another lie. "It's nothing much, just a small cottage. I don't need a lot of things around me to be happy." There was some truth to that statement, but the truth only went so far because there *were* things that Hayley wanted around her, lovely things that would make her happy, things like books and a real painting done on canvas, something signed by the artist. "And you?" she asked.

"Right now, I'm sharing an apartment with a friend from business school," Ethan explained, "but come fall I'm going to start looking around for something to buy. I mean, I'm twenty-eight. I should own a place of my own."

"What kind of place?" Hayley asked.

"I'm not entirely sure yet," Ethan admitted. "I'm hoping to get married one day, and I definitely hope to have a family, so there's probably a big backyard in my future. You know, a swing set and maybe a small pool and a grill for sure. But as it's just me now, a smallish condo is probably what I'll decide on."

To own a piece of real estate, something tangible and substantial. That was a goal Hayley had never dared set for herself. And now she knew that Ethan intended to marry. But she doubted he would be eager to marry a liar. So she would never let him know that she had lied. . . .

"Here's another question," Ethan said suddenly. "I mentioned that I went to Harvard but I never asked where you went to college."

Hayley forced a smile she hoped conveyed a sense of nonchalance she didn't feel in the least. "I did two years at a local college," she said, "and then decided to take a few years off. I feel that real-life experience is invaluable. I'll go back one day, maybe start over. In the meantime, I keep up with my reading."

"I think that was brave of you," Ethan said earnestly. "School will always be there."

Hayley turned away to toss the banana peels into the compost container. *What am I becoming?* she thought. In the space of less than ten minutes she had told no fewer than three lies, more than she had told in as many years. And though she had felt uncomfortable lying she had done it pretty spectacularly. What that said about her character was best left unexplored.

Ethan stood. "I'd better get going," he said. "I promised Marisa I'd fix the door to one of the bathroom cabinets upstairs and I need to run to the hardware store first." And then he laughed. "If you hear a crash you'll know I messed up. Bye."

When Ethan had left the kitchen, Hayley went to the window that looked out on the side drive. She watched as Ethan walked briskly to his car and slid into the driver's seat. Only when the car was out of sight did she return to the snack she had been preparing. And as she poured apple juice into two sippy cups she saw her mother's care-lined face as clearly as if she were standing right before her.

I'm doing this for her, she told herself. *It's the right thing to do.*

Chapter 58

The sun was blazing into the office, causing Amy to wonder if she should retrieve her sunglasses from her car. But Cressida had been in her bedroom all morning, and Amy didn't want to run the risk of her mentor emerging only to find her protégé missing, even if only for a few minutes. So she turned away from the window—not that it made much of a difference—and with a tissue pulled from the box on Cressida's desk she dabbed at her sweaty forehead.

Suddenly, Amy's phone alerted her to a text from Cressida. *Meet me in the hall.*

Amy got up from the desk, puzzled by the summons. In the past week or so Amy had noticed that Cressida's moods could change so radically and so quickly. Maybe it was the same with all seriously successful people; they hadn't gotten where they were by being bright and cheery all the time. They had to focus and make tough and often unpopular decisions, and all that pressure must make them prone to bad moods and quick tempers.

"I'm not to be disturbed," Cressida said when she appeared at the door to the office. "You can wait for me in the kitchen."

Amy nodded as Cressida closed the office door behind her. As she made her way to the kitchen it occurred to Amy that almost every day at some point Cressida retreated to her office with the instructions that she was not to be disturbed. Maybe she made a daily call to her office in Atlanta to get an update on important business matters. If so, it would be good if she shared what she was doing with Amy, who as Cressida's protégé was supposed to be learning about . . . Amy suddenly wasn't quite sure what it was she was supposed to be learning about. One thing was interesting, though. When Cressida emerged from her office she always seemed energized. Dealing with the company's home office must really get Cressida's adrenaline going.

Today was no exception. After about twenty minutes Cressida joined Amy in the kitchen with more than the usual spring in her step. Even her eyes looked bigger and brighter.

"I've had the most marvelous idea," Cressida announced. "Why don't you come live with me year-round at my home in Atlanta? You could be my right-hand woman. Isn't that a fantastic idea? I don't know why it took me so long to think of it."

Amy was stunned. From protégé to right-hand woman in only a few weeks? "What exactly would be involved in being your right-hand woman?" she asked.

Cressida waved a hand in the air. "Oh, we'll figure out the details as we go. The point is that you would have your own suite of rooms and a brand-new wardrobe. No offense, Aimee, but those outfits you wear will not work in the offices of Prior Ascendancy."

Amy glanced down at her knee-length fitted skirt and white blouse, pieces she had thought looked professional enough. "I'd be going to your office?" she asked. She had a sudden vision of a massive steel structure with gleaming glass windows and shiny metal elevators and sleek men and women in designer suits hurrying through the white marble lobby, all like something from a movie.

"Of course," Cressida said.

"What would I be doing there? I mean, would I have an official position?"

Cressida winked. "You just might."

"It's just that I—"

"Think of the bigger picture, Aimee!" Cressida cried.

Amy nodded. "Okay," she said. "It's a very interesting idea. I—"

"Good, that's settled. I'm off to get a pedicure, though the salons around here are fairly horrid."

And with that Cressida left the kitchen with her usual rapid stride. Amy took a seat at the island. While she hadn't actually promised Cressida she would accept the job, she had been about to promise that she would consider the offer. Sure, she already had a job lined up for fall, and yes, she had promised her friends she would take the fourth bedroom in the apartment Stella's father had earmarked for them in one of the buildings he owned. But this might be one of those opportunities a person would be crazy to turn down. A real job at Prior Ascendancy might be her ticket to a successful life. It might . . .

Suddenly Amy remembered the harsh comments Cressida had made about Jordan and Rhiannon and Noah the other day and felt a sense of queasiness settle over her. She remembered how Cressida had declared that all old people were self-centered. She thought of those former employees of Prior Ascendancy, the ones who had claimed age discrimination. Suddenly Amy wanted to hear her mother's voice. She took her phone from her pocket, went to her contact list, and put the phone back in her pocket. She was fine.

After dinner Amy sat at her desk and opened her laptop. The momentary queasiness she had felt that afternoon had passed, leaving only a sense of excitement in its place. Atlanta.

She would definitely not tell her mother about the offer yet, as she strongly suspected Leda Latimer would be 100 percent against it. Amy didn't understand why her mother was so anti-Cressida, unless it was that she was intimidated by her success. If that was the case, then Amy thought she might have a legitimate reason to feel disappointed in her mother. What was a hooked rug compared to a corporate takeover? Well, assuming Cressida had ever been involved in a corporate takeover. What was a tapestry compared to a technological innovation? Not that Prior Ascendancy was a tech company, but still.

Anyway, it might be fun to live somewhere new. Amy logged on to the Atlanta Chamber of Commerce website. It didn't take long to see that there was way more to do in Atlanta than there was in sleepy little Yorktide. There was the Atlanta Botanical Garden and the Georgia Aquarium. There was the High Museum of Art, too, with jazz in the evenings. Not that Amy was a big fan of jazz, but it might be a fun way to spend a few hours, sipping a cocktail and people watching. And her new black sequined purse would be perfect for such an evening!

There had to be fantastic shopping in a big city like Atlanta, too, and as an employee of Prior Ascendancy Amy would be earning a good salary. But there again was that niggling question. A right-hand woman was an employee, wasn't she? Cressida hadn't mentioned specifics like a salary, but she had said they would work out the details as they went along. It was like the figurative handshake deal they had about Amy's being the family's nanny. Nothing to worry about.

After a quick search, Amy found information about a place called Phipps Plaza where there was an Armani, and a Fendi, and a Dior shop. And at Lenox Square, another mall, there was a Bulgari and a Cartier store. Amy remembered Cressida showing her that Bulgari gemstone ring and the gold Cartier bracelet and thought that if things turned out well working for Prior Ascendancy, then one day maybe she, too, would be able to buy a piece of important jewelry from one of those high-end jewelers. If things worked out well, she . . .

Amy frowned, assailed by the memory of Cressida's asking her to make the call to her great-aunt's nursing home, of Cressida's intention of having Amy witness the firing of an employee, of Cressida's unpleasant comments about her husband. How would she handle being subjected to Cressida's tough and erratic behavior if she had nowhere to which she could retreat, like her own apartment?

But Amy quickly dismissed the worry. Everyone had days when they were snappy or anxious or overly critical of the people around them. Besides, Amy had always believed in forgiving and forgetting. It was what a good person did. It was what her mother and her grandparents had taught her.

Grandma. Amy thought of her favorite photo of her grandmother as a young woman. In the photo, Anne Gleeson was wearing a fringed shawl around her shoulders. Amy had always thought the shawl made her grandmother look glamorous and mysterious. It almost didn't matter what else you were wearing when you topped it off with a gorgeous fringed shawl.

Amy looked back to her laptop. She needed a shawl. And she knew just where to get one.

Chapter 59

Vera was sitting on the love seat in Leda's studio with Winston sprawled across her lap. "What are you feeding this thing?" she asked with a frown.

"If by 'thing' you mean Winston," Leda said from her seat at her worktable, "he gets what he's always gotten. Everything he wants. Within reason, of course."

"Of course. Ow. He's bruising my leg!"

"Vera, don't be so dramatic and pay attention. Guess what I did this morning? I Googled the people for whom I was nanny the summer I was seventeen."

Vera's eyes widened. "You did?"

"I did, and it brought the Stirlings down to size. That's their name, Stirling, Lance and Regan."

"Wait a minute," Vera said. "Lance Stirling? The painter? I've seen some of his work. It stinks. He can't even draw."

"I know. But when I was working for him I thought his work was some of the most beautiful I'd ever seen." Leda shook her head. "The ignorance of youth."

"So, what did you feel when you found the evil duo?" Vera asked.

"Absolutely nothing. It was amazing. It was like a dark cloud lifting. I can't believe I didn't hunt them down sooner."

"You might not have been ready sooner," Vera pointed out, while vainly trying to move Winston off her lap and onto the cushion next to her. "I bet something inside you told you that you were finally ready to let go."

"An instinct," Leda agreed, "and that reporter asking for an interview right after Phil's urging me to submit a piece to the competition. Both seem to have given my self-esteem a boost."

"So, maybe now you'll be ready for romance?"

"No," Leda said firmly. "Why should I be?"

Vera shrugged. "I don't know."

"I saw Margot Lakes the other day in town. Did you know she volunteers at an animal shelter on Saturday mornings?"

"Nice try, Leda," Vera said.

"Why is it okay for you to swear off romance but not for me?" Leda demanded.

"It just is, okay? So, tell me more about the Stirlings."

"There's not much more to tell. He hasn't had a solo show in years, and there was no mention of Regan's ever having earned the degree in Egyptian history she was pursuing that summer. Their daughter is doing well, though. She's studying for a degree in environmental science."

"Good for her. For God's sake, Leda, get this monster off me."

Leda laughed. "He'll get off when he wants to get off. By the way, do you have any plans for the Fourth of July?"

"The restaurant will be open per usual," Vera said. "And then I thought we'd go down to the beach to see the fireworks that evening."

"That's exactly what I was thinking," Leda said. "Why don't you come here for dinner first? I'll do the classics, corn on the cob, hot dogs, strawberry shortcakes."

Vera nodded. "It's a deal. Now seriously. Can you get this monster off me?"

Chapter 60

Hayley slowed to a stop behind a row of cars on Forest Road. There was an accident up ahead; she could see several police cars with their blue lights flashing. Hayley said a quick prayer for the people involved. She didn't really believe in God, but she couldn't see how it hurt to ask some potentially greater power to protect a human being in danger.

A greater power who would certainly not approve of her lying in an attempt to ensnare an innocent person into a marriage. Hayley frowned and tapped her pointer finger on the steering wheel. Her conscience would not stop nagging at her, no matter how often she reminded herself that there was plenty of precedent for what she planned to do. Women had banked on their charms since the dawn of time. Famous courtesans and mistresses had achieved money and security and even respect via their looks.

There was the Marquise de Pompadour, a common-born woman who became the mistress and, more important in the end, a friend and advisor to King Louis XV of France. And there was Mrs. Alice Keppel. She was Edward VII's favorite mistress and made quite a bundle from her association with the king.

Of course, Hayley thought, becoming the mistress of a married man was out of the question for all sorts of reasons, not the least of which was the fact that her mother would be devastated. Her father wouldn't care, not as long as there was something in it for him. He probably wouldn't care if she was brutally murdered by some rampaging serial killer as long as he could sell the story to a national rag and make a few thousand dollars out of it.

One thing was for sure, she thought, inching forward as the car ahead of hers moved a few feet. As she had told Amy, she absolutely would not get pregnant. In this day and age very few men would feel the need to marry the mother of their child just to confer legitimacy. Besides, it would be cruel to bring a child into the world only for the benefits she might reap from his existence. And what if she and the child were left high and dry? It wasn't as if Hayley had family who could lend a hand in raising her offspring. No, everything about the scenario seemed to her deeply wrong and undesirable.

And there was another scenario Hayley hadn't fully considered. As Ethan's wife, she would most likely be expected to have children with him. She had never really wanted children of her own, because she had only ever envisioned her life as a slightly better version of her mother's. But in the security of a marriage to a man like Ethan Whitby, things would be different. She could raise children in a safe environment and provide them with not only the basics but also wonderful things like travel and exposure to the arts. But what if one day Ethan learned the truth about the woman he had married, that she had lied to him about her past? Would he sue for sole custody of her dearly loved children?

Hayley shook her head. What a mess she was creating! And who was she to classify herself with those famously successful women like Mrs. Keppel and the Marquise de Pompadour? As her father had told her time and again, she was a nobody.

No, Hayley told herself firmly. She was *not* a nobody, and what she was doing was thoroughly practical, and if that made her a cold-hearted opportunist, so be it. There were worse things to be, like a wife beater and a drunk. Or, like her mother, a defeated woman, satisfied with an entirely unsatisfying life.

Finally, the road was opened for traffic and Hayley drove on. By the time she arrived at Amy's house she was exhausted by the topic of scheming for a better life. She found Amy at the little round table in the backyard.

"I thought you'd be here earlier," Amy said. There was a bottle of pale pink nail polish on the table, along with a few fashion magazines; a plastic bowl filled with chunks of watermelon, cantaloupe, and pineapple; and two plastic forks.

"Sorry," Hayley said, dropping into a chair. "There was an accident on Forest Road and traffic was stopped for almost half an hour. There was no ambulance, so that's a good sign." Hayley speared a chunk of pineapple with one of the plastic forks and held it out to Amy. "Do you want some?" she asked.

Amy shook her head. "No thanks. I've never been fond of pineapple."

"You've never been *fond* of pineapple?"

"That's what I said."

"It's just that I've never heard you use that term before," Hayley noted. "Usually you like or don't like something."

"What's wrong with using the expression 'fond of'?" Amy asked. "Cressida uses it all the time."

"Ah, now I see! Who are you, anyway? It's like you're not Amy anymore but Cressida Prior's mini-me. Wait, you're *not* Amy! You're Aimee!"

"Laugh if you must," Amy said, "but I'm learning so much working for Cressida. It's like, there are all these things about the world I didn't know."

Hayley raised an eyebrow. "You mean Cressida is teaching you things like science and history?"

"Well, no," Amy admitted. "She's teaching me practical stuff like how to win at office politics and the importance of the right clothes for the right occasion and what wines go with what sort of food. Did you know that some reds work really well with certain types of fish?"

"How does that information help Cressida?" Hayley asked. "Didn't you tell me she doesn't drink alcohol and eats only raw vegetables?"

"Not only raw vegetables," Amy corrected. "Just mostly. But next week she's starting a different eating program."

Hayley rolled her eyes. "Look, as someone who's had to go without decent food on more than one occasion I don't have a whole lot of tolerance for people who spend thousands of dollars on the latest fad diet."

"This new *program* isn't a fad," Amy argued. "There's a book about it and everything."

"Oh, well! That makes it totally legitimate! Look, are you sure Cressida isn't anorexic?"

"Of course not," Amy protested. "That's a horrible thing to say!"

"It's not an insult," Hayley argued. "Anorexia is a disease. Her life could be in danger."

"Well, she's not sick."

"Do you know about the character of Cressida in ancient Greek mythology?" Hayley asked.

"I don't think so," Amy admitted.

"Cressida was a young Trojan woman in love with Troilus, a young Trojan man," Hayley explained. "They were pledged to marry, but when Cressida's father defected to their enemy, the Greeks, Cressida left Troilus and switched allegiance with her father. Then she fell in love with a Greek soldier named Diomedes. Of course, Troilus was devastated by her faithlessness and got himself killed in battle pretty soon after that."

"What's your point?" Amy asked with a frown.

"Just that the character of Cressida has come to stand for faithlessness and double-dealing."

"You're one to point the finger!" Amy cried. "Double-dealing is the least of what you're doing with Ethan!"

Hayley cringed. "All right," she said. "Point taken."

"Well, I'm sure Cressida's parents didn't know that story when they named her. They probably just liked the way the name sounded."

Hayley grinned. "It's like a parent naming her daughter Jezebel or her son Attila and not expecting all sorts of preconceived notions to be associated with her kids. And don't forget the teasing by kids with more mainstream names like, well, like Amy and Noah."

"Noah is in the Bible."

"Yeah, but his character isn't associated with anything bad," Hayley pointed out. "By the way, have you seen Noah lately?"

Amy suddenly found the bottle of nail polish very interesting. "I've seen him."

"And?" Hayley asked.

"And nothing. And I still think Cressida is a pretty name."

"Watercress. It makes me think of watercress." And then Hayley laughed. "Come on, Amy, I'm just teasing you."

"I know that," Amy said hotly. "By the way, do you know if Noah is seeing anyone? Because I saw him with someone in town. They looked pretty . . ." Amy shrugged. "Close."

Hayley restrained a smile. So, Amy was finally coming around. "Not that I know of," she said. "I could find out if you want."

"No!" Amy cried. "I mean, don't bother. I don't really care. I was just wondering. You know."

"Yes," Hayley said, smiling at her friend. "I know."

Chapter 61

"I think this is the new main entrance. Yes, right through here."

Amy followed her mother into the long, low wooden building that housed the studios of a group of artists and craftspeople collectively known as the Blue Heron Circle. Amy had accompanied her mother a few times before and had always found the excursions enjoyable. But this morning the building looked shabby to her, and the odors coming from various chemicals used by the artists made her feel slightly sick to her stomach. She would have preferred to be at Cressida's house, but Cressida had told Amy not to come in to work until noon, as she had booked a private masseur for a three-hour session. And as Will and the children would be spending the day at the Farnsworth Museum in Rockland, there was no need for Amy's presence. For about a second Amy had felt disappointed that she hadn't been asked to accompany Will, Jordan, and Rhiannon. Then again, why would Will have required her help? Her position in the Prior household was not really that of nanny, was it?

"Missy's studio is at the end of this hall," her mother said, leading them down a long concrete corridor off which were ten or more rooms, all messy and chock-full of print-making and painting and metal-working equipment.

Amy lamely returned her mother's smile. And then she felt bad. She had agreed to come along. The least she could do was to pretend interest. At the very end of the hall they found Missy Greene, potter. She greeted Amy and Leda enthusiastically and ushered them into her studio.

"I'm so glad you came this morning," she said, linking her arm through Leda's. "I'm dying to show you my new work."

Missy wore her long gray hair in a massive plait down her back. Her eyeglasses were the largest Amy had ever seen, huge plastic circles in the same shade of bright red as her lipstick, some of which had wound up on her teeth. As for her clothes, well, Amy wasn't quite sure how to describe what Missy was wearing; it was something like a cross between a colorful caftan and a tent, the kind you slept in when you went camping.

No doubt Cressida would be horrified by Missy's appearance. Cressida's friends were probably all successful businesspeople like she was, people who didn't have the time to grow their own organic vegetables and make their own clothing. Then again, Cressida had never mentioned any friends, but of course she had them. Everyone did. Amy had no doubt they were all probably as thin and expensively dressed as Cressida. And neat. With no lipstick on their teeth.

While Missy and her mother chatted, Amy wandered the studio. There was a potter's wheel with a foot peddle and a stool attached to it. On shelves tacked to the wall there were bits and pieces of pottery; a small painting of a bowl of pears; and an old tin can stuffed with brushes, markers, and pens. And there were books, lots of oversized art books, piled precariously on the floor and worktables.

Amy frowned. Her office at Prior Ascendancy in Atlanta—she would have an office, wouldn't she?—would probably be the complete opposite of this space, decorated with contemporary furniture and abstract prints and beautifully tended potted plants. People in Yorktide who had thought Amy not very bright or ambitious would be so surprised if she went off to become someone important at Prior Ascendancy. The thought made her smile.

Amy's attention was caught by a woman passing by in the hall. Well, it wasn't the woman who caught her attention as much as the massive muffin she was biting into. Amy frowned and remembered how Hayley had mocked Cressida's eating programs. Hayley seemed dead set against Cressida and she hadn't even met her, not that Amy wanted *that* to happen. An instinct told her that Cressida would take against Hayley as deeply as Hayley had taken against Cressida.

Amy glanced across the studio at her mother, talking animatedly to Missy. Next to Hayley meeting Cressida, the last thing she wanted was for Cressida and Leda Latimer to meet. Luckily, her mother spent most days in her studio, and when she wasn't there she was doing the grocery shopping or hanging out with Vera at Over Easy, and neither activity would likely bring her into contact with Cressida, who went into Ogunquit and Yorktide only for the spas and high-end shops.

In fact, Amy wasn't at all sure why Cressida had chosen southern Maine as the family's holiday destination, as she didn't seem in the least bit interested in any of the usual features that appealed to visitors—the famously rocky coastline; steamed lobsters available at every turn; blueberries baked into all sorts of yummy desserts; beautiful farmland; pristine beaches. And another thing was odd, Amy thought, continuing her listless wandering through Missy's studio. The other day Cressida had told Amy that she didn't hold with celebrating any of the big commercial holidays. "The whole thing is just so pedestrian and wasteful," she had said dismissively. "Of course, we won't be waving flags and eating apple pie on the Fourth of July," she had added. "You'll come in to work as if it were any other day." Amy hadn't really understood what Cressida had meant about holidays being pedestrian and wasteful, but of course she hadn't asked for an explanation. True, she was disappointed to be missing the town's Independence Day festivities, but that was all right. Parades, hot dogs, and brass bands really were overrated.

Amy found herself in front of a cabinet in which several pairs of earrings were displayed. A small card announced that the earrings had been made by Missy's sister Melly. One pair in particular caught Amy's attention. They were constructed with a very pretty pink center stone surrounded by shimmery glass beads. Then Amy frowned. The earrings definitely couldn't be called important jewelry.

"Amy?"

Amy turned abruptly from the cabinet. "Sorry," she told her mother. "I was . . . I was looking at these earrings."

Her mother smiled. "Come here and take a look at these pots. They're lovely, aren't they? The glaze is a formula Missy developed."

"Wow," Amy said, forcing a smile. She knew what Cressida Prior would say about the pots, and it was not that they were lovely.

"Here," Missy said. "I want you to have one. Pick the one you like the best."

"No, I couldn't," Amy said quickly.

"I insist. Now, it's your choice."

Amy cast her eye over the pots and suddenly saw that they were indeed lovely as her mother had said. The colors were so deep and intense. "I'll take that one," she said, indicating a small green pot with a tall neck. "If you're sure."

With a smile, Missy wrapped the pot for Amy and then hugged both Amy and her mother. Amy followed her mother out of the studio, the pot held close to her chest. Missy might be a bit of an odd duck, but she was an awfully nice person. But Cressida probably wouldn't see past Missy's interesting exterior. Amy felt uncomfortable. She didn't like to criticize Cressida but sometimes . . .

"How about we get some lunch?" her mother suggested when they had left the building.

Amy managed a smile. "Sorry, Mom. I have to be at work in twenty minutes."

"Of course. How could I have forgotten?"

"Thanks for asking me to come along this morning," Amy said. "It was fun." And really, it had been sort of fun, at least at the end.

Her mother beamed. "My pleasure," she said, unlocking the car.

Chapter 62

Leda was in her studio that afternoon finishing a dozen new coin purses for Wainscoting and Windowseats. The demand for accessories rose crazily in the summer, and it was at times like these that Leda wished she could afford to hire an assistant. Or, she thought with a grim smile, maybe she could be a mentor to a protégé. She was sure she would do a far better job at mentoring than Cressida Prior was doing with Amy.

Earlier, Leda had told Missy about entering her work in the FAF's annual competition and Missy had been thrilled. She had also suggested that Leda might want to participate in an open studio tour organized by the director of the gallery at Yorktide Community College, Harry Carlyle. Any artist in the area was welcome to participate. The entry fee was small, and the majority of the money raised through the visitors' tickets would be donated to the art department of the local grammar school. The idea of anyone other than one or two visitors at a time in her studio made Leda a little nervous, but she had promised Missy she would consider the idea, and she would.

Leda reached for a zipper and turned back to her sewing machine. Amy had seemed bored at Missy's studio that morning. She hadn't even wanted to buy a pair of the pretty beaded earrings made by Missy's sister. And Leda had also noticed that lately Amy hadn't been wearing any of the woven bracelets she had made for her. Cressida Prior's influence once again?

Before she could gloomily ponder that possibility, an e-mail from Margot popped up on her computer screen. Leda scooted over to her laptop—a wheeled chair was a must—and saw that Margot was forwarding information about a reading being given by one of her friends who was a poet. *I thought that you and your friend Vera might enjoy Tricia's work*, she had written. *Hope to see you there.*

Leda made note of the time, date, and location of the reading and forwarded the e-mail to Vera. Margot's invitation was clearly a sign of her interest in Vera, no doubt about it. Leda had run into Felicia McCarthy, a woman from Margot's church, quite by accident at the farmers' market the day before and had ever so casually asked Felicia if she knew Margot. "Oh yes," Felicia told her. "She's a great asset to the choir as well as to our parish's version of Meals on Wheels. We call it Soup and Smiles. We're so glad she joined our church." Leda wasn't sure how she was going to use all of the positive information she had gathered, especially if Vera insisted on being adamantly against the possibility of romance, but she was committed to try.

Before Leda could ponder this question further her cell phone alerted her to a call from Phil.

"Any news from the FAF?" he asked.

Leda groaned. "No, and it's killing me! I've never been so impatient about anything in my life."

"I've got just the thing to take your mind off the waiting. A bottle of chilled Prosecco and homemade cheese straws."

"I'll be there as soon as I can," Leda assured him. "And I'll bring a dozen new coin purses while I'm at it."

Leda went back to her sewing machine to complete her work. She felt seriously lucky to have such good friendships with such an interesting variety of people. In that way, Leda felt sure she was far richer than Cressida Prior. Far richer and far more blessed.

Chapter 63

"So, what's everybody doing for the Fourth?" Michelle asked.

Sarah shrugged. "The usual. I'll take the kids to see the parade in the morning, and then the bosses are hosting a bash at the house. What about you, Hayley?"

"I've got the day off," she told the other nannies. "The Whitbys are going to a friend's house in Cape Elizabeth for a barbeque."

"Amy?" Cathi asked, with what Hayley thought was a sly smile. "What's the almighty Cressida got planned?"

Amy shrugged. "Nothing, actually. She doesn't believe in celebrating the big holidays."

Hayley was the only one who didn't laugh at this statement. She knew how much Amy loved all the pomp and circumstance of July Fourth.

"So," Elizabeth said, "you'll have the day off, too?"

"No," Amy said, fiddling with the edge of her paper napkin. "I have to go in. It'll be a day just like any other day."

"You won't be the only one having a lousy holiday," Cathi said, leaning forward over the table. "I've got a bit of seriously juicy gossip. Mrs. White found Mr. White in bed with one of her friends."

There was a collective gasp of surprise and disbelief, followed by a few choice comments about Mr. White's character.

Cathi shook her head. "My mouth was on the floor when Mrs. White told me."

"I can't believe she *did* tell you," Michelle replied. "I mean, you're her kids' nanny, not her friend. But I guess she had to explain her husband's absence somehow. She must be so embarrassed."

"Embarrassed and furious," Cathi went on. "She threw him out immediately and was on the phone to her lawyer about a minute later. And I always thought they were a good couple. It just goes to show."

Hayley only half listened to the ensuing conversation about what punishments should be inflicted upon Mr. White. Her thoughts had turned to Ethan. She hadn't seen him since she had lied about Brandon and her living arrangements. And about why she had left college without a degree. She wondered when she would next have the opportunity to talk with him. She wondered what lies she would tell him then.

"I just saw a photo of Anna Nicole Smith's daughter online," Sarah said. Hayley had no idea how the conversation had turned to celebrities. "She's her mother's mini-me."

"Anna Nicole really was very pretty," Michelle said. "Not that it mattered in the end. What an ignominious death."

"Did she ever get the inheritance from that ancient husband?" Cathi wondered.

Elizabeth shook her head. "I'm not sure, but her entire life was a pity, and her poor son overdosing as well. I hope her daughter is doing all right. What a legacy to leave for your child."

"I feel sorry for her," Madeleine added. "If she had been a *real* schemer she might be alive and well now, married to another old geezer and draping herself in diamonds."

"Like Barbara Piasecka Johnson," Sarah said.

"Who's that?" Amy asked. Hayley had noted that unlike the rest of the friends, who were drinking beer or wine, Amy was drinking water. And she hadn't ordered any food. Evidence, no doubt, of Cressida Prior's influence.

"She married John Seward Johnson of the Johnson & Johnson

fortune," Sarah explained. "She came to the U.S. from Poland with one hundred dollars to her name and a master's degree in art. Johnson's wife hired her as a cook, I think. Long story short, she impressed Mr. Johnson with her knowledge of art and eventually became his wife. There was over forty years' difference in their age. When he died, his kids sued her for the money he'd left her, but for some reason they settled out of court. Barbara got the bulk of the money."

Hayley was aware that Amy was stealing glances at her, as if looking for signs of discomfort. The conversation *was* making her uncomfortable, but there was no way she was going to reveal that discomfort.

"How do you know all that?" Cathi asked.

Sarah shrugged. "I read it somewhere. She must have been one smart cookie, whether or not she set out to marry the old goat."

"Maybe she really did love him," Hayley suggested, "if not in a romantic way. Maybe it was a marriage of companionship."

"Hayley is right." Amy shot another glance at her friend. "She might have been a very nice woman with no ulterior motive."

Elizabeth frowned. "That's beside the point. I think it's ridiculous to be advocating marriage as a way to get ahead in the world in this day and age. It's demeaning to both men and women."

"Who said I was advocating it?" Sarah argued.

"I wouldn't say it's a wonderful idea, but I believe it's as valid an option now as it ever was." Madeleine shrugged. "Women should have the freedom to live their lives as they see fit."

Sarah leaned forward. "I was reading another article online and it really opened my eyes. The writer pointed out that women are most often better looking than men, right? And men usually make more money than women no matter how unfair that is. So, the chances of a good-looking woman marrying a man who makes more money than she does are pretty high. There's really nothing unusual in that and certainly nothing inherently wrong."

"I still say the Cinderella story ruined the lives of generations of women," Elizabeth said grimly.

Michelle laughed. "Come on! It's just a story. Besides, I think the real theme isn't so much about marrying the prince as it is about the fact that Cinderella goes from a life of obscurity and abuse to a life of being in the spotlight with someone who respects her for her kindness and goodness."

"That's an awfully positive spin!" Elizabeth exclaimed. "No, the story is all about having a man rescue you when you should be rescuing yourself."

"Not every woman has the resources to rescue herself," Hayley pointed out mildly. "What's so wrong with asking for help when you need it? Anyway, Cinderella didn't ask for the Prince to be in love with her. It just happened." But she hadn't lied to him, Hayley thought. And that made a difference.

"But did she really love him, or was she just using him?" Elizabeth pressed. "Was she really so good and pure, or was she just a grasping whore?"

"Women shouldn't use the word *whore* or *tramp* when talking about other women," Amy said firmly. "It makes us as bad as misogynists."

Madeleine nodded. "I agree. Did you know that in the French version of the story by Perrault, Cinderella forgives her wicked stepsisters and lets them marry noblemen? But in the German version by the Grimm brothers, the magic birds that protect Cinderella throughout the story peck out the eyes of her evil stepsisters at her wedding."

Suddenly the image of her own eyes being pecked out for bad behavior by birds, magic or otherwise, caused Hayley to stand abruptly. "I'm off," she said. "I've got to run an errand on my way home."

Cathi looked at her quizzically. "At this time of night?"

"Hannaford is still open," Hayley said. "My mom needs some aspirin." Her mother needed no such thing, but Hayley felt that if she didn't get out of the pub as soon as possible she would do something stupid like scream. She waved to the group and hurried off.

Hayley walked to her car, her mind buzzing. She was proud of her good reputation and had always fought to distinguish herself from her father and brother, people who routinely stooped to lying and cheating. What would the residents of Yorktide think of her if she were to marry someone like Ethan Whitby? Some might think her lucky, but others would suspect her of low intentions. Even if Ethan truly loved her and she truly loved him, there would always be those who assumed she had married him for his money alone. But what was she thinking? A marriage of mutual love between her and Ethan could never be the case.

Never.

Chapter 64

"It's cool we can see the fireworks from here, isn't it? I don't know why Mom and Vera had to go down to the beach and deal with the crowds when they could have stayed right here in the backyard. I mean, I used to like going to the beach to see the fireworks but not now."

Amy's words had fallen on deaf ears. Hayley, sitting across from her at the little table in the backyard, seemed lost in thought. She was probably thinking about Ethan Whitby. Amy suspected her friend had left the pub so abruptly the other night because the conversation had come too close to home. Poor Hayley.

Amy took a sip of her water with lemon slices. Cressida sometimes drank water with lemon slices. She said it was cleansing, and maybe water with lemon slices had something to do with Cressida's having been in such a good mood all day. She had praised Amy's punctuality and complimented her outfit, both of which had sort of made up for Amy's missing the Independence Day celebrations. And Cressida's encouragement had prompted Amy to tell Hayley about the offer of a job at Prior Ascendancy. Not that Amy expected Hayley to be thrilled, but she had to tell someone her secret or bust.

"Hayley?" Amy said. "Are you paying attention? I have something big to share with you."

"What is it?" Hayley asked, with not very much interest, Amy thought.

Amy outlined Cressida's offer, from the promise of her own suite of rooms to a new wardrobe, from the title of right-hand woman to . . . well, that was about all there was to tell at the moment. "So, what do you think?" she asked when she had finished.

"I think it's a lousy idea," Hayley said sharply. "And you won't be able to wear your new fur hat in a southern climate."

Amy frowned. There had been no need for Hayley to mention the hat. "Well, I think it's a great idea," she countered.

"What exactly is so great about it?" Hayley asked. "And why do you have to live at her house? Why can't you have your own place? If you live with the Priors you'll have no privacy. You'll always be at their beck and call. Is that what you want?"

"No," Amy said automatically. "I don't know. Anyway, I'm sure I'd have time to myself."

"And what about those friends you promised to share an apartment with?" Hayley asked. "If you back out they'll have to find another roommate, and that's not always easy."

"They'll be fine," Amy said. "Stella's father owns the building. I'm sure he'll cover my rent until they find someone to take my place." And then she sighed. "I shouldn't have told you about the offer. I knew you'd be totally against it."

"Sorry," Hayley said. "Look, if you're determined to go through with this, forget about a handshake being good enough to seal a deal. Ask for a contract detailing exactly what being a right-hand woman involves and what sort of compensation you can expect. Sick days. Vacation days. Health insurance. Have a lawyer read the contract," Hayley went on, "make up a list of changes you want made, and then sit down to negotiate the deal that works for you. Better yet, let the lawyer do the negotiating."

"I can't ask Cressida for a contract," Amy protested. "She'd think I didn't trust her."

Hayley laughed. "You shouldn't trust her. You shouldn't trust anyone you've known for only a few weeks, let alone go off to live with them. Wake up, Amy. You can't really be that naïve."

"I'm not naïve," Amy argued. "Maybe I'm just taking a leap of faith. Isn't that how you move ahead with your life, by taking chances?" *It's what Cressida has told me over and over again*, Amy thought. *Don't be afraid to take risks. Women especially need to take risks in order to succeed.*

"Okay," Hayley said. "Let's say you take this leap of faith. Do you really want to move so far away from your mom? You guys are joined at the hip, at least you were until Cressida Prior came along."

Amy hadn't really given much thought to this. Atlanta *was* pretty far away from Yorktide, not like Boston.

"And don't forget that Cressida is offering you a job," Hayley went on, "not a life."

Suddenly Amy felt angry. "I wish you wouldn't always be so—"

"So what?" Hayley asked sharply. "I'm only looking out for your best interests."

"I can look out for my own best interests, thank you very much." Amy was sure that she could. Almost entirely sure. "So, what's going on with Ethan?" she asked, feeling a bit mean-spirited. "Any progress? You ran out of the pub pretty quickly last night when the subject of marrying for money came up."

"I did not run anywhere," Hayley protested. "And things are going fine."

"Just fine?" Amy pressed.

Hayley stood and reached for her bag. "I promised my mother I'd be home before nine. She wants me to watch some reality show with her. See you around."

When Hayley had gone, Amy remained at the little table. Hayley's comments had made her feel uncomfortable and unsure. The prospect of a life in Atlanta didn't seem as wonderful as it had only a few minutes earlier. Why did Hayley—why did everyone!—have to be so negative about anything having to do with Cressida Prior? Okay, she could be difficult and she didn't hold with celebrating holidays, but . . .

As abruptly as Hayley had stood up and left for home, Amy stood up and stomped into the house. There was a box of cookies in the cupboard. One stupid cookie wouldn't be breaking her diet. Besides, it was a holiday and everyone had the right to celebrate. Didn't they?

Chapter 65

The breakfast crowd at Over Easy had mostly gone when Vera joined Leda and Phil at Leda's usual table, a large cup of coffee in hand.

"So, why did you want to see us?" Phil asked.

"I want to show you guys something," Leda told her friends. "Well, I don't actually want to show it to anyone. In fact, I wish I had never seen it, but it's too late now."

"What are you talking about?" Phil asked.

Leda sighed. "Well, I was visiting the website of the *Journal of Craftwork* this morning when I saw a comment someone made about my work. See, the *Journal* ran a notice that I would be featured in next month's issue."

"What did this person say?" Vera asked.

"Here." Leda reached into her pocket and pulled out a piece of paper. She handed it to Phil. "Read it for yourself."

Phil cleared his throat and read the note aloud.

"I checked out this woman's website. Why did you feature her work? It's awful. My three-year-old could do better. I took a class a few years ago in knitting so I should know. She should give up."

"Garbage," he said, passing the paper to Vera. "And why in God's name did the editors leave this comment up on the site?"

Instead of returning the printed page to Leda, Vera tore it in half and in half again. "Ignorance," she said. "There's nothing that makes my blood boil like a bold display of ignorance. This woman clearly has no idea of the time and effort it takes to create a piece of art. One knitting class and she's an expert on the creative process?"

Leda shook her head. "I don't know," she said, and she could hear the plaintive note in her voice. "Maybe I'm in over my head. Maybe I should withdraw from the competition."

"No," Phil said firmly, "absolutely not. Leda, if you're going to offer your work to the world you have to learn how to accept constructive criticism and to ignore abusive comments. This was an abusive comment, and what you do with those is throw them away."

"There will always be haters," Vera pointed out. "There will always be people who feel the need to attack and demean, and the Internet has made those people more powerful than ever. And don't get me started on poor spelling and grammar! The angrier the rant, the worse the presentation."

Leda considered her friends' words. Of course they were right, but that didn't mean their advice was easy to follow. "Do you think I should respond to this person?" she asked.

"And say what?" Vera asked. "Thanks for being an idiot and ruining my day? No. The only way to deal with haters without losing your mind is to ignore them."

Phil nodded. "Vera is right. Try to imagine for a moment how unhappy and negative a person must be to take the time to attack someone she doesn't even know. I feel sorry for haters. I'd bet the person they hate more than anyone is themselves."

"You're probably right," Leda admitted. "And I don't want to think of how Amy would judge me if I quit now. I'm sure the great Cressida Prior has never backed away from a challenge or let an uninformed critic get her down."

"If that's the truth, then she's not human," Vera said. "And if she claims that's the truth, then she's lying."

Phil reached across the table and took Leda's hand in his. "You'll be fine," he said reassuringly. "By lunchtime you'll have forgotten all about this little incident."

Leda smiled ruefully. "By lunchtime?"

"Okay, then, by dinner. Seriously, Leda, put it out of your mind."

Before Leda could promise Phil that she would try, the bell over the door tinkled. Leda turned to see who was coming in.

"Margot," she said with a smile and a wave. "Come and join us."

Vera stood abruptly. "I hear Bud calling me," she said, and scurried off to the kitchen.

"It couldn't have been something I said," Margot noted, taking a seat at the table and nodding in the direction in which Vera had hurried off.

"Crisis in the kitchen," Leda said hurriedly.

"The chef can be testy," Phil added.

Margot smiled, but Leda was pretty certain that she hadn't believed the reason for Vera's taking off. "I was in the mood for an omelet," she said. "I hear the omelets here are the best in town."

"They are indeed," Phil assured her. "And the coffee's not bad, either."

"I really enjoyed your friend's poetry reading," Leda said. "I bought a copy of her book."

Margot smiled. "I'm so glad. And I'm sure Connie is, too. I'm sorry I didn't get to chat with you. No one expected such a good turnout."

"I'm sorry Vera couldn't make it," Leda said, and immediately wanted to kick herself. It wasn't her place to make Vera's apologies.

"Did she say why?" Margot's tone was casual, but she didn't look up from the table.

"She said something about a business meeting," Leda lied. In fact, when Leda had asked Vera if she planned on attending the reading, her answer had been a flat no.

Margot looked up and smiled. "Of course," she said. "Business always comes first."

"But only after food," Phil said heartily. "May I recommend the Western?"

Chapter 66

"Remind me why I'm here at this ridiculous hour?" Amy asked, rubbing her eyes with her fingertips.

Hayley swallowed before replying. "Because I asked you if you wanted to meet for breakfast and you said yes."

"Why did I say yes? I hate mornings."

Hayley shrugged. In truth, she wasn't quite sure why she had asked Amy to meet that morning. Lately their conversations seemed to degenerate into cantankerous arguments. Hayley disliked Cressida Prior and the way she treated Amy, and Amy disapproved of Hayley's idea of getting Ethan Whitby to marry her as a way out of near poverty. Frankly, Hayley didn't see a way to resolve either issue without more argument.

"That's an awfully big breakfast," Amy noted. "Pancakes *and* sausage?"

"Have you ever spent the morning running after two active toddlers? I need all the fuel I can get." Hayley eyed Amy's half a grapefruit. "And just because you're starving yourself doesn't mean the rest of us have to."

"I'm not starving myself," Amy said petulantly. "I'm just not very hungry. Look, I'm sorry I was so bitchy about your leaving the pub early the other night. It's just that I still don't think setting out to trap Ethan Whitby into a marriage is the right thing to do."

"Keep your voice down," Hayley said with a quick glance over her shoulder. "And don't use the word *trap*."

"What word should I use?" Amy asked.

"My plan to leave behind this life I've been living and to make a brighter future for myself and my mother."

Amy sighed. "Then rely on yourself and not on a man. You're smart, Hayley. I wish I was half as smart as you are. Why don't you just use your brain!"

"You need more than a brain to succeed in life," Hayley replied, putting her fork and knife on her empty plate. "You need luck, which is something I never seem to have."

"Cressida didn't need a rich husband to succeed. She did everything all on her own."

"Really?" Hayley said. "Didn't you tell me Cressida is from a wealthy family who sent her to an Ivy League school? I don't have that leg up, Amy. I couldn't even finish my degree from a freakin' community college because my mother needed the money I'd saved to pay six months of back rent. Six months! How we weren't thrown out of the place I don't know. The landlord is a saint. Not like the last landlord we had, who did throw us out, not that I could blame him after my idiot father broke almost every window in the apartment."

Amy pushed aside her plate. "I don't care what people say. Money doesn't buy happiness. It just doesn't."

"Maybe not," Hayley said, "but it pays the mortgage and buys the groceries and gets you good medical care, all of which seems like stuff that would make any normal person happy."

"Okay, maybe that's true, but money can't buy love."

Hayley laughed. "Who said anything about love? I'm not expecting love."

"Well you *should* expect love," Amy argued. "Everyone should."

"Amy, you are such an innocent!"

"Be that as it may, has Ethan made a pass at you yet?"

Hayley took a final sip of her coffee before answering. "No," she admitted. "Honestly, I don't think he even sees me as a woman."

"Maybe he's gay," Amy suggested.

"No. He's not gay. And I'm pretty sure he doesn't have a girlfriend, though I do know he wants to be married one day. Anyway, I've been charming and—"

"What?" Amy laughed. "Hayley, you're a lot of good things, but charming isn't one of them."

Hayley frowned. "I can be charming."

"You're too prickly and suspicious to be charming. Remember the time you accused that poor old man at The Razor Clam of trying to grope you and all he was doing was swatting away a wasp that had landed on your shoulder?"

"How was I supposed to know he was trying to do me a favor?"

Amy sighed. "Look, I might not like what you're doing, but you're my best friend and I'll always support you. You know that, right?"

"Yeah," Hayley said. "I do. Thanks."

The girls left the diner shortly after and went on to their respective jobs, Amy yawning as she got behind the wheel of her car and Hayley resisting the impulse to scold Amy once again for not having eaten a proper breakfast.

Hayley arrived at the Whitbys' house fifteen minutes later to find Marisa in the twins' room, preparing them for a bath.

"It's just us girls today," Marisa said as Hayley fetched clean towels from a tall chest of linens. "Jon and Ethan were going to drive up last night, but there was some issue that kept them at the office."

"Oh," Hayley said. "I mean, I hope it gets settled. The issue."

She was surprised at the depth of her disappointment. It wasn't lost on her that if she considered Ethan a mere instrument that might help her achieve a goal and not an individual worthy of real affection, she might not feel so let down. It was all that ridiculous talk about everyone deserving love. Amy was so naïve.

"Can I talk to you about something?" Marisa asked suddenly.

Hayley's stomach knotted. Had Marisa caught her out somehow, divined her thoughts in the way some women could?

"Sure," Hayley said. "Of course."

"There's this student in my class I just can't figure out. I mean, she's perfectly nice and always on time, and she completes the assignments I give, but she seems to have absolutely no aptitude for languages. She can memorize vocabulary but not rules of grammar, and she's completely unable to speak a coherent sentence." Marisa paused. "I can't quite figure out why she signed up for the course. It's not inexpensive, and clearly she's not getting much out of the experience. I hesitate to talk to her about her work—the class isn't a part of a degree program—because I'm not quite sure what I'd say. Any thoughts?"

Hayley considered for a moment. "How old is this woman?" she asked.

"I'd guess in her late sixties."

"Does she socialize with the other students?"

Marisa nodded. "Yes. She's very friendly."

"I think," Hayley said with a smile, "that your student is lonely. I think she signed up for the class to be with people. It probably doesn't matter that she's not absorbing the lessons as long as she's out of the house and interacting with others."

"Of course!" Marisa said with a laugh. "Thanks, Hayley. I think I'll just let my student alone. And now if you can handle the girls' bath I'd better get going. I hope they're good for you today. You will be good for Hayley, won't you?"

Both girls chorused, "Be good!" Marisa kissed her daughters good-bye and left the bedroom.

When Marisa had gone, Hayley realized that she felt disoriented. It was rare that someone treated her as an intelligent equal. Sure, her mother relied on her for just about everything, but being asked for advice from someone like Marisa Whitby was different. It had made her feel validated in some way to have an educated, sophisticated person seek her advice. Validated and disoriented.

"Bath time," Hayley announced, lifting each girl into an arm. "Grab your rubber duckies."

"Rubber duckies!" Layla cried.

"Rubber duckies yellow!" Lily added.

Hayley kissed each girl's head. Children rule, she thought. And nobody should ever forget that.

Chapter 67

Amy tried in vain to suppress a yawn. She was still groggy and wondered why she hadn't had a second cup of coffee at breakfast. Maybe Hayley had a point about eating a good breakfast to set you up for the challenges of the day. Didn't people say that breakfast was the most important meal of the day? She debated going down to the kitchen to see what sort of snack she could grab but decided that probably wasn't a good idea. She had never eaten anything of her own accord under the Priors' roof. Amy wasn't sure how the situation had come about. There had been nothing in the guidelines she had been given at the start of the summer about staying away from the fridge.

Anyway, at any moment Cressida might need her. In fact, Amy thought, maybe she should check to see if Cressida needed anything now. For the past half an hour she had been in the room the family was using to store their luggage, doing something or other.

Amy left the office and turned right into the hall. The spare room was two doors down on the left. As Amy approached she heard the low murmur of a voice other than Cressida's. When she was a few feet from the open door she stopped. Will was in the room with Cressida; Cressida was in the process of lifting a plastic storage box filled with files. Amy began to turn around to go back to the office when she saw Will reach out to take the box from his wife's hands. And then she saw Cressida deliberately let go of the box and slap her husband's face. Amy flinched as she heard the crack of flesh on bone. "Don't touch me," Cressida spat. "I can do it myself."

Amy didn't hear what Will said in response; maybe he said nothing. She dashed back to the office, and a moment later she heard footsteps heading toward the bedrooms at the back of the house. It dawned on Amy then that she had no idea where Jordan and Rhiannon were that morning.

Her heart pounding, Amy sat upright in the chair across the desk from Cressida's. What she had just witnessed had upset her deeply. All Will had been trying to do was to help his wife. He hadn't deserved to be hit for his efforts. But maybe he had said or done something wrong before Amy had arrived. Still . . . How, Amy wondered, could anyone tolerate a marriage in which physical violence played a part?

She thought about the easy compatibility her grandparents had shared, the way her grandmother had made her grandfather breakfast every morning of the week, the way her grandfather had lovingly maintained his wife's loom and sewing machine. Their relationship had been built on love and respect and kindness.

Unlike the relationship between Nora and Eddie Franklin. Amy shuddered to think of what might happen if Nora needed practical assistance from her husband. He certainly wouldn't be there for his wife if she got sick, and at the rate he was going he almost definitely wouldn't be alive to care for her in her old age. That's where Hayley's scheme came in. Hayley was attempting to set in place a safe and secure future for her mother, as well as for herself. Really, Amy thought, who was she to judge?

Nervously, Amy glanced toward the door of the office. Earlier, she had hoped to ask more about the Atlanta offer but now realized she didn't have the nerve to broach the subject, not after the violent scene she had witnessed a few moments earlier.

Amy looked at her watch; her mother had given it to her for high school graduation. It was only ten thirty in the morning but already the day seemed way, way too long.

Chapter 68

Leda was reviewing her bank statement. The water bill had been significantly higher last month than the month before. Well, Leda thought, the summer had been a dry one and gardens did need to be watered. And there had been an unexpected expense in the form of a new tire for her Subaru. Still, at the moment things were all right, but come September and Amy's move to Boston there would be a fairly big outlay, especially if Amy hadn't been saving as much money as she was supposed to be saving.

And that was likely. The evening before, a package had been delivered for Amy. Usually Amy loved receiving packages and was always eager to show her mother what was inside. But not this time.

"It's just a little something I bought," she had said with a dismissive wave of her hand.

"Come on," Leda had urged.

With obvious reluctance Amy had opened the package to reveal a large red shawl fringed with glittering black beads. "It's real velvet," Amy had told her mother. "And the beads are Swarovski. That's why they have so much sparkle. Isn't it gorgeous?"

"How much did it cost?" Leda asked quietly.

Amy had lowered her eyes to the shawl draped across her arms. "It was on sale for half price. Two hundred dollars."

With Leda's professional wholesale discounts, she could have made a very similar piece for a fraction of that. "Where are you planning on wearing it?" she asked.

Amy kept her eyes lowered. "I don't know. When I'm in Boston. It will go with the black sequined evening bag." And then she had looked up at her mother. "Come on, Mom, I'm making real money this summer. I can afford a few splurges."

"As long as you're putting away a significant amount of money each week," Leda reminded her. "You know I can't foot the entire bill for the relocation."

"I am saving, I swear. And doesn't the shawl remind you of the one Grandma is wearing in that old photo?"

That shawl, Leda remembered, had been a cheap cotton thing and borrowed at that. "Yes," Leda said. "I suppose it does a bit."

Leda gave her accounts another quick check and closed her laptop. She had been very lucky that for the past several years she had been able to support herself and her daughter on the profits she earned from her craftwork. Still, Leda was well aware that one day she might be required to take a part-time job in order to make ends meet. After all the years working from home as her own boss and under her own steam it would be difficult to make the transition to someone else's employee, to doing work that didn't engage her the way crafting did.

Suddenly, Leda recalled one of her favorite quotes about creativity. Creativity, Albert Einstein had said, is intelligence having fun. And if the fun didn't involve balloons and cake, it was valid all the same. Right then and there Leda decided to place a call to the YCC art gallery, the organizer of the open studio tours each October. At the very least she could obtain what information she needed and decide later on whether to actually participate. More exposure might mean more income, and that dreaded part-time job might never have to become a reality.

Chapter 69

"Baa baa blah shee, have oo ana wuul!"

Hayley smiled. "Yes, Lily. That's very good." Lily loved to recite her favorite nursery rhymes. Layla, while enjoying the rhymes being read to her, let her sister do the talking.

Hayley and the twins were sitting on the floor of the den among a slew of toys, coloring books, and puzzles. It was ridiculous but Hayley had been hoping for some word from Ethan. While it was true they hadn't exchanged contact information, it was conceivable that Marisa might have given him her cell phone number. Maybe something she had said the last time they spoke had turned him off. Maybe he had found out the truth about Brandon. It would be relatively easy to do; he could have overheard a bit of gossip in the convenience store on Main Street or at the gas station closest to the Whitbys' house. But to say that Ethan was avoiding her was to assume that he was visiting Maine in order to see *her*; and of course he wasn't. He came to visit his family.

As the girls occupied themselves with their toys, Hayley's thoughts turned to what Amy had told her the night before about that half-baked idea of moving to Atlanta to be Cressida Prior's right-hand woman. Hayley could all too easily imagine her friend making a terrible mistake abandoning all of the good things about her life in Yorktide—and her sensible plans for a spell in Boston—

for a very sketchy and uncertain future. It might be a mistake that could be reversed, but it would be a mistake that would take a very heavy toll.

"Look!" Layla directed Hayley's attention to the sisters' latest project—grouping a handful of brightly colored rubber shapes by size and color. It warmed Hayley's heart to see siblings at play together. It was likely that Lily and Layla would be dear companions for life; twins most often were. Maybe if she and Brandon had been born closer than six years apart they might have developed a friendship, but maybe not. Brandon had begun to show signs of antisocial behavior long before Hayley had come along, and it had only gotten worse over time. One incident in particular was burned into Hayley's memory. She must have been about six. Brandon had pinched the skin on her forearm so hard and for so long it had actually broken. She couldn't recall if Brandon had been punished. Her mother must have inflicted some sort of penance on him, but if she had it had had no curative affect.

Hayley uncrossed her legs and stretched them before her. It might be nice to have two or three children within a year or so of each other, she thought, so they stood the chance of enjoying a warm sibling relationship. But you didn't miss what you never had. That's what "they" said, but Hayley had always taken issue with that blanket statement. She believed that you could indeed miss what you'd never had; imagination and empathy could easily show you the nature of something potentially good, even wonderful. If you had never tasted root beer you wouldn't be likely to miss it. If you had never seen the movie *Jaws* you wouldn't likely miss that, either. But travel? Access to great art in museums? A beautiful home? A good marriage? A child of your own to love and cherish?

"I want!" Layla cried, pointing at her sister, who was clutching a pink rubber doughnut to her chest.

Hayley scolded herself for daydreaming when there was a potential toddler crisis to solve. "Lily," she said in her most bright and reasonable tone, "how about you keep the pink doughnut for a few minutes and then let Layla have it for a few minutes."

"No!" Lily shouted. "Mine!"

Hayley sighed. So much for a two-year-old's concept of sharing.

Chapter 70

Hayley was sitting at the Latimers' kitchen table, head in her hands, a scowl on her face.

"You look furious," Amy said, sitting across from her friend. "What happened?"

Hayley brought her hands away from her head and slapped them onto the table. "What happened," she said, "was that my mother was conned out of one hundred dollars we could ill afford to lose!"

"Oh my God, how?" Amy asked. "Was she hurt?"

"Only her pride was damaged. Get this. She was coming out of the post office when a guy going inside bumped into her. She says that *she* bumped into *him,* but believe me it was the other way around. The guy had been holding a box and dropped it when they collided. My mother said she heard tinkling glass and the man got upset. He said there had been a vase in the box that had belonged to his great-grandmother. It was the only bit of her the family had left and he was sending it to his dying mother to comfort her."

Amy shook her head. "And your mother . . ."

"Right," Hayley said. "My mother felt so bad for this guy that without any hesitation she offered him everything she had in her wallet, which happened to be the grocery money for the week."

"And he took it. What a jerk."

"When she told me what had happened," Hayley went on, "she

still had no clue that she had been conned. Can you believe it? That's one of the oldest scams in the book!"

"Your mother has a good heart," Amy said. "She thought she was helping someone. And at least it was only a hundred dollars." But the look on Hayley's face told her that had been a spectacularly unhelpful thing to say. "Sorry," she added quickly, remembering with discomfort the two hundred dollars she had spent on the shawl, the one hundred fifty dollars on the evening bag, the ninety dollars on the fur hat.

Hayley rubbed her forehead. "Why does she allow her life to be so dismal?"

With a twinge of discomfort Amy remembered the conversation she had had with her mother and Vera about people who allowed themselves to be victims. Both had rejected Cressida's opinion that such people got what they deserved as harsh and unsympathetic. At the time, Amy hadn't been so sure Cressida was wrong. Now, witnessing Hayley's weariness, she felt troubled. "Maybe your mother can't help being the way she is," she said lamely.

"But doesn't she ever think about what she's done to me by being such a *victim*?"

"Your mom is a good person," Amy said stoutly. Her feelings were clearer now than they had been a moment ago. "I don't believe she would ever do anything she thought would hurt you."

Hayley laughed bitterly. "So, she's oblivious to the example she's setting? That makes it even worse."

"I didn't mean that she was oblivious." Amy thought she might be getting a headache. "Come on, Hayley. You're not your mother. You won't wind up like she did."

Hayley laughed bitterly. "Won't I? Still think my idea of getting Ethan to marry me is crazy?"

"Yes," Amy said firmly. "I do, even though I'm beginning to understand your motives. Still, you'd be bored out of your mind as a trophy wife. You'll never learn how to keep your mouth shut and smile and nod like you really care about what your husband and his cronies are talking about."

"I won't be bored," Hayley argued. "I'll find things to do. Charities. I'll support charities. That's what rich women do, right?"

"You'll laugh too loud and you'll never remember to use the proper fork. You'll have nothing in common with the other women in Ethan's world who probably all grew up in wealthy families and went to finishing schools in Switzerland and were groomed for the life of a consort from the start."

"All clichés," Hayley said dismissively. "And archaic thinking. It won't be like that. People are always moving up into a better class. This is America. Our culture is fluid. We're the home of the self-made person."

"I don't know about that. You were always way better in history than I was. And speaking of me," Amy said, "how do I fit into this uptown future? Am I going to be an embarrassment to you?"

Hayley sighed. "Amy, you could never be an embarrassment to me. Not like my family."

"And speaking of family," Amy said, "what will you tell your children about your childhood? You'll have to lie to them, too, like you've probably lied to Ethan. You have lied about your family, haven't you?"

"Yes," Hayley admitted. "A little."

"Okay, so how are you going to keep those lies going over time? Your past will catch you up. Hayley, I know I'm the stupid one in this friendship but come on, this time I know I'm being smarter than you are!"

"You're not stupid," Hayley replied fiercely. "And I appreciate that you're so concerned about what I'm doing, I really do. But it's something I have to try, no matter the risks."

"Well, I can't stop you. And I promise to be here when Ethan leaves you and you're all alone."

"I won't be all alone," Hayley countered. "I'll have money."

Amy sighed. She knew Hayley was being purposely flippant. She knew that her friend was pretending a callousness she was constitutionally unable to feel.

"Look," Hayley said, "maybe things won't turn out horribly. Ethan and I are both really interested in history. We have that in common."

Amy laughed. "It takes a lot more than a hobby to keep two people together for life."

"Anyway," Hayley went on, slumping in her chair, "I've seen Ethan only three times this summer. Nothing will probably come of the stupid idea, anyway."

Amy felt a wave of pity wash over her. She loved Hayley. Hayley didn't deserve to be so unhappy. "You need something to cheer you up," she said.

"And what would that be?" Hayley laughed grimly. "The hundred dollars my mother lost magically reappearing in my wallet?"

"No. I mean, I'd make it happen if I could. Look, why don't we get some onion rings at The Razor Clam?"

"What would Cressida say if she knew you were eating fried food?" Hayley asked, already reaching for her bag.

"I don't care what she would say," Amy declared, and at that particular moment she meant it.

Chapter 71

Leda had made a chicken casserole and was pleased to see that Amy had eaten a decent portion of it and not once had she asked suspiciously if butter had been involved. Her strange and irregular diet didn't seem to be getting badly out of hand.

"How are things at work?" she asked.

"Okay," Amy said. "Cressida told me that she does two hundred sit-ups every morning. I don't think I could do even one."

"Me neither," Leda admitted, reaching for a slice of French bread. Cressida's sit-up record hadn't impressed Amy. Interesting.

"I don't think Hayley has any respect for the idea of marriage," Amy said suddenly. "She talks about wanting her mother to leave her father like it's no big deal."

"She has no other marriage to observe up close," Leda pointed out. "The family is scattered, and as far as I know Nora and Eddie never socialized with other couples. All she knows is what she's observed at home, and that's been pretty grim."

"I know. It's just seriously hard for Hayley to understand what keeps her mother in the marriage."

"I think it's hard for a lot of us to understand," Leda said, "but we have to accept that it's Nora's decision to stay."

"Is it really her decision?" Amy pressed. "I mean, maybe she doesn't believe she has the power to leave the marriage, and if that's the case, she isn't really making a decision, is she?"

"That is a point to consider," Leda admitted. "And there's the religious vow she took when she married Eddie Franklin."

"But Hayley doesn't know if her mother even believes in God anymore." Amy sighed. "Hayley's too young to be so bitter. I wish she didn't hate her father, but I guess I understand why she does. Every time I've met him he's given me the creeps. Maybe that's because of what Hayley's told me, but still."

"She certainly has reason to dislike him," Leda agreed. "He's never been anything but trouble for his family. There was a brief time very long ago when I and probably everybody else in Yorktide had hope that Eddie Franklin was turning his life around. He stopped drinking and managed to keep a job at a mechanic shop for almost five months. It was so good to see Nora with a smile on her face. But then something went wrong," Leda went on. "The next thing you know Eddie was sailing down Main Street one morning, rip-roaring drunk and the whole mess started up all over again. After that Nora seemed more downtrodden than ever. I think her husband's reverting to his old ways really took the spirit out of her. Sometimes I wonder if it might have been better for Nora if Eddie had never attempted to get well. It gave her false hope. I know that's a horrible thing to say, but still, I wonder."

"False hope," Amy said with a grim smile. "I think Hayley stopped hoping anything would change at home the day she was born."

Leda got up from the table and brought her empty dish to the sink. "I'm taking a piece to a client's house. I should be back well before eight."

"Okay," Amy said, rising from the table as well. "I'll clean up."

The drive to the heavily wooded area where Leda's newest client lived was always a pleasant one but more so when the air was clear and cool as it was this evening. Leda drove with all the windows opened, and as she turned onto a particularly picturesque lane she was delighted to spot an owl flying low through the trees.

The conversation over dinner had got her thinking about the different marriages she had known. There was Lance and Regan

Stirling, who had chosen to construct their union with infidelity as an integral part of it. She wondered if it had been something on which they had both agreed, or if Lance Stirling had strong-armed his wife into accepting the inevitable.

There was her own brief but contented marriage to Charlie. What would have become of the marriage had Charlie lived? Would they have stayed together? Would Leda have come to love him as deeply as he deserved to be loved? Would they have had more children? Charlie had wanted a big family.

Leda thought, too, about her parents' marriage, which had been a genuinely happy one. And then, of course, there was the Priors' marriage. Leda didn't know much about it, but what she did know hardly indicated a state of marital bliss. The truth was there were as many blueprints for marriage as there were people to pledge at the altar to love and cherish each other until death parted them. To prescribe a particular blueprint as universally best was impossible, though it was something Leda bet most people spent a good deal of time pondering.

Leda turned onto Wysteria Lane and pulled into her client's driveway. She should probably have parked down the road so that she could add a long walk to her almost nonexistent exercise routine. No doubt that's what Cressida Prior did, take every advantage to burn off another calorie. But Leda Latimer was not Cressida Prior, and for that she was thankful.

As Leda made her way up the drive Rosie Kirby opened the door and waved. She held her one-year-old son on her hip, and her four-year-old son clung to her left leg. Leda waved back. She very much hoped that Amy would one day marry and have children. So far, Amy had expressed little interest in relationships. She had dated but not much and had never been in love. Sometimes that worried Leda, but when she remembered her own first experience of love, the sheer insanity of it, she was glad that Amy had managed to avoid an early romantic disaster. Amy was warmhearted; one day she would fall in love and most of Yorktide, including Leda Latimer, wouldn't be sorry if it were with Noah Woolrich.

"Come in," Rosie said warmly when Leda had reached the door. "I can't wait to see what you've brought."

Chapter 72

"Damn," Hayley muttered. Her car's engine was making an ominous sound. She had bought the 2005 Kia Spectra three years earlier from a former neighbor for the proverbial song and guarded it as if it were made of solid gold. The last thing she wanted was her father or her brother getting anywhere near it. Neither man had a good record with vehicles.

The engine complained again, and Hayley sighed. Well, the car *was* thirteen years old. It would have to be replaced at some point. And her mother's car as well, though she hoped not at the same time. Hayley wasn't at all sure she could make that financial necessity work.

Nora Franklin. Hayley's mouth set in a frown. Her mother had repeatedly apologized for having fallen prey to the con man outside the post office. Her apologies had made Hayley feel guilty. The truth was that she had half-deliberately caused her mother to feel ashamed about her behavior. What sort of person was she to derive satisfaction from causing a person she loved emotional distress?

And that wasn't all that was bothering her. The other day Amy had used the term *trophy wife* and it had caused Hayley almost physical pain. She had sworn to her friend a confidence in her intentions she didn't really feel. In truth, Hayley wasn't sure about anything. Amy was right. Maybe she wouldn't be able to handle a world so vastly different from the one she had known to date. Maybe she really was meant for an obscure and depressing existence, playing referee for her parents and scraping off the mold in other people's shower stalls, her good looks wasting away while her brain rotted for lack of intellectual stimulation and her deep need for beauty withered in the face of peeling paint and sidewalks littered with junk food wrappers.

Hayley turned onto Hawthorne Lane and parked in the Latimers' driveway. She found Amy in the backyard at the little table. She was scowling.

"What's up?" Hayley asked, dropping into a seat.

"What's up," Amy said, "is that my mother turned down a new custom client because she thought he was too difficult. I mean, that's insane! I thought that with entering the FAF competition and being interviewed by that journal she might be becoming more professional."

"Your mother has been working with clients for years," Hayley pointed out. "She knows a difficult one when she meets one. It sounds to me as if she made a totally professional choice."

Amy shook her head. "She has absolutely no business sense."

"She manages to pay the bills on time, doesn't she?"

"Yeah," Amy admitted. "Yeah, but she doesn't have any real *ambition*. If she had, maybe we'd be living in a bigger house and have better cars and be able to afford a real vacation, not just staycations."

"You shouldn't complain," Hayley snapped. "Your mother has done a really good job of providing for you. You have a good life with her."

"Don't tell me I shouldn't complain about my mother," Amy snapped back. "Look at the things you say about your mom!"

"Sorry," Hayley said. And she was.

Amy opened the issue of *Vogue* that was sitting on the table and was immediately absorbed in its glossy pages. Hayley, fiddling with the bracelet Mrs. Latimer had made for her, felt her conscience kick at her again. She knew that she shouldn't criticize her mother, but the brutal truth was that Nora Franklin was no Leda

Latimer. There had been many times in Hayley's life when she wished she could have moved in with Leda and Amy to escape the alternately dour and angry atmosphere in her own home. That dream had come true once, if only for a short while.

When Hayley was about nine Nora Franklin was set to be admitted to the hospital for an operation and hadn't wanted to leave her daughter in the care of her father and brother. She had asked Leda if Hayley could stay with her for the duration, and Leda had agreed. And what a wonderful ten days they had been, Hayley remembered, waking up in a big, comfy bed; the cats—Winston and Harry's predecessors—chasing each other up and down the stairs; Leda laughing her bell-like laugh at their antics; Amy goofing around with hand puppets her mother had made. Hayley remembered doing her homework at the big kitchen table with no noisy interruptions from Brandon. She remembered how everyone was in bed at a reasonable hour, with no TV blaring into the night or doors slamming shut or anyone stumbling in after midnight. Meals were served at regular hours. Hayley's mother had been in the unfortunate habit of holding dinner for a husband who might or might not show. "A family should eat dinner together," Nora would say, to which Hayley would reply, "But we're not really a family, are we? Dad doesn't think so. If he did he'd be here, not letting his kids go hungry."

Mrs. Latimer, on the other hand, never served dinner later than six o'clock. Homemade mac 'n' cheese. Hamburgers cooked on the grill behind the house. String beans that were perfectly crispy, and peas that didn't come from a can so they weren't all gray and mushy. Angel food cake with fresh strawberry sauce on top! Hayley thought it likely that even in her dying moments she would see in her mind's eye Mrs. Latimer bringing the cake to the table, the sauce chunky with bits of strawberry, the red fairly gleaming against the alabaster of the cake. Amy had said, "We're having angel food cake *again*?" Hayley had been shocked. It had never occurred to her that her best friend was spoiled.

"Anything interesting?" Hayley asked, weary of reminiscing about those idyllic days long gone.

Amy looked up from the magazine. "I'm reading an article about a new wrinkle filler. It's supposed to be way better than Botox. I am so going to get fillers when I'm older. I bet Cressida sees an A-list dermatologist."

Hayley managed a smile. She thought of her mother's worn face, a face that had witnessed too much hardship in her forty-seven years. With any luck one day Hayley would have the money to take her mother to spas for massages and facials and expensive haircuts. She would probably have to wrangle Nora into accepting such pampering, but wrangle her Hayley would. And Nora Franklin's life would be better for her daughter's efforts. Hayley was sure of it.

Chapter 73

Since the morning that Amy had witnessed Cressida slap her husband's face she had been struggling to come to terms with the upsetting event. She had spent a lot of time reminding herself that what she had witnessed was a private moment. For all she knew a slap was nothing new to Will. For all she knew Will hit his wife. She hoped not, but it was possible. In the end Amy decided to forget as best she could what she had seen. She told herself that it had been minor in the scheme of things. And she knew she had grown up in a particularly warm and fuzzy home. Amy doubted Hayley would have been half as shocked as she had been, witnessing a moment of physical violence between a husband and wife.

The important thing, Amy thought as she climbed the few steps to the Priors' front door, was that she not let Cressida see any of her discomfort. The important thing was that Cressida continue to consider her as someone worthy of being a protégé and a right-hand woman.

"You'll be watching the children this morning," Cressida announced when she opened the door to admit Amy. "I sent Will to Portsmouth on an errand."

Amy felt panic rise in her. It was the first time that summer she had been asked to supervise Jordan and Rhiannon. What was she supposed to *do* with them? The words she had read so many times on the agency's website came back to her. A nanny was supposed to see to the children's every need, be it physical or emotional. So far, the only needs Amy had been required to meet were Cressida's.

Cressida solved Amy's dilemma by instructing Amy and the children to play an edition of Timeline. Cressida went upstairs to her office and Amy, Jordan, and Rhiannon sat at the kitchen table. As usual, Rhiannon was dressed in head-to-toe black. Jordan was wearing a Ralph Lauren polo shirt. It was a nice shirt, but Amy doubted an eight-year-old boy cared about wearing designer clothing.

"I've never played this game before," Amy said, with a smile. "Is it fun?"

"It's not about having fun," Rhiannon stated. "It's about proving how much you know."

Amy's stomach sank. "Oh," she said. "You'll have to explain the rules to me."

Rhiannon did, and the game began. Neither child seemed to take any real pleasure in it even though one or the other of them won each round easily. Amy had never felt her lack of general knowledge so keenly. She was relieved when Will returned home around eleven. Clearly the children were too, as they rapidly left the table to join him by the pool.

Amy went to the powder room, and when she returned to the kitchen she found Cressida, peeling cucumbers and slicing them into the blender. Amy cast about her mind for something of interest to say. As a potential right-hand woman she needed to appear well informed. Didn't she?

"My friend Hayley," Amy said suddenly, "the one who's working as a nanny for the Whitbys this summer, they're the people renting that big old house on Overlook Road, anyway, Hayley told me that someone is building a new convention center in Portland." Amy paused. "At least, I think it was Portland."

"Jon and Marisa Whitby?" Cressida asked with a frown.

"Yes. Do you know them?"

"I know them," Cressida said sharply. "The wife is insanely jealous of me. Every time I buy a couture item Marisa has to run right out and buy the exact same piece. As if she could ever look as good as I do in Chanel!"

"She really buys the exact same piece?" Amy asked.

"Would I lie?" Cressida snapped.

"No, of course not," Amy said quickly.

"And Jon. Dumping his first wife for a woman almost thirty years younger than him? What a cliché! Marisa will be done with him in another year or two and he'll be left a laughingstock like so many of his sort. Idiots." Cressida picked up the glass of pureed cucumber. "I'll be in my office," she said.

Cressida had only been gone a moment when Will came back into the kitchen from the patio. He went to the freezer and pulled out a box of frozen pops. "Don't tell Cressida," he said with a conspiratorial smile. "They're all-natural but she doesn't like the kids to snack between meals."

Amy managed a smile in return. It was the first time she had come face-to-face with him since witnessing that awful scene, and she felt awkward and embarrassed.

"You haven't had a full day off since you started working here, have you?" Will asked.

"No," Amy said. "I mean, not really."

"Don't you think you deserve some time off each week?"

"No," Amy said quickly. "What I mean is, I don't mind a crazy schedule. Not that it's crazy. I didn't mean that."

Will shrugged. "Thanks for playing Timeline with Jordan and Rhiannon earlier."

"It's my job," Amy said automatically. And then the absurdity of the situation hit her. What was her job here, really?

Will went back out to the patio, and Amy stood uselessly by the marble-topped island. An upsetting idea occurred to her. She wondered if Will were going to approach Cressida about the issue of vacation days. She hoped he wouldn't. She didn't want Cressida to think she had been complaining. She didn't want Cressida to be mad at her. She especially didn't want to lose her job. Sure, Cressida could be moody and sometimes even unpleasant, and she hadn't mentioned the Atlanta job after that first time, but . . .

"Aimee!"

Amy jumped at the shouted summons and hurried off to Cressida's office.

Chapter 74

The sun was strong that morning. Leda was wearing her favorite floppy straw sunhat, woven by a woman she knew from the Blue Heron Circle, and the lightest, loosest linen pants and top she owned. Even so, she felt uncomfortably hot and sticky. She had come into town only for a carton of milk and a loaf of bread and was eager to get back to her studio and the big standing fan that worked wonders on days like this.

As she turned onto Main Street she noticed that walking toward her was Nora Franklin. She was carrying a string bag in one hand and a plastic shopping bag in the other. She wore no hat or sunglasses, two items it was dangerous to be without on such a summer day.

It would be good to say hello to her, Leda thought; she hadn't spoken to Nora in almost a year. Leda raised her hand in greeting, but instead of returning the gesture Nora made a sudden turn at the corner and in a moment was out of sight.

Leda lowered her hand and frowned. She was sure that Nora had seen her and just as sure that she had abruptly turned the corner because she had not wanted to stop and chat. That was no surprise. The poor woman had looked bedraggled, as though the weight of her rotten domestic life, devoid of simple attentions except for what her dutiful daughter could give her, was finally marking her outwardly as no doubt it had marked her inwardly long before now.

Leda continued on toward her car. With Yorktide being a small community, everyone knew about Eddie Franklin's behavior, and there could be no way for Nora to hide whatever shame, embarrassment, or anger she must be feeling. In such a case it could be argued that there was benefit in the relative anonymity of urban life. If Nora lived in Portland, for example, she might be able to walk down certain streets unnoticed and unknown, something that might feel like much-needed relief from the scrutiny of her neighbors. But Nora didn't live in Portland.

As Leda passed by the toy shop on Clove Street she caught sight of an old-fashioned scooter in the window, and an image of Brandon Franklin as a small boy came to her. He had had the most adorable little smile in a cherubic, chubby-cheeked face. Until he was three he had carried a favorite stuffed animal everywhere, a floppy beige dog he called Spot. It broke Leda's heart when she thought of what had become of that little boy, and no doubt it broke his mother's heart as well. Leda knew that Hayley had little sympathy for her brother, and that was understandable. By the time Hayley had come along when Brandon was six he had already started to display cruel and careless behaviors. While the little girl could have benefited from the protective attention of an older brother, all she had met with was teasing and bullying.

Leda reached her car, slid into the driver's seat, and headed for home, suddenly very conscious that in spite of that nasty encounter with the Stirlings when she was seventeen, and in spite of losing her husband so shortly after their wedding, her life, unlike Nora Franklin's, had been so very good. She had been raised by loving parents. She had a wonderful daughter and dear friends who never failed to cheer her on when times were tough and to celebrate with her when times were good. She had been the subject of an interview by a major journal. She had acquired several new clients since the start of the year. She had found the nerve to enter a piece of her work in a national competition.

Yes, Leda thought as she headed for her lovely and secure home on Hawthorne Lane. She was a very lucky woman indeed.

* * *

The first thing Leda did when she arrived home, after putting the milk in the fridge and the bread in the breadbox, was to check her e-mail. There was a message from Margot Lakes, asking if she might drop by the studio the following afternoon. And there was an e-mail from an editor at a popular crafting journal called *Needle and Thread*, asking if Leda would be interested in writing a piece describing her creative process.

Leda sat back in her chair. This was a challenging topic about which to write, and honestly one she had never given much thought. But why not finally take the time to articulate what it was she did and why she did it? She might just learn something about herself as a result of such a challenge. The fact that there was a two-hundred-dollar stipend on acceptance of the completed article was almost unimportant. Without further hesitation Leda sent a reply in the affirmative to the editor, and immediately after, she opened a new document.

And then she froze. It had been years since she had written anything other than brief descriptions of particular works for her website. She realized that she had no idea where to begin. But maybe, she thought, writing an article was like fashioning a work of fiber art. You just picked up a pencil and sketched whatever came into your head until at one unexpected moment an idea began to take form and then, for better or worse, you pursued that idea. *Just write what comes into your head*, she told herself. *Don't censor yourself.*

Leda took a deep breath, turned the setting on the standing fan from medium to high, and began to write.

My art isn't something separate from my life. It's an integral part of who and what I am. It's a part of how I live each and every day.

My home is my studio; my studio is my home.

My art is a language in which I speak to strangers so that they don't remain strangers.

Creation brings happiness. It calms us at the same time it inspires us. Art heals us.

Pablo Picasso supposedly said that inspiration exists but that it must find you working. I believe that absolutely.

Suddenly Leda's fingers stopped typing. That was okay. What was important was that the creative process had begun, and that was always an exhilarating feeling. Leda laughed out loud. In spite of the sticky weather and the sad almost-encounter with Nora Franklin, this was turning out to be a very good day.

Chapter 75

It was ten o'clock on a Thursday morning. Marisa, staving off a nasty summer cold, was at home with the girls and in desperate need of the latest novel by Charles Todd. "The Bookworm is holding a copy for me," she had told Hayley. "Would it be an imposition for you to pick it up?"

Hayley smiled at the memory. Going to a bookstore an imposition? Still, it had been very nice of Marisa to ask. Hayley had gladly driven to downtown Yorktide, and while at the store she had rapidly browsed the used book section, finding a paperback copy of Kathryn Hughes's biography of George Eliot for three dollars. Treasures paid for and in tow, Hayley stepped out onto the sidewalk and headed in the direction of the small parking lot behind the old-fashioned pharmacy.

"Hayley!"

Hayley stopped and turned. Striding toward her, his hand raised in a wave, was Ethan Whitby. He was wearing slouchy jeans and a white T-shirt. His auburn hair flopped over his forehead as he walked briskly along. His arms, she noted, were slim but muscular.

"Hi," Hayley said when he had joined her. She liked the freckles along the bridge of his nose. "I didn't know you were visiting."

Ethan smiled. "It's a surprise. I haven't even been to the house yet. I hope Marisa doesn't mind my popping in for a few days."

"I'm sure she won't," Hayley told him. "And the girls will be happy to see you. So, what are you doing downtown?"

Ethan indicated the small paper shopping bag he was carrying. "I know Marisa is partial to the scones at Bread and Roses. What about you?"

"Bookstore run for Marisa. And I scored a biography of George Eliot for three dollars."

"Excellent. Don't you love when you stumble across just the gem you were hoping for?" Ethan asked.

Hayley laughed. "I do. But I should get back to the house. Marisa's battling a cold and I don't want to leave her tending to the girls too long."

"I'll walk you to your car, if that's okay," Ethan said.

"Of course," Hayley replied. When, she thought, was the last time someone hadn't simply assumed that she would be happy to accept his company? This family with whom she was to some extent sharing the summer was unlike any family she had ever known. For a brief moment, Hayley thought she might cry at the strangeness of it all.

"So," Ethan said as they walked along, "is this the first time you've worked as a nanny?"

"Yes," Hayley told him. "Though I've been babysitting since I was ten."

"Do you know any of the other women—and men, I suppose—working as nannies in Yorktide?"

"I've met a few," Hayley told him. "There's a sort of informal network. My friend Amy is one of the group. She's working for the Priors this summer. Cressida Prior of Prior Ascendancy."

"I know who she is," Ethan said with a frown. "Well, I don't know her personally, but let's just say that her reputation precedes her."

"What do you mean?" Hayley asked.

Ethan hesitated a moment before going on. "She's over-the-top self-involved. Some would say she's a narcissist, and she can be pretty ruthless. I'll give you an example," Ethan said. "She poached a few key employees from one of my father's friends, and she went about it in a particularly devious way. And along with buying the employees she bought their competitively valuable trade secrets. Dad's friend suffered a fairly substantial business loss as a result."

"Unethical but not illegal?" Hayley asked.

"As far as I know, yeah." Ethan shook his head. "But maybe Cressida Prior is different on the domestic front. Maybe she's all warmth and fair play."

"I don't think she is, not if what Amy has told me is true. And there's more. Cressida calls Amy Aimee. She told Amy it sounded more sophisticated, and Amy didn't protest."

Ethan frowned. "A person's name is so much a part of her identity. To have someone take it away isn't right."

"Amy doesn't see it that way," Hayley told him. "She was flattered. It was like she was suddenly dissatisfied with the name her mother had given her."

"People like Cressida Prior have huge powers of persuasion," Ethan said grimly, "and they use them to bully those around them."

Hayley and Ethan arrived at the corner of Grove and Main Streets just as the light turned green for pedestrians. They had stepped into the street with the rest of the crowd when a midsized car came flying through the intersection against the light. Several people screamed. Ethan grabbed Hayley's shoulders and pulled her back to the sidewalk. A child began to sob.

"My God," Ethan muttered, releasing Hayley. "Are you all right?"

Hayley nodded. With a trembling hand, she reached for her cell phone and called 911. "Someone just ran a red light at the corner of Grove and Main in Yorktide," she told the dispatcher, her voice shaking. She then spelled out what she had caught of the license plate number and described the car before ending the call.

"Are you sure you're okay?" Ethan asked quietly, running his hand gently down Hayley's arm. "I hope I didn't hurt you when I grabbed you."

Hayley took a deep breath. "You didn't hurt me," she said. "And thank you." Ethan might just have saved her life. She could still feel his strong hands on her shoulders and again thought that she might cry. Suddenly she realized that Ethan was looking at her intently. She could swear he wanted to kiss her. And if he did kiss her . . . "My car is right across the street," she said suddenly, taking a step away from him. "I should be getting back."

Ethan cleared his throat and nodded briskly. "Of course. I've got to get on, too. A friend of mine is staying at the Beachmere. We're meeting for lunch."

"Okay," Hayley said, taking another step away. "And Ethan? Thank you again. For . . . for before."

Hurriedly, Hayley crossed the street, opened her car door, and slid inside. Her hands trembled as they gripped the steering wheel. Something had just happened. Something serious. But it was not the kind of something that was supposed to happen. There had been a real connection between her and Ethan Whitby, there *had* been, she had felt it, but there couldn't be! She couldn't allow there to be. Emotions were dangerous. Love just messed everything up. Look at what had happened to her mother; her life had been blighted by romance. No, Hayley thought, she had to keep her wits about her and her heart locked firmly away if she was ever to succeed in her plan to—

Hayley's hands slipped from the steering wheel. If she was ever to succeed in her plan to—to be safe.

Chapter 76

"Oh, I love this song," Amy said to the interior of her car as she turned up the volume on the ancient radio. She was in a pretty good mood this morning. The sun was shining, the new lip color she had bought had turned out to be a perfect nude, and when she weighed herself the night before she found that she had lost two pounds.

She was almost at the Priors' house when her phone alerted her to a text. There were no other cars on the road, so Amy risked looking down at the phone on the passenger seat. *Don't need u today* Cressida had written.

Suddenly, Amy's good mood plummeted. She wondered why Cressida had told her not to come to work. Maybe one of the children had complained about her, claimed she had cheated at Timeline, though how you could cheat at the game was beyond Amy's imagination. Maybe . . . Amy frowned and, at the next turn in the road, headed back toward Hawthorne Lane.

"What are you doing home?" her mother asked when Amy appeared in the kitchen fifteen minutes later.

Amy shrugged and went to the counter to pour her second cup of coffee. "Cressida said I don't need to come in today."

"When did she tell you?" her mother asked.

Amy took a seat at the kitchen table. "A few minutes ago. She sent a text."

Leda frowned. "She could have given you some notice. You could have slept in this morning."

"Oh, I don't care!" Amy shook her head. "Sorry. I didn't mean to raise my voice."

"Did she say why you weren't needed?"

"No. Maybe one of the kids is sick." That shouldn't be cause for telling the nanny to stay home, but Amy was the nanny in name only, wasn't she? It was more likely that Cressida didn't want Amy around. Maybe Will had told Cressida that she was upset about not having agreed on days off and Cressida had gotten angry that Amy hadn't come straight to her as she had commanded that first day on the job and was punishing her by keeping her at a distance.

Amy's mother got up from the table and brought her cereal bowl to the sink. "Since you're home," she said, "maybe you could help me with the gardening."

"I thought I'd go to the beach," Amy blurted. But she had thought no such thing. It was wrong to punish her mother for Cressida's punishing her. If that's what Cressida was doing. "Okay," she said. "I'll help."

"Great. Maybe we could go somewhere fun for lunch. We haven't been out to lunch once this summer. That's not a criticism," her mother added quickly. "I know you've been working hard."

Amy managed a smile. "Sure," she said. "We could go to that taco place you like."

"Excellent idea. Let me grab some gardening gloves and we can get started."

When her mother had left the kitchen, Amy put her fingers to her temples. She was getting a headache. She was in no mood to do anything other than shut her bedroom door behind her. Besides, a Mexican meal would make her regain the two pounds she had lost.

With a sigh, Amy went to change out of her work clothes. Not even the perfect nude lipstick could make this day a good one.

Chapter 77

A tall, thin woman was coming out of The Yellow Buttercup, the highest of the high-end boutiques in Yorktide. She was noticeable because she was the only one among the throngs of vacationers and random locals who was dressed as if she was heading to a business meeting in New York. Leda recognized a Gucci bag slung over the woman's shoulder. She didn't know where the pantsuit and heels had come from, but she knew quality workmanship when she saw it, even from a distance.

Suddenly it occurred to Leda that the woman had to be the infamous Cressida Prior. Leda watched as Cressida Prior—if that was her—walked through the crowd of casually dressed tourists. Her impression was of a woman unhealthily thin. The set of her shoulders and the angle of her head seemed to declare to the world that she would tolerate nothing less than perfection from others and expect nothing less than obedience to her every whim.

Leda sighed. How neutral could her assessment possibly be? Love and admiration transformed an average-looking human being into an angel of beauty. Contempt and dislike transformed an average-looking human being into a goblin. Leda disliked Cressida Prior. Of course she would find her unattractive.

In a moment Amy's so-called mentor had disappeared from sight. Leda decided she wouldn't tell Amy she had seen Ms. Prior.

What would be the point? She made her way to Wainscoting and Windowseats to find Phil behind the checkout counter, a look of puzzlement on his face.

"What's wrong?" Leda asked.

"Nothing," Phil said. "It's just that Sadie Jones returned this table runner of yours a few minutes ago with the complaint that it wasn't properly finished. See? These threads have unraveled from this bound edge."

Leda looked at the piece and immediately felt her self-confidence plummet. "How could I have been so careless?" she said, putting a hand to her heart. "This is awful."

"Wait a minute." Phil held the damaged edge of the runner close to his face. "Just as I suspected," he said after a moment. "The threads haven't just come loose. They've been torn. Look."

Phil handed the runner to Leda, who further examined the damage. "Yes," she said. "I think you're right. But I don't understand."

"All you need to understand for now," Phil said firmly, "is that the damage is not your fault. Leave this to me."

Leda shook her head. "What do you mean it's not my fault?"

"What I mean," Phil explained, "is that my esteemed customer has a reputation around town for returning items in mysteriously bad shape and demanding refunds. Invariably there's no receipt—she claims to have lost it—and store return policy means nothing to her. She's been known to show up a year or more after making a purchase expecting her money back or a replacement."

"How awful," Leda said. "What sort of a person would act so reprehensibly?"

"A very sad person," Phil said. "Go home, Leda, and put it out of your mind. I'll deal with Ms. Jones."

Leda had been pacing her studio for what seemed like hours. In spite of Phil's assurances, she couldn't get the thought of those unraveled threads out of her mind. She knew that at times she made mistakes, but when she did she usually noticed the mistakes right away and corrected them. What if Phil was wrong about what had happened? This was the worst possible time for her to be losing her touch, what with the media having noticed her and her work about to be judged in the FAF's competition.

The phone rang, and Leda dove for the landline on her desk. It was Phil.

"It was just as I thought," he said. "Ms. Jones's dog was responsible for the damage to the runner. I shamed her into telling me what had really happened. We shop owners should band together and agree not to let her and her ilk abuse us any longer."

"I'm so relieved," Leda said. "Did she apologize?"

"What do you think?" Phil said. "People like Sadie Jones don't apologize, because they don't ever feel that what they've done is wrong."

Leda sighed. "Thanks for investigating, Phil. In spite of her bad behavior I'd be happy to repair the damage."

"I wouldn't bother," Phil told her. "She wouldn't pay you and she wouldn't be grateful for your generosity."

Phil was right, Leda realized. She would be wasting her precious time catering to someone like Sadie Jones. "Okay," she said. "I'll let it go." After thanking Phil again, Leda ended the call and sank onto the love seat. In spite of the happy ending the incident had really shaken her.

For so long Leda had been hiding from the larger world, emerging only far enough to make a comfortable if conservative life for herself and her daughter. But now she was venturing further abroad, and it was a fact that whenever you put yourself out into the world, in whatever form that might be, you risked being hurt or cheated or ignored. But the risk was usually worth it. At least, it was supposed to be. And yet Leda had been so quick to accept blame for a wrong she hadn't committed, so quick to doubt her abilities. Clearly, she still had a long way to go before her pride in her work was a constant matter of fact.

And could the same be said about love, Leda thought, glancing at the photo of Charlie taken only days before his untimely death? Was love always worth the risk of rejection or misery? Here she was urging Vera to take another chance at romance and yet she herself didn't seem to be able to take that brave leap.

Leda shook her head. Thoughts of romance could wait. She went to her desk and opened the file that contained the article she was writing for *Needle and Thread*. She was enjoying the challenge. She was learning about herself as she finally articulated her creative process as best as such a thing could be put into words. And she had never been more grateful for spell-check. Never.

Chapter 78

Hayley was perched on a rock at the top of Ogunquit Beach. The experience was all so familiar and yet all so wonderful. The expanse of white sand; the clusters of fabulously shaped shells; the wild call of the seagulls. The beach was a gift, one that Hayley knew she didn't always properly value.

Finally, Hayley saw Amy approaching along the sand. There was an air of dejection about her. Hayley wondered if this was the right time to share with Amy what Ethan had told her about Cressida Prior's unethical business practices. She doubted Amy would believe her, but forewarned was forearmed, and if Amy was still considering moving to Atlanta to work at Prior Ascendancy . . .

"Hey," Amy said when she joined Hayley. Her tone was flat. "Why did you want to see me?"

Hayley waited until Amy had perched next to her. "Look," she began, "Ethan told me a few things about Cressida Prior I think you should know."

Amy frowned. "Like what?"

Hayley related the story Ethan had told about his father's friend's unhappy experience. "She has a reputation as a narcissist," she said finally. "So just be aware."

"There's no way Cressida would have done something so underhanded," Amy declared when Hayley had finished her tale. "I mean, she can be—tough—but she's not, I don't know, underhanded."

Hayley shrugged. "Why would Ethan lie? Why would his father's friend lie?"

"Because they're men," Amy said, "and men resent powerful women. Cressida told me that pretty much every man she encounters hates the fact that she's a success. If they're not trying to sabotage her business they're spreading lies about her personal life. Cressida would say you're naïve if you believe what Ethan told you."

"I don't care what Cressida Prior would say about me," Hayley said firmly. "Who made her an oracle? Seriously, you've known this woman for a matter of weeks and already you're taking everything she says as gospel? You even let her change your name!"

"She didn't change it," Amy argued. "She just—adjusted it. Anyway, Cressida told me a bunch of stuff about the Whitbys you should probably know."

"Stuff I absolutely don't need to know, thanks."

"I'm going to tell you anyway," Amy announced, and she did.

When she was done, it was all Hayley could do to restrain a hearty laugh. "First of all," she said, "Jon and Marisa Whitby are very happy together, and don't ask what do I know of happy marriages. It doesn't take a genius to recognize when two people enjoy each other's company and treat each other with respect."

"But the age difference," Amy said. "You have to admit it's kind of huge."

"There's nothing unusual in an older man marrying a younger woman, you know that, and if the age difference doesn't bother them, why should it bother anyone else? And Marisa jealous of Cressida?" Now Hayley did laugh. "Why would she be jealous? She's got everything, including the most important thing, a family she loves and who love her. From what you've told me, Cressida Prior's marriage isn't exactly warm and fuzzy, and as for her relationship with her kids, well, all I can say is good luck to them."

Amy didn't reply.

"And as for Marisa one-upping Cressida with couture," Hayley went on, "that's just ridiculous. Even if she does own expensive designer clothes, she's not the type to get involved in a petty rivalry."

"How do you know?" Amy pressed. "You don't really know Marisa at all."

"Well, you don't know Cressida, either," Hayley pointed out.

Amy's face grew alarmingly flushed. "I know her better than you know Marisa."

Hayley sighed, weary of the ridiculous exchange. "Look," she said, "we're going to have to agree to disagree."

"We've never fought before," Amy said miserably, tears springing to her eyes. "Not ever."

"Oh, come on," Hayley said. "I don't like your boss and you don't like mine. It's nothing to cry about. Hey, has she mentioned the Atlanta offer again?"

Amy wiped her eyes with her fingertips. "No. She's very busy."

"Are you still considering it?"

"Of course," Amy snapped. "Why wouldn't I? Are you still set on getting Ethan Whitby to marry you?"

"Of course," Hayley snapped back, remembering the feel of his hands on her shoulders, the look in his eyes, the . . . "Why would I change my mind?"

Amy stood abruptly. "I have to go," she said. And then she strode off in the direction of the parking lot.

Hayley stared out at the calm blue water lapping gently against the shore. The exchange with Amy had upset her. What was going on this summer? Neither she nor Amy seemed to be in their right minds. In fact, in some ways Hayley hardly recognized herself or her best friend. How had they gotten to this crazy place where they were each acting so wildly out of character, refusing to listen to reason, snapping at each other like middle school girls? None of it made any sense. If only they could . . .

If only they could what? Abruptly, Hayley got up from her seat on the rocks and strode off to her car.

Chapter 79

Cressida still hadn't given Amy a reason for her telling her not to come to work the other day. Amy wished that she had. Sometimes, Amy felt as if she didn't know where she stood with Cressida. Did Cressida really consider her a protégé and a friend, or did she see Amy as merely . . . as merely an accessory?

Like today. Cressida hadn't told Amy they were driving up to Portland. If she had given Amy some notice, Amy would have worn something nicer, like maybe her new brushed cotton skirt. It had cost kind of a lot, but it was such a pretty shade of pink Amy hadn't been able to resist.

Now, entering the city, Amy said a silent prayer of thanks to whoever might be listening. Cressida had driven way beyond the speed limit the entire way. For the duration of the forty-minute ride Amy had gripped the edge of the passenger seat with her right hand, hoping Cressida couldn't see the sign of her anxiety. Cressida probably despised people who experienced anxiety.

Once within the city limits, Cressida parked the car in a garage, complaining loudly though there was no one but Amy to hear that the prices were outrageous. Then she led them with her rapid pace down to Commercial Street and to a boutique called The Stellar Woman. Amy didn't often get to Portland, and when she did she mostly window-shopped. When she did have some money to spend it wasn't enough for stores like The Stellar Woman. Not even on the salary Cressida was paying her. The least expensive item Amy had seen so far was thirty-five dollars, and that was a tiny hair clip.

"This is gorgeous," Cressida announced.

Amy turned to see Cressida fingering the sleeve of a lightweight bomber-style jacket in a buttery yellow leather. While Amy wasn't sure the color would complement Cressida's complexion, the jacket itself was really beautiful. And it was locked to the rack.

"Excuse me," Cressida called across the store to the middle-aged saleswoman who was assisting another customer. "I'd like to see this jacket."

The saleswoman smiled. "As soon as I've finished helping this lady I'll be right over," she said.

Before the saleswoman could turn away, Cressida raised her voice. "Do you know who I am?" she demanded. "I am Cressida Prior, and I am entitled to good service."

"Every customer is entitled to good service, ma'am," the saleswoman said in a remarkably calm voice. "I will be with you as soon as possible."

"Too bad," Cressida spat. "You just lost a very valuable customer."

Shamefaced, Amy followed Cressida from the shop. An image of Cressida's hand making sharp contact with her husband's cheek hovered in her mind. She was terrified of speaking but somehow courageous enough to do it anyway. "The saleswoman was all alone," she said, striding along next to her mentor. "I'm sure she didn't mean to insult you."

"Well, she did insult me," Cressida snapped. "I should call the owner of that shop and get her fired."

Amy cringed. She so hoped she hadn't made the situation worse by voicing her opinion. If that saleswoman got fired because of her . . . "Where are we going now?" she asked.

"We're going to lunch," Cressida said. "I'm simply starved."

Amy lay stretched on her bed, her old plush panda in her arms. She was utterly exhausted from the day she had spent with Cressida in Portland, and the ride back to Yorktide had been a nightmare. Cressida had driven even faster than she had on the way north, weaving in and out of traffic until Amy actually prayed for a police car to stop them. When Amy had stepped out of the car her legs had almost buckled under her, so dizzy had she felt. Dizzy and relieved that she was in one piece.

Things had gone from bad to worse that afternoon. After the debacle at The Stellar Woman, they had gone for lunch at a restaurant called Luna's. There was a pasta special Amy really wanted to order, but she knew that Cressida would disapprove so she ordered a house salad instead. It was what Cressida ordered. The dressing, Cressida told the waiter, should come on the side, and they would not need any bread. Cressida left half of her undressed salad on her plate. She informed the waiter that the arugula was wilted and had given him no tip.

But that wasn't the worst. When they were leaving the restaurant, a teenaged boy wearing what was recognizably a feminine outfit was passing by. Amy was impressed. Here was a young person on the verge of discovering his style, daring to appear in public in clothing that proclaimed a gender fluidity. It must take an awful lot of courage, Amy had thought, for someone who didn't fit the norm to stand up and be seen for who he was. She smiled kindly at the boy, and he gave the ghost of a smile in return.

And then Cressida had burst out laughing. "What on earth is that?" she cried. "How ridiculous!"

The boy had blushed furiously and hurried on.

Amy was stunned. This was much worse than what Cressida had done to the saleswoman earlier. Amazingly, once again she found the nerve to speak. "You embarrassed him," she said, her voice shaking.

"So?" Cressida shrugged. "If he's going to walk around in that sort of ridiculous getup he's going to have to learn how to take criticism."

But it wasn't criticism that Cressida had offered, Amy thought as she followed miserably in Cressida's wake. It was mockery.

Amy rubbed her eyes. She so needed to reconcile the good parts of Cressida with the bad parts but was finding it increasingly difficult to do so. Could she really have been so wrong about her employer's character? God knew she had been spectacularly wrong before. There were even a few incidents she had never told her mother because it embarrassed her to be so foolish in her judgment. Like the time she had given a scruffy young guy ten dollars because he told her his car had been stolen and he needed money to get home to Falmouth. She had believed his sad tale, and the memory of his drawn face and hollow eyes had haunted her all afternoon. That is until she came across him again sitting with a group of other scruffy young men and women at a café, drinking beer and laughing. She had felt like such an idiot. When Hayley had told her about her mother's falling for that broken vase scheme Amy had practically squirmed with discomfort. It was exactly the sort of scheme she knew she would fall for.

Amy squeezed her old panda for comfort. She remembered what Ethan had told Hayley about Cressida's unethical business practices. She remembered the article her mother had found about the lawsuit against Cressida by her employees. She remembered the sight of Cressida slapping Will's face. How could she seriously consider moving to Atlanta with someone who could treat people so carelessly and cruelly and not be bothered by guilt and self-recrimination? Or maybe, Amy thought, Cressida's conscience *did* nag her late at night. Maybe Cressida would spend this very night wide awake, rebuking herself for her bad behavior. But even if she did, how did that remorse help the people she had abused?

Amy rolled onto her side and curled into the fetal position. Cressida Prior, her relationship with Cressida Prior . . . it was all so difficult to comprehend, and at that moment, in the safety and security of the bedroom she had slept in almost every night of her entire life, Amy didn't think she was properly up to the task.

Chapter 80

The cats were at their bowls, loudly crunching their breakfast and slurping the fresh water Leda had put out for them. Leda had devoured a bowl of cereal and two pieces of toast and was halfway through her first large cup of coffee. Amy, however, had barely touched her high-fiber, no-sugar-added cereal, a recommendation from Cressida, and had taken only a sip of her coffee.

Since dawn Leda had been reading and rereading her article for *Needle and Thread*. It had come together far more quickly than she had imagined it would, but that didn't mean it was any good.

"May I read you the most recent draft of my piece?" Leda asked, looking up from her papers. "I think reading it aloud might help me to hear any awkward lines or transitions."

Amy shrugged. "Sure," she said.

Leda cleared her throat and began to read. Twice she glanced at Amy to find that she was staring at her cup of coffee with a sort of dull expression, her mind clearly miles away.

"So?" Leda asked when she had finished reading the draft. "What do you think?"

"It was fine," Amy said.

Leda thought her daughter had looked ill or unhappy ever since she had returned from Portland late yesterday afternoon. "Are you coming down with something?" she asked.

"No," Amy said flatly. "I'm fine."

"Are you sure?" Leda pressed. "Is there something on your mind you want to talk about?"

Amy roughly pushed her chair back from the table and stood. "No," she said. "I've got to go."

Amy left the kitchen without a farewell, and a few moments later Leda heard her car leave the driveway. Leda sighed. She shouldn't have pushed Amy to talk about what was on her mind. It was a good bet whatever it was had to do with Cressida, but Amy's thoughts and feelings belonged to her. She had a right to keep them to herself.

It was a scenario that had never occurred to Leda when she had worried about her daughter being abused by an employer. The fact was that women could be just as unscrupulous as men. They could wield power just as dangerously, with little if any regard for the damage they inflicted on those in a position of weakness or subordination. Look at how that supposed new friend of Amy's back in freshman year of college had treated her. Look at Regan Stirling, wife of the man who had seduced Leda's seventeen-year-old self.

With a bit of a struggle Leda put thoughts of Amy aside and read through the article yet again, pencil in hand. This time, she was satisfied. She would send it that afternoon. Leda folded the papers and slipped them into the pocket of her bathrobe. As she was on her way to the stairs she heard something coming through the mail slot in the front door and went to see what had been delivered. Along with a few bills there was the latest issue of the *Journal of Craftwork*. Eagerly Leda retrieved the magazine and searched the table of contents for her interview. She flipped to page 15, and there in black and white were her very own words.

She felt a surge of joy. Her first instinct was to show the interview to Amy the moment she got home from work that evening. And then reason stepped in. No, Leda thought, she would share the interview with Amy at a later date when she hoped Amy would once again be interested in her mother's career. Leda couldn't quite see when that day would come, but until it did there were others who would be more than happy to share in Leda's joy. Leda took her cell phone from the other pocket of her robe and called Vera.

"It's here," she announced when Vera had answered. "The interview."

"I'm on my way over," Vera assured her. "I absolutely can't wait to see it!"

Chapter 81

It was amazing how much gear was needed when bringing small children to the beach, Hayley thought. Just as she had finished packing her car with diaper bags, a small cooler, a beach chair, and a sail bag stuffed with a blanket and towels, Ethan had come dashing from the house, carrying a canvas bag, asking if she would mind if he came along. For a moment Hayley thought she had misheard, but when he stood there, smiling and obviously waiting for her reply, she hurriedly told him that of course she didn't mind. Ethan ran back to the house for another beach chair, checked that the girls were securely in their car seats, and got into the front passenger seat.

"Thanks again for letting me join you," Ethan said when they were settled—and it had taken some time—on the sand midway between Ogunquit and Wells.

There was no need for Ethan to thank her, Hayley thought. He was a Whitby. The girls were his sisters. He had a right to be anywhere they were. But she could expect politeness from Ethan. He had shown her that more than once. "Sure," Hayley said with a smile.

Ethan smiled back and opened the book he had brought, a copy of *The Dante Club* by Matthew Pearl. Hayley, too, had brought a book, the Eliot biography she had bought the other day, though she didn't expect to do much reading, not when there were energetic toddlers to keep an eye on. At the moment, though, the girls were quiet, busy filling plastic pails with sand, patting the sand with plastic shovels, and dumping the sand, only to repeat the process again and again.

After a while, lulled by the heat of the midday sun, Hayley began to wonder if people passing by assumed that she and Ethan were a couple, here in Ogunquit with their children to spend a quiet week at the seaside. . . . Hayley shuddered. The fantasy—and that's what it was—alarmed her. It made her feel warm and fuzzy, and that was a dangerous way to feel. Her goal was to keep her emotions entirely out of her plan for betterment and escape. If it wasn't already too late for that. She remembered the absolute surety of the connection she had felt between herself and Ethan as they had stood so close to each other on that corner the other morning, after he had rescued her from sure disaster. . . .

Hayley shot a glance at Ethan. He was not gazing at her with longing. He was frowning in concentration over a page of his book. So much for connection. Hayley sat up straighter in her chair. She became aware that an elderly woman in a diaphanous caftan seemed to be making her way toward them.

"Your children are absolutely adorable," the woman said as she approached. "You must be such proud parents."

Hayley gripped the arms of her chair. She was unable to reply.

Ethan laughed and gestured between Hayley and himself. "We're not together," he said. "These are my sisters. But they are adorable, aren't they?"

"Oh, pardon my mistake," the woman said, putting a hand to her cheek, before continuing on her way.

Ethan resumed reading. Hayley released her grip on the arms of her chair. What an idiot she was! How quickly Ethan had denied their being a couple! It only proved what she had already known, that fantasizing was a very stupid thing. And to think she had supposed he had wanted to kiss her that morning in Yorktide.

"You okay?" Ethan asked. "You're frowning."

Hayley managed a smile. So, he had been looking at her. "I'm fine," she said. "My mind wanders."

"Laylay hat," Lily announced loudly. Indeed, her sister had taken off her hat yet again and had tossed it aside.

Hayley watched Ethan lean forward and gently place the sun hat back on Layla's head. "Who's your favorite Disney princess?" he asked when he had sat back in his chair.

The question took Hayley by surprise. "I don't know," she said. "Belle, I suppose."

"Because you love to read?"

"Yes," Hayley said. "That, and I always thought the Beast looked pretty sexy. Not that that has anything to do with why I like Belle," she added hurriedly. It had been an idiotic thing to say.

"I think my favorite Disney princess—" Ethan laughed. "Hey, don't look so surprised. I watched all the movies growing up; guys aren't immune to pop culture."

"Sorry," Hayley said. "I know that."

"Anyway, I think my favorite princess might be Merida from *Brave*."

Hayley smiled. "That came out only about six years ago."

"I might have borrowed a DVD from a friend," Ethan explained with a shrug.

"So, why Merida?" Hayley asked. He really was awfully cute, admitting to watching Disney movies as an adult.

"Because she's an individual. She's courageous, and she involves herself in clan politics for the good of the community. And Mulan," Ethan went on. "She's impressive, too. And Tiana. All those characters are determined to live their own lives, but none of them pursues their futures without regard for their families and friends. They're tough, but they have a heart. In comparison, the older Disney princesses seem pretty passive. Of course, they were a product of a time and place, but still, if I were going to choose someone to spend the rest of my life with I'd choose Merida over Cinderella any day." Ethan smiled. "Assuming, of course, she chose me back."

Hayley managed a smile. It didn't come as a big surprise that Ethan admired strong, independent women, not women who looked to a man to give them a free ride through life. Hayley felt terribly uncomfortable. An honest man like Ethan would probably never even suspect he was the target of a gold digger, even a gold digger who wasn't sure she had the coldness it took to snare a millionaire.

"I know our culture isn't perfect," Ethan went on, "but I'm glad my sisters will grow up in a world that allows them to be strong individuals. It would be horrible if they had to grow up in a society that forced them to conform to old stereotypes or to have to rely on a man for a purpose."

Hayley tried again to smile but failed. If Ethan only knew what she had been planning! *Had* been? Was she really no longer interested in ensnaring Ethan? No. She wasn't. She was interested in *knowing* him. That was different. That was impossible. That was another stupid fantasy.

Ethan's phone rang, and he looked at it with a frown. "It's my office. I really should deal with this, and the paperwork is at the house. I'll walk back. Can you manage on your own?" he asked as he rose from his chair and began to pack his bag.

"Of course," she snapped. "I've sat for triplets in the past. These two are no problem."

Ethan looked confused. "I just meant that I could come back later and help you pack up."

Hayley shook her head and smiled. "Sorry. I mean, thanks. I'll be fine."

"See you back at the house, then." Ethan gathered his things and, with a wave, headed off.

Hayley sighed. Almost every experience in her life thus far had taught her to be ready to take offense. To be ready to fight. To be ready to defend herself. All Ethan had intended was a kind offer of help, but what had come first to her mind was the assumption that he was doubting her ability to do her job. Amy was right. There was no way she would ever be able to fit easily into Ethan Whitby's kinder, gentler world, not after the life she had led. No. Way.

"Layla," Hayley said with a sigh. "Why is your hat off again?"

Chapter 82

Amy was alone in the Priors' kitchen with nothing to do but wait until Cressida came out of her office, where she had retreated some time earlier. All morning Amy had been feeling bad that she hadn't paid more attention to the piece her mother had written for *Needle and Thread*. In fact, she hadn't really heard a word of it. Now she vowed that when the interview for that journal was published she would read it really carefully, and when the article for *Needle and Thread* was in print she would do the same.

It was almost noon. Amy's stomach growled. Maybe Cressida would be coming out of her office soon, not that noon necessarily meant lunchtime to her. On the bright side, Cressida had been in a pleasant mood that morning. Whatever had caused her bad behavior that horrible day in Portland seemed to have been resolved. That was a very good thing because Amy had worn herself out engaging in rationalizations. Maybe Cressida had been suffering from PMS. It could be seriously bad. Or maybe there had been a crisis at the headquarters of Prior Ascendancy. Maybe Cressida and Will had had a nasty fight that morning. Of course, no matter what had happened Cressida shouldn't have behaved so abominably, but on occasion everyone said and did things they shouldn't. Right?

Amy heard footsteps on the stairs, and a moment later Cressida came into the kitchen. She was wearing running gear. Her pupils looked dilated and she was sniffing.

"Are you getting a cold?" Amy asked, hoping Cressida wouldn't think her interfering. "My mom's friend Vera swears by this herbal stuff. I could get you a bottle if you want."

Cressida waved her hand dismissively. "No, no, I'm fine. Just dust. The stupid housekeeping team must have forgotten to properly vacuum my office. I'll have a word with them. I'm going for a run."

"Is there anything I can do for you while you're out?" Amy asked.

Cressida suddenly smiled. "Just be here, Aimee." And then she was gone.

Amy looked helplessly around the kitchen, hoping to find something that needed doing, but every dish and gadget and pot or pan was perfectly in place, as if none of them had ever been used. Just as she was about to wander into the living room Rhiannon came in from the patio. Once again, she was wearing head-to-toe black.

Rhiannon cocked her head to one side and studied Amy. "You're just like the other one," she said after a moment. "Not exactly like. You're prettier."

"Thanks," Amy said. "But what do you mean by the other one?"

Before Rhiannon could reply—and Amy had no idea if she would or what she would say if she did—Will appeared in the doorway.

"There you are," he said brightly, as if he had been looking for his daughter for hours. "Couldn't you find the trail mix?"

"I'll get it for you," Amy said hurriedly. She went to the breadbox that never contained any bread and handed the bag to Rhiannon.

When Will and his daughter had gone back outside, Amy rubbed her forehead. She had the strange feeling that something was being kept from her. The way Rhiannon had looked at her with such scrutiny. Who was "the other one"? And why had Will appeared just as Rhiannon might have been about to tell Amy what she now realized she wanted to know?

Or did she want to know? Amy sighed. How had it come to feel like another interminable day?

Chapter 83

It was not often that Leda found herself with time to spend enjoying a day in Portland. Truth be told, she didn't really have the time now, not with all of the jobs on which she was working and those that were waiting in the wings. But, she thought, if you didn't take a few hours every once in a while to refresh your senses and fill them with new sights and sounds, you could very easily go stale. And for a craftswoman that was a real nightmare.

Helping her to make the decision to leave Yorktide by ten that morning was an invitation she had received from one of the artists who had a studio at the Birch Tree Fellowship, an artists' studio and collective in Portland's West End. Sam, a printmaker she had met several times over the years at various craft fairs, suggested she come by to see some of his more recent work and to take a tour with him of the site.

Leda left her car in a garage close to the Old Port and arrived at the Fellowship's headquarters at about eleven, where she was greeted warmly by Sam. After catching up, Sam guided Leda through the print shop, the woodworking shop, a large space for artists who worked in clay, and the gallery where artists took turn displaying their work. Leda was impressed to learn that the Fellowship ran fund-raisers and sponsored sales and presented talks by the various members and affiliated guests.

"This is just an extraordinary place," she told Sam when they had completed the tour.

"I'd argue if I could," he replied with a smile. "I swear my work has taken directions it might never have taken since I've been a part of this community."

After studying Sam's latest works, Leda made her farewells and walked back toward downtown Portland. There was such a strong sense of community at the Fellowship, she thought. It had appealed to her, especially now that she was taking steps, however small, to become more than a solo practitioner in the world of creative enterprise. Well, maybe the steps weren't so small after all. She had agreed to the interview with the *Journal of Craftwork* and had shared its publication with Vera and Phil, though not yet with Amy. Adelaide Kane, owner of The Busy Bee quilt shop in Yorktide, had called to congratulate Leda on the piece and to invite her to one of the shop's open house evenings.

She had also agreed to write the piece for *Needle and Thread* and had just received word from an editor there that her essay had been accepted and that the check for $200 was on the way. And, perhaps most courageously, she had submitted one of her works to the FAF's annual competition. If all that didn't count for something, then Leda didn't know what did.

When Leda reached the Arts District, centered on downtown Congress Street, she stopped to chat with a young man selling miniature watercolors. He told her he was a student at Maine College of Art majoring in painting. Leda could see why. His work was extraordinary. She asked him why he had chosen to paint in miniature, and with great enthusiasm he explained his inspirations. Leda was moved by his passion and bought one of his works. The young man thanked her profusely, and Leda went on her way with a smile.

Her next stop was the Maine Jewish Museum. It was housed in a restored synagogue that had been built in 1921. Leda had never been to the museum before and was thrilled to learn of its many wonderful programs and events. While there she was able to view an impressive and very moving photography exhibit by a woman who had survived the Holocaust. To experience the horrors of such an event and yet to come through with her creative spirit still intact and perhaps even stronger than it had been before. . . . Leda wished she could meet the woman, now long deceased, and profess her thanks. Her own occasional struggles with her work, her own habit of self-doubt, seemed trivial, even ridiculous, compared to the struggles this artist must have faced. Leda left the museum moved and chastened.

A glance at her watch told her it was time to head back to Yorktide. As Leda made the journey toward the Old Port where she had parked her car, she realized that she hadn't walked so much in years. Her legs felt rubbery, but her spirits felt very robust indeed. The little watercolor safely in her bag, Leda knew that this day had been one of the most profitable and inspirational days she had spent in a very long time.

Chapter 84

That evening the group at The White Hart consisted of Hayley, Cathi, Michelle, and Sarah. Amy had pleaded a headache. Madeleine was accompanying her employers to a performance at The Ogunquit Playhouse, and Elizabeth had given no reason for her absence. That wasn't unusual. She kept to herself most of the time.

Hayley wasn't really in the mood to socialize, but her mother had told her that Eddie Franklin had invited a buddy over to the apartment for dinner, and though a part of Hayley felt she should stay to help her mother cook and serve the men, who would no doubt be entirely ungrateful, another, ever so slightly stronger part of her allowed her to walk away from a situation for which her mother was largely responsible. If Nora Franklin could learn to say no to her husband, even once. . . . Hayley picked up the menu. As long as she was here she was determined to enjoy herself as best she could.

But before Hayley could scan the menu to see what caught her fancy, some instinct made her look over her shoulder. Taking a seat at the far end of the bar was Ethan Whitby. Her heart beat more quickly. She hadn't seen him since he had left the beach the day before. By the time she got back to the house with the girls, he had gone off to an event at the Portland Museum of Art. When she had arrived at the Whitby house that morning there had been no sign of him. She had felt disappointed but had ruthlessly pushed the feeling away. Ethan had a full life that had nothing to do with his sisters' summer nanny. The nanny who had hoped to catch his attentions for her own selfish purposes. The nanny who, in spite of her best laid plans, had developed an affection for him.

"I'll be back in a minute," Hayley said to the others at the table. She got up and walked toward the bar. "Hi," she said when she was standing at Ethan's side.

Ethan looked up from the menu he was studying and smiled. "Hey! This is a nice surprise. What are you doing here?"

Hayley gestured toward the large table at the back of the room. "Hanging out with some of the other summer nannies. What about you?"

Ethan shrugged. "Marisa invited a few of her colleagues from the college for dinner, and I didn't want to be in the way."

"You've come to the right place if you want sports talk."

"Good. I can hold my own when it comes to the Red Sox."

"The Red Sox pretty much rule around here."

"Okay. Good."

An awkward silence followed this awkward exchange. Ethan held Hayley's gaze. She held his. She felt slightly sick to her stomach. This was what she wanted, wasn't it, to capture Ethan's interest? But no. Not like this. Not like—

"I should get back to the others," Hayley blurted.

Ethan cleared his throat and nodded. "Right. See you tomorrow."

Hayley hurried back to the table.

"So, who was that?" Cathi asked when Hayley had slipped into her seat. "He's very attractive."

"He looks like that guy from *Grantchester*," Michelle said. "The one who plays the vicar. Swoon! Or, wait, maybe that guy from *Outlander*, the one who plays Jamie! Double swoon!"

"He's the son of my boss," Hayley explained. "He lives in Connecticut, but he comes to visit his sisters. Well, his half sisters."

"Does this person have a name?" Cathi asked.

Hayley took a sip of her beer before answering. "Ethan," she told them.

Michelle leaned in. "Are you . . ."

"Absolutely not!" Hayley declared.

"Wise," Cathi said. "It's never a good idea to get too close to an employer—or his handsome son."

Sarah nodded. "It's always an abuse of power when someone in charge allows himself to get sexually involved with an underling."

"Did I ever tell you guys about my friend Jessica?" Michelle asked. "About three years ago she fell hard for the son of the family for whom she was working. His parents found out and threatened to cut him off without a dime if he didn't drop Jessica, and of course he did. She was heartbroken."

Hayley took another sip of her beer; her throat suddenly felt parched. Back when she had decided on her so-called plan to ensnare Ethan into marriage she hadn't considered the possibility that opposition from the Whitbys might prevent anything at all from happening. God, how stupid she had been!

"It's like we're servants really, not employees," Sarah was saying. "And we're certainly not members of the family no matter how much we kid ourselves that we matter."

Michelle nodded. "And yet sometimes they act like we're part of the family. Don't spread it around, but both Mr. and Mrs. Morris walk around in their underwear. At first I was like, what? And then I realized it's just what they do when they're home."

"That sort of behavior isn't about considering you part of the family," Sarah contradicted. "That's about their not acknowledging that you're a person. Take my bosses. They talk about all sorts of personal things right in front of me. It's as if they think I'm just part of the furniture. It never seems to occur to them that if I was an unscrupulous sort I could very easily tell the entire town their personal business or use the information to my advantage."

"So, Hayley," Michelle asked, "tell us what oddities you've been subject to under the Whitby roof?"

"None, actually," Hayley said.

Cathi laughed. "Oh, come on. Don't tell me that like Amy you're in awe of your employer?"

"Not at all," Hayley assured the others. "I'm sure Mr. and Mrs. Whitby have their quirks and their quarrels but never when I'm around. They treat me as a professional. They treat me with respect." And how, Hayley wondered, had she repaid that respect? By scheming and lying and . . .

Sarah frowned. "Lucky you."

"I wonder if Elizabeth deludes herself into thinking she's part of the Buchanan family," Cathi mused.

Sarah shook her head. "More's the pity if she does. And I bet Madeleine believes her perfect employers consider her indispensable. She's so complacent about her position with them. It drives me nuts when she goes on about all the perks she gets. Like going to the theatre tonight."

"I wouldn't want to spend my free time socializing with my boss!" Michelle shuddered.

"Hey, Hayley," Cathi said, "what's with Amy and the Priors? What do they really need her for?"

Hayley shrugged. She didn't feel comfortable giving an opinion on Amy's unusual arrangement with the Priors, especially when Amy wasn't present. "I have no idea," she said.

Michelle laughed. "It's not Will Prior who wants her around. It's Cressida who needs Amy at her beck and call."

"It kind of gives me the creeps," Sarah admitted. "Something about the way Amy talks about her boss seems wrong."

Cathi leaned in, her eyes wide. "Do you think there's something sexual going on?"

"No," Hayley said firmly. "It's not sexual."

"What we do is so, I don't know, so boring," Sarah pronounced.

"I hardly think caring for someone else's children counts as boring," Cathi argued. "I think it's pretty important. Okay, even when it's boring."

Michelle grinned. "I love those psycho nannies from the movies. *The Hand That Rocks the Cradle* always freaks me out, no matter how often I see it."

"Ugh," Cathi said with a grimace. "I hate horror stories. Give me *Jane Eyre* any day. I love how Jane Eyre stands up to Rochester, knowing he could fire her and she'd be nowhere. And then when she comes back to him in the end, knowing she's facing social ruin but willing to do so just to be with him. Sigh. So romantic."

Sarah shuddered. "So sickening, you mean. *Jane Eyre* is a horror story! Rochester is a monster! Keeping his insane wife locked up like an animal and trying to trick Jane into marrying him, which would totally ruin her if the truth that he was already married ever came out. Selfish bastard."

"Yeah, but Rochester says *he* was tricked into the marriage to Bertha," Cathi argued. "He married her for her money without knowing she was mad. What choice did he have once he discovered the truth but to lock her up to keep her from harming anyone? Insane asylums of the time couldn't have been much better than an old attic."

Tricking someone into marriage. . . . Hayley smiled vaguely while the talk flowed on around her. She was acutely aware that Ethan was only yards away. . . .

"Would you ever hire a manny?" Michelle asked the group.

Sarah shook her head. "Absolutely not. I would only hire a woman to watch my kids."

"Men are nurturing, too," Cathi pointed out. "I'd rather hire a nice guy than a bitchy girl."

That comment evoked laughter and agreement. Hayley thought of how good Ethan was with his sisters. He would make a fine father one day. A fine father and a . . . Hayley could no longer resist the desire to turn toward the bar. Ethan was looking directly at her. He smiled, got up from his seat, and lifted a hand in a gesture of farewell. Hayley lifted her own hand in return. She felt a terrible urge to leave with him, to walk along the darkened beach at his side, to feel the warmth of his hand in hers. . . .

Hastily, Hayley turned back to her companions. Each one of the women was eying her with an inquisitive, penetrating look.

"Hey," Hayley said brightly. "Should we get an order of nachos?"

Chapter 85

Amy had left for work very early that morning at Cressida Prior's last-minute command. Again, there had been no reason given for the summons. Amy hadn't had time for coffee or breakfast. Hopefully, Leda thought, Cressida would provide more than cucumber juice or a kale shake for lunch.

Leda looked at her watch. Hayley was coming by shortly to pick up a few fabric samples to show to Marisa Whitby. The day before, Marisa had contacted Leda about ordering a set of throw pillows for her house back in Connecticut. They had discussed ideas, and Leda had offered to drop off a few fabric samples for Marisa to examine. Marisa had thanked Leda for the courtesy. "I'm a bit overwhelmed with my class this week," she admitted. "I'd love to visit your studio, but at the moment I'm in over my ears!"

But Leda's plan to deliver the samples to Marisa that morning had been foiled when the dishwasher suddenly wouldn't function. A repairman was due between eight and noon, which made leaving the house during that window out of the question. And then it had occurred to Leda that Hayley might be willing to take the samples with her to work. Luckily, she had caught Hayley just as she was getting into her car.

When Hayley arrived, Leda offered her a cup of coffee, which she declined, and then handed Hayley the canvas bag full of fabric samples.

"It's very nice of you to bring these to Marisa," she said. "Thank you."

"It's no worry," Hayley assured her.

"What do you think about Amy's relationship with Cressida Prior?" Leda asked suddenly.

"It doesn't matter what either of us thinks, does it?" Hayley said. "Amy is obviously smitten, but crushes usually don't last for very long."

"I certainly hope this one doesn't." Leda hesitated before going on. "Look, you'll tell me if you see or hear anything, well, anything really worrisome, won't you?"

"I wouldn't feel comfortable breaking Amy's confidence," Hayley said promptly.

"Of course not. I didn't mean that." Leda smiled. "I don't know what I mean, really."

"Don't worry, Mrs. Latimer. Amy will be fine. The Priors will go back to Atlanta at the end of the summer and Amy will belong to us again."

"I certainly hope so. Will you apologize to Mrs. Whitby for my not delivering the samples in person?"

"Sure," Hayley promised.

When Hayley had gone off, Leda went up to her bedroom to get dressed. How sensible and mature Hayley was, Leda thought. Nothing shook her equilibrium for long. And Hayley certainly would never find herself in the situation Amy was in; she was too level headed and sharp eyed to be taken in by anyone.

Leda opened her closet and pulled out a comfortable sheath dress. She so wished Hayley would meet a good man who wouldn't allow her family's poor conduct to diminish her value as an intelligent and kindhearted individual. But the question remained, Would Hayley ever allow herself to fall in love and to be happy? Leda had a sorry suspicion that she might not.

Chapter 86

"Um, why did you want me to come in early today?" Amy asked. "I mean, it's fine," she added hurriedly, "no problem at all. I just wondered."

"Because I've got an important call at seven-thirty and my idiot husband isn't here to supervise the children." Cressida sighed. "He's gone off to the local emergent care facility."

Amy's stomach tingled. "Is he all right?" she asked.

"Of course he's not all right," Cressida snapped. "He was bleeding all over the place. It was disgusting."

Amy didn't dare ask how Will had gotten hurt. She didn't want to know that Cressida might have had something to do with it.

"He'll definitely need stitches," Cressida went on. "For all I know he might even lose the finger. But that's his problem. If he's stupid enough not to know how to properly use a kitchen knife, then he got what he deserved."

Amy's stomach felt worse. Cressida's lack of sympathy was stunning. But maybe cutting his finger with a kitchen knife was something Will was always doing and Cressida was simply tired of his careless behavior.

"I want you to supervise Rhiannon and Jordan while they play chess," Cressida went on. "I don't want any interruptions."

Then she went off to her office for the important call. It was only the second time that summer that Amy had been asked to spend time alone with the children. Suddenly she remembered the bag of casual clothes she had brought to work with her on the first day. The bag was still sitting on the backseat of her car. The shorts and T-shirt were probably a mass of wrinkles by now.

Rhiannon and Jordan were in the living room, seated across from each other at the low coffee table. Amy wondered if Cressida knew that her children sat on the floor. Even though the house was kept spotless by a team of cleaners, Cressida wasn't likely to tolerate her family sitting anywhere other than on raised and sterilized surfaces.

"Hi," Amy said. She sat on the couch. It was as hard and unforgiving as a park bench. Rhiannon, staring hard at the chess board, ignored her. Jordan gave her a small smile.

Though Amy was very sorry Will was hurt, she was kind of glad he wasn't around. She felt so embarrassed in his presence. She wondered if he knew that his wife routinely bad-mouthed him. He didn't seem downtrodden or depressed, but he had to be. No one could be entirely immune to abusive behavior.

Amy was beginning to suspect that Will stayed in the marriage for the sake of the children; after all, he was obviously the primary caretaker. Maybe Cressida had threatened to withhold custody should he decide to leave. And why didn't Cressida leave the marriage if she despised Will so much? Then again, Cressida's marriage wasn't her business. But Cressida had *made* it Amy's business by telling her things she probably had no right to know, like that Will wore boxers instead of briefs and that he suffered from indigestion.

"That wasn't a smart move."

Amy startled. She had almost forgotten the children were there.

Jordan frowned. "Yes, it was."

"Amy?" Rhiannon asked. "What do you think?"

"I'm sorry," Amy said. "I don't know anything about chess." *So much for meeting the children's intellectual needs*, she thought.

Jordan looked back to the chessboard. Amy shifted uncomfortably on the couch. She wondered what the children really thought of her, when they thought of her at all. Rhiannon often looked at her with a sort of detached, critical gaze; clearly, she had been assessing Amy in relation to "the other one." Amy thought that Jordan might actually like her but that his shyness prevented him from reaching out to her. His shyness and the fact that his mother rarely allowed Amy any interaction with the children.

Rapid footsteps on the stairs alerted Amy to the fact that Cressida was returning to the living room. Oddly, she didn't scold the children for sitting on the floor.

"Your father called," she announced. "He's on his way home."

"Is Daddy okay?" Jordan asked.

Cressida rolled her eyes. "He didn't lose his finger if that's what you're asking."

The little boy flinched. Rhiannon put her hand on his back and led him from the room.

"You should do something different with your hair, Aimee," Cressida said with a frown. "Those curls aren't doing you any favors. They make you look immature."

Amy managed a smile. "Okay," she said.

"I'm going for a run. Don't let the children cause trouble."

When Cressida had gone, Amy put her head in her hands. Why was Cressida always telling her to change? Why was she always finding fault? Amy raised her head and sighed. Maybe Cressida wouldn't mention the job offer in Atlanta again and Amy would never have to give an answer either way. In spite of what she had told Hayley, the idea of moving away with the Priors had come to seem totally unappealing. At the same time, Amy knew she had a very difficult time saying no to her boss. Sitting on the hard couch in this sterile house by the sea, Amy felt trapped by her own weakness.

Suddenly Jordan reappeared. Amy hadn't heard him coming. The boy made so little noise, not like most boys his age.

"I can't get this open," he said, holding out a tube of craft glue. "Can you help me?"

"Sure," Amy said. She was pleased to be of some use to one of the children, and getting the cap off a tube of craft glue was certainly something she could handle. Unlike advice about chess.

"Here you go." Amy smiled and handed the opened tube back to Jordan.

"You're nice," the little boy said.

Nicer than "the other one," Amy wondered. "Thank you," she said. "You're nice, too."

As quietly as he had come, Jordan left the room. A moment later the sound of the front door opening followed by a shouted greeting informed Amy that Will was back. She was tempted to tell him that she wasn't feeling well and that she needed to go home. Will would understand.

But Cressida would not. Besides, Amy thought, if she went home now she would lose the money she would have earned by staying put. Amy rose from the couch and went to greet Will. She would ask if there was anything she could do to help. She hoped that there was. Taking money for doing nothing was wrong.

Chapter 87

"Nice sneakers," Marisa said, pointing at Leda's pale green Keds.

Leda laughed and pointed at Marisa's identical sneakers. "Great minds think alike. I got mine at Reny's."

"Me too." Marisa looked around the studio. "This is a fantastic space," she said. "I'm glad my class got cancelled so I could visit."

"Thanks. The studio was my mother's before I came to share it with her and eventually, after she died, to take it over entirely."

"It must have been nice working side by side with your mom." Marisa laughed. "My mom and I are so totally different we never could share much of anything except a love of cherry pie."

"So," Leda said, "you wanted to talk about a custom bedspread and matching pillow shams in addition to the throw pillows?"

"And possibly curtains, if you don't think that's too matchy-matchy. I know it's a bit decadent, but I just can't seem to find anything I really like in the stores. When Hayley told me about your custom work I thought, Why not? She's really been a godsend this summer, you know. The girls adore her, and I totally rely on her."

"She's an extraordinary young woman," Leda said, "but I'm not sure she knows it."

"Has she had it tough?" Marisa asked. "I've heard a few rumors at YCC but . . ."

"She's had a difficult home life, yes. Honestly, she's like a rose among cacti in that house. The real problem is that Hayley has such an overdeveloped sense of responsibility toward her mother. Too often she ignores her own needs. I just wish . . ." Leda shook her head. "I'm sorry. I've said too much."

"No worries," Marisa said. "Mum's the word."

Leda opened a book of fabric samples and laid out several photographs of work she had done for other clients. For twenty minutes the two women talked through ideas, and Leda took notes and made sketches. When both felt they had made a good start, Leda brought light refreshments to the studio.

"My daughter is nanny for the Prior family," she told Marisa when they were seated at the little table at which Leda entertained her clients, sipping tea and munching cookies.

Marisa's eyebrows shot up. "Really? I can't say I have a very high opinion of Cressida Prior, not that I've met her more than once or twice, and that in a large social setting. Her husband is all right, at least compared to Cressida."

"Amy says he's a very hands-on parent. Do you know if he works?" Leda asked.

Marisa frowned. "I don't think he does. I seem to remember hearing that before the kids were born he worked for Cressida's company, Prior Ascendancy."

"But Prior is *his* last name?"

"As far as I know. I can't quite figure them out as a couple," Marisa admitted, "and frankly I'm not sure I want to. I love those tassels you showed me," Marisa said suddenly.

Leda laughed. "They're great as long as you don't have cats. I keep anything that dangles far away from Harry and Winston."

"No cats. But when the girls are older I think Jon and I will get them a dog."

After another twenty minutes Marisa took her leave. As Leda cleared the tea things she thought about what she had learned about the Priors. It wasn't much, but she was interested to know that she wasn't the only one who was puzzled by the couple. And she was very glad to discover that unlike Amy, Hayley was genuinely appreciated and valued by her employers.

Chapter 88

Nora Franklin was opening a cardboard box of frozen French fries when Hayley entered the kitchen. She had to hand it to her mother. No matter how small or battered the kitchen in which she found herself forced to work, she kept it clean and tidy.

"Your brother called earlier," her mother announced.

That was news, Hayley thought. He hadn't been heard from since that letter she had misdirected back in the spring.

And then she felt a jolt of panic. "He's not coming home, is he?" she asked bluntly. Brandon showing up in Yorktide and wreaking his usual havoc could easily result in Ethan Whitby's discovering the lies Hayley had told him. It could also result in her being fired. Hayley thought it a miracle that Eddie Franklin hadn't already gotten her sacked by showing up at the Whitby's house drunk and demanding money. Then again, he had probably forgotten where his daughter was working for the summer, assuming he had ever paid attention in the first place when his wife had let slip that Hayley was employed by a wealthy family.

"No," her mother said. "At least he didn't say anything about coming home. But he did say he sent me a letter a few months ago. I never saw it. Did you?"

Hayley shrugged. Her conscience was clear. "Nope," she said.

Nora dumped the contents of the cardboard box onto a baking

sheet. The clattering of the frozen French fries bothered Hayley. "Your brother says he needs money."

"My brother needs a job," Hayley spat. "Don't send him money, Mom. We can't afford it."

"We must be able to send him something," Nora pleaded. "He says he hasn't had a decent meal in weeks. Maybe you could ask the Whitbys for an advance in your pay?"

Hayley felt as if her mother had slapped her across the face. It was an insult that Nora Franklin thought nothing of asking her hardworking daughter to sacrifice her pride for the sake of her bum of a brother.

"Absolutely not," she said firmly.

"But why?" her mother asked, a look of sincere confusion on her face. "You said they're decent people."

"They are decent, which is why I'm not dragging them anywhere near our pathetic family problems. The subject is closed."

Nora Franklin hung her head and turned toward the oven. She might have ceased pleading with her daughter, but Hayley knew it was likely her mother would send her next paycheck to her son. As if Hayley wouldn't notice the absence when she reviewed the bank statement at the end of the month.

A feeling of anger tore through Hayley's gut. Why, she wondered, did she even bother to make things right when almost every effort met with resistance or failure?

"I'm going out for a while," she said. "I need some fresh air."

Her mother turned around; her face was a mask of worry. "You won't be gone long, will you?" she asked.

"No, Mom," Hayley said with a sigh. "I won't be gone long."

Chapter 89

"So, what do you think of this dress?" Cressida asked. "It's a Saint Laurent."

Amy restrained a grimace. She didn't like to lie, but there was no way she could tell Cressida the truth, which was that the dress looked awful on her. It wasn't the fault of the dress. It was the fact that Cressida was way too thin.

"Well?" Cressida demanded.

"You look great," Amy said brightly. "The dress looks awesome on you."

Cressida turned again to the full-length mirror that hung on the back of the office door. "It does, doesn't it?"

Amy watched Cressida turn from side to side and wondered what her employer saw when met with her reflection. She suddenly felt slightly sick watching Cressida preen and pose. She thought of that old story, "The Emperor's New Clothes," in which the emperor was so vain and self-deluded he believed he was dressed in the finest ensemble when in actuality he was naked, duped by a cunning tailor and a fawning court. *I'm no better than those characters,* Amy thought, *lying right to Cressida's face.* But would telling the truth really help Cressida? Or was she so far out of touch with reality she was incapable of accepting the truth?

Suddenly, before Amy could attempt to puzzle out the answers to those thorny questions, Cressida was all business. She strode toward the hall and gestured for Amy to follow.

Will and the children were seated at the kitchen table. There was a sketchpad open before Rhiannon, along with a box of colored pencils. Jordan was eating a carton of yogurt.

Will looked up from the day's edition of the local newspaper. "There's fresh coffee," he said.

Cressida poured herself a cup and took a sip. And then she made a face of disgust and threw the cup at the wall. It shattered spectacularly. "Your father can't do anything right," she snapped. "He can't even manage a decent cup of coffee."

Amy felt a sudden cold shock run through her. She knew there was nothing she could say. She wondered if she should clean up the shattered cup and the spilled coffee that was dribbling down the wall and spreading across the floor. But she couldn't seem to move a muscle.

Jordan was staring down at his yogurt; Amy couldn't read his expression. Rhiannon's expression, however, was clear. For a moment, Amy thought the girl was going to shout at her mother. Will must have thought so, too, because he gently squeezed Rhiannon's shoulder, and she was silent though her expression remained tense. It was a supremely uncomfortable moment, one the likes of which Amy had never before experienced.

But things were about to get worse. Suddenly, Cressida strode over to the table and picked up Rhiannon's sketchpad. "That's as good as you can do?" she said with a sneer. "That line is completely crooked, and the perspective is off." She dropped the sketchpad onto the table and went to the fridge, where she removed a bottle of the expensive fizzy water she preferred. Bottle in hand, Cressida stalked from the kitchen. "Come to my office in fifteen minutes, Aimee," she called over her shoulder.

When Cressida had gone, Will busied himself clearing away the shattered cup and spilled coffee. Amy had never felt herself at such a loss. She wasn't sure it was her place to provide the emotional sustenance a mother wouldn't or couldn't give. Besides, she had a feeling that Cressida would be angry with her for stepping into the heart of a domestic situation. But Cressida had left the room. Amy walked over to the table and looked down at Rhiannon's drawing. She was no art expert, but she could see that Rhiannon had talent. "I think your picture is really good," she said.

"Thanks," Rhiannon muttered.

Amy bit her lip. Her heart felt as if it might break. Why had Cressida had children in the first place if she didn't seem to have even one ounce of maternal feeling?

"I like the frog," Jordan said with enthusiasm. "It looks so real."

Rhiannon managed a small smile. "I'm almost out of paper. Do you think we could get another sketchpad, Dad?"

"Absolutely." Will rejoined the children at the table and took his daughter's hand.

"Excuse me," Amy mumbled, turning away. "Cressida needs me in her office."

Chapter 90

"What brought this on?" Leda laughed and returned Amy's bear hug.

"Nothing," Amy said, releasing her mother and going over to the love seat, where she flopped into a corner. "I just thought I'd give you a hug."

"Thank you very much. And here's some good news. I have another new client. Marisa Whitby. She bought one of my pieces from Phil and then contacted me about doing a custom project. She came to the house to talk about options. She's a very nice woman and has a lot of respect for Hayley."

Amy nodded. "Yeah. Hayley said she's cool. Mom?" Amy said suddenly. "What do you think of my hair? Do you think the curls make me look silly or immature?"

It took no great imagination to conclude that Cressida Prior had criticized Amy's naturally curly hair. "No," Leda said firmly, "I don't, but it shouldn't matter what I or anybody else thinks. You should wear your hair the way you want to wear it."

Amy began to fiddle with one of her curls. "I was thinking that maybe I could buy us a new microwave," she said. "They're not expensive, and the one we have now kind of dies when you try to defrost something."

Leda thought of Amy's purchases this summer—the fur hat, the evening bag, the shawl. "Save your money," she said. "Our household budget can cover a new microwave."

"Okay." Amy shifted on the love seat to a more upright position. "You know, the other day I was kind of thinking that I should return that velvet shawl. I mean, when am I going to get to wear it? And then I read the return policy and you can't return sale items. I should have checked before I bought it."

Leda nodded. "Lesson learned," she said. "And it is a beautiful shawl. Life is long, Amy. I'm sure one day you'll have an opportunity to wear it."

"I suppose." Suddenly Amy got up from the love seat and was gone from the studio.

Leda turned to her work. What exactly was going on with her daughter Leda wasn't sure, but she felt a bit of hope take hold in her breast. It seemed that Amy might finally be growing up. At least, she might finally be breaking free of the stranglehold Cressida Prior had had on her these past months. And that would be something worth celebrating.

Chapter 91

"Nice look, Dad." Ethan laughed and smoothed a tuft of his father's hair that had been sticking up comically.

Jon Whitby laughed as well. "I've got a cowlick as bad as Alfalfa's." He looked to Hayley. "Have I dated myself?"

"No," Hayley assured him. "I love *The Little Rascals*. Will you be here for lunch?" Though feeding the adults of the house was not in her job description, Hayley found that she wouldn't mind making sandwiches for father and son.

"Nope," Ethan said. "We're going to play golf with one of Dad's old cronies and have lunch at the club." Ethan grimaced. "We're both terrible players, but it's a game people who work in our business are pretty much obliged to play."

"And the food at the clubhouse is terrible," Jon added. "They can't even make a decent chicken salad sandwich."

Ethan put his arm around his father's shoulder. "Cheer up, Dad. We'll stop for a hot dog at Flo's on the way back. Bye, Hayley. I hope the girls don't give you any trouble while we're gone."

When the men had gone, Hayley headed upstairs to the twins' bedroom. Her heart felt so full she thought she might cry. She couldn't help but wonder if her brother might have been a better person if his father had treated him with affection and respect. If Eddie Franklin had even once bothered to help his son with homework or to take him to the park to toss around a baseball, Brandon might now be a productive member of society rather than his own worst enemy. It was impossible to know for sure what might have been, but it was a question that too often haunted Hayley.

Hayley found both Whitby girls sitting up in their cots.

"I brush my hair," Layla announced, pointing to the dresser on which the hairbrushes, combs, and other toiletries were kept.

Hayley smiled and brought Layla's brush to her. "Lily? Do you want to brush your hair?" she asked. Lily considered the question for a moment before shaking her head in the negative.

As Hayley set about tidying the room, she wondered if there was something she could do for her brother. The problem was, she had no concrete idea of what sort of help might benefit Brandon or even if he would consent to be helped toward a better life. You couldn't force a person to change if he didn't want to, and especially not if he felt he wasn't up to the challenge. It had to be true that sometimes doing nothing to help a person was better than doing the wrong thing. Didn't it? Or was inaction a form of enabling?

Lily suddenly pulled herself to her feet with the help of her cot's rail. "Out!" she demanded, at which her sister stood and demanded the same. Hayley smiled. Her poor brother might be a lost cause, and maybe the same could be said for Hayley in some respects, but here were two children who had a very good chance of becoming healthy and happy adults.

Chapter 92

Amy glanced across the desk at Cressida, her head bent over a thick bound document. Cressida had set her the task of sorting through a large box of plastic-coated paper clips. Cressida preferred to use red paper clips. The others Amy was to throw away. It was a ridiculous task, totally unimportant, not the sort of work a mentor would set for a protégé whose future she took seriously.

Amy restrained a sigh. She wished she could talk to her mother or Hayley or even to Vera about Cressida's odd behavior. For so long she had gone on about how wonderful Cressida was to whoever would listen. To admit that she had been wrong would be a serious blow to her pride, but . . .

There was a knock at the open door. Amy automatically turned to see who it was and quickly turned back. The last thing she wanted was to be a witness to yet another unhappy exchange between Will and Cressida Prior.

"I brought the mail," Will said, approaching the desk.

Amy tried to keep her eyes down but couldn't resist a quick glance upward, just in time to see Will hand an envelope to his wife. Cressida pulled the envelope from him with a grimace. Amy quickly looked down.

Without another word, Will left the room.

At least, Amy thought, there had been no slap. She had never seen Will be anything but pleasant and respectful to Cressida. But when Will was alone, how did he feel about his marriage? Did he resent his wife's success and her attitude of superiority? He simply couldn't be happy, could he? There were people who sought to be punished or made miserable; Amy had learned about them in a psychology course. Masochists, they were called. Maybe Will was a masochist.

Amy returned to the ludicrous chore Cressida had set her. She wasn't in the habit of giving other people's sex lives much thought, but in this case she simply couldn't help it. The Priors shared a bedroom, so there had to be some degree of intimacy, even if they slept in separate beds. But how could Will want to make love to his wife knowing she thought him a failure? If they were having sex it must be mechanical and loveless, simply a marital chore that one or both of them insisted on just to quiet an itch. Amy was a virgin by choice, and she knew she probably harbored an overly romantic view of what sex should or could be, but still, even the most sexually mature person must consider the notion of sex in a loveless relationship less than ideal. Wouldn't she?

"Aimee! Are you working or daydreaming?"

Amy flinched. "Sorry," she said quickly, pulling another red paper clip from the box.

Then Cressida smiled brightly. "I've an idea. Let's go to the kitchen and make those kale shakes you like so much."

With difficulty Amy managed a smile. "Okay," she said. There was no point in saying no to Cressida Prior.

Chapter 93

"Guess who I saw earlier?" Vera said. "Hayley and Ethan Whitby. They were coming out of The Bookworm. They were smiling."

"There's nothing unusual in that, is there?" Leda said. "Books do make people happy."

"The smiling isn't what I found interesting," Vera explained. "It was the fact of their being together, though the Whitby kids were with them. And one of the waiters at the restaurant was being catty to my hostess about girls from the gutter aiming way too far above their heads. It was clear he was talking about Hayley, because he went on to mention Eddie Franklin by name, as if Hayley has any relation to that creature other than an unfortunate biological connection."

"And you stood there and listened to malicious talk?" Leda asked.

"Only for a minute, and then I told them both to get back to work. The point is that people are talking."

"Do you think there's something between Hayley and Ethan?" Leda asked.

Vera shrugged. "How would I know? Though I have to say they look *right* together. I know that doesn't mean anything, but there you have it."

Leda considered. Frankly, it was difficult to imagine a relationship of substance between Hayley and Ethan ever getting off the ground, let alone proceeding smoothly into the future. Leda was not enough of a romantic to believe that love could conquer all obstacles, like a vast social divide, strong family opposition, or in this case Hayley's own well-known aversion to the dangers of romance. Still, wonderful things did happen, assuming that a relationship between Hayley Franklin and Ethan Whitby would be a wonderful thing and there was no way to know. Marisa certainly approved of Hayley as a mature and intelligent young woman, but that didn't mean she wanted her for a daughter-in-law.

"Has Amy said anything about them?" Vera asked, interrupting Leda's musings.

"No. But Amy hasn't been spending much time with Hayley this summer."

"Of course," Vera said. "The almighty Cressida has Amy in her bony grip."

"How do you know it's bony?"

"I've seen her. I'd like to drag her into Over Easy one of these days and force-feed her my blueberry pancake special."

"Forget about Cressida Prior. I just hope that if something romantic is brewing between Hayley and Ethan Whitby, Hayley stays on her usual guard." Leda frowned. "So many things might go wrong. I would hate to see her get hurt."

"Everyone gets hurt at least once in romance, and I should know. But I understand what you're saying. The kid has had enough thrown at her what with that family of hers. So," Vera asked, "how are you handling all this waiting around for the FAF to announce the winners?"

"Not well. To be honest, it's driving me a bit crazy, but I have plenty of work to keep me busy."

"Work is the antidote to so many unpleasant things," Vera said. "Retirement is overrated."

Leda smiled. "I'm not sure everyone would agree with you."

"No, I suspect most people wouldn't. But then again, I am an oddball, aren't I?"

Chapter 94

"This place is great," Ethan said with a smile. "Well, I suppose anywhere you can have lunch with the ocean a stone's throw away would be."

Hayley smiled. "I don't often get to The Razor Clam. When you suggested we have lunch I thought, now's my chance."

Ethan laughed and dug into his fried clams.

The day before they had run into each other at The Bookworm, where Hayley had taken the girls for story hour. Before they had parted Ethan had asked if she wanted to meet for lunch today. "I know you probably have lots to do on your day off," he added hurriedly. "But . . ."

"Sure," Hayley had said promptly. But she had hardly slept the night before, not with memories of their chance meeting at The White Hart, the feel of Ethan's hands on her shoulders as he pulled her from the path of the speeding car, the image of his lovely face running through her mind. Hayley had finally gotten out of bed at five that morning. A hot shower and several cups of coffee had revived her enough to face what might turn out to be a verifiable date with Ethan, an event about which she felt very, very confused.

And now here they were at noon, sitting across from each other at a picnic table, a man and a woman, not really friends, not lovers, not . . . Hayley took a long gulp of her ice water and prayed she wouldn't do or say anything embarrassing. Or wrong. Or . . .

"I read this interesting article last night," Ethan said suddenly. "It made me think of what you told me about your taking a break from college to explore other avenues. According to this writer there's a sort of grassroots movement among young people today against going right into college after high school. In some areas, there's even a feeling against going to college at all. I can understand that. I mean, college costs are insane these days. It's just that it certainly doesn't hurt to have a degree." Ethan frowned. "That said, some of my college classmates graduated more ignorant than when they started."

"Partiers?" Hayley asked.

"Yeah," Ethan admitted.

"The idea of people throwing away their college years makes my blood boil. If you're lucky enough to have the money to go to college, then you shouldn't be stupid enough to waste the opportunity!"

Ethan smiled. "You sound just like my father. He's totally self-made, the first in his family to go to college, the first to pursue a career rather than a job. He knows what it's like to struggle. One of the reasons I have so much respect for him is that he never stooped to anything unethical or criminal to get ahead. That's not always the case with people who've reached the heights he's reached."

Hayley squirmed. You could very easily argue that what she was planning to do—what she *had been* planning to do, entice someone into a marriage for her own convenience—was seriously unethical.

"Do you think he's lucky as well as being smart and hardworking?" she asked. Luck was a topic about which everyone had an opinion.

"I don't know how to answer that," Ethan said. "I'm not sure I believe in luck. Bad things happen to everyone and good things happen to everyone. I guess what makes a difference between one life and another is how the person living that life deals with the good and the bad."

Hayley poked at her fried clams and considered. Some people believed that you made your own luck. Were they right? Was it possible to mold your future into a form that would benefit you without necessarily hurting others? Up until this summer Hayley's life had felt totally outside of her control. She had seen setting her cap on Ethan as a way to grasp control from the universe, to make her own luck. But in doing so she *would* be hurting someone. Ethan.

"You're very good with my sisters," Ethan said suddenly.

Hayley looked up from her clams and smiled. "Thanks," she said. "I love children."

"Then you must be excited to have a family of your own."

Hayley hesitated. "I look forward to having a family with the right man," she said carefully.

"I love kids, too," Ethan said, "and I definitely want a family. Only one problem. I haven't met my children's mother."

"Has there been someone serious?" Hayley asked. It was a normal, conversational question, wasn't it?

"Yes, there was," Ethan said. "I was almost engaged—I'd even started to shop for the ring—when she broke things off because she'd fallen in love with another guy."

"I'm sorry," Hayley said earnestly.

"I was, too," Ethan admitted. "I had no idea she was seeing someone behind my back, and someone I knew at that. That was three years ago. I'm still an unrepentant romantic but a wiser one."

"What was she like, your almost fiancée?" Hayley asked.

"She's a software designer," Ethan told her. "She has her own company now."

Of course Ethan's former girlfriend owned a software design company, Hayley thought a bit wildly. And this was the man she thought she could entice into marrying her, a woman who had achieved no more in her life than not quite two years at the community college and sometimes, only sometimes, being able to keep her mother from harm. Hayley managed a smile. "How did you two meet?" she asked.

"We were both traveling in Europe the summer after graduate school," Ethan explained. "We met in London through a mutual friend. Thinking back, I see that I was fooling myself from the start. I wasn't in love with Patricia as much as I was in love with the idea of someone wanting to get married and have kids. It was for the best that the relationship ended."

"Is she married to the guy she left you for?" Hayley asked.

"Yes," Ethan said. "There's no animosity between Patricia and me. I'm glad she's happy."

Hayley stared at the untouched pile of French fries on her plate. Of course Ethan was glad for his former girlfriend. He was a kind and generous man.

"Penny for your thoughts?" Ethan asked.

"Sorry," Hayley said, managing another smile. "I was . . . I was just thinking about an article I read the other day in *Town and Country*. It was about destination weddings. Italy is really popular. And the Caribbean islands are always in the top ten."

Ethan looked at her with surprise. "I didn't have you pegged as someone who reads *Town and Country*."

Hayley bristled. The entire conversation had gotten badly out of control. "Why not?" she demanded.

"I've seriously stuck my foot in my mouth now," Ethan said hurriedly. "I supposed you didn't read glossies because you seem so interested in more important things than debutante balls and destination weddings. But now that I know you do read about debutante balls and destination weddings . . . I still think you're really intelligent. I don't mean—"

Hayley laughed, ashamed of her earlier defensiveness. "Stop! It's okay, I get it. I *am* intelligent but that doesn't mean I don't enjoy some mindless downtime on occasion."

"Me too. Have you ever watched *Pawn Buddies*? It's a pretty good show. You can learn a lot about history."

"I'll take your word for it," Hayley promised. He really was adorable when he was being earnest.

"So, have *you* ever had your heart broken?" Ethan asked suddenly.

Hayley hesitated. She could lie again but . . . no. She couldn't lie. She just couldn't. "I haven't, actually," she admitted. "I guess it's because I've . . . I've never been in love."

"Some would say you're lucky," Ethan pointed out.

Hayley smiled. "We're back to the subject of luck."

Ethan leaned slightly forward and looked steadily at her. "Maybe I *do* believe in luck after all," he said.

Hayley looked steadily back at Ethan with no idea of what message her eyes were conveying. Could he possibly be referring to their having met this summer? She thought he might be. But of course not. That would be too perfect, and perfect things didn't happen to Hayley Franklin. To any of the Franklins.

Hayley was aware that the silence between them was beginning to stretch uncomfortably. Ethan must have thought so, too. "Maybe we should be going," he said suddenly, lowering his gaze.

Hayley got up from the bench. "Yes," she said. "All right."

Ethan carried their trays to a trash can and then rejoined Hayley. They began the walk to Ethan's car, parked at the edge of town. They had not gone far when Hayley heard someone call, "Ethan! Over here!"

Ethan turned in the direction of the voice, and a frown appeared on his face.

"A friend?" Hayley asked, looking at the man who had caught Ethan's attention. He was standing with his arm slung around the slim shoulders of a woman.

"No," Ethan said shortly. "Someone I work with. Come on. We'll have to say hello now that they've seen us."

As they approached the man and woman, both of whom looked to be around Ethan's age, Hayley swiftly took in the huge diamond ring on the woman's left hand, the handbag with a designer logo, the clothing that fit her perfectly. Though the day was sweltering, the woman looked perfectly cool and composed. Hayley was acutely aware of the sweat running down the back of her neck. The contrast between this woman and Hayley was glaring. At least it felt glaring to Hayley. For a brief moment, she wondered if Ethan noticed the extreme contrast and felt embarrassed to be seen with her. No, she thought. Maybe some men, but not Ethan.

"Imagine running into you here," the man said when Ethan and Hayley had joined the couple. Hayley took an instant dislike to him. If she had been a superficial sort, the weak chin and beady eyes might have turned her off, but it was something more significant that repelled her, a sense of assumed superiority that virtually oozed from him.

At the same moment that Ethan was saying, "Jeff, Marie, this is my friend Hayley," Hayley was saying, "I'm the Whitbys' nanny."

Hayley cringed, but Ethan smiled. "Hayley is nanny to my sisters this summer," he went on.

Marie extended her hand. "Nice to meet you," she said.

"You as well," Hayley replied.

Jeff did not extend his hand. Instead, he looked Hayley up and down in a way that was not only inappropriate but downright rude. Her blood began to boil and she was afraid her self-control was going to snap, but before she could slap him down with an acid comment, he was saying: "So, Hayley. Do you wear a French maid's costume when you're on duty?"

The anger that had flooded Hayley quickly morphed into shame. She had never felt so humiliated. The sweat pouring down the back of her neck seemed a cascade now, and she thought she felt a trickle making its way down her temple.

"Hayley is not a maid," Ethan said firmly. "She's a professional child-care expert."

"I had a nanny once," Marie said quickly, smiling at Hayley. "She was a godsend to my mother. I'm one of five kids."

Hayley managed a small grateful smile in return.

"We need to be off," Ethan said abruptly, taking Hayley's elbow in his hand, a gesture that at any other time and by any other person she would have resented. Then he was hurrying them away in the direction of his car.

"He's a jerk," Ethan muttered as they walked. "And mark my words, before long Marie will be sorry she agreed to marry him. I swear I'll never understand why otherwise intelligent women can make such idiotic mistakes when choosing a husband."

"Why do you think she chose Jeff?" Hayley asked, her voice a bit uneven.

Ethan frowned and took his hand from Hayley's elbow. "Money. His father makes mine look like a pauper. But all the money in the world won't make Marie happy living with that specimen. I just hope she realizes that before they have children. Without children, she'll be able to make a clean break."

Hayley felt ashamed. Maybe she and Marie were more alike than she had supposed.

When they reached Ethan's car Hayley walked around to the front passenger side door. "I usually fight my own battles," she said before getting in. "Thank you for defending me."

Ethan held Hayley's gaze over the roof of the car for a long moment. "It was my pleasure to defend you," he finally said. "I'm only sorry the need arose in the first place."

Chapter 95

Amy paced restlessly around her mother's studio. Harry and Winston were curled up back to back on the love seat. Every once in a while one of them would open a green eye just a little bit and track her progress to nowhere.

Amy was troubled. Maybe if she mentioned to her mother in a casual sort of way how harsh Cressida could be with her family, her mother might have a word of wisdom to offer, a bit of advice that might help Amy handle another uncomfortable situation at the Priors' house. She would not, however, mention the slap Cressida had given Will or the cup she had thrown against the kitchen wall. That might be giving away too much.

"It's funny how different people have different parenting styles," Amy said.

"Funny how?" her mother asked without looking away from her loom.

"Well, like how some parents are always praising their children for doing good work even if the work isn't really all that good. They just want to encourage their children so the children don't grow up with low self-esteem."

"And other parents?" her mother asked.

Amy shrugged. "Cressida, for example. She doesn't coddle Jordan and Rhiannon at all. In fact, she can be kind of, I don't know, tough on them. Like the other day, Rhiannon was drawing with some colored pencils and Cressida criticized her work pretty roughly. I thought the drawing was good and so did Will and Jordan. I don't know. I guess I don't see why a parent can't be nice about a child's efforts."

"Do you think the children are being mistreated or abused?" her mother asked, finally looking away from the loom. "Because if you do, you have a duty to report the behavior."

Amy paused. Did witnessing your mother throw a cup against a wall mean you were being abused? She just didn't know the answer to that question. "Nothing like that," she said quickly. "It's just different from how I grew up, so it surprises me. That's all. Really, Mom, forget it."

"All right." Her mother did not immediately turn back to her work. "By the way," she said, "do you know if Hayley is involved with Ethan Whitby?"

Amy swallowed hard. "I don't know. I don't think so. Why? Did someone say something? Because I don't know anything."

"Vera said she saw them coming out of The Bookworm one afternoon. That's all."

Amy felt relieved. "They probably just bumped into each other. You know."

"Well, if something is going on, I just hope Hayley doesn't get hurt. By the way, do you know what occurred to me the other day?" her mother asked suddenly. "I remember you mentioning at the start of the summer that there was a pool at the Priors' rental. But I haven't seen a wet bathing suit in our bathroom."

"That's another thing," Amy blurted. "Back when I started working for Cressida she told me there wasn't enough chlorine in the state of Maine to get her into the pool. She hates germs. But she lets the children swim in the pool. It seems inconsistent somehow."

"Maybe Will overruled his wife on the issue," her mother suggested. "But that doesn't answer my question. Why haven't you been using the pool? We've had some real scorchers this summer."

Amy began to flip through a book of fabric samples on her mother's worktable. "I just assumed Cressida didn't want me to," she said. "I mean, she never suggested I use it, so . . ."

"There's always the ocean if you want a swim," her mother said blandly before returning to her work.

Amy felt that she had been dismissed. She left the studio and headed for the stairs to the second floor. She wondered if she should have told her mother more of the odd things that had been going on at the Priors' house—there were so many from which to choose—but the opportunity was lost. Wearily, Amy climbed to her room. There was still a lot of tidying up to do there, like the bottom of the closet to clear out and the weird stain on the windowsill to scrub off. Maybe she would tackle one of those chores. Or maybe not. Probably not.

Chapter 96

Over Easy had closed for the day, but the staff was still busy putting the place to rights and planning for the following morning's crowd of diners. Leda and Vera were sitting in Vera's cramped office, drinking coffee and nibbling crullers.

"How does a girl from the Midwest know about crullers?" Leda asked, licking her lips appreciatively. "I always think of them as a New York City thing. Years ago, I met a woman vacationing from Brooklyn and we got chatting about pastries and such, don't ask me how, and she told me about crullers and bialys. Before then I'd never heard of either."

"It's my job to know about breakfast foods," Vera pointed out.

Leda nodded. "Of course. By the way, I asked Amy if there was something between Hayley and Ethan Whitby and she was pretty evasive, which leads me to think that something is indeed going on between the two. I suspect Hayley swore her to secrecy. I can't imagine Hayley wanting the scrutiny of every busybody in Yorktide."

"Really. Can you imagine what some would say about a member of the Franklin family presuming she was good enough to date a member of the Whitby family?" Vera shook her head. "There are always people who love to see the downtrodden kept down. Anyway, there's something I want to tell you. I'm thinking of opening a second, year-round restaurant. Well, I'll close for a few weeks around Christmas, of course."

Leda was surprised. "What about traveling during the winter months?" she asked. "Are you going to give up the spas and the canyons?"

"I'll have to for a while," Vera said, "at least until we've gotten through a few seasons and I know I can trust my manager, whoever that will be."

"So, what's behind this decision to expand your empire?" Leda asked, eyeing the plate of crullers on Vera's desk.

Vera shrugged. "Now that I'm eternally single I have more time to devote to my career. And like I said the other day, work is a perfect antidote to all sorts of unpleasant things."

Leda frowned. She had fallen down on the job of bringing Margot and Vera together, though it wasn't entirely her fault that both women remained single. Vera was the real roadblock, refusing to attend the poetry reading Margot's friend had given, dashing into the kitchen when Margot made an appearance at the restaurant.

"Eternally single?" Leda said, reaching for another cruller. "Isn't that a little dramatic?"

"So what if it is?" Vera asked. "I'm allowed to make an opera out of my love life or lack thereof if I want to."

"Of course. Sorry." Leda hesitated before going on. "If I can change the subject for a moment—"

"Please do!"

"Amy came to me with her concerns about the way in which Cressida treats her children. She swears they're not being abused, but she is surprised by the harsh way in which Cressida deals with them."

Vera shook her head. "Poor kids. No doubt Amy is right to be concerned. But you can look at her coming to you in a relatively bright light. The almighty Cressida Prior has flaws after all, and Amy is finally able to admit that."

"You're right. Still, I wish she'd never gotten involved with that woman in the first place."

"And I wish I were the Queen of Sheba." Vera got up from her chair. "Well, you know what I mean. Now, skedaddle and take the rest of those crullers with you. I want to get out of here before dinnertime."

Chapter 97

Nora Franklin was working an overtime shift at the grocery store and would be home before long, tired and hungry. Eddie Franklin . . . well, Hayley didn't know where her father was and didn't much care, as long as he didn't show up until after she and her mother had finished dinner. He was a sloppy eater, and it made Hayley feel sick watching him wipe his mouth with the back of his hand and take up spilled ketchup with his thumb.

Hayley was paying just enough attention not to slice her fingers as she topped and tailed the green beans. The major part of her mind was reflecting on the upsetting incident that had taken place earlier. Hayley was used to men eyeing her but never quite in the manner that toad Jeff had, and in front of his fiancée too. Ordinarily, faced with such a creep, Hayley would have lashed out, but this time it hadn't only been shame that had held her tongue. It had been respect for Ethan, a desire to spare him embarrassment in front of his colleague, no matter how odious that colleague was.

The encounter had been demeaning and had made Hayley's flesh crawl, but one good thing had come from it. Ethan had introduced her as his friend, not only as an employee of the family. Of course, Hayley couldn't be sure if he had used the word out of mere politeness or for lack of a more accurate term, which might be *acquaintance*. Still . . .

And the way Ethan had taken her elbow to usher her away from the scene of her humiliation. . . . It had been such a lovely gesture, a sign of genuine concern and respect. But maybe it hadn't meant all that much to Ethan. Maybe it had been nothing more than an automatic response. He had probably seen his father take his mother's and his stepmother's elbow on certain occasions and had absorbed the old-fashioned, gentlemanly habit.

Green beans washed and drained, Hayley turned to scrubbing and slicing a few potatoes for boiling. Snippets of the conversation over lunch at The Razor Clam ping-ponged through her memory. Patricia, Ethan's almost fiancée. His desire for children. *I'm still an unrepentant romantic but a wiser one.* That final, enigmatic comment about his believing in luck after all.

Hayley put the halved potatoes into a pot of roiling water and sank into a seat at the kitchen table. She felt disoriented. Happy. Sad. Uncertain. Ethan had asked her to have lunch with him. Could it possibly be that he liked her for who she was? But he didn't *know* who she was! She hadn't allowed him to know.

Hayley rubbed her head. A terrible, dreadful thought had come to her as Ethan drove her to the library that afternoon. (Of course she couldn't allow him to take her home.) Was it possible that she was falling in love? She had developed genuine feelings for Ethan Whitby, the man she had planned to use to her own advantage. *Genuine* feelings. That much she knew. But did those feelings translate to love?

Hayley heard a key in the door, and she jumped up from the table. A moment later her mother joined her in the kitchen.

"Dinner is almost ready," Hayley said with an attempt at a smile. Nora looked exhausted, the skin under her eyes bruised with weariness.

"Is your father home?" Nora asked, her tone flat.

"No," Hayley said. She couldn't tell from her mother's expression whether she was glad about or merely indifferent to Eddie Franklin's absence. "Sit down," she directed. "Have a glass of lemonade."

Her mother took a seat and poured a glass of lemonade out of the carton on the table. "Thank you, Hayley," she said after she had taken a sip.

Nora Franklin looked so small and stooped and worn out. Hayley swallowed past a lump in her throat. She was her mother's guardian. Maybe it shouldn't be that way, but it was. No matter what happened she could never, ever leave her.

"You're welcome, Mom," Hayley said quietly. "Dinner will be ready in a moment."

Chapter 98

Noah waved and jogged across the street to join Amy. "Hey," he said with a smile. He was wearing a T-shirt with the logo of the Meadtown Brewery. For the first time in their long acquaintanceship Amy noticed just how blue his eyes were, almost azure. How had she not noticed that before?

"Hi," she said. "How's it going?"

"Good." Noah stuck his hands in the back pockets of his jeans. "Look," he said, "I know it's last minute and all, but we just got a gig tonight at that new place out on Ridge Road. Do you think you can make it?"

"Sure," Amy said brightly. "I'd love to come."

Noah smiled. "Great," he said. "We start at eight. If you don't mind sticking around until the end of the last set, maybe we could hang out for a while and talk."

"That would be awesome," Amy said, and she meant it.

"Cool." Noah took his hands out of his back pockets and shoved them into his front pockets. "So . . ."

Amy felt herself blush. Since when had she felt shy around Noah? "I have to run," she said quickly. "I'm supposed to go right back to the house after I pick up Cressida's prescriptions at the pharmacy."

"Right." Noah took his hands out of his front pockets. "Then I'll see you tonight."

"Right," Amy said. "Tonight." Amy watched him jog back to his truck, a smile on her face.

"I want you to spend the night here, Aimee."

Cressida was dressed in a pair of leggings and a racerback athletic top. Amy realized she had never seen her employer in the same athletic wear twice. Athletic wear wasn't cheap. Not that Amy had ever had an interest in buying athletic wear.

"Are you and Mr. Prior going out?" Amy asked, surprised by this announcement.

"No," Cressida said flatly. "You don't have plans, do you?"

Amy hesitated. She really wanted to hear Noah's band. She still felt badly that she hadn't protested when Cressida had mocked him and wanted to make it up to him in some way, even if it was just by going to hear him play. But maybe if she stayed the night, Cressida would pay her the equivalent of overtime. The more money she could earn this summer, the less she would have to borrow from her mother come fall. Amy decided. She would apologize to Noah and promise to come to his next gig. He was a nice person. He would understand.

"No, no plans," Amy lied. "I'll just need to go home first and get my things."

"Nonsense," Cressida said with a wave of her hand. "You can wear one of my nightgowns, and the bathrooms are stocked with fresh toothbrushes. Unless you need some sort of special medications from home?"

"No, no medications," Amy said lamely.

Cressida smiled brightly "Then it's settled. You're a treasure, Aimee. I don't know what I would do without you. Now I'm going for a run."

When Cressida was gone, Amy sent a text to her mother and left a message for Noah at the brewery. And then she felt a sort of dread descend upon her. She wasn't at all sure she had made the right decision. Maybe the idea of spending the night with the Priors would be more acceptable if she considered it an adventure of sorts, though it wouldn't be a fun adventure if she was asked to play a game with the children that was beyond her intellectual capacity. And it certainly wouldn't be fun if Cressida decided to throw another cup against a wall or to lash out at her husband.

Suddenly, Amy recalled one of the conversations that had taken place among her fellow nannies at The White Hart earlier in the summer. Last year, Cressida had hired two nannies from two different employment agencies, and both experiences had ended in disaster for the women hired. Could Cressida Prior be banned from working with the established agencies? Was that why she had hired Amy privately? Yes, Amy thought. That very well might be the case.

"Damn," she muttered. "What did I get myself into?"

Chapter 99

Leda dragged the large box of craft supplies through the living room and into the studio. Her back hurt. She was out of breath. The usual UPS driver was always willing to lend a hand with the heavier deliveries to 22 Hawthorne Lane, but this driver had been new and patently not willing to do more than dump the hefty box on Leda's doorstep.

With a grunt, Leda shoved the box with her foot, and it came to rest against a leg of her worktable. She sank into her chair and opened her laptop to check her website. Lately she had become much better about keeping up with its maintenance and replying to messages and orders. And she was finding that it wasn't so horrible a task as she had once found it.

Leda glanced at her watch and compared the time to what appeared on the upper right of her computer screen. Ten o'clock. She had been woken that morning at seven thirty by a call from Amy. She hadn't told Leda much about her night at the Priors' other than the fact that she had eaten dinner with the family and then, in Amy's words, pretty much hung around while Will and the children disappeared to their bedrooms and Cressida read on her Kindle. Only when Cressida finally retired to bed just before one o'clock had Amy been sent off to the guestroom. She had been woken at six o'clock by a loud knock on the door. Cressida, it seemed, didn't need much sleep.

As for payment for her overnight services, Amy had told her mother—rather gloomily—that Cressida had given her the usual hourly rate. There had been no additional payment for her inconvenience. Amy had come very close to admitting that she should have clarified the issue of compensation before agreeing to spend the night. That, Leda thought, was progress. Amy's critical faculties, such as they were, hadn't been totally diminished.

Leda was busy replying to a few inquiries that had come in via the website when at ten forty-five her cell phone rang. She didn't recognize the number but answered nonetheless. A pleasant male voice introduced himself as a member of the FAF's panel of judges assigned to select this year's winners. Leda's heart began to pound. She knew what was coming next. She hadn't won. The call was a courteous way of telling the losers the bad news. It really was very nice of the FAF to choose a personal touch . . .

"Congratulations, Mrs. Latimer," the man went on. "Your tapestry entitled Stars Streaming was chosen in the Best Emerging Talent division."

Leda opened her mouth, but the only sound to emerge was a sort of gurgle.

"Mrs. Latimer?" the man said. "Are you there?"

"Yes," Leda croaked. "I'm here. Are you sure? Are you sure I won?"

The man laughed kindly. "I'm perfectly sure. In fact, you were the judges' unanimous choice for the prize. Congratulations. You'll be receiving a check in a week or two and the promised mention in the October issue of the FAF's newsletter."

Leda thanked the man profusely and ended the call. Tears began to leak from the corners of her eyes. Her first thought was to tell Amy, but she suspected Cressida Prior didn't approve of her employees taking personal calls at work. Instead she called Vera.

"Hot damn!" Vera cried. "You go, girl! I knew your work would be chosen!"

Leda laughed. "You knew no such thing, Vera."

"Okay, but I had a very good feeling."

Phil was no less enthusiastic; his praise brought more tears to Leda's eyes.

When they had ended their call, Leda grabbed her keys and headed out to the car. She would buy a bottle of Prosecco and raise a glass in a toast to herself. She had never done such a thing before. She deserved it. She really deserved it.

Chapter 100

The weather was downright idyllic—eighty degrees, low humidity, and only a few scattered clouds to mar a bright blue sky. Hayley, Ethan, and the girls were under the expansive awning over the back patio, the girls playing in their plastic wading pool, the adults stretched on lounges.

As usual, Ethan had a book in hand, this one a battered old paperback copy of *The Sun Also Rises*. His beautiful auburn hair flopped over his forehead. Hayley badly wanted to run her hands through it. Maybe, hopefully, she wasn't really falling in love with Ethan as much as she was simply attracted to him sexually. That would be more acceptable. That she could handle.

A half an hour or so passed and Hayley, her own book in hand, felt positively lulled by the calm ordinariness of the moment. Adults reading. Children playing. Was this what it was like to be part of a family not torn apart by strife? But this *wasn't* her family, Hayley reminded herself firmly, Ethan and Layla and Lily. Her family was Nora and Eddie and Brandon, and it would never truly be otherwise. She had to stop this dangerous tendency of fantasizing whenever she was with Ethan Whitby. She had to stop it now.

A buzzing from Ethan's phone took him away from his book.

"What is it?" Hayley asked when he had put his phone back

down on the little table by his lounge, his face set in a frown. "Not bad news, I hope."

"My friend Dan and his wife are getting divorced," Ethan said quietly. "I don't understand. They've been married less than a year. I was a groomsman. I saw how they looked at each other at the ceremony. They both had tears in their eyes."

"Maybe they weren't really meant to be together," Hayley suggested carefully. "Maybe it was only after the excitement of a big wedding and honeymoon wore off that they realized they weren't really in love."

Ethan sighed. "But after less than a year? And they've known each other for close to five years. You'd think after all that time a person would have a pretty good idea about his partner being The One."

Poor Ethan, Hayley thought. He was genuinely distressed. She wished she could say or do something to relieve some of that distress but . . . "Did your friend say why the marriage failed?" she asked softly.

"No. I'm sure he'll tell me when we speak in person." Ethan sighed again. "I dread the idea of a divorce, though I understand it can happen in what had once been the best of marriages."

Suddenly, Lily burst into tears. Layla looked stricken. She loved to splash in the little pool; clearly, while Hayley's attention had been focused on Ethan, she had gotten too wild. Hayley leaped from her lounge, and only as she was reaching for Lily did she realize that Ethan was at her side, reaching for Layla. He brought the penitent child to his lounge where she curled up in his arms, her head on his chest. Hayley brought Lily to her own lounge where, tears forgotten, she found great interest in the buttons on Hayley's shirt.

Ethan bent his head and kissed the top of Layla's strawberry blond head. "I often wondered why my parents didn't have more kids," he said, "but it's not something I feel I can ask about. Anyway, when my father remarried I got my wish for siblings. Not the way I imagined it would come about but. . . . You know," he said suddenly, looking over to Hayley, "contrary to what people might believe, my father didn't leave my mother for Marisa. My parents' divorce happened before my father met Marisa, and it was a mutual decision."

"Do you believe that?" Hayley asked.

"I do, though I'd like to know more of what led to the decision to part ways." Ethan shrugged. "I never saw my parents fight or even disagree about anything significant, but then again, marriage is a private thing."

"What's your mother doing now?" Hayley asked. "Is she remarried?"

"No," Ethan told her with a smile. "She's happy being single, at least for the moment. She spends most of her time traveling. She just got back from Hong Kong, and next month she's off on a cruise to Alaska."

And what would her mother do if she divorced Eddie Franklin? Hayley wondered. Nora Franklin wouldn't have the money to travel as far as Boston, let alone Hong Kong. And if she met another man, Hayley believed the chances were good that he would be cut from the same cloth as Eddie Franklin. Her mother simply didn't know any better.

"How often do you see your mother?" Hayley asked.

Ethan laughed. "Not often. Still, I have a feeling that once I'm married and my wife and I have a child, Grandma will be around a heck of a lot more often."

Hayley suddenly wondered if her own mother ever yearned for grandchildren. Strangely, it was a thought that had never occurred to her. "You seem to get along really well with Marisa," Hayley noted.

"I do," Ethan agreed. "It was a bit odd at first, having a stepmother only a few years my senior, but it wasn't long before I came to know Marisa as a person in her own right."

"How did she meet your father?" Hayley asked. Had it been a chance meeting? she wondered. Had it been the result of luck, a force in which Ethan said he might just believe?

"They met at a conference on contemporary Italian culture," Ethan told her. "Marisa was one of the speakers, and Dad was in the audience. He's passionate about Italy. In fact, he's in the process of buying a villa not far from Florence. Anyway, he went up to Marisa after the session to discuss some point or other, and that was pretty much that. They were married four months later."

Hayley smoothed a lock of hair from Lily's forehead. "So it was a whirlwind romance," she said. And then she looked over to Ethan to find him looking back at her steadily with those wonderful blue eyes.

"My father says you know when you know."

Before Hayley could react to these words, either in heart or in mind, Ethan's phone buzzed again, breaking the undeniable connection that had once again leaped to life between them.

"Sometimes I hate the phone," Ethan muttered. "It's work. I'm sorry." Gently he got up and put Layla securely on the lounge.

A few moments later Hayley followed him inside the house, girls in tow. Her heart was beating painfully and she felt ever so slightly sick. Ethan was nowhere in sight, and for that she was glad. She needed to think. She badly needed to think. Once the girls were thoroughly dried, changed, and settled on the floor of the den with a few toys, Hayley sank onto the couch near to them and rubbed her forehead.

Marriage. A sacred union whether or not you believed in a god. Hayley wondered if she had ever truly grasped what a marriage meant until now, this summer, in the company of the Whitby family. Until Ethan had come into her life. But why was that? He was no proselytizer, and she was no naïve acolyte. Could it simply be that her feelings for Ethan—of which sexual attraction was only a part, she knew that now—could it be that those feelings of admiration and respect and—

"A liddle lam a liddle lam a liddle lam!" Lily cried.

"Feece as white as snooo!" Layla responded.

Hayley shook her head. Wool gathering—she cringed at her own pun—was not allowed when two little lives were in your care.

Chapter 101

Amy yawned widely. She was alone in the kitchen the morning after the second night spent with the Prior family.

The experience had been even more strange than the first. The children had been silent at dinner; Amy had wondered if their discomfort was due to her presence or if dinners at the Prior house were always tense, what with Cressida monitoring what everyone ate and Will's few attempts at conversation shut down with a withering look from his wife. At one point during the meal Jordan had knocked over his glass of water. His eyes had gone wide with horror, and Amy had tensed, sure there was going to be a strong reaction from Cressida, but she had just turned to Will and asked him to wipe up the spill.

Again, Cressida had stayed up late, requiring Amy to sit with her in the living room while she read. Cressida had finally gone to her room close to midnight. A few hours later Amy thought she heard someone moving around in the house. Carefully she had opened the door of the guest room a mere inch, but it was enough to see that Cressida, wearing a thin white nightgown, was moving through the living room below. The word *wraith* had popped into Amy's mind before she had hurriedly closed the door again.

She hadn't slept after that, and two cups of strong coffee at seven a.m. had failed to revive her strength or her spirits. She was contemplating a third cup when Will came into the room, dressed in his ubiquitous T-shirt and cargo shorts.

"Good morning," he said. "I hope you slept well."

Amy returned his greeting but didn't respond to his comment. Will didn't need to know that the sight of his wife wandering the darkened house had unnerved her and sent all possibility of sleep running.

Will set about pouring a bowl of high-fiber cereal, humming while he did so. Amy, deciding against caffeine overload, brought her cup to the dishwasher.

"What are you two doing in here together?"

The cup dropped from Amy's hand onto the dishwasher's top rack. She whirled around to find Cressida in the doorway, a look of fury on her face, hands clenched at her sides. "Nothing," Amy said quickly. "I—"

Cressida took a step into the room. "Don't make excuses," she spat. "I told you on your first day of employment you were to come to me for instruction, not Will. And now I find you going behind my back after all I've done for you. It's insubordination. I should—"

Amy jumped as Will slammed the glass of juice he had been holding on the marble countertop. "Cressida," he said loudly and firmly. "That's enough."

His tone of voice made Amy flinch. She had never heard him speak in anything but a soft and gentle tone. She shot a glance in his direction. His expression was cold. Amy looked back to Cressida and held her breath.

"Of course," Cressida said after a moment. She seemed completely composed. "I'm just off the phone with my director of R and D. There's a problem he can't solve. My head was elsewhere. I'll be in my office."

It wasn't an apology, but it seemed it was all Amy was going to get. Amy waited for Will to say something, but he turned back to preparing his breakfast as if nothing extraordinary had just happened. She wondered if she should thank Will for interfering, but the words simply wouldn't take form. Quietly, she left the kitchen.

* * *

At around one thirty that afternoon Amy was with Cressida in her office. Her stomach was still in knots from the morning's confrontation. She snuck a look at her watch and willed the afternoon to be over.

"About earlier," Cressida said suddenly, looking up from her laptop and across the desk at Amy, who was occupied with sorting through a box of colored rubber bands. Cressida preferred to use only red rubber bands.

Amy tensed. She should have known the storm hadn't entirely blown over.

Cressida shook her head. "I really should fire the head of R and D. I can't be expected to deal with every little problem that comes up. That's what he's getting paid for."

"Right," Amy said. Agreeing with Cressida always seemed the right thing to do. She wondered if Will was going to suffer consequences for standing up to his wife that morning. Another slap across the face? She didn't want to imagine the scene.

"I knew you'd understand," Cressida said briskly. "Here. I have something for you." Cressida opened a drawer of her desk and with her clawlike hand she began to rummage through the contents. Amy remained rigid in her chair, wondering if she could somehow flee the room and never come back. Finally, Cressida's hand emerged holding a compact mirror. She thrust it toward Amy, who had no choice but to stand up and take it. The cover of the compact was made of mother-of-pearl tiles. One tile was missing a corner. "It's from the 1950s," Cressida explained. "Not my sort of thing at all, but Jordan gave it to me a few weeks ago—Will took the kids to some dusty, old antique place against my orders—and until a few moments ago I'd forgotten all about it. It's yours now."

Amy mutely stared at the compact in her hand. It wasn't until she had finally made her escape from the office—Cressida had sent her to fetch the mail—that the full awfulness of what had just happened struck her. Cressida Prior had just tossed away a gift given to her by her own son, a little boy who in spite of his mother's erratic and sometimes cold behavior nevertheless loved her. Amy came to a halt halfway down the stairs from the second floor. She wanted nothing more than to march right back to the office and tell Cressida Prior that she was wrong to have rejected her son's gift. But she knew she would do no such thing.

Amy continued toward the front door, her thoughts troubled. Cressida's gifts weren't about the recipient at all. They were payoffs for bad behavior. They were a way for Cressida to get rid of items that no longer served a purpose or that no longer pleased her. They were attempts at buying affection and loyalty. Her gifts were tainted with self-interest.

Amy retrieved the mail from the floor just inside the door and turned to trudge back up the stairs, but she stopped cold when she saw Will standing a few feet away. "Cressida said you can have the rest of the afternoon off," he said. His tone was pleasant and low. "I'll take the mail."

"Thanks," Amy said, holding out the small stack of bills and flyers. As soon as Will had taken the stack, Amy turned and left the house, grateful for the reprieve and wondering if her dismissal had indeed been Cressida's idea after all. But it didn't matter. She was free, at least until tomorrow. And she couldn't wait to see her mother, her wonderful Best Emerging Talent mother.

Chapter 102

"I think you'll like this new design." Leda placed her most recent sketch on the worktable. "I've colored in this end to give you an idea of the palette I have in mind."

"Your friend Vera," Margot said, keeping her eyes on the design.

Leda swallowed. "What about her?" she asked.

"Is she single?" Margot's tone was studiedly casual. "Just that I've never heard anyone mention she had anyone special. . . ."

"Most definitely single," Leda assured her.

"Was she ever in a long-term relationship?" Margot asked, still keeping her eyes on the tapestry sketch.

"What's your definition of long term?" Leda asked carefully.

"Over two years."

"Then, no," Leda admitted. And then hurriedly she added, "Not for lack of trying, mind you."

Margot finally looked up from Leda's sketch. "Can I ask you another question? Why have you been asking people about me?"

Leda grimaced. "You know."

"Small towns, big mouths."

"I'm really sorry. I was only trying to help bring you and Vera together. If I was assured that you weren't, um, nutty, I'd feel justified in trying to nudge things along. Assuming, of course, that's what you want, and I think that maybe you do, inviting us to the poetry reading . . ."

Margot gave a crooked smile. "And what did you find while you were checking my credentials?"

"That you're eminently *not* nutty," Leda said firmly. "See, in the past Vera has had rotten luck with women. It's not as simple as her always choosing the wrong person. Not that she hasn't made bad choices on occasion. Who among us hasn't? But even the ones who seemed perfectly normal turned out to be liars or obsessives, or worse, criminals."

"Criminals?" Margot's eyes went wide.

"Don't ask," Leda told her. "If it weren't so tragic it'd be funny. Let's just say Vera's become convinced she's meant to be alone for the rest of her life. But I don't think she really wants to be alone, and I know she likes you well enough, so I thought I'd help out a bit, at least get you two talking. Are you angry with me?"

"Of course not," Margot said. "I'm flattered you thought I might be a good match for your friend."

"Thank you. Vera knows nothing about my sleuthing, of course."

"Your secret is safe with me," Margot assured her. "So, do you think I stand a chance?"

Leda nodded. "If you can get her to drop the wall she's put up between herself and romance."

"And how do I do that?" Margot asked.

Leda smiled wanly. "I have absolutely no idea. Persistence?"

"I can be persistent, but don't worry, I won't cross the line to being a stalker."

"Good. Vera had a stalker once. It was very frightening."

Margot put a hand to her heart. "Oh Lord."

"I didn't mean to scare you away," Leda said hastily. "Really, Vera is a very normal and down-to-earth person."

"If you say so." Margot cleared her throat. "Now, about this design. Could it be worked in a different palette? Maybe a more neutral one?"

"Of course," Leda told her. "Let me grab some colored pencils and we'll experiment. And I'd like to invite you to a party Phil is giving in celebration of my winning the FAF competition. Vera will be there. It would be a convenient and no-pressure way for you to spend some time together."

"Sure," Margot said. "I'd love to come. It will also be a good way for me to meet more of my new neighbors."

Leda selected pencils in taupe and beige, cool gray and soft blue, and began to color in another section of the sketch. "What do you think of these colors?" she asked after a moment.

"Perfect," Margot said. "And, um, what about those criminals?"

"There were only two," Leda said quickly. "And one was a long time ago. Really, you have nothing to worry about."

Margot gave a half smile. "If you say so."

Please let me be right, Leda thought. *Please!*

Chapter 103

"Why did I suggest we come downtown today?" Ethan asked, giving Hayley a slightly pained look.

Hayley laughed. "I have no idea. A desire to play tourist?"

"I guess that's it. And I am a tourist, aren't I?"

Ethan was pushing Layla's stroller while Hayley steered Lily's down the sidewalk. The double stroller was simply too wide for the narrow, tourist-crowded streets of downtown Ogunquit. Still, in spite of the crowds and the snail's pace at which she and Ethan were forced to move, Hayley was enjoying the little excursion. She was with Ethan. She liked being with him. And at the moment she was not prepared to agonize over this fact.

Suddenly, through the throng on the sidewalk Hayley spotted a head of dark brown curls that looked awfully familiar. Amy Latimer.

Amy suddenly waved and made her way toward them. "Hi," she said, slightly out of breath.

"Ethan," Hayley said, "this is my friend Amy. She's the one working for the Priors this summer."

Ethan put out his hand to shake Amy's. "Nice to meet you," he said. Then he turned to Hayley. "Is this your friend whose mother made that beautiful tapestry Marisa bought for the Connecticut house?"

Hayley nodded. "Yes. Leda Latimer. And Marisa commissioned more work from Amy's mother."

Ethan looked back to Amy. "Your mother is really talented."

Amy smiled. "Thanks. She just won this big nationwide craft competition for Best Emerging Talent. She was also interviewed for a magazine, and another magazine asked her to write an article for them."

Ethan smiled. "You must be proud of her."

"I am." Then Amy looked down at the twins. "Who is who?" she asked.

Hayley introduced the girls. "Where are your charges?" she asked.

Amy flushed. "Their father has them today. Cressida is waiting for me back at the house. I just came into town to get her some things she needed. I guess I should be getting on."

"It was nice to meet you," Ethan told her.

"You too," Amy said, and hurried past them as best she could.

"Have you two known each other long?" Ethan asked as they continued to inch along the sidewalk.

"Since we were little kids," Hayley told him. "I don't remember actually meeting Amy. She's just always been there. Amy and her mother. Since Amy's father died, Mrs. Latimer has been on her own. She seems happy, though."

"Better to be alone and happy than in a relationship and miserable."

"Yes," Hayley said. That was something she truly believed. And yet . . . a marriage of convenience must be one of the loneliest places ever to find yourself. Who in her right mind . . .

"How's Amy holding up working for Cressida Prior?" Ethan asked.

"According to Amy," Hayley said, "everything is fine. But I have a feeling the truth is beginning to dawn. At least, I hope it is. Amy is a thoroughly good person, and that can be a liability at times."

"Like when you come under the influence of someone not so good," Ethan suggested.

"Exactly." Hayley smiled a bit. "I tend to see the negative or the possibility of the negative before anything else. With Amy, it's the other way around."

"I'm sorry you see the world that way," Ethan said feelingly. "Why do you think that is?"

"I don't know," Hayley answered with an exaggerated shrug and a laugh. "Just lucky, I guess."

"Ice cream!" Lily twisted in her stroller and looked fixedly at Hayley. For the quieter of the twins, she could be surprisingly forceful.

Layla seconded the demand. Loudly.

Ethan smiled. "Permission to stop at the ice-cream shop?" he asked.

"Permission granted," Hayley told him. "No extras for the girls, but you can have anything you want," she added, resisting the urge to lay her hand gently on his cheek.

"Yes, dear," Ethan said with a laugh.

Hayley followed Ethan as he navigated through the crowd toward the ice-cream shop. Her heart had started to beat wildly. What was she doing playing house? It was ridiculous. Nothing good could come of it. She was sure of it.

Ethan suddenly looked over his shoulder at her and winked.

Hayley smiled. She couldn't help it.

Chapter 104

When Cressida told Amy that she was sending her to downtown Yorktide on an errand, Amy's spirits rose. Anything to get out of the house for a while. Even the fact that the errand was to pick up a brand of seriously strong laxatives at the pharmacy didn't dampen her mood. As soon as she was behind the wheel of her car she texted Hayley in the hopes that she would also be in Yorktide that afternoon. Yes, Hayley had replied. She was taking the girls to the charming little park by the WWII memorial.

Errand completed, Amy sat on one of the benches in the park and waited for Hayley to show. She had bad news to deliver. Cressida had demanded she spend the night again and Amy hadn't had the guts to say no. Not that she wasn't upset with her lack of nerve. She was.

Look at what had happened the first time she had agreed to stay at the Priors' overnight. She had cancelled her date with Noah and hadn't heard again from him after he had sent her a text acknowledging the message she had left for him at the brewery. Anything Noah had felt for her might now be dead. And here she was about to let down her closest friend in favor of her boss. The radical idea of quitting her job had occurred to Amy but only briefly. Her grandfather had taught her the importance of not walking away from responsibility. She would finish out the summer as Cressida

Prior's . . . whatever it was. Besides, actually telling Cressida face-to-face that she wanted to quit was a terrifying thought.

There was Hayley, pushing the girls in a double stroller. She waved when she saw Amy.

"I can't go to the Mexican Kitchen with you tonight," Amy blurted the moment Hayley had joined her. "I'm sorry. I promised Cressida I'd stay over at the house."

"Another last-minute summons?" Hayley frowned. "You're being taken advantage of, Amy. What is this, the third time you've been asked to spend the night with little or no notice? What's involved with these night shifts, anyway?" Hayley asked, peering down at the two sleeping girls.

"You know, the usual things," Amy said with a shrug. "We eat dinner and—"

"And what?" Hayley asked. "What do you do for the rest of the night? Does Will stick around?"

"No," Amy admitted. "He goes to bed, I guess. Cressida reads one of her business journals and I read, too. And then she goes to bed and so do I."

"So, you don't actually *do* anything on these nights?" Hayley pressed.

"Right. The point is that I'm *there*."

"You get overtime for these do-nothing nights, I hope?"

"I get paid," Amy said. She had been wrong to assume that she would be compensated more grandly for night hours than for day hours. She supposed she could count the tokens Cressida had given her as the equivalent of overtime. There was the designer bag Cressida didn't want because it was last year's It model. That the lining of the bag was badly ripped didn't seem to matter to Cressida. And there was the silk scarf from Coach. The colors were gorgeous—teal and deep purple—but it was only after Amy had gotten home that she realized there was a large grease stain covering one entire corner of the scarf. Amy could only hope that whatever castoff Cressida decided to give her tomorrow wouldn't be something one of the children had given her, like Jordan's vintage compact.

"Well, I think it's odd," Hayley said.

Amy said nothing. She was tired of arguing that what she was asked to do for Cressida was normal or fair when in fact she knew that it was neither. "So," she said, "are you going to go to the Mexican Kitchen anyway?"

"Sure, why not? I enjoy my own company, and I'm not missing out on free chips and salsa. Anyway, good luck tonight."

I don't need luck, Amy thought. *I need* . . . But she didn't know how to finish the thought.

"It was nice meeting Ethan," she said. "He didn't act like I thought he would."

"The Whitbys are good people. Money doesn't corrupt everyone."

Amy wondered. Would Cressida be a nicer person if she didn't have such financial power, or did gaining financial power in the first place require a certain ruthlessness? But what about Will? He didn't seem corrupted by the cushy life he lived. Or had he in effect sold himself to the highly successful Cressida in exchange for those very comforts?

And what about herself? Had her own head been turned by the bundles of cash Cressida handed her at the end of each week? Had money blinded her to the truth about her employer? She remembered the unnecessary and impulsive purchases she had made that summer and regretted them. Amy sighed. Life was so complicated. People were so hard to figure out. At that moment, she felt very young and very clueless.

"So, how *are* things with Ethan?" she asked. "You two looked pretty cozy pushing those strollers the other day."

Hayley looked away. "Fine," she said.

Well, Amy thought, that was an evasive response. Maybe her question had hit a nerve. Maybe Hayley's scheme wasn't working as she had hoped, or maybe she had chosen to abandon it. But if either of those possibilities were the truth, why hadn't Hayley told her what was going on? Amy felt a twinge of guilt. Why *would* Hayley have come to her when all Amy seemed able to talk about was her fantastic mentor? The sad truth was that she hadn't been there for Hayley this summer. And if she hadn't been there for Hayley, she certainly hadn't been there for her own mother.

Amy rose abruptly. "I'd better get back," she said. "Cressida will be wondering what took me so long."

Amy lay on the bed in the guest room and stared blindly at the ceiling, wondering yet again how she had let herself get sucked into the dynamics of this family. There had been another upsetting incident that evening. When told to come to the table for dinner Rhiannon, in the living room watching a movie on the big-screen television, had called out that she would join the others in a minute. When two minutes had passed and Rhiannon hadn't made an appearance, Cressida had gotten up from the table and marched into the living room. Amy had sat frozen, hearing but not wanting to hear Cressida's shrill voice raised in anger. Then there had come the sound of a slap, followed by the pounding of feet running up the stairs.

When Cressida returned to the table her expression was grim. Neither Will nor Jordan said a word but continued to eat, eyes on their meal. Amy continued to poke at the plate of steamed vegetables before her, her appetite gone.

But there were only a few weeks left of the summer and then Amy's responsibility to the Priors would be over. And there was no way she would accept the offer of a job in Atlanta, assuming it was still on the table. She wasn't sure how she was going to say no to Cressida, but she would find a way. She hoped she would be able to find a way.

Lying there in the guest bedroom it occurred to Amy that while Cressida claimed to be a feminist she was nothing of the kind. The way she kept Amy in a state of uncertainty and inferiority was abusive. The way she refused to really empower her so-called protégé by setting her serious tasks proved that she had no respect for Amy. And the way Cressida spoke about her colleagues and employees was telling. Clearly Cressida favored competition over collaboration, and that seemed pretty classic male behavior. Amy had learned about such things in a class called Gender Politics. Too bad the lessons had slipped her mind.

The sound of a door opening and closing and then the creak of a floorboard caused Amy's heart to beat faster. Quickly she got out of bed and carried the white ladder-back chair to the door of the room, where she wedged it under the doorknob. She didn't really know what she was afraid of, but the memory of a wraithlike Cressida roaming the house in her long white nightgown suddenly frightened her.

Amy looked at the digital clock on the dresser. It was only two. Four more hours before she would be summoned.

Chapter 105

Leda sat at her usual table in Over Easy, sipping a cup of excellent coffee. "So, is this a new item on the menu," she asked when Vera joined her. "The challah French toast. Or have I just not noticed it before now?"

"It's new," Vera explained. "It seems to be a hit, too."

Leda put down the menu. "I have something to admit," she said carefully, "and I don't want you to be angry with me."

"What could you possibly have done that would make me angry? Unless you gave away my top-secret recipe for lemon curd. That just might be unforgiveable."

"Nothing like that." Leda sighed. "The thing is, I took it upon myself to ask around about Margot Lakes. You know, in case one day you and she might . . ."

"What do you mean ask around? Like, you did a background check?"

"An informal one, of course," Leda added hurriedly, "and I kept your name out of it. And the consensus is that Margot Lakes is perfectly normal. No criminal record. No secret husband. No obsession with worms like that woman you dated last year. Who keeps worms as pets?"

Vera shrugged. "She liked the fact that they were quiet."

"And Margot asked about you the other day. She wanted to know if you were single."

Vera looked down at her coffee. "Oh."

"I told her that you were. Are you mad at me?"

"No," Vera said, looking back to Leda. "I'm not mad. And thanks for telling me that Margot is interested. But I'll say it again. I'm permanently off the shelf. My sell-by date is a thing of the past. I've formally retired from the world of wooing and being wooed."

Leda sighed. "Okay. I give up. I formally resign from the world of matchmaking."

"Don't look so down. Thank you for caring so much about me, really. I appreciate that you're only looking out for what you believe are my best interests. But I'm just fine the way I am."

"Vera—"

"I don't badger you about getting out there and meeting someone, do I? Wait, don't answer that. Look, from now on neither of us will try to prod the other to date. Deal?"

Leda hesitated before replying. There really wasn't any need to mention to Vera that she had invited Margot to Phil's party. "Deal," she said.

"Are you excited about the party?" Vera asked, as if reading her mind.

"Excited and nervous," Leda admitted. "I wish Phil wasn't going all out for me."

"Nonsense. It will be fun. Is Amy coming?"

"Of course. Why wouldn't she?"

Vera shrugged. "Cressida Prior might require her presence again."

"Amy would never miss this celebration. She found the issue of the *Journal of Craftwork* with my interview the other day and was upset that I hadn't shown it to her when it first came in. I couldn't tell her that at the time I thought she wouldn't be interested. She cares, Vera, she really does. And I think Cressida Prior's spell is wearing off."

"The Wicked Witch of Yorktide." Vera frowned. "I'll need to see her melting to believe it."

Chapter 106

Hayley had lain awake all night, haunted—that was not too strong a word—by the memory of yesterday's outing in Ogunquit. She had known full well that playing "happy family" with Ethan was potentially dangerous and for all sorts of reasons. But she hadn't been able to remove herself emotionally from the moment no matter how hard she tried. And she had tried. She had tried very hard.

Things had really ratcheted in intensity once they had gotten their ice-cream cones and taken the twins to a small park off the main thoroughfare. Ethan and Hayley had sat side by side on a slatted wooden bench, the girls in their strollers set facing each other. Nothing much had been said, certainly nothing of great consequence, but the longer Hayley sat next to Ethan, her thigh just about touching his, her shoulder occasionally grazing his shoulder, the more she had felt almost faint with desire.

"Turn to me," Ethan had said abruptly. Hayley had turned, half expecting . . . With his paper napkin, Ethan gently wiped ice cream from the corner of her mouth. They had never been so physically close as they were at that moment, their faces mere inches apart, their eyes locked on one another. The tension had been almost unbearable until once again a child had interrupted the potentially explosive situation by making herself known, and loudly at that. Layla had turned her ice-cream cone upside down on the little tray of her stroller. Lily, finding this amusing, quickly followed suit and then, realizing that her ice cream was now not so easy to eat, had shrieked in dismay.

The incident had shattered the intimate moment. Ethan had laughed and righted Lily's cone, saving what he could of the ice cream. Hayley busied herself wiping Layla's face, covered with sticky vanilla goo.

They had gone back to the Whitby house after that. Ethan went off to his room to work, and Hayley hadn't seen him again. Lying in the bed that night she had realized she didn't know how much more of his proximity she could take without . . . without what? Her plan, that wretched thing, had long been abandoned, if indeed she had ever really embraced it in the first place. So, what now? What happened next? Nothing? Everything?

At four a.m. Hayley had given up on the possibility of sleep. She got out of bed, careful not to wake her mother. (And her father? He might be home or he might not be.) She had showered and dressed and left the apartment by five. The roads were largely deserted but for the occasional farmer bringing his produce to a market and a few others whose workday started well before nine. She had driven to the beach, where she had sat in her car—the morning was chill—and stared at the ocean, steely and gray, almost without conscious thought. When it was finally time to head to the Whitby's house, Hayley took a deep breath and started the car. Would Ethan be there? She hoped he wouldn't be. She hoped he would be.

She turned onto Overlook Road shortly thereafter, parked, and went into the house. As was her habit she headed directly to the kitchen.

Ethan was there. He was alone. "Hi," he said. He was wearing a rumpled chambray shirt, open to the middle of his chest. Hayley thought he might have slept in it. His jeans, too, looked as if he had spent the night tossing and turning in them on some uncomfortable surface, rather than in his own bed.

"Hi," Hayley said. She stood just inside the door, clutching the strap of her bag slung over her shoulder.

"Marisa is out," Ethan said. "The girls are asleep." Hayley could see him swallow hard. An electric sensation streamed through her, the likes of which she had never known.

"Hayley—" Ethan began.

After, Hayley couldn't remember how what had happened next had happened. All that mattered was that they found themselves in each other's arms, their lips pressed together as if their very lives depended on it. Hayley had no idea how long this glorious experience lasted. It could have been minutes. It could have been hours. When finally their lips parted, they clung to each other still.

Ethan traced the line of Hayley's cheek with his forefinger. "'The Brightness of her cheek would shame those stars as daylight doth a lamp.'" He smiled. "I played Romeo in my senior year of high school."

"I bet you were wonderful," Hayley whispered.

"Maybe not wonderful. Hayley," Ethan went on, his tone urgent, "I've wanted to kiss you almost from the first moment I saw you, but I felt it would be wrong. My father is your employer. I didn't want to put you in an awkward situation. I was going to wait until after the summer to ask you out." Ethan shook his head. "But this happened. I'm sorry."

Hayley thought that no one, not even the Latimers, had ever been so considerate of her feelings. "Please, don't be sorry," she said feelingly. "Just don't."

"I can't help but be. My father would be furious if he thought I'd compromised the peace of mind of one of his employees."

"I know. But I'm not without blame, too." Hayley smiled and put the flat of her palm against Ethan's chest. "Until now I wasn't sure you had any interest in me," she said. "Not romantically."

"When all along I was . . . I love you, Hayley Franklin. I really do."

Hayley felt faint and held Ethan more tightly. "And I love you, Ethan," she said. "Truly."

And then the sound of the front door opening . . .

"Give me your number," Ethan whispered. "I'll leave through the back door and get in touch with you later."

Hayley did, and gave Ethan another quick kiss.

Ethan smiled. "I really do believe in luck now. No, let's call it Fate with a capital F."

And then he was gone.

As footsteps made their way to the kitchen Hayley tried desperately to compose herself. It was not easy. A part of her wondered if she would suddenly wake to find that the past moments had been only a dream. How cruel that would be. . . .

Marisa appeared in the doorway, dressed in baggy sweatpants and sweatshirt. "Hi," she said brightly. "I thought I'd take a stroll this morning before heading out to YCC. It's a lovely day, isn't it?"

Hayley managed a smile. "Yes," she said. "It is."

"Is Ethan still here?" Marisa asked. "I left a message with him about my being out."

Hayley reached for a dishtowel and swiped at a nonexistent mark on the counter. "No," she said. "He left. He told me you were out."

Marisa went over to the coffeepot and poured herself a cup. She seemed in no hurry to leave. "Remember that student I told you about earlier this summer," she said conversationally. "The one who wasn't able to grasp most of what was going on but who seemed to enjoy coming to class?"

Hayley nodded.

"You'll never believe how things have turned out. Another of my students, one of the quickest learners in the class, has been tutoring Marjory for a few hours each week. They've become friends, and Marjory is finally absorbing the lessons. Isn't that fantastic?"

"Yes," Hayley said. "It is." She so wished Marisa would leave. She didn't know how much longer she could fake a normal conversation.

As if subliminally detecting Hayley's wish, Marisa looked at her watch. "Oops," she said. "I'd better get ready for work. I'll check on the girls while I'm upstairs."

Finally, finally Hayley was alone. She held on to the counter for support. She had kissed Ethan in his father's house. It wasn't like her to be reckless. How could she have been so . . . But she couldn't be angry with herself, not entirely. She was in love. For better or worse it had happened. She was in love.

Chapter 107

Amy's mother was making dinner. *She is such a good person*, Amy thought, slumped in a seat at the little table in the backyard. Even after a long, hard day at work she was always happy to make them a meal and ready to listen to whatever news Amy might need to share. *I don't deserve her*, Amy thought, digging a hole in the grass with the toe of her sneaker. *But what would I do without her?*

From the pocket of her lightweight jacket Amy removed a small, blue velvet box. The morning after the third odd night spent in the Priors' house, Cressida had given Amy another gift, this one for being "a star." It was a silver ring set with what for a split and mind-numbing second Amy had thought was a diamond, but that Cressida explained was a good-quality cubic zirconia. Amy had wanted to ask what Cressida, who by her own admission collected only "important" jewelry, was doing with a fake, but she didn't. Instead, Cressida offered an explanation that had left Amy feeling humiliated.

"I ordered it from one of those websites that sell mid-level costume jewelry," Cressida said. "One day you just might be ready for a real diamond of your own."

Later that morning Cressida had vaguely mentioned Amy coming with the Priors to Atlanta, but again she made no reference to a specific job at Prior Ascendancy. Amy was glad. She was not moving to Atlanta no matter how real a job she was offered.

And maybe it wasn't a good idea to move to Boston, either. She had allowed herself to be taken advantage of this summer, and that certainly didn't say much for her maturity. If she did decide to stay in Yorktide come September she would have to let Tracy, Stella, and Megan know as soon as possible so they could start the search for another roommate.

Amy opened the blue velvet box and stared at the ring inside. The awful thing was that she liked the ring. It was really pretty, but how could she ever wear it knowing from whom it had come and the spirit in which it had been given? Where was her pride? Why couldn't she throw it away? She felt an overwhelming flood of frustration. She wanted to turn the clock back to the spring, before she had first started thinking about working as a nanny this summer so that none of this craziness would have happened. But that was magical thinking. Magical thinking got you nowhere.

"Amy!" her mother called from the house. Amy—not Aimee—stuck the ring box into the pocket of her jacket and with a heavy heart went inside for dinner.

Chapter 108

Leda couldn't sleep. All day long she had been thinking about the notion of finding oneself at a crossroads, neither here nor there, betwixt and between. That's where she was at this moment in her life, at the proverbial crossroads. The truth was that at some moment in everyone's life a choice had to be made—this path or that path. You chose one and you lived with that choice, whether it turned out to be a good choice or bad.

Leda stared up at the ceiling fan slowly twirling its way to nowhere. At this moment in time she could either retreat or advance. She could refuse further interviews and requests for articles. She could keep her website small or even let it lapse. She could go on as she always had, reasonably content within a limited scope. Or she could open herself to a wider community of craftspeople and those who appreciated their work.

But the choice had already been made, hadn't it? By accepting Phil's formal gesture of acknowledgment—the party he was giving in her honor—Leda was in effect choosing the path that for her represented more risk, and quite possibly far more rewards. In the past few weeks, Leda had come to understand that there was a reason prizes were awarded and medals were bestowed, apart from the largely self-serving aspect in certain exalted circles. People needed to acknowledge in others talents they didn't themselves possess.

To accept that acknowledgment gratefully and thankfully was okay. It was more than okay.

Leda turned on her side and tucked her hands under her pillow. She wished her parents could be here with her now to share in this time of celebration. Funny, she thought. No matter how old you were, a part of you still wanted to make your parents proud. And Charlie. Poor Charlie. She would like it if he were by her side now, too. In a way, she supposed he was still with her. Amy was his daughter, and Amy embodied the best of Charlie Latimer.

It was no use. Sleep would come when it wanted to. Leda tossed the covers aside and went to the little desk in a corner of her room. There, she opened a sketchpad and with sure and rapid strokes she began to sketch a very intriguing idea that was blossoming in her mind.

Chapter 109

Hayley was alone but for a few stars and a sliver of a moon. It was ten o'clock. She was sitting on one of the benches in the parking lot at Ogunquit Beach. She didn't usually venture out at this hour, but her troubled thoughts had propelled her from the small apartment in search of air. In search of space in which to think.

Ethan. The thrill of their kiss, the ecstasy of having been told she was loved, it had been all too quickly replaced by a flat and certain realization of futility. There was no true romantic future for Ethan Whitby and Hayley Franklin. She had known that earlier in the summer, but she had let that truth be blinded by unruly emotion.

That Ethan had been telling the truth when he declared his love for her Hayley had no doubt. She also had no doubt that Ethan was in love with a fake. The real Hayley Franklin was unlovable. Who could love someone who had been compelled to physically restrain her own father in an attempt to prevent him from beating her mother? Who would ever believe that she had taken absolutely no pleasure or pride in such an action? Who would ever believe such a person wasn't forever tainted by such negative experience?

Hayley pulled the sleeves of her sweatshirt over her hands and crossed her arms over her chest. Alone at the edge of the ocean she realized that she was completely isolated. There was no one in her life to whom she could turn for comfort. Given the circumstances of her home life she had always been somewhat alienated, but to feel now at the tender age of twenty-one that she was completely alone in the world was truly awful. Would it always be this way?

Yes, Hayley thought. Because her past had made her what she was. Her past had made her a deceiver. And Ethan's past had informed his character; it had made him noble. Maybe that was an old-fashioned concept, but Hayley believed that nobility of character still meant something in this world. A noble person was a person concerned with the good of others, a person willing to put aside his desires for the sake of another's happiness or safety. And by not acting on his romantic feelings for Hayley for so long, that was just what Ethan had done. He had been protecting her. And what had she done for him in return? Nothing but consider him someone to use in order to achieve her own selfish ends.

Even if she were to come clean and admit to Ethan that she had lied and why, even if he were to forgive her and ask her to be his wife, one day he would realize that his love had been sorely misplaced and then he would leave her. Worse, he would stay with her for the sake of their children, and Ethan and Hayley would be prisoners in a loveless, resentful marriage.

Hayley shivered in the damp night air. Her father had just lost his most recent job. He swore it wasn't his fault. Her mother was sporting a suspicious bruise on her arm, a bruise she swore was a result of tripping over the living room rug and stumbling into the door frame. Her brother had left yet another drunken voice mail on her phone, asking for money because someone he thought a friend had stolen his last few dollars.

Would Eddie or Nora or the real Brandon Franklin ever be welcome guests at Jon Whitby's Italian villa or at the dining room table in their lovely Greenwich home? Would the Franklins and the Whitbys ever be able to engage in civilized, intelligent conversation about politics, or religion, or art, or even about the future education of their grandchildren? The answer to these questions was a resounding no.

It was better to end things with Ethan now before anything had really begun. It was for his own good. Hayley would tell him the truth about herself. He would probably hate her for lying, but she hoped he would forget her before too long. Hayley knew that she would never forget him, and that would be her proper punishment—a lifetime haunted by the memory of the only man she had ever loved. A good and decent man.

Wearily, Hayley got up from the bench overlooking the water and headed for her car. Who knew what mess she would find when she got home.

Chapter 110

"Why aren't you wearing the ring I gave you?" Cressida demanded. She was dressed in a racerback running top and leggings that came to just above her calves. Amy knew that "thigh gap" was a coveted thing among models and wealthy women, but this was ridiculous. Amy felt slightly sick to her stomach faced with the skin-and-bones woman before her.

"I didn't think it would be a good idea to wear it while I'm working," Amy said quickly. "In case it got damaged. It's so pretty."

Cressida seemed to accept that explanation. "I need you to watch the children tonight," she said. "Will and I are dining out."

Amy's stomach tensed. "I'm sorry," she blurted. "I can't. My mother's celebration party is tonight."

Cressida frowned. "Her what?"

"I told you." And she had, though Cressida hadn't seemed the least bit impressed. "She won Best Emerging Talent in a national fiber arts competition. There's a party tonight at Phil Morse's house."

"Phil Morse?" Cressida waved a hand dismissively. "I don't know him. Anyway, you'll just have to show up late. I need you, Amy. Remember, you *were* hired to watch the children. We'll be home before nine, and you can pop into the party then."

Before Amy could further protest—and she wasn't sure that she would have had the nerve to—Cressida strode out of the room. A moment later Amy heard the front door open and shut. Amy stood alone in the kitchen. She had a completely unexpected desire to pull every stemmed glass from where they hung over the microwave and throw them to the floor. Her anger frightened her. She took a deep breath and forced herself to calm down. Will. Maybe she could appeal to Will. It would be risking Cressida's wrath, but . . .

"What did your mom win?"

Amy jumped. Jordan had appeared, silently as always.

Amy managed a smile and told him.

"Is she nice?" Jordan asked.

Amy smiled again at the dear little boy. "She's very nice," she said. "She makes the most amazing angel food cake, and she used to sing me to sleep when I was little and afraid of thunderstorms."

"We're not allowed to eat cake," Jordan replied, "but sometimes my dad gets us cupcakes when we're out." Suddenly, his eyes grew wide. "Don't tell my mother, please," he begged.

"I won't say a word," Amy assured him. She wanted to enfold him in a hug but wasn't at all sure he would welcome such a gesture.

As suddenly and as quietly as he had come, Jordan left the kitchen via the door to the patio.

The moment he was gone, Amy burst into tears. How in the world was she going to break the news to her mother, her wonderful mother, that she would miss a good deal of her victory party? How?

Chapter 111

Phil was impeccably turned out as always in a slim tan suit. His pale blue shirt coordinated beautifully with his vibrant blue pocket scarf, and his taupe suede shoes were downright gorgeous.

Leda glanced around Phil's backyard. It was tended by a professional landscape company and was always in perfect shape, the lawn thick and even as a carpet, the rhododendron and azalea bushes trimmed, and the large maple tree flourishing. For the evening's festivities, the granite-topped table and wrought-iron chairs that usually stood on the flagstone patio had been put away and replaced with a long drinks table covered with a smooth white cloth. There were bottles and bottles of wine along with sparkling water and a nonalcoholic fruit punch. In the center of the table sat a tall vase sporting a stunning assortment of yellow and green flowers, Leda's favorite color combination. Phil had hired waiters to pass platters of hearty appetizers, classics like deviled eggs and shrimp wrapped in bacon, as well as more sophisticated options like tuna tartare on toasts and blinis with caviar and sour cream.

It was wonderful to see so many friendly faces, Leda thought, like Adelaide Kane and Cindy Bauer of The Busy Bee quilt shop. As fellow fiber art enthusiasts, they had been Leda's friends through thick and thin. Verity Peterson, a sculptor and instructor at Yorktide Community College, was there as well, along with her fiancé, David Wildacre, the head of the English Department at the college, and her daughter Gemma, herself a budding artist. Missy had been one of the first to arrive and already seemed to be the life of the party, circulating expertly.

The one noticeable absence among the crowd was Amy. She had sent Leda an apologetic text around one o'clock, explaining the situation in which she unexpectedly found herself. She promised to be at the party by nine and offered her mother use of the red velvet shawl and black sequined evening bag. At three and then again at six Amy had called, adding to her initial apology and promising to get to Phil's as soon as the Priors returned from their engagement.

It was interesting, Leda thought, watching the guests laughing and raising glasses. Only weeks earlier Amy's absence at an important event like this would have left Leda feeling devastated. But at this particular moment, her confidence boosted by the attention her work had been receiving as well as by her ability to finally put the past in the form of Lance and Regan Stirling to rest, she was able to take her daughter's absence somewhat in stride. Sure, she was disappointed that Amy couldn't be at the party from the start. But Amy was an adult, and she had made a choice, much as Leda was an adult and was now making a choice not to depend so heavily on her daughter's emotional support. It was a lesson she was learning the hard way, but learning it she was.

When Leda had first arrived at Phil's an hour before the festivities were due to begin, he had complimented her on her outfit. Leda had been pleased. Phil did not offer hollow compliments. She had agonized over what to wear that evening. She had spent a full forty-five minutes going through her closet and had finally decided on a black linen sheath dress, over which she wore a long vest of her own design and execution. The bright blues and pale greens of the vest popped against the black of the dress and worked well with the turquoise-and-gold stud earrings Vera had given her for her last birthday. Amy's offer of the shawl and the bag had been kind, if guilt driven, but both items were far too fancy for an evening in Yorktide.

Leda suddenly was aware of two new arrivals to the party. She didn't recognize either the man or the woman. Only when Leda saw them shake hands with Phil did she realize that the bags slung across their shoulders were camera bags. Her stomach fell. When the reporters had gone to the drinks table, Leda dashed over to Phil.

"Reporters? What are they doing here?" Leda whispered, grasping his arm.

"I invited them," Phil said simply. "That's Bob Hurley from the *Yorktide Daily Chronicle* and Sue Harris from the *Portland Press Herald*. You're a local interest story, Leda."

"Phil, you shouldn't have!" Leda protested.

"Nonsense. It's good publicity for the both of us. People will read about you and come flocking to the shop for your work. Well, those who don't come to you directly for custom work. Remember, when Bob and Sue approach you, be charming and be sure they get the spelling of the shop correctly."

Phil moved off to greet more arriving guests. Well, Leda thought, taking a fortifying sip of wine, she had made the choice to walk along the more public path, hadn't she? She could handle Mr. Hurley and Ms. Harris. Of course she could.

Leda accepted a blini from one of the circulating waiters, and as she did she spotted Hayley among the crowd. Though she was nicely dressed in a taupe dress, she looked pained. Leda wondered if her mood had anything to do with the supposed relationship with Ethan. She had heard no further gossip about the two, so maybe if something had indeed begun it had already ended. Hayley suddenly caught sight of Leda and made her way through the throng.

"Your mother couldn't come?" Leda asked, though she hadn't expected to see Nora Franklin.

"She sends her best," Hayley told her. "Congratulations again, Mrs. Latimer."

Before Leda could thank Hayley, Phil called the guests to attention. He raised his glass and asked everyone to raise their glasses to the woman of honor.

"Speech! Speech!" Vera cried after Phil's brief toast.

"Go on, Mrs. Latimer," Hayley encouraged.

Leda cleared her throat. The last time she had spoken in front of a crowd was at one of Amy's Girl Scout meetings ages and ages ago. "Thank you all for coming," she said, hoping she was pitching her voice to be heard. "This has been an amazing experience. I especially want to thank Phil Morse for believing in me from the start and for never allowing me to give up, even when I was sorely tempted to do just that. He's been my friend, my knight in shining armor, my greatest supporter. To Phil!"

When the applause had died down, Leda found Hayley gone and Vera by her side. Vera was wearing a pair of dark denim flares, a crisp white blouse, and a fitted navy blazer with shiny gold buttons. "I see you and Margot have been chatting," Leda said.

"Yeah," Vera said. "She's nice. More than nice, really. And she's cute, don't you think?" Suddenly, Vera's expression turned serious. "I don't know, Leda. Do you think I'd be totally insane to give love another chance?"

"No," Leda said firmly. "I don't. I think you'd be insane not to."

"You know, you should take your own advice."

Leda laughed. "I thought we had a deal not to force each other to date. Besides, I've enough on my plate at the moment, thank you. Like keeping up with all the orders that have been coming in since the award was announced."

"Woman does not live by work alone," Vera pointed out. "At least, not for long."

"Unless she loves her work as I do."

"Point taken. So, where is Amy?" Vera asked, scanning the crowded backyard.

"Cressida required her attendance this evening," Leda explained. "Amy didn't sound happy about it and swore she'd be here by nine."

Vera frowned. "She should be here now, to hell with what Cressida requires. You're her mother and this is a big moment for you."

"Don't be too hard on her," Leda said. "Like I said the other day, I've a feeling Amy's had just about enough of Ms. Prior."

"About time," Vera said robustly. "The summer is almost over. Then again, better late than never."

"Yes, and Margot is alone over by the drinks table."

Vera nodded. "I'm on it. Wish me luck."

"Luck," Leda promised.

And gazing around at the large crowd Phil had gathered in her honor, Leda wondered if luck had had something to do with her winning the FAF's annual competition. Maybe it had, but that didn't really matter. What mattered was that she felt so very grateful for the people who had believed in her. And those people included one Leda Latimer.

Chapter 112

Hayley opened the door to the apartment and went inside. The kitchen and living room were dark. She walked over to the old couch and sank gratefully onto it. The evening at Phil Morse's had been a trial. She had barely been able to stand the laughter and good feeling. One sip of wine had brought on a headache. She had had no appetite for the plentiful food.

It hadn't helped that Hayley had recognized several of the guests at the party as staff at Yorktide Community College, most significantly David Wildacre, the head of the English Department. He had greeted her warmly, and while in a way it had been nice to see him, in another way it had been downright painful. Hayley had taken two courses taught by Mr. Wildacre; each had been a fantastic experience, and she had kept all of her notes and papers. Not that she would ever have use for them again.

At about eight o'clock Ethan had sent her a text.

Miss you.

To which Hayley had replied truthfully: *I miss you, too.*

That message had been followed by a line from Shakespeare. *Who could refrain that had a heart to love and in that heart courage to make love known.*

Do you have the entire works memorized? Hayley had asked.

Wish I could say yes but I can't lie to you. Xxx

"I can't lie to you." Hayley whispered the words aloud. The next time she saw Ethan Whitby would be the last.

With a sigh, Hayley got up from the couch and tiptoed down the hall to her parents' bedroom. She carefully opened the door just wide enough to see that her father wasn't there. Nora Franklin was snoring slightly, her work-worn hands tucked under her cheek. For the moment, she seemed at peace.

Hayley closed the door and went to her own room. She undressed and crawled into her bed. She was asleep almost before her head touched the pillow.

It was some time after midnight that Hayley was awakened by her cell phone. She fumbled for it on the night table, hoping and yet dreading that it would be Ethan. But it was not Ethan. It was Brandon. Hayley stared at the screen and let the call go to voice mail. And then she deleted the message without listening to it.

Chapter 113

Amy stood at one of the large windows that looked out on the front lawn and drive. She could see nothing but darkness. It was eleven thirty. She felt anger building inside her. It scared her that for the second time in one day she felt so close to losing her temper. By now she strongly suspected that Cressida had purposely kept her from attending her mother's victory celebration.

At eleven forty-five the lights on Cressida's red Tesla came into view. The moment the car had come to a stop in the drive Amy threw open the door. Cressida didn't as much as look at Amy as she came inside and walked directly to the staircase. Will followed a moment later.

"She has a headache," he said.

Amy didn't bother to reply. She dashed from the house and down the drive to her car. Ten minutes later she pulled up outside Phil's house. It was dark. Ten minutes after that, Amy was quietly opening the front door of her own home. She removed her shoes in the front hall and tiptoed upstairs. The door to her mother's room was closed. For a moment, Amy considered knocking and then decided that another sincere apology could wait until morning. Her mother needed sleep.

Amy went on to her bedroom and changed into her favorite summer nightgown. She was still angry, but now she was also very clear about something. Cressida had used her. Since the day Amy had met her at The Atlantic, Cressida Prior had been using her.

With a sigh, Amy lay down on her bed. She had been crazy to even consider the Atlanta offer. She doubted that Cressida had even bothered to discuss with her husband the idea of Amy's moving in with the family. She probably planned to announce the arrangement as a done deal. And how would poor Jordan and Rhiannon feel about a virtual stranger living down the hall, a stranger their mother seemed to favor over her own children?

The entire situation was sick. She could quit first thing in the morning, but she wanted whatever money she could get from Cressida Prior. And every cent of it would go into the bank. From this point on she would be on her guard, and when the summer was over and the Priors went back to Atlanta she would be free of them forever. End of story.

Amy pulled the cord on her bedside lamp and miraculously was asleep within moments.

Chapter 114

"Coffee?" Leda asked.

Vera nodded. "Intravenously, if possible." She had brought an apple strudel with her from the restaurant. It was a new recipe she was considering for the menu and needed, she said, an honest opinion.

"It's an apple strudel," Leda said, sitting across from her friend at the kitchen table. "You know I've never met an apple strudel I didn't like. I'm hardly the one you should be asking."

Vera shrugged. "I just wanted an excuse for making off with it. Now, cut me a slice please."

Leda did and passed the plate to Vera. Then she cut a slice for herself and took a bite. "OMG," she said. "That's yummy."

"So, what did Amy have to say for herself this morning?" Vera asked.

"She couldn't stop apologizing for having missed the party," Leda told her. "And there was definitely a note of anger about the fact that the awesome Cressida Prior let her down."

"Amy should be angry," Vera said. "I wouldn't be surprised to learn that Cressida kept Amy away from the party on purpose. After all, it wasn't to celebrate Cressida, was it? It was to celebrate you."

Leda thought that Vera was probably right. "Did you see the *Chronicle* this morning?" she asked.

Vera nodded. "Fantastic picture of you. And I read the *Press Herald*'s write-up online. Very nice. I'm proud of you for handling it all so well."

"I was a nervous wreck at first," Leda admitted. "But then, I don't know, something came over me and I started to enjoy talking to the reporters."

"Getting used to the fame and fortune already?"

Leda laughed. "Fortune? I'll believe that when I see it in my bank account. So, did you and Margot make plans to get together?" Leda asked, cutting another thin slice of the strudel.

"As a matter of fact," Vera said, "we did, but I'm not promising anything will come of it. Why is it so important for you that I settle down?"

"Not settle down as much as . . . be happy." Leda shrugged. "I don't know, Vera. I guess I am still a romantic at heart."

"And there's nothing wrong with that. Hey, did you see that awesome silver necklace your friend Missy was wearing?"

Leda nodded. "I did. It was made by her friend Gary. She told me he's participating in the open studio event this October."

"Excellent," Vera said. "I think I'll buy myself a little gift. A girl always deserves a little gift from herself. A gift and daily pastry. That's my story and I'm sticking to it."

Chapter 115

Hayley had asked Ethan to meet her at a small pond on one of Yorktide's backroads. The pond was largely ignored by beings other than frogs, wild ducks, and egrets. It was an appropriately isolated place for lovers to meet for the last time.

Hayley had purposely arrived a bit early. She was waiting for Ethan by a stand of tall grasses when she heard the sound of tires leaving the road. She turned. The sight of Ethan striding toward her, a look of sheer happiness on his face, made her heart pound in her chest. He had become so dear to her in such a short time. She felt sick at the thought of never seeing him again.

"I haven't stopped thinking about you for a moment," Ethan said when he reached her. He gathered her in his arms. Hayley didn't protest, though she knew that she should. Instead she buried her face in his chest and held him tight. Ethan lowered his head then and kissed her passionately. Hayley didn't protest this, either.

"I have something for you," Ethan said when their lips finally parted. From a small shopping bag Hayley hadn't noticed he was carrying he withdrew a thick, square package and handed it to Hayley. *I can't accept a gift from him,* she thought. *I can't hug him or kiss him. I can't.*

Carefully Hayley unwrapped the package and gasped. She held

in her hands a mid-nineteenth-century edition of *The History of the Decline and Fall of the Roman Empire* by Edward Gibbon, Volume 1.

"It's pretty fragile," Ethan said. "I found this copy online in a small bookshop in England. I was going to wait until summer was over and I could officially ask you out before giving it to you but, well, things happened."

Hayley gazed at the worn leather cover of the book in her hands, a book that had been held and read by generations of people long since gone. "'History . . . is, indeed, little more than the register of the crimes, follies, and misfortunes of mankind.'"

Ethan smiled. "You're as good at quoting as I am."

"Thank you, Ethan," Hayley said, looking into his beautiful and earnest blue eyes. "It's the most wonderful, thoughtful gift I've ever received." And it was. But she had to speak. "Ethan, I . . . I'm so sorry. Nothing more can happen between us. I'm sorry."

Ethan looked stricken. More, he looked confused. "But I'm in love with you, Hayley," he said. "I love you."

"And I love you, Ethan," she said. "I truly do."

"Then why are you ending things before they've even begun?" he asked.

"Because our being together wouldn't be fair to you," Hayley said firmly. "Your world is so vastly different from mine. I'd only wind up embarrassing you, Ethan, trust me."

Ethan shook his head. He laughed, but it wasn't a joyous laugh. "What are you talking about?"

Hayley took a deep breath. "I lied," she said. "I had to quit college. I didn't leave because I wanted to. My mother needed money to pay the rent."

"There's no shame in helping family," Ethan pointed out. "If that's all—"

"I lied about other things, too," Hayley interrupted. "My brother isn't a successful lawyer. He's . . . he's trouble. He's not a good person."

Ethan looked perplexed. "I don't understand," he said. "Why would you lie about your brother?"

Hayley swallowed against a lump in her throat. "I didn't plan to lie," she said. "The words just came out, and the lie wasn't something I could take back without alienating you from the start. Like I've alienated you now."

"You haven't alienated me." Ethan reached for Hayley's free hand, the one not clutching the precious book, but she thrust it behind her back.

"I won't be able to say what I have to say if you touch me," she said, her voice trembling. "I'll lose what little courage I have."

And then Hayley told Ethan the bitter truth. That her family had spent time in a shelter for the homeless. That on occasion they had gotten their meals from one of the local food banks. That they had lost their home to foreclosure due to her father's gambling habits. That her father and her brother had been incarcerated. That her father was violent toward her mother. That she did not live on her own in a cozy cottage but rather with her parents in an attempt to protect her mother from total despair.

"Now you see why we can't be together," she finished. Her eyes brimmed with tears. Her throat was dry. Her hands trembled.

Ethan shook his head. "Who was I talking to all summer?" he asked quietly.

"Me. Just a better version of me."

A flash of something like anger appeared in Ethan's eyes. "Do you think so little of me," he asked, "that you'd assume I'd reject you based on the circumstances in which you were brought up?"

"I'm so sorry, Ethan," Hayley whispered. "I can't tell you how sorry I am."

"None of those things you told me about your parents and brother, or about your family's financial circumstances, are your fault," he went on urgently. "You're totally innocent."

Hayley shook her head. "You can't understand," she said sadly. "You can't understand what it's like to be poor and afraid. And I wouldn't want you to know what it's like to sleep in a room full of strangers, every one of them as desperate and hopeless as you. I wouldn't want you to understand what it feels like to be thrown out of your home and be standing on the sidewalk where everyone can see you, everything you own piled up around you, with no idea of how you're going to get your stuff to the next miserable little apartment. . . . I would never want you to know what it's like not to be able to rely on your parents to keep you safe and clean and fed."

"Oh, Hayley," Ethan murmured. He reached for her again, but she stepped away. "I don't care about your past," he went on. "I mean, I'm sorry that you were unhappy as a child, but how does that stand in the way of us in the here and now?"

Hayley shook her head. She had never felt so utterly sad. "It just does," she said. "Trust me, Ethan. I know what I know." And then she held out the book for Ethan to take. "You'll want this," she said.

"No." Ethan's voice was rough with emotion. Tears brimmed in his eyes. "Keep the book. I want you to have it. I'm sorry for everything that's happened to you, Hayley. Truly sorry. And if it means that we can't be together, well, I can't force you to have faith in me the way I have faith in you. You won't hear from me again."

Ethan lowered his eyes and strode off. Alone, Hayley collapsed to the ground in a torrent of tears. She felt as if she were crying for every little wound she had received in her life. The Christmases her family had to go without presents and a turkey because there was no money to spare for extras. The puppy she was never able to adopt because her mother was afraid that Brandon would be cruel to it. The times she had been too embarrassed to go to a school dance because she had nothing decent to wear. The angry landlords pounding on the door. The electricity being turned off because a bill hadn't been paid.

She didn't know how long she had sat crumpled on the ground, holding Ethan's book to her heart, before she finally found the strength to stand and to make her way to her car. When she got back to the apartment she hid the book under her mattress. If her father found it and was smart enough to guess it might be valuable (it was doubtful, but odder things had happened) he would hurry off to sell it for what he could and no doubt spend it all at the pub. Hayley felt that if the book came to harm, her heart, already broken, would somehow manage to break once again.

A few minutes later Hayley heard the door to the apartment

open. She tensed. "Hayley?" her mother called. Hayley cleared her throat. "Coming, Mom," she called back. And then she went to join her mother, the person for whom her deception had largely been in service. But the deception had also been for her own sake. She had acted from selfish motives, and she deserved to be punished. She had glimpsed a world of love and it had been denied to her, and that was entirely her own fault.

Chapter 116

Amy was sprawled on her unmade bed. It had been a trial of a day. She had barely been able to look at Cressida without wanting to demand an apology for causing her to miss her mother's celebration. Of course, Cressida hadn't apologized, and she had been particularly short-tempered, snapping at the children when they passed through the house and sending Amy from the office because it seemed that Amy was breathing too loudly. Amy had almost laughed at that but had simply gone downstairs and out to the patio, glad for the respite.

On the shelf over Amy's desk sat the small, green glazed pot her mother's friend Missy had given her. Crumpled up next to it was the stained scarf Cressida had tossed Amy's way. What a difference, Amy thought, between the manner and motive of the two women! Missy's gift had been offered in a spirit of true generosity. Cressida's gifts had been offered as gestures meant to bind Amy to her and create a sense of debt. That small, green pot meant so much more to Amy than any of the damaged items Cressida had thrown her way.

Amy got up from her bed and went downstairs. She found her mother in her studio, a tapestry spread out on the worktable.

"That's a gorgeous piece," Amy told her.

"Thanks. I'm racing against the clock on this order."

Amy squeezed her mother's shoulders. "I love you, Mom," she said. "I don't tell you that enough."

"You're not still feeling guilty about missing the party, are you?"

"Yes," Amy admitted. "And I should feel guilty, for a lot of things. For one I should never have accused you of not believing in me. I know you believe in me, and I know you always have, even at times when I didn't believe in myself."

Her mother merely smiled. "Vera's coming over for dinner, by the way. In fact, she's bringing it."

"Cool," Amy said. She needed to be around women whom she could truly respect, women like her mother and Vera and Hayley. Women who didn't feel the need to undermine everyone around them in order to feel good about themselves.

Women who didn't find it difficult to be nice.

Chapter 117

Vera had made peppers stuffed with lamb, rice, and Middle Eastern spices. Leda noted that Amy ate as if she hadn't had a meal in weeks. There was some truth in that.

"I was thinking I'd attend the FAF's annual show next spring," Leda said, helping herself to another pepper. "It would be wonderful to meet other craftspeople from around the country. I could learn so much, and I've never been to Dallas before. I've never really been anywhere."

"I think that's a fine idea," Vera said. "Creativity needs both solitude and community."

"What about that open studio event?" Amy asked. "The one your friend Missy told you about?"

"I've already contacted Harry Carlyle. He's the director of the gallery at YCC and the one organizing the event. I'm signed up and ready to open my doors!"

"I can't wait to see what comes next for you, Mom." Amy reached for the dish of pita bread and the bowl of hummus.

"Also," Leda went on excitedly, "I was thinking I'd like to offer a free course for kids at Strawberry Lane come fall. What with arts education funding being cut so drastically, I feel I have to do something. Kids need to learn visual thinking and creative problem solving."

Vera nodded. "Life without art is stupid. The sooner kids learn that, the better."

"I've never seen you so inspired, Mom," Amy said with a smile. "It's cool."

Vera turned to Amy. "How's your boss these days?" she asked.

"She's the same," Amy said shortly. "I don't really want to talk about her."

The glamour is gone, Leda thought. The glitter had worn off.

"Did your mom tell you I'm planning to open a second restaurant?" Vera asked Amy. "This one will be year-round. I'm starting with just dinners five or six days a week, and I'll see from there."

"That's awesome, Vera. You should definitely put these stuffed peppers on the menu. And the hummus."

Leda took a sip of her wine and watched as Vera and Amy engaged in animated conversation about menu options and décor. She couldn't help but feel that the old Amy was back—at least a wiser and more tempered version of the old Amy. She hoped this Amy would be able to survive the remaining few weeks of summer with the Priors. So much could happen in a few short weeks. . . .

"Remember that cake Mrs. Franklin used to make, like a bazillion years ago?" Amy was saying animatedly. "The one with the funny name? Anyway, wouldn't it be great if somebody—and I'm not saying who—if *somebody* would give Mrs. Franklin the chance to sell her cakes and stuff to a restaurant? She could be the pastry chef. I mean, if she wanted to. She was awfully talented once upon a time."

"The key phrase there is 'once upon a time,'" Leda pointed out. "It's a lovely idea, Amy, but possibly not the most practical."

Vera nodded. "I'm all for lending a helping hand when it makes sense," she added, "but why don't we take things one step at a time."

Amy shrugged. "Of course. But we can keep the idea in the back of our heads, can't we?"

Leda laughed.

"Yes," Vera said. "*We* can."

Chapter 118

True to his promise, Ethan did not reach out to Hayley. She wasn't surprised to learn that Ethan was a man of his word. She was, however, miserable but was trying her very best not to let her low spirits affect her work for the Whitbys.

At the moment, Hayley and Marisa were in the kitchen while the girls were napping. Marisa was seated at the counter, mending Lily's favorite plush rabbit. Hayley was unloading the dishwasher, a mindless-enough task and one that allowed her to hide her face from her employer. She knew there were dark circles under her eyes and there was little chance of her raising a smile.

"Ethan texted to say he won't be coming to Maine this weekend," Marisa suddenly announced. "I'll be sorry not to see him, as will the girls."

Hayley put two coffee mugs in a cupboard. "The girls really love him," she said, neutrally. "And he's so good with them."

"Will you be sorry not to see him, Hayley?"

Hayley startled. She didn't turn to face Marisa. "What?" she said. "No. I mean . . ."

"It's all right, Hayley. I'm not blind."

Slowly, Hayley turned around and faced Marisa. "There's nothing between us," she said quietly. *Not now. Not since I told him the truth about me,* she added silently.

Marisa smiled kindly and put down her sewing. "Really? A busy young man coming all the way to Maine from Connecticut almost every weekend. No, there was more to Ethan's visits than just family obligation."

"I'm sorry," Hayley said, fighting a terrible feeling of distress. "I feel so embarrassed. I never meant to . . ."

"You don't have anything to be embarrassed about," Marisa assured her. "You didn't allow Ethan's attentions or your feelings for him to prevent you from doing your job thoroughly. You do feel about him the way he feels about you?"

Hayley nodded. "But there can't be anything between us," she said.

"Why not?" Marisa asked.

"I can't . . . There just can't be."

Marisa sighed. "I know I'm prejudiced because I'm married to his father, but I can honestly say that Ethan is a fine person, even extraordinary in ways. Don't underestimate him, Hayley. Look, I suspect I know what's behind your reluctance. You think that given your upbringing you won't be right for him."

Hayley felt shocked and slightly sick. "How did you know?" she asked. "Did he say something to you about my family?"

"No," Marisa told her. "Other people talked. I might be a temporary resident, but I heard things, none of which tarnished my opinion of you in the least. I hold you in high regard, Hayley, as does Jon."

Hayley simply couldn't prevent the tears that came to her eyes. She remembered how isolated she had felt only a few days earlier. Here was a completely unexpected ally.

"I know what some people probably think of me when they see I married a wealthy older man," Marisa went on. "But I try not to let their prejudice bother me. What's important is my love for Jon and his for me. We're true friends, and in the end that's what survives all the fuss and bother of courtship. A devoted friendship. And I suspect that's something you could have with Ethan if you allow it."

"Thank you," Hayley murmured, wiping her eyes with her fingertips. "I'm sorry you had to get all mixed up in this. . . ."

"No apology necessary. Look at the time! I'm going to be late for class. I'll finish repairing Mr. Floppy later."

When Marisa had gone, Hayley sank onto one of the stools at the counter. She could hardly believe what had just occurred. How incredibly lucky she had been this summer to work for such wonderful people. She would miss the twins come September. She would miss them all; the Whitbys had shown her a better way to be a family. She would forever appreciate all they had done for her.

And though it was kind of Marisa to express her support of her stepson's interest in Hayley, it was also naïve. There would be no love and devoted friendship between Hayley Franklin and Ethan Whitby.

There simply would not.

Chapter 119

Cressida was standing at the kitchen counter, juicing yet another bunch of cucumbers. Amy, with nothing to do, sat on the stool farthest from her employer, studiously staring at the wall. Amy knew that since the night of her mother's party she hadn't been projecting her usual enthusiastic self at work, but Cressida hadn't seemed to notice the change in her demeanor. Most times Cressida saw only what she wanted to see. Herself.

"Aimee," Cressida suddenly instructed. "Go and get my reading glasses. They're on my desk unless my idiot husband moved them."

Dutifully, Amy went up to the office. The reading glasses weren't immediately visible. In fact, the desk was unusually cluttered. Amy moved aside a file folder and an open magazine, and there under the magazine were the glasses, right next to . . . right next to a small plastic bag of white powder. Amy's heart began to pound painfully in her ears. She stepped back from the desk. *This can't be real,* she thought. And maybe it wasn't. The white powdery stuff could be anything. It could be . . . But nothing reasonable came to mind. Why would someone keep sugar or talcum powder or dishwasher soap in a ziplock baggie on top of her desk?

Cocaine. The questions crowded Amy's mind at once. How

could Cressida be so careless as to use drugs with children around? Did Will know about his wife's habit? Did she allow drug dealers into the house?

Rapidly Amy reviewed all of the times she had been made uncomfortable by her employer's behaviors. The strange, often inane tasks she had set Amy. Keeping Amy from her mother's victory celebration. Insisting Amy spend 90 percent of the workday with her and not with the children. Her wildly shifting moods. Her bursts of temper. The dilated pupils and runny nose.

Amy took a deep breath and returned to the kitchen, where she handed Cressida the reading glasses she had been sent to find.

Cressida looked at her quizzically. "Are you all right?"

Amy nodded. "Fine," she said.

"Well, I hope you're not getting sick. I can't stand being around sick people."

I am sick, Amy thought. *Just not in the way you imagine. I'm sick of this relationship.*

There had never been a longer afternoon than that afternoon alone with Cressida Prior in the big white house overlooking the Atlantic. As Amy fetched bottled vitamin water and performed mindless tasks, she prayed that Cressida wouldn't ask her to spend the night again. She couldn't do it—she wouldn't—but it would be difficult to refuse Cressida face-to-face before she had had time to prepare her thoughts and to craft those thoughts into words that would brook no argument. Mercifully by four o'clock Cressida was in a listless mood and told Amy with a lazy wave of her hand that she was free to go. "Will can feed the kids," she murmured as she sank into a deck chair by the pool. *And who will feed Cressida,* Amy wondered as she grabbed her bag and left the house. When Amy was gone, who would take her place as paid companion or conspirator or servant, whatever you could call the strange position Amy had held this summer?

As Amy drove home to Hawthorne Lane she found herself checking the rearview mirror more than was necessary, half wondering if Cressida had changed her mind about letting Amy go and was following her with the intention of coercing her back for the night. Only when Amy was pulling up outside the home she shared with her mother did she breathe a sigh of immense relief. Only when Amy had closed and locked the front door behind her did she realize there were tears in her eyes.

Chapter 120

"Look what came in the mail today," Leda announced. "The new issue of *Needle and Thread*."

"Wow, this is so cool," Amy cried, jumping up from the kitchen table and reaching out for the magazine. "You're in print!" Amy read aloud the opening paragraph of her mother's piece. "I didn't know you were such a good writer, Mom," she said when she had reached the final line.

"I didn't, either," Leda admitted. "I'm not saying it was easy or that I'm going to take up a new creative career, but I would like to write more about the role of craft in our lives."

"We need to buy a few copies of this magazine for the archives. And I'll put a link to the article on your website. With the interview in that journal and your winning the competition and now this, you'll be a household name before long!"

Leda laughed. "Only in the crafting community, but that would certainly be an honor. Look at the time. I'd better get dinner started. Any requests?"

"Whatever you want, Mom," Amy said. "And put me to work."

Leda did. While Amy chopped garlic and shredded parmesan, Leda washed the fresh basil she had bought earlier. There was little more delicious than pesto sauce with big chunks of ripe tomatoes over pasta.

"I haven't heard you talk much about the move to Boston," Leda remarked. And as far as she knew Amy hadn't seen her future roommates since her graduation party, but that didn't mean she hadn't been speaking with them. "We really need to be making plans. We still haven't booked a U-Haul or decided what furniture you want to take with you."

"I'll take care of things, Mom," Amy said hurriedly. "It's not your responsibility."

"But I want to help," Leda said, smiling at her daughter. "I could pack your winter clothes if you like."

Amy smiled distractedly. "Really, Mom," she said. "I'm on it."

Leda shrugged. "If you're sure." And as Leda poured olive oil on top of the basil, garlic, cheese, and pine nuts already piled in the Cuisinart she wondered if Amy was having doubts about the move. She wouldn't be surprised if that were the case, not after the craziness Amy had experienced this summer. Well, if her daughter wanted to stay in Yorktide that was fine. There would have to be changes, of course—Amy would have to pull a lot more weight around the house than she was at the moment—but that was all right. Life was all about change. And Leda had a pretty good feeling that Amy was learning that lesson rapidly.

Chapter 121

Hayley sat slumped on the battered old couch in the apartment's tiny living room. Her head hurt. Her heart hurt. She wished she could talk to Amy about what had happened with Ethan. She missed her friend.

Only weeks ago, Hayley had believed that personal happiness was overrated. But she hadn't understood what happiness meant. She knew now that being with Ethan would make her happy in ways that counted, in ways that had nothing to do with money or education or social position. Being with Ethan would make her happy in an essential way. Happy in love.

Except that she couldn't be with Ethan. In spite of what Marisa thought, Hayley knew she would be poison to him.

"Hayley? Are you all right?"

Hayley looked up to see her mother standing at the entrance to the living room.

"Poor Hayley," Nora Franklin said, coming toward her. "You work so hard." Nora sat next to Hayley on the couch and put her arm around her shoulders.

It was such an unexpected and rare event that for a moment Hayley didn't know how to react. The truth was that her mother's touch felt not comforting but alien, unwanted. With a jerk of her shoulder she dislodged her mother's arm and got to her feet.

"I'm fine," she blurted.

The look of shock and dismay on her mother's face caused Hayley an almost physical pain. "I'm sorry, Mom," she said hastily. "I'm sorry. It's just that . . . I have a headache. I'll go and lie down for a while."

Hayley hurried from the room, ashamed that she had caused her mother such distress. But she simply hadn't been able to help it. She was the one to offer support to her mother. She was her mother's caretaker. Not the other way around. It had never been the other way around.

Chapter 122

Amy thought she had never eaten a more delicious meal than the simple one she had helped her mother prepare that evening. She had eaten until she was satisfactorily full. She had almost forgotten what it was like to enjoy a meal without a critical voice in her car, scolding and disapproving.

Now Amy was in her bedroom, dressed for sleep but not quite ready to drift off. Earlier she had evaded her mother's questions about Boston because she had come to the conclusion that moving away was *definitely* not the right thing to do. She remembered her mother's good advice, to choose the family for whom she would be working as carefully as they chose her, and with hindsight she deeply regretted that she had dismissed the words of wisdom. If she had taken her mother's advice she might not have fallen prey to an unscrupulous and seductive employer. That the seduction was not of a sexual nature made no difference; what Cressida had done to her was almost if not equally as powerful as if she had enticed Amy into becoming her lover.

It had occurred to Amy only days before that Cressida might have hired her *because* she was underqualified—and hiring her privately, for whatever reason, had also definitely been to Cressida's advantage. Cressida might have taken one look at Amy's résumé and immediately seen a person she could manipulate. Suddenly

Amy recalled Hayley telling her that Cressida Prior had a reputation among her colleagues as a narcissist. Amy thought she knew what a narcissist was but she wasn't entirely sure, so she went to her desk and opened her laptop.

A little bit of online research yielded the information that people with narcissistic personality disorder—if indeed that was what Cressida suffered from—were prone to periods of depression. NPD, Amy read, was also associated with anorexia. That might explain Cressida's extreme diets and her conviction that she looked fantastic when in fact she looked sickly. Or it might not. The problem with trying to make a diagnosis based on Internet research alone was the fact that unless you were a medical professional you could very well make a *misdiagnosis*. Amy remembered the time Vera had convinced herself that she was suffering from a dread form of psoriasis when it turned out that she just had an allergy to a new detergent.

Still, it couldn't hurt to read a bit more. People suffering from NPD also often battled with substance abuse, and the substance most often abused was cocaine. While Amy had no proof that the white powdery stuff she had discovered on Cressida's desk was cocaine, the odds seemed pretty high that it was. She recalled the day that Cressida had offered her the nebulous job in Atlanta and suspected that Cressida must have been high. What else might explain such an impetuous offer?

Amy closed her laptop. She recalled her initial thrill at being singled out by Cressida, a thrill that had worn off after time to be replaced by a deep weariness, a weariness that had finally been replaced by a feeling of repugnance. Yes. Repugnance was not too strong a word to describe how Amy had come to feel about the relationship. She had never in her entire life experienced a relationship that had progressed from bliss to disgust in so short a time. Maybe if she was experienced in romance she would have recognized this dynamic—the initial thrill, the gradual awareness of small disappointments, followed by the hard-hitting realization that the relationship was all wrong and the desire to get away as quickly as possible. In a way, Amy thought, you could call her relationship with Cressida a whirlwind romance. Cressida had been the seducer, older and powerful, the one who had blinded the younger and less experienced person with visions of favor and promises of power, visions that were ultimately revealed as phantasms, promises that were revealed as empty.

Amy yawned and realized she was finally ready for sleep. With her beloved plush panda in tow she crawled into bed, her mind at peace. By this time tomorrow she would be free.

It was with some trepidation—would Cressida hit her as she had hit Will?—but with an unshaken resolve, that Amy set out the following morning to confront her so-called mentor. It had taken her months to see through the thin and brittle surface glamour of her employer. Cressida was an unstable, toxic person who had lured Amy into her unhappy household for some bizarre reason Amy couldn't fathom. The pathological need to manipulate? A desire to dominate someone so obviously weaker than herself? Whatever the reason, the thought that she once had very much wanted to be a part of the Prior household filled her with shame.

Amy pulled into the driveway and got out of the car. She was wearing her favorite sundress. She took a deep breath, stood as tall as she could, and walked up to the front door. Cressida was not waiting for her there. Her hands fumbled with the key, but after a second try she managed to insert the key into the lock and open the door.

"Hello?" she called, but there was no reply. Neither was there any immediate sign of Will or the children. The house was so quiet that for a moment Amy wondered if anyone was there but herself. Maybe Cressida had gone out.

"Aimee! Is that you?"

Cressida was home. Amy went up to the office. Cressida's head was bent over a paper file on the desk. Through her thinning hair, Amy could see white scalp. Cressida's shoulders looked bonier and frailer than ever. Strangely Amy felt a sense of pity for the formidable but troubled woman before her. Cressida was the weaker person in their relationship at that moment and Amy the one with the power, and though Amy was about to defy the woman who had hurt her, she had no desire to hurt her in return.

Cressida suddenly looked up. "You're looking quite tidy today," she noted. "In spite of the sundress."

Amy refused to be cowed. "Thanks," she said. "Are Will and the children at home?"

"No. I sent them away. Peace and quiet."

"There's something I need to discuss. I mean," Amy went on, "there's something I need to tell you."

"Yes?" Cressida said sharply.

"I've decided not to accept your offer of a job in Atlanta," Amy announced. "It was a very generous offer, but it's not what I want for my life. Of course," Amy went on hurriedly, "I'll finish out the summer as per our verbal agreement."

There followed a terrible silence. Cressida remained perfectly still. When the silence had gone on for longer than Amy felt she could bear, she desperately cast about her mind for something to say. Before she could find it, Cressida spoke. Rather, she shouted.

"What the hell are you saying?"

Amy flinched under Cressida's assault but stood her ground. "I'm saying that I'm not going to Atlanta with you."

"Why not?" Cressida demanded.

Amy gulped. "Because I don't want to," she said.

"You're crazy," Cressida spat. "Only an idiot would turn down a possibility for success like the one I offered you." Cressida rose to her feet, her face distorted in a snarl. "I'll fire you immediately unless you change your mind."

Sweat might have broken out under Amy's arms and at the back of her neck, but she felt a deep calm come over her. She had done it. "I'm not changing my mind," she said.

"After all I've done for you," Cressida went on, leaning forward over the desk. "You're an ungrateful little bitch! I can't believe I thought you had it in you to be someone of consequence. As of this very minute you're—"

Amy laughed. She couldn't help it; the entire situation was just so ludicrous. "You can't fire me," she said. "I quit. I don't want your money. It's dirty, just like you're dirty. Your house might be spotless, but your heart isn't."

Cressida fell back in her chair as if she had been shoved.

"My mother is worth a hundred of you," Amy went on. "I should never have listened to you belittle her work. And the nasty things you said about my friend Noah. You called him a coward, and yet he's one of the bravest, most noble people I know. And one more thing. My name is Amy, not Aimee."

Amy turned and strode toward the door of the office. When she reached the threshold she was tempted to look back. She wondered what she would see. A hint of weariness on Cressida's face? Cressida's hand shaking as she reached for a bottle of the expensive vitamin water she was so fond of? But Amy continued into the hall, down the stairs, and out the front door. As she walked to her car she thought she detected a hint of autumn in the air, a time to let the old crumble away and the new to take its place. She slid behind the wheel of her car and another laugh escaped her.

Chapter 123

Earlier in the summer Amy had suggested that the house be cleared out of what she had referred to as junk. In one way, Leda had realized, Amy was right. There were boxes of old papers and who knew what else cluttering up the attic, and now was as good a time as any to clear away what was no longer needed or necessary.

On a day on which the temperature was only due to rise to the midseventies, Leda mounted an excursion to the attic. Still, she brought with her a standing fan, as until deep winter the attic was fairly stifling. A quick glance around the low-ceilinged room showed that Leda had her work cut out for her. Boxes and trunks and plastic storage bins were piled willy-nilly. It was all very daunting, but Leda was in the mood for a purge.

She started by opening a trunk in which she discovered some of the beautiful clothes her mother had made for her when she was a child. It seemed a shame to keep such lovely garments stored away. Leda wondered if she might incorporate some of the pieces into her quilt work. A photo of each item of clothing as it currently existed would preserve the original, and she could go from there. Satisfied, Leda dragged the trunk to the door of the attic. She would ask Vera to help her manage it down to the second floor.

Next Leda attacked a stack of box files. In the first she found a bundle of test papers from high school, several lined notebooks with yellowed paper dating back to her grammar school years, and one of her first sketchbooks. The sketchbook she would keep, but the school-related items Leda threw into the large plastic garbage bag she had brought with her.

Before she closed the file and moved on to the next in the stack, she realized there was a piece of folded paper partly stuck to the bottom of the box. Gently she pulled it free. Carefully she opened the page to find one of the poems Lance Stirling had written her that long-ago summer. Leda was stunned. She clearly remembered throwing out what she thought had been every scrap of paper that had come from Lance Stirling. Somehow this page must have survived.

The poem was pretty bad, the language florid, with lots of aching limbs and thumping hearts. With a genuine laugh, Leda tore the paper to shreds and tossed the pieces into the plastic garbage bag along with her childhood school things.

At noon, hot, sweaty, and covered in dust, Leda decided to break for lunch. On the way down to the kitchen to wash up and grab something to eat, she was suddenly overcome by a powerful feeling of intense pride. But the pride had nothing to do with Leda. Rather, it was centered entirely around Amy. Amy had done something wonderful. Leda knew it as absolutely as she knew her own name. How else to interpret the euphoria that was now pulsating from her heart?

Leda shook her head and chuckled. No doubt she was just hungry. And thirsty. Dehydration could do funny things to people. It could make them imagine all sorts of silly things. Leda hurried on to the kitchen and the half pound of sliced turkey waiting in the fridge.

Chapter 124

Hayley was sitting with the girls in the park by the World War II memorial when Amy texted, asking where she was. Hayley assumed that Amy was on another errand for Cressida. How else would she have gotten out of the looney bin that was the Prior household?

Amy appeared ten minutes later. She was wearing one of her prettiest sundresses. Hayley hadn't seen her wear a sundress since early summer. They really looked wonderful on her.

"What's wrong, Hayley?" Amy asked, sitting next to her on the bench. "I've never seen you look so miserable, and that's saying something."

Hayley busied herself adjusting the girls' sunhats. She hadn't planned on telling Amy what had occurred between her and Ethan. Not yet, anyway. It was all so raw. "I'm fine," she said with an attempt at a smile.

"Come on," Amy pressed. "What's going on? I'm worried."

Hayley sighed. She would have to tell Amy at some point. It might as well be now. "What's going on," she said, "is that my whole stupid plan backfired."

"What do you mean it backfired?" Amy asked.

"I mean that I fell in love with Ethan Whitby. But I can't be with him, Amy," Hayley went on hurriedly. "You were right. I was crazy thinking I could fit into Ethan's world. The whole thing is a mess."

Amy shook her head. "Wait, back up a minute. Did you tell him how you feel?"

"Yes," Hayley admitted. "Things had been building all summer, but neither of us acknowledged it. Finally, we kissed. It was . . . It was incredible. He told me that he loved me and I told him that I loved him. And then I came to my senses. The next time we met, I told him we couldn't see each other again."

"Oh, Hayley!" Amy cried, her hand to her heart. "You poor thing. Why didn't you tell me before now?"

"Because I don't like to ask for help," Hayley admitted. "You know that. Besides, all you seem to care about lately is Cressida Prior."

"You're right," Amy said promptly. "I'm sorry. My head was so turned by Cressida I wasn't able to see or hear anyone but her. Look, I have something to tell you, too. I quit. I haven't told my mom yet, but I will tonight."

"You quit?" A smile came to Hayley's face for the first time in days. "That's fantastic. Tell me everything."

So Amy did, starting at the very beginning.

"I'm really impressed," Hayley said when Amy had finished her tale. And then she smiled ruefully. "You know, our experiences this summer couldn't have been more different. Even though we're the best of friends it's like we've been living in two entirely different worlds. You could see my mistakes so clearly and I could see yours and yet neither of us was really able to help the other."

"Tell me about it," Amy agreed. "And how odd is it that I never met Marisa and you never met Cressida. You really love your charges and I hardly got to know mine."

"The Whitbys are excellent employers, while the Priors are far from it."

"And the Whitbys have a stable marriage, while the Priors have a rotten one." Amy shuddered. "I feel I've been tainted by being in the presence of such a miserable husband and wife."

Hayley smiled kindly. "You'll get over it. You're strong, Amy."

"Thanks. So are you."

"Am I?" Hayley shook her head. "Honestly, I'm wondering how I'll ever get over Ethan. How could I have fallen in love with someone I'm so entirely unsuitable for?"

"Don't say that!" Amy protested. "You're a wonderful, intelligent, beautiful, kind person. Anyone would be thrilled to marry you."

"I'll argue that some other time. Tell me about your romantic life this summer. I've been so wrapped up in my own woes I never asked if anything was finally going on with you and Noah."

"Nothing, I'm afraid," Amy said with a sigh. "You know, Cressida saw Noah once when we were in town. She said horrible things about him and I didn't stick up for him. I feel so ashamed about that. Noah is sweet and smart and talented. I'll be lucky if he still agrees to talk to me after I cancelled a date because Cressida needed me to spend the night."

"He's not going away that easily, Amy," Hayley assured her. "Everyone knows he's been in love with you since we were kids."

"I don't know about in love, but . . ."

"You'd make adorable children. At the very least they'd have amazing hair."

Amy blushed. "Kids! Isn't that leaping ahead a bit? We've never even kissed."

"Then it's about time you did," Hayley scolded. "Why don't you ask him out? Apologize again for cancelling the date and suggest a picnic on the beach one evening."

Amy smiled. "I guess if I can stand up to Cressida Prior I can handle just about anything, even rejection by a guy I really admire."

"There's the spirit. You know, back in the spring when we first talked about being summer nannies we never thought we'd wind up where we are, did we? Our lives turned upside down."

Amy nodded. "The question is, Did we learn anything of value this summer? Are we going into the fall any wiser than we were a few months ago?"

"I don't know about wiser," Hayley admitted, "but I definitely feel chastened. I had so little idea of what love felt like, romantic love I mean. I had so little respect for it. What about you?"

"Wiser, I think. At least I hope so. I don't want to get caught up by another manipulative person like Cressida Prior ever again. It's pretty embarrassing how I just ate up whatever she fed me." Amy laughed. "Not real food, of course!"

"Speaking of real food, how about we hit the Mexican Kitchen soon?"

"I'm there," Amy said. "Just name the day."

"We make a pretty good team when we actually pay attention to what the other is saying," Hayley noted. She could feel tears pricking at her eyes. She didn't think Amy had ever seen her cry, not even when she had sprained her wrist falling off the slide in the playground when they were kids.

"We do make a good team," Amy agreed. "We definitely do."

Chapter 125

Amy looked around her bedroom. During the course of the summer she had made a few attempts at tidying up but had never really succeeded. That was okay. There were a lot worse things to be in life than a messy, curvaceous woman with curly hair who liked to wear sundresses and the bracelets her mother made for her, a woman who liked to cuddle her cats and eat a decent meal. A woman who loved and respected her mother.

Amy knew that she was partly responsible for what had happened this summer. Did she really present such a blank slate to the world that a person felt that she could choose what to write upon her? If that were the case then things had to change, and before much more time was wasted. She needed to know her own mind and to make it known to others.

She thought about those who loved her for who and what she was. There had been her grandparents, and there was always her mother. For a few months, there had been her father, too. By all accounts he had adored his infant daughter, and Amy had the photos to prove it. There was Hayley, and like Hayley had said, they made a pretty good team. And there was Vera, and maybe there would even be Noah Woolrich. She bet her father would have approved of Noah. To lose sight of those people as she had almost lost sight of them that summer was simply wrong. It was also dangerous.

Now, Amy thought, to tell her mother what she had done that morning. She knew her mother would be proud.

Chapter 126

Leda was in the living room, reading another of the cozy mysteries she adored, when Amy came into the room and plopped into an armchair.

"Winston, come sit on my lap," Amy called. He did, and Amy laid her hand on his furry back.

Harry had followed his friend into the room and was glaring up at Amy. Leda patted the couch. "Come sit on Mamma," she called. With a last accusing look at Amy, Harry leaped onto the couch and with elaborate deliberation settled on Leda's lap.

"Mom?" Amy said. "Can we talk?"

Leda put her book aside. "Sure. What's up?"

"I quit my job working for the Priors."

Leda was stunned. "You did?" she said. "Tell me everything."

"It's a long story," Amy said, "but I'll try to make it brief. A few weeks ago, Cressida offered me a position in Atlanta as her right-hand woman. She was never very specific about what being a right-hand woman involved, but I considered the idea for a while. And then I started to really pay attention to how Cressida was actually manipulating me while pretending she was my mentor and friend. I started to really pay attention to all of the weird things about her relationship to her husband and the cold way she treated her children and the callous way she regarded pretty much everyone else until finally I realized there was no way I wanted to move into the Priors' home to be a sort of menial servant."

Leda shook her head. "I wish you had told me about this offer. I could have . . . no. I was going to say that I could have helped you to think about it, but I don't think you would have allowed me to help."

"You're right," Amy said. "I wouldn't have. I did tell Hayley, and she thought the idea sounded insane. She tried to talk me out of it, but I wouldn't listen."

"So, what happened?" Leda asked. "I mean, how did it go when you quit?"

"I didn't intend to quit when I went to tell Cressida that while her offer was very generous I had to turn it down." Amy grimaced. "She threatened to fire me if I didn't change my mind, and I told her I wouldn't and that she couldn't fire me because I quit. Then I kind of told her off. She'd said lots of unkind things about . . ." Amy felt herself blushing. "Well, about people I know, and I finally spoke up for them and for myself. And then I marched out of the house."

"Congratulations, Amy," Leda said feelingly. "I'm proud of you. I know it must have taken a lot of courage to stand up to someone like Cressida Prior."

Amy laughed. "It did! I still feel kind of wiped out. But what happened this summer was partly my fault, Mom. I chose not to listen to the good advice of people close to me. So that leads me to a big question. Would it be okay if I stayed here at home instead of moving to Boston?"

"Of course it would be okay," Leda told her. So, her suspicion had been on target.

"I have a lot of growing up to do," Amy went on, "and honestly, after what happened this summer—after what I allowed to happen—I'm thinking it would be best to postpone a move. I thought I'd talk to Vera about a job at the new restaurant she's planning to open. And I intend to help you grow your business, too."

"I'd love nothing more," Leda admitted.

"I was so flattered by the attention and the praise," Amy went on musingly. "I thought, wow, I must be really worth something if this powerful woman is taking such notice of me. But just because a person is powerful in an obvious and public way doesn't mean she's fundamentally better than someone who's powerful in a more subtle and quiet way. Like you, Mom. You knew all along that something wasn't right in the relationship between Cressida and me. I'm sorry I didn't listen to you."

"Sometimes trying to prevent a loved one from making a mistake isn't necessarily the right thing to do," Leda pointed out. "Maybe if I hadn't fought you so hard about Cressida you might have seen the truth earlier."

Amy smiled. "Better late than never, right? There's something else, Mom. The other day Cressida asked me to fetch something from her office, and while I was looking for it I came across this plastic bag of white powdery stuff. It was sitting right there on her desk. I can't be sure, but I think it was cocaine." Amy shook her head. "Cressida had these weird mood fluctuations. She'd be listless one minute and then she'd go into her office and close the door for a while and when she'd come out she'd be full of energy. For so long I had no idea what was causing her shifting moods. I guess I thought that she was just stressed."

"I doubt drugs are behind everything frightful about that woman," Leda said. "But they certainly can't be helping an already emotionally unstable person." With shame, Leda recalled feeling disappointed in her daughter earlier that summer for being blind to her boss's flaws. But look at what Amy had accomplished. And Leda's instinct had told her so that very afternoon; her own heart had known that Amy's good heart had finally triumphed over Cressida Prior's powerfully problematic behavior.

"I'd like to share something with you," Leda said, deciding as she spoke. "It's a bit difficult for me to talk about."

"Sure," Amy said, her hand stroking Winston's back. "You can tell me anything."

"There was a reason I was so against your taking a job as a nanny," Leda began. "It had to do with my own experience as a nanny the summer I was seventeen."

"I never knew you worked as a nanny," Amy said in surprise.

"I did, but it didn't end well." Leda sighed. "The husband was a very charming man. I was a very naïve teenager. He led me to believe that he was unhappy in his marriage and that he had fallen in love with me."

Amy grimaced. "Not that line."

"After weeks of being seduced by charming words and intimate little gestures," Leda went on, "I went to bed with him. It was just the once but that seemed to be all he had wanted, because immediately after he told me that our relationship was over. I begged to know why, but he had nothing more to say. And then I learned from his wife that he routinely seduced young women and then dropped them. She told me she tolerated his affairs because she knew he would never leave his family. And that was the end. I literally ran from the house and never looked back."

"Mom," Amy said, shaking her head. "How awful! You should have told me before now."

"It's hardly the kind of thing you're eager to tell your daughter," Leda pointed out, "that you allowed yourself to be seduced by a married man when you were only a teen. I mean, I've always taught you to respect the bonds of matrimony, but I didn't exactly act on that advice myself."

"You can't blame yourself, Mom," Amy said firmly. "You were a kid. It was their fault, not yours."

"Anyway," Leda went on, "I know it was silly of me to suppose that the same thing might happen to you, but that's what I was afraid of."

"You weren't entirely wrong, were you?" Amy noted. "I did get seduced, just not in the way you thought I might. Did you ever tell my father what happened?"

"I never told anyone but Vera and now you," Leda admitted. "I suppose if you hadn't gone through what you did this summer I wouldn't ever have said a word to you."

"Was my father a rebound? I don't mean that in a blame sort of way," Amy added hurriedly. "I mean, were you so distraught about having been used by that couple that you sought refuge and security with someone kind?"

"I cared a great deal for your father," Leda said after a moment, surprised by the wisdom of Amy's guess. "He was a good man, and for the short time he had with you he was a wonderful father. I missed him terribly when he passed away."

Amy was silent for a long moment. When she finally spoke, her tone was thoughtful. "Cressida said she was my mentor, but she never really taught me anything of value. A mentor is supposed to encourage a protégé's individual growth. But Cressida didn't want me to set out on my own path. I think she just wanted to mold me into her mini-me. I think she's seriously lonely, but I don't think she can admit that to herself."

Leda nodded. She had thought a lot about loneliness over the years. "To admit that you're deep-down lonely," she said, "must be a terrifying thing. It must make you feel as if something is very wrong with you, not to be able to connect with another person in a meaningful way."

Amy sighed. "I wonder if Cressida's husband will ever have what it takes to break away. If there weren't any children, then he might find it easier to leave. But there *are* children." Amy sighed. "I wonder what will happen to them."

"You know, I did something this summer I'd never done before," Leda told her daughter. "I went online to search out that couple I'd worked for. I'm not going to tell you their names, but I do want you to know that their daughter is doing very well for herself. She's getting a Ph.D. in environmental science. At least she's been able to flourish intellectually. There's hope for Jordan and Rhiannon. Children can be remarkably resilient."

"I suppose," Amy agreed. "So, how did you feel about the parents when you saw their faces after all these years?"

Leda smiled. "I don't know what I expected to find, but it wasn't two average sixty-somethings. I guess I'd never thought about their being vulnerable to time and circumstance. I realized: These people are only flesh and blood. Why was I so afraid of them? They had no power to hurt me, not once I'd left. And I knew that by confronting them I was finally setting the past to rest."

"Good," Amy said forcefully. "And I'm going to set the past to rest by reporting my experience with the Priors on the nanny websites. I'm not going to mention the cocaine, though, even if that is what I saw. The last thing I want is for the Priors to say I'm lying and sue me. But I will talk about the phony job description, the lack of a written contract, and the fact that Cressida hired me privately, which was definitely not to my advantage no matter what she claimed."

"It's the right thing to do," Leda affirmed. "I never reported my experience because I felt so culpable. Still, I was an underage girl who had been taken advantage of. I should have said something. Who knows how many other young people those two might have harmed since then?"

"You did what you could do at the time, Mom," Amy said firmly. "It's over."

"Yes," Leda agreed. "It's over. So how about we celebrate putting the past to bed?"

Amy smiled. "Deal. But can we do it with ice cream? Or cake. Or maybe both."

"Tired of Cressida's abstemious eating habits?" Leda asked.

Amy shuddered. "If I never see another stalk of celery in my life I'll be a very happy person."

Chapter 127

Hayley inserted her key in the door of the apartment. Before she turned the key, she moved closer to the door. There was a noise coming from inside, an erratic banging and a . . . Hayley whirled around. "Mom," she directed. "Stay in the hall. I'll go in."

"It could be a burglar," Nora whispered fearfully, grasping Hayley's arm.

"Doubtful. Stay here," she directed again. She took a fortifying breath, turned the key, and went into the apartment. The banging, and now a crash as if a piece of furniture had been overturned, was coming from the direction of the bedrooms. Hayley walked softly toward the back of the apartment. Then it became clear that Eddie Franklin—who else could it be if not Brandon?—was in her bedroom.

Hayley felt a surge of fierce anger rise in her. It frightened her in its intensity. She felt at that moment as if she could manually strangle the man who was partly responsible for having given her life. In that moment, she hated her father. She hated him.

"Stop that!" she cried, standing in the doorway of her bedroom. Her father, his eyes glittering with malice, looked up from the drawer he was clawing through.

"Where's the money?" he spat. "I know you've been keeping my money from me!"

Hayley took a step back. Her father wasn't drunk; she had seen him drunk often enough to know when he wasn't. And it was this fact that unnerved her badly. Usually her father's outbursts of violence went hand in hand with drunkenness.

Before she could protest that there was no hidden stash of money—would she be so stupid as to keep cash around for the male Franklins to find?—her father strode the few steps across the room and tore the pillows and bedclothes from the bed.

"What are you doing?" Hayley cried. The book. Ethan's book. . . . "Stop it!"

Hayley came forward a step and then jumped back as Eddie Franklin yanked the mattress from the bedframe, knocking over her makeshift bookcase. And there, atop the box spring, lay the precious gift Ethan had given Hayley only days before.

With a roar of disgust, Eddie Franklin grabbed the old and fragile book and threw it. The book opened as it flew through the air, hit the wall, and then landed on the floor with a thud. Hayley cried out and ran to retrieve her gift. The spine felt loose. Hot tears began to course down her cheeks. She was right to have let Ethan go. He didn't deserve to be made any part of this.

"Where's my money?" her father roared again. Hayley turned around to see him coming toward her menacingly. "It's mine by rights. I'm the head of this house."

Hayley took a step back and then another until her back was against the wall. She hadn't felt so frightened and helpless since she was very young, in the days before she had learned how to fight back with cunning and at times with physical force. But all fight seemed to have gone from her. She clutched the book to her chest, unable to move even when Eddie Franklin lifted his meaty fist before her face.

"You'll touch her over my dead body!"

The sound of the voice behind him, loud and shrill, served to stun Eddie Franklin. Hayley watched in disbelief as her mother strode into the room, her hands clenched into fists, her expression stern and determined. For a split second, Hayley thought that she must be imagining the moment, or that this woman coming to her rescue wasn't her mother at all, just someone who vaguely resembled the Nora Franklin Hayley had left cowering in the hallway moments ago. Her usually stooped shoulders were thrown back in determination, her usually dull eyes sparking with purpose.

Nora Franklin now stood at her daughter's side, resolute. And then, to Hayley's utter astonishment, Eddie Franklin lowered his fist. The look on his face was one of deep confusion.

"I mean it, Eddie," her mother spat. "You touch her, you're out of here. Head of the house? Don't make me laugh. You're pathetic and we've all known it for years. You want money? Keep a job like a real man."

Eddie opened his mouth but no words came out. He took a step toward his wife and daughter, and for a terrible moment Hayley was sure he was going to beat the two of them to a pulp.

And then Nora put up her hand. "One more step and I call the police," she said in a deadly quiet tone, "and this time I won't drop the charges. And when you get out of jail you'll come home to find us gone, and gone for good."

It was these words that seemed to reach what there was of Eddie Franklin's reason. He retreated out of reach. All of the meanness and menace was gone from his face and his attitude. Hayley realized that she was holding her breath; she had absolutely no idea what would happen next.

"Nora," her father said, softly and with a whine in his voice. "Please. You can't leave me. I'm sorry. Really, I'm sorry."

Hayley had never, ever heard her father plead or apologize. And yet there was something in his tone that made Hayley think he might indeed be sorry for his misdeeds. But she continued to stand frozen to the spot, her eyes shifting from one parent to the other.

Nora folded her arms across her chest and frowned. "We'll see. One more wrong step and it's over. I mean it, Eddie. Never. Again."

Hangdog, Hayley thought. That was the word to describe the look on the face of her bully of a father. Downright hangdog.

"I'm going out," he said.

"You can pick up half a gallon of milk while you're at it," Nora instructed. "Dinner will be on the table at six thirty. If you're not home by then, clean and sober, you can spend the night in the hallway, and I don't care how loudly the neighbors complain."

Without another word, Eddie Franklin left the room, and a moment later the women heard the door to the apartment close. It did not slam.

Nora began to pick her way out of her daughter's bedroom, righting the overturned bookcase and closing the drawers her husband had left hanging open. Hayley followed her mother to the living room, where Nora sank onto the couch, her hands clasped in her lap.

"Mom?" Hayley asked gently, sitting next to her. "Are you okay?"

Her mother laughed a bit wildly. "I think so," she said. Suddenly she turned and took Hayley's shoulders in a firm grip. "You need to get away from here," she said fiercely. "At least for a while. Take all the money you've saved. It's yours. I have no right to ask you to stay with me. I'm your mother. I shouldn't be dependent on you. I want the best for you, and that means living your own life."

"But Mom—" Hayley began to protest.

"I mean it, Hayley," her mother said forcefully. "Handling your father is my responsibility, not yours. I'm sorry I haven't done my job in the way I should have. I never intended to . . . to let you and your brother down." Nora removed her hands from Hayley's shoulders and folded them in her lap again.

"Where did you find the courage, Mom?" Hayley asked. "What happened to make you take a stand against Dad just now?"

"Do you remember when a few days ago I tried to comfort you and you pushed me away?" she asked.

Hayley felt a rush of shame. "Mom, I—"

"Let me say this," her mother went on. "It's been preying on my mind that my own child could find her mother's comfort so alien. I've felt so ashamed. And just now, when I saw your father menacing you, something just snapped and I couldn't let him hurt you any more than he already has. Can you forgive me for being a coward all these years?"

"Of course I forgive you, Mom," Hayley said, giving her mother's hand a gentle squeeze. "But I've never understood why you stay with Dad, and I don't think I ever will."

"I'm sorry," Nora replied. "But if you can't understand, are you willing to try to accept that it's been my choice?"

Hayley hesitated. Accepting the fact that your mother would choose to remain in a domestic situation fraught with anger and alienation was not an easy task. But above all Hayley wanted peace between them. "Yes," she said finally. "I'll try to accept that your choices are yours. But did you really mean what you said to Dad, that you'll leave him if he makes another wrong move? Because you know he probably will. Nothing will change overnight, and even if things do get better over time they might not stay better. I'm sorry, Mom, but that's the brutal truth."

"I know," Nora admitted. "I don't have huge expectations of your father. Well, I have no expectations of him, really. But I do finally have expectations of myself." Nora shook her head. "I never thought I'd have the nerve to speak back to your father the way I did earlier. Never. So who knows what I might be capable of in the future?"

Hayley gave her mother a hug. "Promise me you won't let Brandon push you around any longer, either," she said. "It's high time he grew up. You know you're not doing him any favors by bailing him out of trouble."

"I know. But Brandon was never as smart as you. He was never as good and decent, not even as a child." Nora sighed. "I guess I thought that if I just paid enough attention to him he might become a better person. But that doesn't make sense. I see that now."

"I know you did what you thought was best," Hayley said reassuringly.

Nora pointed to the book Hayley still held. "The book," she said. "It looks old. Where did it come from?"

Hayley ran her finger across the embossed title on the front cover. "A friend."

"This friend must care very much for you," her mother said gently.

Hayley's voice trembled when she replied. "I believe he does."

"And you care for him?"

Hayley nodded.

"Is he from around here?" her mother asked.

"No," Hayley told her. "He's from very far away."

"Love," Nora Franklin said, "is always the strongest bridge over great distances. Believe that, Hayley."

Hayley wiped tears from her eyes. "I'll try," she said. "I'll try."

Chapter 128

It was a rainy afternoon, perfect for staying indoors and doing nothing more taxing than flipping through fashion magazines or, as Hayley was doing, sitting on the living room floor dangling a toy for the cats.

Amy, curled in an armchair, had decided not to tell her mother or Hayley about the time she had witnessed Cressida slap her husband. She had done enough damage to the man by repeating his wife's cruel criticisms. The least she could do was to spare him the further humiliation of being known as a physically abused husband.

"Will Prior sent me a text asking if I'd meet him for coffee tomorrow," she said now to Hayley.

"Are you going to meet with him?" Hayley asked.

Amy nodded. "I am. I want to hear what he has to say."

"It could be unpleasant," Hayley pointed out. "Cressida is a nut, but she is his wife. Do you want me to come with you in case you need reinforcements?"

"No," Amy said. She was not afraid of Will Prior. "Thanks, but I'll be okay. I just can't help but think about the children. My mom says children are resilient, but I wonder if one day Jordan and Rhiannon will rebel against their parents in some spectacular, destructive way."

"I guess no one can know how a child will react to his past as he grows into adulthood," Hayley said. "Maybe he'll embrace it wholeheartedly, maybe he'll reject it entirely, or maybe he'll pick and choose what examples of his parents' behavior to live by."

"Well, I hope that Jordan and Rhiannon manage to forget the lessons Cressida's been teaching them. But even if they do, the fact remains they missed out on so much love and warmth, and if you don't get that when you're little, how do you know what to look for when you grow up?"

Hayley sighed. "That's a question I've been asking myself all my life. In Jordan and Rhiannon's situation, I could see how their father's affections might become suspect at some point. They could turn against him for not having better protected them from a toxic mother."

"I guess we'll just have to hope for the best. Anyway, I've decided I'm going to report my experience with the Priors on the nanny websites. I'm hoping my story might spare someone else from being caught up in their weird dynamic."

"Good for you," Hayley said forcefully. "Women have to stick together in ways that make a difference. And speaking of women sticking together, I have something to tell you, though you're not going to believe it when you hear it."

Amy smiled. "Don't keep me in suspense!"

"My mother, the long-abused Nora Franklin, finally stood up to my father, and in a pretty spectacular way." Hayley went on to relate what had happened when she and her mother had discovered Eddie Franklin tearing apart Hayley's bedroom.

"You're right," Amy said when Hayley had finished speaking. "I don't believe it, except that you're not a liar so I have to believe it."

"Well, I wouldn't say I'm not a liar. I lied to Ethan about plenty of things."

"That's different," Amy said firmly. "You were desperate. You weren't really you."

"I'm not sure that excuses me. Anyway, when it was all over, my mother encouraged me to take all the money I have saved and get away. She said that handling my father was her responsibility. And she apologized for not having been able to protect me before now."

"This is amazing," Amy said. "It's like your mother has been reborn or something."

"Don't expect a total revolution just yet," Hayley warned. "She might easily backslide, and I wouldn't blame her if she did, not after all the years she's spent being subservient to my father."

"She'll need encouragement. Maybe my mother can help in some way. I can tell her what happened, can't I?"

"Yeah," Hayley said. "Maybe if your mom can just, I don't know, have coffee with her. Some small gesture of friendship might go a long way at this point."

"Sure. So, *are* you going to leave Yorktide?" Amy asked.

"I haven't given it any real thought yet," Hayley admitted. "I mean, I'd have to go someplace where I could get a decent job, or else why bother. And I'm not sure I can walk away from my mother, not when she's only just begun to assert herself."

"Don't be mad at me for saying this," Amy began, "but maybe you're just as stuck as your mother is. Leaving home means you'd have to change. You'd have to start thinking about your own life as most important, and that will be hard to do. But Hayley, you have to try. You can't let fear stand in your way."

Hayley didn't say anything for a very long moment but sat staring down at the cats, who, tired from their exertions, were lying on their backs, airing their furry tummies. Amy began to worry that she had gone too far with her version of tough love, but then Hayley raised her eyes and smiled a tentative smile.

"Maybe I *should* leave town," she said. "Maybe I should have faith in my mother's ability to cope without me. And maybe I should have faith in my own ability to cope without her."

"That's the spirit!" Amy suddenly snapped her fingers. "I have a brilliant idea! I told you that I'm not going to Boston. Why don't you take my room in the apartment? I'm sure the other girls won't mind, and it will save them the hassle of trying to find another roommate. As for a job, I know you can find something. There are always jobs in big cities."

Hayley nodded. "Okay," she said. "Why not? I'll do it. If you're sure your friends won't mind."

"I'll talk to them today," Amy promised. "I can totally vouch for you being the most responsible person I know."

"Thanks, Amy. You're a good friend. And Boston isn't too far away, so I can easily come home if my mother needs me. Not," she added quickly, "that I'll be making excuses to come home. At least I'll try not to be."

"Good. So, do you think your mother will forgive your father for all the stuff he's put her through?"

"I expect she already has," Hayley said. "And maybe one day I'll be able to forgive him. Let's see if he gets his act together now that my mother has found her voice."

"What about Brandon?" Amy asked. "Do you forgive him for all the trouble he's caused?"

"I'm not sure how to answer that," Hayley admitted. "I don't think he had all that much of a choice when it came to being a good person. My mother thinks he was born with some innate deficiencies of character, and growing up in a home like ours certainly didn't do him any favors."

"I can't pretend I ever liked him," Amy said. "Still, I don't think he's evil or anything."

"Probably not. But can you forgive someone for behavior they aren't sorry for? Can you forgive someone who doesn't want to be forgiven, someone who doesn't think he needs to be forgiven?"

Amy laughed. "I don't know the answer to those sorts of questions, Hayley."

"Does anyone?" Hayley asked with a grin.

Chapter 129

When Leda had finished telling Vera about how Amy had stood up to the great Cressida Prior, Vera raised her fists in the air. "Good for Amy!" she cried. "I knew she had it in her. Well, to be honest I wasn't quite sure, but I'm glad she proved herself stronger than I gave her credit for. I'm glad she proved me wrong."

"Me too," Leda admitted, pouring boiling water into two teacups. "There's another thing. Will Prior asked to meet her, and she agreed."

Vera frowned. "You think that's such a good idea?"

"I don't know. Part of me thinks she should have refused. But I understand her need for closure. Maybe Will can shed some light on what went on this summer."

"I hope so," Vera said, bringing her cup of tea to the kitchen table. "I'd like to strangle that Cressida Prior for what she put Amy through."

Leda joined her friend. "I don't think that would do Amy any good," she pointed out, "but there is a way you might help. Do you think you might find a place for her in the new restaurant? I know she has no experience, but she is a hard worker when she's given the chance to be."

"Does she want to work for me?" Vera asked.

"She mentioned talking to you about a job. But I don't want you to feel compelled," Leda added hastily.

"Do I ever? No, I'd be glad to give Amy a real chance, not that mentor nonsense Prior tried to unload."

"Amy seems pretty clear about a lot of the dynamic Cressida established between them. I think she made a very big stride toward adulthood this summer." Leda took a sip of her tea. "So," she went on. "Have you seen Margot since the party?"

Vera busied herself rearranging the shortbread cookies she had brought from the restaurant on the plate Leda had provided. "Yeah," she said finally. "Once or twice."

"And?" Leda prompted.

Vera shrugged. "And, you know."

"No," Leda replied patiently. "I don't know. And stop fiddling with those cookies."

"If you must know," Vera said with a put-upon sigh, "we've been to dinner and for a walk on the beach. And we've talked on the phone. But only a few times. And we text. That's all."

Leda smiled and reached for a cookie. "Now we let Nature take its course."

Chapter 130

Hayley brought an empty coffee cup to the dishwasher, checking to see that the twins were still eating their Cheerios and milk and not tossing the cereal around the room. Being with the sisters had gotten her to thinking about Amy's questions regarding Hayley's feelings toward Brandon, and she had come to acknowledge that it really would be a good thing to allow more compassionate feelings to take the place of her usual criticisms and judgment. And maybe once compassion became a habit she might find the determination to offer her brother a more tangible form of help. It would be up to him to accept or to reject that help, but offering it might be the right thing to do.

"Good morning!" Marisa came into the kitchen wearing a T-shirt emblazoned with the words THIS IS WHAT A FEMINIST LOOKS LIKE. She hadn't mentioned Ethan after her last conversation with Hayley, and for that Hayley was grateful.

"Another perfect summer day," Marisa commented, smiling at the girls and pouring herself a cup of coffee.

"We learn to enjoy them as much as possible," Hayley said. "In the dead of our long winters, summer seems such a distant memory."

"Speaking of long winters, I've been wondering what your plans are after we've gone back to Connecticut," Marisa said, sitting on one of the stools at the countertop. "If you don't mind my asking."

"I don't mind," Hayley told her. "I'm going to Boston. It's a last-minute decision."

"Where will you live?" Marisa asked. "There are some lovely neighborhoods in the city but also just outside. The T makes it really easy to get around."

Hayley had only been on the T once. Marisa didn't need to know that. "I'll be sharing an apartment in Allston," she said, "with a few of my friend Amy's friends from school. The rent is manageable, though I need to find a good-paying job pretty quickly. You know from my résumé that I have experience cleaning houses." Hayley smiled awkwardly. "There are always people who need help cleaning their houses."

"I might just know of something that would be of more interest to you," Marisa said. "My friend Jillian Roseveare is a professor of medieval literature at Boston University. She's starting a year-long sabbatical come the fall, and her plans are to undertake the research for a book she's planning to write. I know she's been looking for a research assistant. I could give her a call and suggest she talk to you. What do you think?"

What Hayley thought was that she might faint. And then she laughed a bit wildly. "But I know almost nothing about research methods," she said.

"You'll learn," Marisa said robustly. "If Jillian is willing to give you a chance, would you be willing to take it?"

"Yes," Hayley blurted. "Of course."

"Good. I can't say the money will be great, and you'll probably need a second job to make ends meet. But I think the experience would really benefit you going forward." Marisa smiled kindly. "Teachers at YCC talk. I know you were an excellent student. I know you didn't want to leave school. And I suspect you want to continue your education at some point. Am I right?"

Hayley nodded. "Yes," she said, her voice quavering. "It's my dream."

"Then why not start making that dream a reality? Let me call my friend, and if she's already hired someone I'm sure there's some other academic we know in desperate need of an intelligent, hard-working assistant."

Hayley swallowed hard. "I don't know what to say. Working in academia would be like a dream come true. Thank you."

Marisa got up from the stool and put a gentle hand on Hayley's arm. "I like you, Hayley," she said. "We all do. The girls will miss you. I'll miss you. You were a great help to me this summer. Without your good care of my children I wouldn't have been able to teach the class at YCC. And teaching is something I really enjoy."

"It was my pleasure. It's all been . . ." Hayley took a steadying breath. "It's all been such a good experience."

"Even getting to know Ethan?" Marisa asked softly. "I don't believe all is lost there, Hayley. I really don't."

Before Hayley could protest, Layla picked up her bowl of Cheerios and dumped it over her head. Lily started to scream with laughter, which set Layla off as well, and neither Hayley nor Marisa could resist joining in.

"I'll get a washcloth," Hayley gasped.

Marisa hurried to the broom closet. "And I'll get a mop."

Chapter 131

It was with some degree of curiosity that Amy had agreed to meet Will Prior that afternoon. After all, he was not entirely innocent. He had stood by while his wife mistreated an employee working in their home. He didn't seem to care that his wife largely ignored their children. And what about his wife's drug use? There was no way he could be ignorant of Cressida using drugs unless willfully. Denial might be a normal reaction to an unpleasant or stressful situation, but at bottom it was also a supremely selfish reaction.

With a steadying breath, Amy pushed opened the door to the coffee shop. There were only a few people inside apart from the baristas. A woman with pure white hair cut in a sleek bob sat at the counter that ran along one wall of the café; she was reading a hardcover book and sipping a large cup of tea. A young man with a small child in a stroller sat on a cushioned bench that ran halfway down the opposite wall. He was drinking from a tall paper cup while the child studied intently the plush rabbit in his hands.

And then there was Will, seated near the back of the shop at a table for two. Amy wondered who was watching the children. As Amy approached Will she noted for the first time an overall weariness in his bearing. No doubt it had been there all along, but Amy, blinded by the flash that was Cressida Prior, had failed to notice.

"Thank you for coming," he said.

Amy nodded and sat at the table.

"What would you like to drink?" he asked.

"Nothing," Amy said. "I'm fine."

Will cleared his throat. "This is probably too little too late," he began, "but I would like to apologize for my wife's behavior this summer."

"Why did she want me to spend so much time with her?" Amy asked, leaning forward. "My job was supposed to be to care for the children, not to be her personal servant."

"There have been other young women," Will said with a shrug. "She tries to groom them to follow in her footsteps and to be her friend but . . . it never works out. She chooses girls who are obviously . . . unworldly."

Amy felt slightly sick to her stomach. "You mean vulnerable," she said.

Will nodded.

Amy recalled the day Rhiannon had mentioned "the other one," and now much more became clear. "And yet you let her do it all over again," she said, "manipulate another young person into turning against people she holds dear and giving up things she enjoys just so . . . just so Cressida Prior can have a personal plaything?"

Will's expression darkened. "I can't really stop her, can I?"

Amy thought about that for a moment. She supposed Will was right. One adult might have the right to tell another adult how to act, especially if the second adult was behaving in a manner that most people would find objectionable, but what power did the first adult have to compel the second adult to change her ways? Not much.

"She treats you like dirt," Amy blurted, the sound of Cressida's hand cracking against Will's cheek loud in her memory. "She ridicules you in front of your children. How can you put up with it? Don't you see that by treating you disrespectfully she's teaching the children that it's okay to have no concern for the happiness and dignity of others, even the happiness and dignity of their own father?"

Will's lips compressed into a thin line, and Amy wondered if she had gone too far. And if she had, so what?

"It's not ideal," Will said after a moment. "I try to counter her influence on the children. And she's not always so critical. There are times when . . ." Will shook his head and said no more.

"She doesn't have any friends, does she?" Amy asked.

Will frowned. "No."

"Why do you . . ." And then, sympathy for the man seated across from her made Amy stop. "Sorry," she said. "Never mind."

"You want to know what's in it for me?" Will gave her a wry smile. "I'd tell you if I knew."

"Do you know that your wife uses cocaine?" Amy asked.

Will frowned down at his coffee mug and was silent for a moment. "Yes," he said then. "I know."

"Why don't you do something about it?"

Again, Will smiled wryly. "What, turn her in to the police?"

"You could demand she not keep drugs in the house where your children can find them!" Amy realized that she had spoken more loudly than intended and quickly glanced around the coffee shop. No one was staring at them; she hoped no one had heard her outburst.

"It's not as easy as you think," Will replied, "getting someone to stop using. Anyway, she's highly functional. She's not addicted. It's not hurting her like it does some people."

Of course it's hurting her, Amy thought. It had to be. Will Prior was indeed in denial, and probably about more than just his wife's use of recreational drugs. She wanted to ask Will if he had ever even *liked* his wife but wasn't sure she wanted to know the answer to that question.

"Look, I know I'm not an expert," Amy went on, "but I think that Cressida might have a narcissistic personality disorder or something. Maybe you could get her some help."

"She doesn't want help. She doesn't see that anything is wrong. She can't. Look," Will said, reaching into the back pocket of his jeans, "I want you to accept this check. You earned it."

Amy took the check without hesitation. Before putting it into her wallet she noted that it was drawn on an account in Will's name alone. Did he have his own money? Did Cressida give him an allowance? There was so much about the Priors' relationship she just didn't know or want to know, like how two such seemingly different people had come together in the first place.

"I have something for you, too." Amy reached into her bag and withdrew the vintage compact. "Here," she said. "Cressida gave it to me and she shouldn't have. I know that Jordan bought it for her. And I shouldn't have taken it, but at least I'm giving it back."

Amy thought she saw a flicker of anger cross Will's face as he accepted the compact, but she couldn't be sure. "Thanks," he said gruffly.

"I'd ask you to tell the children I said hello," she said, rising from the table, "but I spent so little time with them this summer I'm not sure they'll remember me by this time next week."

"Take care of yourself, Amy," Will said, ignoring her remark.

"I will," she said. It was a promise to herself.

Chapter 132

Leda looked at her watch. An hour earlier Amy had gone off to meet Will Prior. Leda had been trying not to worry—what so terrible could happen in a coffee shop?—but to no avail. The deepest traumas could easily be caused by words instead of deeds, and though as far as she knew Will had never treated Amy badly, he might feel it was time to start.

Suddenly Leda remembered a passage from a book that had belonged to her grandfather, and she went to the living room to hunt it down. She found it on the third shelf from the top of the bookcase, where it had sat untouched for years. *How to Win Friends and Influence People* by Dale Carnegie. It took only a moment or two before Leda found the passage she was seeking.

If some people are so hungry for a feeling of importance that they actually go insane to get it, imagine what miracle you and I can achieve by giving people honest appreciation this side of insanity.

Leda wondered. Did Cressida Prior's need for a feeling of importance run so deep that it had sent her crazy seeking notice, alienating people in the process by her bullying and self-regard? It seemed likely. And how did the need for a feeling of importance differ from the need to feel *appreciated*? By winning the FAF's prize for Best Emerging Talent, Leda had been granted a nod of recognition from her fellow craftspeople, and that was enough. She didn't need to feel *important*, but she did need—everyone needed—to feel genuinely appreciated for her efforts.

At the sound of the front door opening Leda hurriedly returned the book to its place on the shelf. A moment later Amy appeared in the living room.

"How did your meeting with Will Prior go?" Leda asked quickly.

"Okay," Amy said, flopping into an armchair. "He gave me a check. And he apologized for Cressida's behavior, but I don't think anything is going to change in that marriage. I didn't get the sense that he was willing to *make* change happen." Amy smiled. "But what do I know? The worst judge of character ever."

"Don't be so hard on yourself," Leda advised, sitting in a chair close to Amy's. "At least you're learning."

"I hope so." Amy leaned forward. "What I can't figure out is why I was so in awe of Cressida's power and position. I've never cared about those things in the past. Why now?"

"Cressida *is* a bit of a celebrity," Leda noted. "You did tell me you'd first heard about her in that business class."

"Yeah," Amy admitted, "but I'd almost forgotten all about her. I didn't even recognize Cressida's name when I applied for the job. But the minute I saw her face-to-face and realized who she was, well, I was hooked."

"Keep in mind that people like Cressida—bullies and narcissists—are powerful but not all-powerful," Leda said. "You can learn skills that will allow you to shut them down."

"I know. Remember all those workshops I had back in middle school about bullying behavior? But you forget that adults can be bullies, too. I don't think bullying is something people grow out of all that easily. Oh," Amy said, "and speaking of bullies, I forgot to tell you that Hayley thinks it might be a good time for you to reach out to her mother again, now that she's stood up to Mr. Franklin."

Leda nodded. "Nora could use a friend. Hayley's moving on is going to be tough on her."

"I so hope Hayley gets that job working for Marisa Whitby's professor friend."

"That would be fantastic," Leda agreed. "I wish I had a magic wand so that I could make it happen."

Amy smiled. "You don't need one. Marisa turned out to be Hayley's fairy godmother."

"More reliable than a knight in shining armor." Leda smiled slyly. "Not unless his name is Noah Woolrich."

"Mom!" Amy cried but with a twinkle in her eyes. "You're impossible!"

Chapter 133

One of the longtime librarians at the Yorktide branch of the public library had been more than happy to allow Hayley a small office in which she could conduct an early-morning FaceTime interview with Professor Roseveare. There was no possibility of attempting the interview at the Franklins' apartment, not with the threat of Eddie Franklin knocking noisily about the place. He might be on good behavior at the moment, but that didn't make him entirely civilized. Besides, Hayley knew that her mother hadn't yet told her father that their daughter was leaving home. Nora Franklin needed to make that announcement in her own time; it would be an announcement that would bring with it very great change for the family.

Hayley had been more nervous about the interview than she had been about anything else in her life, but with an encouraging word from Marisa Whitby and another from Ms. Cumming, the librarian, she had handled herself professionally. After ten minutes or so she had found herself relaxing enough to ask an excited question about the full scope of Professor Roseveare's projected book. Another ten minutes later and Hayley had emerged from the library office beaming with relief and happiness. She had gotten the job. As Marisa had anticipated, the pay wasn't fantastic but Hayley knew she could find another job easily enough to help make ends meet. And she had liked Jillian Roseveare, young and eager to make a prominent mark in her field of study. More important, a woman eager to extend a helping hand to another woman.

When Hayley got back to the apartment at the end of the workday, she found her mother in the living room reading a paperback romance. Nora Franklin looked up eagerly.

"Did you get the job?" she asked, putting the book aside.

"I did," Hayley said. "I can hardly believe it, but I did." She sat next to her mother on the old couch. "Are you sure you're okay with my leaving Yorktide?" she asked. "I can always say that I changed my mind." Changing her mind was the very last thing Hayley wanted to do, but her habit of service and duty was not one to be broken overnight.

"You'll say nothing of the sort," her mother said firmly. "You'll go to Boston and you'll be a great success."

"I don't know about that," Hayley demurred. "Mom? There's something I've always wondered about. Back in grade school when my class took that trip to D.C., the one we couldn't afford, I remember overhearing you on the phone with someone. I got the impression the person was offering to pay my way. And I heard you say no. What really happened?"

Nora looked down at her hands folded in her lap and sighed. "The teachers had taken up a collection among themselves to fund your taking part," she said. "And I turned them down. I was too proud to accept what I saw as charity. But for your sake I should have put my pride aside and accepted the gift."

Hayley felt an uncomfortable mix of emotions sweep through her—anger, self-pity, regret—but they quickly subsided. The past was the past. It was over and done with. Hayley put her hand over her mother's clasped hands. "Don't worry about it, Mom," she said. "I'll get to D.C. and lots of other places, too."

Her mother looked up to Hayley with a watery smile. "I know you will," she said.

Heavy footsteps in the hall alerted Hayley that her father had come home. Her mother sat up straighter as her husband inserted his key in the door to the apartment. Eddie Franklin appeared a moment later, and Hayley immediately noticed that he was sober and that his hair had recently been trimmed. He looked at his wife and daughter with what Hayley thought was the tiniest bit of trepidation. But maybe that was wishful thinking.

"Hayley and I will be going out for dinner tonight," Nora Franklin announced. "There are makings for a sandwich in the fridge."

Hayley sat perfectly still as her father took in this bit of startling information. "All right," he said. Then he cleared his throat and made his way to the bedroom he shared with his long-suffering wife.

"Why are we going out?" Hayley asked when her father had disappeared behind the closed door.

"To celebrate!" Nora laughed. "It's been so long since we've had something to celebrate!"

Hayley reached over and gathered her mother in a tight hug. "Thank you, Mom," she whispered. "Thank you."

Chapter 134

Amy pulled up outside the Meadtown Brewery. Her stomach was home to butterflies. Lots of them.

The other day her mother had referred to Noah as a knight in shining armor. Whether he would turn out to be her own personal hero she didn't yet know. Of course, much would depend on whether Noah wanted her to be his own personal hero in return.

As luck would have it Noah was just coming out of the brewery as Amy approached.

"Hi," she called. "I hope you don't mind my dropping by."

Noah smiled. His shoulders had never looked so broad. His beard was nicely trimmed, and his thick blond hair was pulled back into a neat bun. Amy had a sudden desire to undo that bun and run her fingers through Noah's hair. Instead she took a deep breath.

"Not at all," he said. "I'm between projects and wanted some fresh air."

"Okay. Good." Amy suddenly found she didn't know what to do with her hands. She stuck them in the pockets of her sundress. She took them out. She folded them in front of her. "How are your parents?" she asked.

"Okay," Noah said. "They're the most optimistic people I know, so that's a real blessing."

Amy smiled. "I remember the time there was that really bad storm and a massive oak crashed through the Hendersons' roof. They had no insurance and everyone was worried they would lose the house, but your mother came to the rescue. Before you know it she had managed to collect enough money in donations to repair the roof with a little left over."

Noah laughed. "That's Mom."

"And your uncle?" Amy asked.

"Feeling better, actually," Noah told her. "Now that he's got me to take over the heavy lifting as it were, he's been able to get the rest he needed."

"I'm so glad. He's such a nice man." *Enough small talk*, Amy told herself. It was time to get to the important matter. "I came here for another reason, actually," she told Noah. "I mean, not just to ask about your family. I'm sorry I didn't go to your gig that night. When my boss asked me to stay over I should have told her that I had previous plans."

"Boss from hell," Noah stated, sticking his hands into the back pockets of his jeans. "Word gets around. I'm sorry you had to put up with her."

"Thanks. But it was totally my fault for not quitting before I did. At least I finally came to my senses."

Noah smiled. "I'm glad you did."

"Me too. Look, I was wondering if you would like to go somewhere with me, maybe take a picnic to the beach one evening or go for a walk or something? I totally understand if the answer is no," Amy finished hastily.

"I'd love to," Noah said. "A picnic sounds like fun. I'll bring some of the new mead we've just perfected."

"Cool," Amy said, feeling a great surge of relief. "Great. Is tomorrow okay?"

"Perfect. So, what's this I hear about you not moving to Boston?"

Amy nodded. "Yorktide is where I belong. It's where I've always been happy."

"Me too," Noah agreed. "I knew that after graduation I'd be back, and I don't regret my decision."

"Noah!"

"Gotta go," Noah said, nodding in the direction of the colleague who had called for him. "Pick you up at seven tomorrow?"

"Do you still like Swiss cheese on your sandwiches?" Amy asked.

Noah smiled again. "You remember that?"

"I remember a lot of things," she assured him. "Like the note you wrote me in first grade."

Noah leaned down and gave Amy a quick kiss on the cheek. Then he hurried off into the brewery.

Amy felt tears of happiness pricking at her eyes as she walked to her car. She was so very pleased that Noah had agreed to a date after the careless way in which she had treated him. She remembered what Cressida had said about the wedding rings Will had given her, how she had called them pathetic. If one day Noah were to slip a ring on her finger she would never, ever belittle such an important gift from the man she had sworn to love for the rest of her life.

Amy had one more stop to make before going home, and that was to Over Easy. She found Vera in her tiny office off the kitchen.

"Coffee?" Vera offered. "I just brewed a pot."

Amy declined the offer.

"So," Vera went on when Amy had taken a seat across from Vera's desk. "You want to work in my new restaurant."

"If you'll have me," Amy said. "I'll work hard, I promise."

Vera smiled. "That's job requirement number one."

"What's it going to be called?" Amy asked.

"I'm thinking of calling it Seasonings," Vera told her. "Or maybe The Butternut. I don't know, something will come to me."

"How about Vera's Place?"

"No. That sounds like a diner. Not that there's anything wrong with diners."

Amy smiled. "Doughnuts and coffee."

"Now I'm hungry again and I just ate lunch." Vera laughed. "Anyway, you need to understand that the restaurant industry isn't glamorous. It's challenging and often frustrating. But the payoff can be good. Not that I'll be giving you Cartier watches I no longer want or Hermès scarves I've tired of," Vera warned.

"Don't worry. All I want from you is what you can teach me. And a salary."

"Good," Vera said with a nod. "You're learning already. Requiring proper compensation for a job well done is a sign of self-respect." Vera looked at Amy then with compassion. "You had a tough go of it this summer. I'm sorry."

"Don't be," Amy told her. "Everyone has to grow up at some point. You know, it's funny. When I started to work for Cressida Prior I looked at her life and thought, Wow, this woman has it all, a great career, a husband, kids, tons of money. But I was so wrong. She doesn't have it all. She doesn't have love." Amy hesitated for a moment before going on. "I asked Noah Woolrich on a date. He said yes."

Vera smiled. "Good for you! I'll let you in on a little secret. When I made the decision to open a second place I did so partly because being single again gave me all this time on my hands. Now that I might—and I only say might—have someone in my life, well, it will be a scramble."

"You'll handle it all beautifully," Amy assured her. "I know you will."

Vera abruptly got up from her desk. "It's your fault, Amy," she said. "I can't fight it any longer. I just have to have a doughnut with my coffee. Let's go to the kitchen and see what the guys can whip up."

Laughingly, Amy followed.

It has been quite a day all in all, Amy thought as she sat cross-legged on her bed, her back resting against a pile of pillows her mother had made from velveteen, calico, and linen. First, she had made peace with Noah. Then she had gone on to meet with Vera to discuss working at her new restaurant. The best part about that meeting, of course, had been the cinnamon doughnuts one of the sous-chefs had made for them.

After, she had enjoyed a quiet dinner with her mother, Harry and Winston hovering in case random bits of food fell from the table. Now she was alone in her room, and though she was very tired she wanted to think about how to tie up a few loose ends before she left this crazy phase of her life behind. One of those loose ends was how to dispose of the "gifts" Cressida had given her this summer. Amy was glad she had returned the vintage compact. She had no idea what Will would do with it, but that was not her concern.

Amy had already decided not to consign any of the items Cressida had given her; she didn't want to profit by them. As for the bag with a torn lining, well, she would never donate that to a thrift store without first having the lining repaired, and while her mother could easily handle that task, Amy didn't want to burden her with something so unimportant. The bag would go into the garbage.

The stained Coach scarf. . . . Amy frowned. She did really like the colors, but the scarf was tainted for her now, and the taint had nothing to do with the permanent stain. The scarf, too, would go into the trash. The silk blouse that was too small she would give to a thrift shop.

But there was one more item to consider. Amy reached into the open drawer of her bedside table and removed a small, blue velvet box. Carefully, she opened it and looked at the sterling silver and cubic zirconia ring tucked inside. Why didn't this ring feel tainted like the bag and the scarf Cressida had given her? Would keeping it and wearing it prove there was something shallow in her nature that could never be avoided? Amy just didn't know the answers to those questions. She closed the box and put it back in the drawer. She would hold on to the ring for a while. It really was awfully pretty.

Suddenly a huge yawn escaped Amy. She scooted down in the bed, turned off the bedside lamp, and within minutes she was asleep, another landmark day behind her.

Chapter 135

"When's the bus due?" Amy asked.

Leda checked her phone. "It's scheduled to depart at eleven, so it should be here pretty soon."

"It doesn't matter if it's a few minutes late," Vera pointed out. "Hayley doesn't have to make a connection after all. And it's too bad Phil came down with that nasty cold. I know he really wants to be here."

"Did you know Phil gave Hayley a check as a going-away gift?" Leda asked. "He wasn't sure it was the right thing to do, but I persuaded him that Hayley wasn't stupidly proud."

Vera sighed. "What a sweetheart he is."

Amy linked arms with her mother and Vera. "This is so exciting. I can hardly believe that Hayley's leaving Yorktide. I'll miss her, but I'm so happy for her."

"Any regrets that you're not the one getting on the bus?" Leda asked her daughter.

"Not one," Amy said promptly. "This is where I belong."

Vera smiled. "Good, because I'm relying on you to show up for work once construction is completed. Maybe one day you'll be my right-hand woman."

"Ugh, don't use that term!" Amy cried. "It's something She Who Must Not Be Named used to say."

Leda was glad that already Amy seemed to be able to speak lightly of the woman who had manipulated her so thoroughly this summer. As Amy and Vera got into a discussion about plans for the opening of the new restaurant, Leda looked to where Hayley was standing with her mother. She recalled how early in the summer she had fantasized about a miracle happening for Hayley, if not a knight in shining armor then the appearance of someone who would believe enough in Hayley to go to some lengths to help her move onward and upward. She felt grateful to Marisa Whitby for having the kindness and the wisdom to act on Hayley's behalf.

Hayley left her mother to speak with Amy, and Leda thought it the perfect moment to approach Nora with a gesture of renewed friendship. There was something different about Nora Franklin this morning, something lighter and less burdened. Leda didn't think she was imagining the change.

"Hayley has a perfect day for traveling," Leda said when she had joined Nora. "Not a cloud in the sky. I think it's a good omen."

Nora smiled. "Thank you for being a friend to my daughter."

"It's always been my pleasure," Leda said sincerely. "She's a remarkable person."

Nora shook her head. "I don't know where she comes from, I really don't."

Leda ventured to put her hand lightly on Nora's arm. Nora did not pull away. "Come to my house for coffee this week. Say, Thursday afternoon around three if that doesn't interfere with work?"

"I will," Nora said. "Thank you. And . . . and why don't I bake something for us?"

Leda smiled. "That would be wonderful," she said earnestly. "A lot of people in Yorktide miss your baking. I especially miss your famous raisin scones."

"I'll have to dig out my old recipes. I remember one for cherry strudel that was always a favorite with Father Mark." Nora smiled. "In fact, I think I'll pop into the rectory after work later today and say hello. It's been a while."

A peal of laughter caused Leda to turn. Amy and Hayley had their arms around each other's shoulders. Leda glanced at Vera, who was smiling fondly at the girls, and then back to Nora Franklin, still standing by Leda's side. These people were her family. This was her community. What an amazing summer it had been for them all.

Chapter 136

It was an auspicious day to begin a journey; there wasn't a cloud in the very clear blue sky. And, Hayley thought, this was only the first step of her journey. Who knew where it would eventually take her?

Volume 1 of *The History of the Decline and Fall of the Roman Empire* was tucked safely in her roomy travel bag, a bag borrowed from Vera. Mrs. Latimer had made Hayley a totally gorgeous bracelet with lapis beads. From it hung a genuine sterling silver charm on which were engraved the words CARPE DIEM. Amy had given her a little shopping bag of special soaps, lotions, and hair products. Nora Franklin had prepared a hearty lunch for her daughter. And Phil Morse had given her an astonishingly large check to help cover her initial expenses in Boston. Hayley had never felt so loved and appreciated. She knew that she would never forget this moment, the feelings of anxiety and sadness mingling with feelings of anticipation and gratefulness.

Her mother returned from a conversation with Mrs. Latimer. "Take good care of yourself, Hayley," she said.

"I intend to," Hayley promised her. "You'll call me if Dad gets out of hand again, won't you?"

"Don't worry about me," her mother said firmly. "You just work hard and learn new things. Promise me."

"I promise," Hayley said.

"Here. I have something for you." Her mother reached into her old leather bag and withdrew a small, round medal on a chain. "It's Saint Michael the Archangel," she said. "My grandmother gave it to me when I was a girl. You know I haven't been to church in years, but I still believe in God and I believe this will help keep you safe."

"Thanks, Mom," Hayley said. She took the medal and secured it around her neck. Maybe her mother's belief would be strength enough for the both of them. She glanced at her watch. The bus would be here at any moment now. If she had any thoughts of turning back from the path she had chosen, now was the time to do it. But she had no such thoughts. Her only regret, and it was one she felt keenly, was that she had hurt Ethan Whitby in the way that she had.

It was at that moment Hayley's attention was caught by a gray BMW turning smoothly into the station lot. It was another moment before Hayley recognized the car.

The driver's door opened and Ethan stepped out. Hayley felt her heart begin to thump painfully. As Ethan strode toward her, Hayley could see that his expression was one of purpose, though his blue eyes looked pained. Hayley was vaguely aware that her mother was no longer at her side. She found herself stepping forward to meet Ethan.

"What are you doing here?" she asked when they stood mere inches apart. Her voice was trembling.

Ethan looked directly into her eyes. "Marisa called to tell me that you were leaving for Boston this morning," he said quietly but urgently. "Don't be mad at her. I just couldn't let you go without one last attempt at convincing you to give our relationship a try. Please, Hayley. I know I promised I'd keep away but . . . I'm sorry. I just couldn't. I just can't."

Hayley felt something blossom in her heart. What had her mother said? Love could bridge even great distances. "It's all right," she said with a sigh of relief. "Don't apologize. Please don't ever apologize."

Ethan moved a little closer. "I fell in love with the person you were this summer, Hayley. And now I want the chance to fall in love with the real, unaltered Hayley. No lies. No half truths. And I promise the same."

"You lied to me?" Hayley asked, smiling through the tears that had begun to leak down her cheeks.

Ethan grinned. "I might have exaggerated my knowledge about the Red Sox. But that's what guys do around a pretty girl. They brag. Wait. I lied again." Ethan took her hands in his. "You're beautiful, Hayley. I want you to know I've thought a lot about what you told me, and I respect your concerns that because we've come from such different backgrounds it might be difficult to make a future together. I really do. And you're right. I'll probably never know what it's like to wonder where the next meal is coming from. But that doesn't change the way I feel about you and our chances for a life together. It just doesn't."

"I don't want to feel beholden to you," Hayley said urgently. "I want us to be equals in whatever is to come."

"I wouldn't want it any other way," Ethan assured her.

"Maybe one day we could go to the Folger Library?" she said.

"And Stratford-upon-Avon. And the Tower of London. And Versailles."

Hayley laughed. "Just two history nerds bumming our way around Europe?"

"Maybe not bumming exactly. I can't put up a tent for my life. But no stuffy hotels. Just charming B and Bs. Maybe we'll rent bikes!"

"And this time I'll be the one to save you from the path of a speeding car. Not that I want any speeding cars in our future," Hayley added quickly.

"Our future," Ethan breathed.

Hayley smiled. "Yes. Let's believe in a future. But Ethan? I need to go to Boston and be on my own for a while. I need to prove a few things to myself. I have to finally embrace the fact that I'm allowed to live my own life, that I have the *right* to live my own life, apart from my parents."

"Of course. I think you're doing the right thing. But we can call each other, and maybe one day you might want to come to Connecticut for a weekend?" Ethan smiled. "You know, to see my sisters."

"Yes," Hayley said. "I'd like that very much. And I'd like to see your father and stepmother, too. Marisa has been so good to me. I'm not sure I deserve all your family has done for me."

"Yes, you do," Ethan said fervently.

"I want you to meet someone," Hayley said suddenly. She took Ethan's hand and led him to where her mother was waiting. "Ethan," Hayley said, "this is my mother, Nora Franklin. Mom, this is my friend, Ethan Whitby. Ethan is the one who gave me the book I showed you."

Nora held out her hand, and Ethan took it in his. "It's very nice to meet you, Ethan," she said. Hayley noted how her mother looked Ethan squarely in the eye, how she smiled pleasantly. There was no sign of deference or embarrassment in her demeanor. It seemed that a miracle had indeed been wrought.

"As it is to meet you, Mrs. Franklin," Ethan replied, with a slight bow of his head.

"Now I'll let you two alone," Nora said, moving away.

"She's lovely," Ethan said earnestly.

Hayley was pretty certain that no one had ever called Nora Franklin lovely before now, and she was grateful for Ethan's kind behavior. "The Gibbon book is in my bag," she told him. "It's the best gift I've ever been given."

And then Ethan embraced her, and with her head nestled against his shoulder Hayley felt more peaceful and secure than she had ever felt in her twenty-one years.

Before letting her go, Ethan whispered in Hayley's ear. " 'Her eyes in heaven would through the airy region stream so bright that birds would sing and think it were not night.' "

"All aboard!"

Ethan's lips met Hayley's in what was an even sweeter and more passionate kiss than the first time they had come together. Then, Hayley made her farewell. While the driver stowed her large bag in the bus's luggage compartment, Hayley, holding tightly to her carry-on, boarded the bus. She found a window seat about midway down the aisle and slid into it. Only when her friends and family were long out of sight did she stop waving. *Life can be so strange*, she thought. At the start of the summer the very last thing she could have imagined was that she would be off to Boston to take a job as a research assistant to a professor of medieval history. Or that she would have met someone like Ethan Whitby—intelligent, kind, a fellow history buff, and above all, someone undeterred by her past.

Suddenly, a text message appeared on her phone.

Hear my soul speak: The very instant that I saw you, did my heart fly to your service.

Hayley smiled and texted back. *Shakespeare?*

The Tempest. Will's words but my sentiment.

So, what was it that did the trick, the plunger or the mud mask?

I'll go with the mud mask. xxxx

Hayley laughed out loud. Maybe, she thought, one day she would tell Ethan the truth about how she had once considered marrying him as an escape from her awful life. She knew for sure that he would understand and forgive.

Chapter 137

Hayley's bus had pulled out of the station, bound for Boston. Mrs. Franklin had gone off to her shift at Hannaford. Ethan had headed to his parents' house before the drive back to Connecticut. Amy stood with her mother and Vera. She would miss Hayley, but she also knew that what mattered most was that Hayley grasp the opportunities she had been given.

"I'm so happy that Hayley and Ethan have worked things out," she said with a contented sigh.

"What really just happened there?" her mother asked. "You knew something had gone on between Hayley and Ethan, didn't you?"

"I was sworn to secrecy," Amy explained. "Let's just say that Hayley couldn't believe someone like Ethan, so educated and cultured, would fall in love with someone like her. But he did, and she fell in love with him, and even though she sent him away for what she thought was his own good he came back. It's so romantic."

Vera smiled. "Romance doesn't always have to end in disaster. I'm trying to believe that."

"Come on, Mom," Amy said. "Let's go home. I want to get started updating your website. And it's almost time for lunch."

The three women began to walk toward their cars, past another bus discharging passengers. One of those passengers, Amy noted, was a jovial-looking man wearing round, old-fashioned spectacles and carrying a beat-up brown leather satchel. When he stepped on to the pavement he suddenly came to a halt and smiled.

"Hello," he said to Leda Latimer.

"Hi," Amy's mother said brightly in reply.

The passenger behind the man nudged him, and with another smile the man with the satchel walked toward the taxi stand.

"What was that about?" Vera asked.

Leda fiddled with the collar of her blouse. "What do you mean?" she asked, her voice a bit higher than usual.

Vera smiled. "The hellos you exchanged with the guy who just got off the bus."

"It was more than a hello," Amy noted, looking toward the jovial-looking man waiting in line for a taxi. "It was like a meeting of the minds or something. Like you've known each other for years."

Vera frowned. "I wonder who he is."

"That's the new heart specialist from New York. Trevor McIntyre."

Amy whirled around to see an elderly woman she recognized from around town. "I saw his picture in the *Daily Chronicle*," the woman went on in a conspiratorial manner. "My niece works at the hospital, and she told me he's been widowed for three years and wanted a fresh start here in Maine."

"Whoever he is," Amy said when the woman had moved off, "he definitely likes you, Mom."

Leda dropped her hand from her collar and blushed. "Don't be silly. What would a heart specialist see in a fiber artist like me?"

"You sound just like Hayley," Amy scolded. "Don't underestimate yourself."

Her mother turned toward the taxi stand. The jovial-looking man waved. Leda waved back.

Amy laughed. "This is too funny!"

Vera linked one arm through Leda's and the other through Amy's. "I think I'll do some discreet checking about this Dr. McIntyre," she said, "and you can't do anything to stop me."

Leda raised an eyebrow. "Did I say that I would?"

The three women continued toward their cars.

"How about tuna melts for lunch?" Amy said brightly.

"Can I invite Margot over?" Vera asked. "I think she's off today."

Amy smiled. "Of course. We're one big happy family here in Yorktide!"

Please turn the page
for a very special Q&A
with Holly Chamberlin!

Q. What prompted you to write a story about two young friends working as nannies for families vacationing in southern Maine?
A. Frankly, the idea of a family hiring a nanny or an au pair has always fascinated me. For one, the notion is so foreign to the world in which I was raised! And I saw in the idea a way for two very different characters—Amy and Hayley—to experience two very different journeys simultaneously. Each young woman's experience with the family for whom she works challenges her in ways that prove necessary for her emotional growth. Plus, there was some fun to be had in the scenes that take place at The White Hart, the pub where all the women working as nannies gather to share their stories.

Q. Writers often use bits and pieces of their own experiences in creating a character or in building a character's experiences. In writing this book did you consciously use any events from your own life to help bring the story alive?
A. I did. The character of Cressida Prior is an exaggeration—though not a huge one!—of two awful bosses I had many, many years ago. I had some fun writing La Prior, and especially enjoyed writing Amy's moment of triumph over the woman who had made her life miserable for an entire summer. Also, an experience I had when I was a little girl in our local library informs Hayley's experience as an eight-year-old reading the biography of Peter the Great. In my case, it was an historical novel about a boy who runs off to sea and has thrilling adventures. I remember being engrossed in the tale until a woman came up to me and said, "You shouldn't be reading that. That's a book for boys." I was thoroughly confused. Why couldn't a girl read about life-threatening storms, pirates, and buried treasure? I'm happy to say that I ignored the woman's remark.

Q. What's next for you?
A. I'm working on a novel about a reunion of dear college friends around the age of forty. The group is gathering for the wedding of one of the women. Though they've all stayed in touch over the twenty years since graduation, each of the characters has a secret or two he or she has been keeping from the others. When these secrets emerge during the course of the week leading up to the wedding, emotional chaos ensues. It's a fun and challenging story to write and a bit different from my most recent novels. I hope everyone will like it!

A READING GROUP GUIDE

THE SUMMER NANNY

Holly Chamberlin

ABOUT THIS GUIDE

The suggested questions are included to enhance your group's reading of Holly Chamberlin's *The Summer Nanny*!

DISCUSSION QUESTIONS

1. There are as many reasons why people stay in an abusive relationship as there are abusive relationships. Talk about Nora and Eddie's marriage and why both parties might choose to stay in it. What about Cressida and Will's marriage? When Amy asks Will what he gets out of the union he says, "I'd tell you if I knew." Why might Cressida remain in the marriage? There are no definitive answers here, so use your imagination!

2. Leda thinks about her husband, Charlie, and admits that "she hadn't really known the man she had married." Talk about Leda's reasons for marrying and compare and contrast those reasons to the reasons that inform Hayley's "plan" to marry Ethan Whitby. In both instances, marriage appears as a sort of refuge or way out of an untenable situation. Is a marriage based on this premise doomed to fail? Or might it on occasion prove satisfactory to both parties?

3. It has sometimes been said that odious women attract the nicest of men. Talk about this observation and how—assuming there is some truth to it—the phenomenon might be explained. Again, use your imagination!

4. Consider how an abusive experience early in life can negatively affect the future of the victim. Consider Leda's seduction by Lance Stirling. Consider Hayley's sad home life. Consider, too, Amy's experience at the hands of Cressida Prior. By the end of the book, how successfully have these women managed to rise above the damage inflicted upon them?

5. Hayley is thinking about her brother, Brandon. "It had to be true that sometimes doing nothing to help a per-

son was better than doing the wrong thing." Do you agree with this notion? Is it futile to offer help to a person who doesn't want help? Is it a duty to do what we can to assist someone we think is in need, even if there's a chance our actions are misguided and might cause more harm than good?

6. Talk about the nature of gifts and givers as expressed in the book. How does Cressida as a giver rate against Leda's friend Missy? How can gifts function as emotional shackles? What does it really mean to give a gift unselfishly and without strings?

7. Consider the notion of success as variously defined throughout the course of the book. How does Leda's definition of success, defined more by hard-won recognition and public appreciation, differ from that of Cressida Prior's definition as something achieved only by winning the top prize? How does Amy's notion of success change during the course of the summer? Discuss the nature of Hayley's dream of a successful life. Consider as well the opening quote by Helen Keller: *Character cannot be developed in ease and quiet. Only through experience of trial and suffering can the soul be strengthened, vision cleared, ambition inspired and success achieved.*

8. Talk about envy as motivation for action. Leda is aware that her envy of Amy's relationship with Cressida Prior largely fuels her decision to enter the FAF's annual competition. How does she feel about this? Discuss competition (male) versus cooperation (female) as two alternative methods for approaching the world. Leda comes to realize that tooting one's own horn isn't necessarily a bad thing, as long as one doesn't let the habit get out of hand. Do you agree?

9. On a related note, what do you think motivates successful women like (the fictional) Cressida Prior who refuse to help other women achieve their career goals? What do you think motivates successful women like (the fictional) Marisa Whitby and Jillian Roseveare, who *do* choose to help other women succeed in their own right?

10. Has anyone in your reading group worked as a nanny or an au pair? If so, would you share your experience with the others in the group? Has anyone hired a nanny or an au pair for her or his children? Was it a positive experience for your family?